Void

Calling upon the library of data stored in his mind, he observed several distant planets, derived their mass, their precession, the length of their seasons, their aphelion and perihelion. The exercise made him smile; he recognized it as an attempt to use mathematics to make chaos predictable. Such ordering was the curse of sentience, an irrepressible desire to engage in an ultimately futile exercise.

Shadow

The guide unslung his ashwood bow, drew an arrow from his quiver, and scanned the swamp. Pools of black water stood to either side of them, steaming in the humidity. The dark trees of the swamp loomed like watchtowers.

Necropolis

Thunder boomed and another lightning flash illuminated the city. Jak caught a clear glimpse of toppled buildings, crumbling megaliths, and broken statues worn by the weather and pitted into anonymity. Sculptures perched atop the roofs of the small, single story buildings in the city's center, the only intact statuary in the ruins. Cale's voice was grim when he said, "Those are tombs."
Jak's skin went gooseflesh. There were a lot of them.

Elsewhere

The nursery opened wide around him, a circular cyst in the earth of his pocket plane. Forty-four paces in diameter, the polished walls of the perfectly spherical room gleamed in the dim green light of a single glowball. Lines of diamonds and amethysts glittered in alternating spiraling whorls inset into the walls.

Book II

THE
EREVIS CALE
TRILOGY

THE
EREVIS CALE
TRILOGY

Book I
Twilight Falling

Book II
Dawn of Night

Book III
Midnight's Mask
November 2005

Also by Paul S. Kemp

R.A. Salvatore's War of the Spider Queen

Book VI
Resurrection
April 2005

Sembia
The Halls of Stormweather
Shadow's Witness

DAWN OF NIGHT

BOOK II

✝

THE
EREVIS CALE
TRILOGY

PAUL S. KEMP

The Erevis Cale Trilogy, Book II
DAWN OF NIGHT

Distributed in the United States by Holtzbrinck Publishing. Distributed in Canada by Fenn Ltd.

Distributed to the hobby, toy, and comic trade in the United States and Canada by regional distributors.

Distributed worldwide by Wizards of the Coast, Inc. and regional distributors.

FORGOTTEN REALMS, WIZARDS OF THE COAST, and their respective logos are trademarks of Wizards of the Coast, Inc., in the U.S.A. and other countries.

All Wizards of the Coast characters, character names, and the distinctive likenesses thereof are trademarks of Wizards of the Coast, Inc.

Printed in the U.S.A.

Cover art by Terese Nielsen
Map by Dennis Kauth
First Printing: June 2004
Library of Congress Catalog Card Number: 2004100684

9 8 7 6 5 4 3 2

US ISBN: 0-7869-3225-2
UK ISBN: 0-7869-3226-0
620- 96549-001-EN

U.S., CANADA,   EUROPEAN HEADQUARTERS
ASIA, PACIFIC, & LATIN AMERICA   Wizards of the Coast, Belgium
Wizards of the Coast, Inc.   T Hofveld 6d
P.O. Box 707   1702 Groot-Bijgaarden
Renton, WA 98057-0707   Belgium
+1-800-324-6496   +322 467 3360

Visit our web site at www.wizards.com

For Jen, A, and B

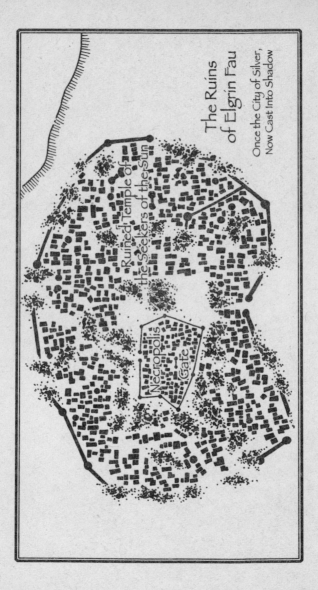

The Ruins
of Elgrin Fau

Once the City of Silver,
Now Cast Into Shadow

Ruined Temple of
the Seekers of the Sun

Necropolis
Gate

And they went forth into the dawn of night.
Long by wild ways and clouded light . . .

—Algernon Charles Swinburne
Tristram of Lyonesse

THE SOJOURNER

Vhostym wished to make one last observation before he began the final stages of his plan. He attributed the desire to nostalgia, to a need to see things as they existed at that moment. For soon, everything would change.

Propelling his projected form upward with the power of thought, Vhostym extended the range of his illusionary proxy to the far limits of his spell—the edge of Toril's sky, leagues above the surface, where the blue of Toril's celestial sphere gave way to the bleak darkness of the cosmos. From there, he looked outward through the eyes of the image and into endlessness. The void of the heavens yawned before him, the massive, limitless jaws of the greatest of beasts. In its infinite expanse, Vhostym bore witness to the immensity of creation, the perfect mathematics of motion, and the insignificance of his own existence.

He, among the most powerful of beings on any world, felt insignificant. The feeling amused him, mostly because it was true. Even his grand plan, as ambitious as it was, faded into negligibility in the face of the endless ether.

The meaninglessness of existence comforted him. Juxtaposed against infinite time and space, even the greatest of beings were small.

Distant but still obviously enormous, Toril's sun dominated his view, once of the countless blazing eyes of the beast. Though he could not see them from that distance, he knew that the fiery star continually spat jets of flame into the cosmic darkness, the smallest of which could have immolated even the City of Brass and all of the efreeti in it. Had Vhostym been looking at the glowing orb through his physical eyes, the light would have blinded him and charred his skin as black as the void. The pain would have lasted only a few excruciating moments before the rays would have reduced him to a heap of seared flesh. Even mild starlight caused his physical form pain unless he took magical precautions—hence his underground existence. His advancing illness had only made his vulnerability to sunlight more pronounced. As a younger githvyrik, he had for centuries sought a spell that would eliminate his extreme sensitivity to light, but to no avail. He could not change what he was.

But he *could* change the world, at least for a time.

The details of his plan marched through his brain, a progression of steps as orderly and logical as those used to solve a complex equation. The scope of his ambition appalled and delighted even him. He could do it though, of that he was certain. He *would* do it.

Other, less grand courses were open to him, of course. Through his magic he could have simply adopted a form that suffered no ill effects from light. He could have faced the sun, as he did then, through the eyes of a projected image, and in that way gain the Crown of Flame. But those were paltry substitutes for the reality, and both were insufficient to satisfy him. Before the end, he would see the crown with his own eyes, feel it against his flesh. And to do that, he needed to stand on the surface of Toril. The thought of it caused him a pang of longing, a desire to feel the coolness of an unfettered breeze against the pale skin of his face.

He set aside his reverie and continued the observation.

In the infinity beyond Toril's sun, innumerable planets and stars spun through the deep, pinpricks of light dancing through the dark. Vhostym observed their motion for a time, his intellect automatically translating their movement into equations that only he could understand. Calling upon the library of data stored in his mind, he observed several distant planets, derived their mass, their precession, the length of their seasons, their aphelion and perihelion. The exercise made him smile; he recognized it as an attempt to use mathematics to make chaos predictable. Such ordering was the curse of sentience, an irrepressible desire to engage in an ultimately futile exercise.

Still, the countless celestial bodies enthralled him. To the uninitiated, the night sky seen from Toril's surface probably appeared to be a veritable ocean of twinkling lights, as though the universe was a sack stuffed full. Vhostym knew that to be fiction. All told, the entirety of the celestial bodies in the universe filled the vacuum of the cosmos no more than fish filled a sea.

The universe, Vhostym knew, was emptiness, a vacuum filled with dust motes and beings ignorant of their own insignificance. The irony was, due to Vhostym's congenital hyper-sensitivity to light, he could see the multiverse only through a projected image, itself a fiction, itself an empty form.

But soon he would see it through his own eyes rather than through the lens of his magic. Then the Crown of Flame would be his. And when he had *that*, he would have everything he wanted.

Millennia ago, not long after the revolution that had freed his people from their illithid tyrants, he had been of a more philosophical bent. Then, he had hopefully pondered how one being could meaningfully affect the cosmic vastness for the better. Initially, he had thought the answer to be ever-increasing power. But as his power had grown—grown so large as to be nearly unparalleled—so too had his understanding. In the end he had come to realize that attempting to affect the universe was the desire of fools. It was too big, too random, too uncaring. He was a dust mote, as was everyone and everything else.

Life had no overarching meaning, he had learned, no grand purpose. Not even his life. There was only sensation, experience, *subjectivity*. That realization, equivalent to an epiphany for a religious zealot, had freed him from his self-imposed moral shackles. In a flash of insight, he had realized that morality was as much a man-made construct as a stone golem. He had come to the abrupt and stunning realization that characterizing an action as good or evil was absurd. He had elevated himself beyond good and evil. What was, was. What one wanted to do and could do, one ought to do. There was no other *ought*, no other objective standard.

That principle had informed his subsequent existence.

He looked down through his slippered "feet" to the spinning sphere below him. The great globe of Abeir-Toril turned its way through the heavens—a whirling green, blue, and brown jewel dusted here and there with a fringe of white clouds. It too was wondrous in its way, a beautiful gear in the clockwork of the universe. True, Vhostym might have improved its symmetry by leveling a mountain range here, or draining a sea there, but still the surface of his adopted world was beautiful.

The surface. Merely thinking about it turned him maudlin. He had set foot on it in his own form only once, as a very young gith, and for only moments. But during that single visit he had seen for the first time the Crown of

Flame, and that vision had birthed in his mind a possibility. He would create the crown himself, and with it walk Faerûn's surface for as long as he willed.

He looked up and to his right, to the silver orb of Selûne, cresting over the horizon line of Toril, and the swarm of her tears. He knew the moon goddess would not be pleased when his plan began to take shape. Neither would Cyric, the Mad God.

It amused Vhostym to think of the divine consternation he soon would cause. He cared not at all, of course. The ire of gods meant as little to him as did the morality of humankind. Gods were little more than men made immortal, driven by the same banal instincts and desires as mortals. Immortality was easy to attain, Vhostym knew. It was living a meaningful existence that was hard.

Vhostym watched Selûne finish its rise above Toril and knew that the time had come to begin, but still he lingered, teetering on the edge of the void. With the object of his desire within reach he felt satisfaction in prolonging the final moments of denial. He knew the reason—consummation of his plan represented a threshold, established a line of demarcation between *before* and *after*. For the moment, he wanted to savor the before, to capture it in his mind like a portrait.

He again looked down on Toril, saw the broad outline of Faerûn, and located the Inner Sea. There, below the cottony clouds, he fancied he could see the island that he had chosen to house the focus for the greatest spell he would ever cast.

Thousands would die, he knew. Perhaps tens of thousands.

So be it, he thought.

He willed what he willed, and so it would be. With that, he decided that it was time to cross the threshold, to begin the *after*. The *before* was boring him.

With a thought, he dispelled his projected image and returned his consciousness to his body. The universe instantly fell away and darkness enshrouded him. As always, it took a moment to overcome the physical and mental torpidity caused by the projection spell. He sat cross-legged on a plush rug. His flesh felt thick and clumsy compared to the lightness of his soaring soul. He imagined he would feel something akin to that lightness when he set foot again on Toril's surface, when he possessed the Crown of Flame and looked into the dark sky with his own gaze.

Inhaling as deeply as his failing lungs would allow, he opened his eyes. The darkness of his pocket plane contrasted markedly with the light of the outer cosmos but he could see clearly nevertheless. His vision extended simultaneously into several spectra, several planes, but his smooth, stone-walled sanctuary looked the same in all of them—unremarkable. He had grown weary long ago of living under the earth. Millennia before, he had pinched off an area of Faerûn's Underdark, essentially creating a pocket plane of his own—a part of Faerûn, but still separate from it. It felt more a prison every decade, not unlike his body.

Several magical gems orbited his head, whirring around at a distance of a few handspans. It was in observing those gems that he had found the inspiration for his plan. Still, he found their incessant hum irritating at the moment. Floating in each corner of the chamber, iridescent glowballs lit the square meditation room, their dim green light an order of magnitude dimmer than starlight and barely perceptible by most beings.

He braced himself, unfolded his legs, and started to rise. His body was weaker than usual. As always, pain wracked his bones the moment he put weight on them.

Refusing to surrender to the wasting disease that plagued his skeleton down to the marrow, he forced himself to stand without magical assistance. That small victory brought him satisfaction. For centuries, his magic had held age and disease at bay. But time was a relentless opponent, and even the most powerful of his magic was losing its battle with the passing years. He had considered lichdom of course, but had dismissed it. He relished the pleasures of the flesh too much even in his old age, though in recent years those pleasures were few. The sensory emptiness of undeath was not for him.

Besides, he had lived a full life in his ten thousand years. He had but one thing left to do. Once it was done he would be fulfilled. With the Weave Tap in his possession he could do it.

He raised his hand to cast a spell but stopped before uttering the arcane words. He stared for a moment at his outstretched hand. The appearance of his flesh disturbed him—bone white, parchment thin, speckled with dark age spots and threads of black veins. His nearly translucent skin wrapped his fingers and hands so tightly that he could distinguish individual bones.

I am almost a lich already, he thought with a touch of sadness.

He had lived too long, and spent too much time underground. The latter problem soon would be resolved. As for the former, well . . . time would claim him when it would.

He fought down a bout of melancholy, admonishing himself for indulging in such weakness. With exaggerated dignity, he straightened his magical gray robes and composed himself. It would not do for his brood of slaadi to see him dismayed. He regarded them as his children; they should not see their father in distress.

Decades ago, needing loyal servants to implement the plan he had conceptualized even then, he had removed the slaads' eggs from the chaos of their native plane of Limbo. Afterward, he had magically altered them in the egg, instilling the raw essence of magic into their still-forming bodies. After their emergence from their shells, he had nurtured them as a father, rearing them on the rarefied nutriment of raw magic and the brains of sentient creatures. They still had a taste for the latter, and a thorough understanding of the former.

Being creatures of chaos, each of his brood had responded differently to the process. Vhostym took a father's pride in their multifarious personalities—Azriim, the intelligent but willful son; Dolgan, incredibly strong and loyal but also somewhat servile; Serrin, fast and merciless; Elura the . . .

Elura the dead, he reminded himself without sadness. Had the brood been able to return her body to him, he might have resurrected her. But divinations had revealed that the priest of Mask and his comrades had reduced Elura to ash. He missed her, in his way. He would have called her the most adventurous of the brood. She had taken pleasure in the males of many species, including Vhostym himself, centuries ago. . . .

Without further waste of sentiment, he put her out of his mind.

In the end, the pre-birth process to which he had subjected the brood had transmogrified them into more than ordinary slaadi. Their magical natures had been enhanced to various degrees. But despite the differences from their ordinary kin, their slaadi biological heritage still ran strong: each felt a compulsion to change from the caterpillar of their current form—that of a green slaad—into the butterfly of the more powerful gray. To do so, they required an influx of arcane power, an admixture of magic known to Vhostym and few others. Vhostym would provide that to his sons upon the consummation of his plan, recompense for their success in retrieving the Weave Tap and serving him for so many years.

Had it been possible, he would have retrieved the Tap himself. But even his power could not have pierced Shar's Fane of Shadows. Only a shadow adept could have done so. So his brood had manipulated the shadow mage Vraggen into gaining them entry. The plot had taken months to unfold, but at last they had succeeded and the time was nigh to move forward.

He spoke a word of power and held his open palm before one of the blank walls of his sanctuary. The magic warped space. The stone wavered, vanished, and was replaced by a door-shaped aperture. Vhostym levitated a few hands breadths off the smooth floor—to ease the strain on his body—and floated through the portal. It sealed shut behind him the moment he cleared it.

In contrast to the austerity of the meditation chamber, the lounge beyond was stuffed with luxuries. Piles of silks, soft cushions, furs, divans, and chairs from many worlds lay strewn haphazardly around the room. As a young man, when he had sought sensation in mistleaf, potent liquors, and the pleasures of the flesh, such things had seemed important to him. No longer. Only one thing was important to him.

Of the hundreds of chambers and rooms that existed in the honeycombed rock of his Underdark pocket plane, that room alone he allowed to remain in such disarray. The chaos of the decor and the decadence of the furnishings appealed to his slaadi. It was their favorite chamber.

Azriim and Dolgan awaited him there.

Azriim sat on a divan on the far side of the lounge in the form of a half-drow, stylishly dressed. Vhostym thought his son enjoyed that body better than his own—a human form was perhaps a more suitable tool for enjoying sensation, he supposed. And what Azriim enjoyed, Azriim did. Vhostym admired that about his son. Of the four slaadi of the brood, Vhostym thought Azriim had taken after him the most.

Seeing Vhostym, Azriim stood and bowed, a reluctant gesture for the prideful slaad.

"Sojourner," he said.

Vhostym smiled. Azriim had never called Vhostym "father" or "master," only "Sojourner." It was enough. Vhostym respected his independence.

On the floor near Azriim, Dolgan crouched on his haunches in his natural form—a hulking, bipedal, toad-like creature with leathery green skin and a face full of fangs. The flesh of his muscular forearm oozed black blood from self-inflicted claw scratches. His dullest son was obsessed with pain—both giving it and receiving it. The fact that the slaadi quickly regenerated their wounds only fed

Dolgan's fetish. Even as Vhostym watched, Dolgan's wounds closed to light scars.

"Master," the big slaad croaked, and abased himself on the floor.

Vhostym looked upon his largest son with impatience and replied, "Stand, Dolgan. You are my son, not my slave."

At those words, Vhostym thought he detected a sneer on Azriim's lips.

Dolgan clambered to his feet, his hind claws scratching against the stone floor, and said, "Yes, Father."

Lightly and quickly, so as not to humiliate his sons, Vhostym extended his mental perception into the brains of his slaadi and brushed their surface thoughts. He found impatience and eagerness. Azriim gave it voice.

"You have studied the Weave Tap for days, Sojourner, and now have been in sanctuary still another."

Had it been so long? Vhostym thought he had been amidst the stars but a few hours. Strange. Still, he did not approve of Azriim's tone. His sons took liberties with him that few in the multiverse would dare.

"You state the obvious, Azriim. And your tone borders on impertinence."

To give his point an edge, he entered Azriim's mind and caressed the pain-receptors of the slaad's brain. Azriim went rigid and bared his perfect teeth.

Dolgan grinned at his brother's pain.

Vhostym released his favorite son.

Azriim shot Dolgan a glare, returned his mismatched gaze to Vhostym, and adopted a more respectful tone.

"I meant only to suggest that we stand ready to begin the next phase."

Dolgan dug his claws into his palms and said, "But first Father must tell us what the next phase is."

Vhostym said, "That is your brother's very point, Dolgan." He looked at Azriim. "You wish to begin the next phase because you desire the transformation? The drive is strong upon you?"

"Now *you* state the obvious," Azriim replied, and his eyes—one blue and one brown—narrowed with perturbation.

At that, Vhostym considered causing more severe pain to Azriim, but decided against it. Instead, he opted for magnanimity and smiled benevolently on his son.

"I do, but my intent in doing so is to teach a lesson."

Azriim took a half step backward, no doubt thinking more pain to be forthcoming, and asked, "A lesson?"

Dolgan too looked puzzled, enough so that he stopped tearing gashes into his own hand.

Vhostym waved his hand in the air, spoke a word of power, and a chalice of two-hundred year old Halruaan wine materialized in his grasp.

"Sit," he said, in a tone of voice that the slaadi dared not disobey.

Both dropped to the floor. Vhostym floated between them and sat on the cushions of a divan. Their eyes followed him to where he sat. He sipped from the wine and sighed—full bodied, and as magically smooth as the velvet he sat upon.

"I am pleased with your success in recovering the Weave Tap. But oftentimes, we learn more from failure than from success."

The slaadi looked questions at him.

"The priest of Mask did not thwart your recovery of the Weave Tap. He failed. Not so?"

They nodded, though Azriim scowled, and his hand went to his abdomen, where the Shadowlord's priest had wounded him.

"His failure has something to teach us," Vhostym said. "Characterize him."

Dolgan looked perplexed. The big slaad looked from Azriim to Vhostym to Azriim again. His confusion caused him to scrape still more flesh from his palm.

"What do you mean, 'characterize him'?" Azriim asked.

Vhostym smiled. He enjoyed these interactions with his sons; they made him feel paternal.

"You, Azriim, are precise. You, Dolgan, are brutal. Serrin is merciless. That is each of your respective characters. Do you understand?"

Azriim nodded.

"Excellent. Now characterize this priest who killed your sister, nearly killed Dolgan, and managed to wound even you."

That tweaked Azriim's pride, exactly as Vhostym had intended.

"This is ridiculous," Azriim said, his tone bitter. "The priest is dead."

"Drowned," Dolgan added.

"Perhaps," Vhostym said. "Characterize him nevertheless."

With typical stubbornness, Azriim refused to answer. He crossed his arms across his chest and looked away. Vhostym could scarcely contain a smile. His slaadi, each of them a powerful, skillful killer when out of his sight, reverted to childishness when in his presence. He supposed the phenomenon was the same across all sentient species.

"Come, Azriim," Vhostym chided, "characterize him."

"Relentless," Dolgan blurted.

Surprised, Vhostym gave Dolgan an approving smile and the slaad fairly beamed. Perhaps Dolgan was not so dull, after all.

"Excellent, Dolgan," said Vhostym. "Relentlessness is an admirable characteristic. But it did not serve him, did it? As Azriim observed, he is likely dead."

"He *is* dead," Azriim said.

Dolgan merely stared.

"Now," Vhostym said, continuing the lesson, "characterize the shadow adept you manipulated into opening the Fane of Shadows."

Before Dolgan could answer, Azriim stared meaningfully at Vhostym and said, "Arrogant."

Vhostym decided to ignore Azriim's implication and said, "Very good. Consider—relentlessness in moderation is dedication. Arrogance in moderation is self-confidence. Learn this lesson. then: All things, when taken too far, become self-destructive and lead to failure." He fixed a hard gaze on Azriim. "This applies equally to both impatience and pridefulness."

Azriim understood the lesson then, and his mismatched eyes found the floor. Vhostym had made his point, so he gave his sons what they wished.

"Remember that," he said, "as the next phase begins."

Both slaadi looked at him sharply.

"It is beginning?" Azriim breathed. "The Crown of Flame?"

Vhostym smiled softly. Azriim did not understand the nature of the crown, only that his father long had sought it, only that once Vhostym possessed it, Azriim would be transformed into gray and freed.

Vhostym took a sip of wine and said, "It began, Azriim, long ago. Now it is finishing."

Vhostym had observed the universe through the eyes of his spell for the last time. Having plumbed the mystery of the Weave Tap, he was ready to put the final phases of his plan into motion.

"And afterward?" Azriim asked.

Dolgan leaned forward, eyes wide, digging his fingers into his flesh.

Vhostym looked upon his sons with approval and replied, "Afterward, my sons, you will have what I have promised to give you: transformation to gray and the freedom to pursue your own lives."

Dolgan, unable to contain his excitement, stood and capered. His dripping hand left a spatter of blood across the carpets. Azriim looked into Vhostym's eyes, as though trying to discern a lie. There was no lie to discern, of course. Vhostym would keep his word.

Azriim asked, "Yet you still will not tell us what the Crown of Flame is, or describe its appearance?"

"When the time is right," Vhostym said. He sent his mental consciousness through the various caverns and rooms of his plane until he located Serrin. The slaad was sharpening his weapon skills by slaughtering some of the penned demons Vhostym kept for research and spell component material.

"Serrin is in the barbazu pen. Retrieve him and bring him to the Weave Tap's nursery. One of its seeds are now ripe. I will explain what you are to do next."

CHAPTER 1

PERDITION

Dark knowledge churned through Cale's mind. Fell power coursed through his veins. He could not quite comprehend it, not rationally, but somehow he *knew* it. His body felt thick and insensate, as though he had been immersed in ice water. He could hear, but only dimly, as though from a great distance. He could see nothing. He felt stupefied; his thoughts ran as thick and as sluggish as tar.

With effort, he fought his way through the mental cobwebs. As he did, memories of the transformation from man to shade rose to the forefront of his consciousness. He recalled shadowy tentacles pulsing with power, piercing his skin, filling him with darkness, stealing his humanity. He pushed the memory out of his mind before it made him scream. He took a deep breath and drank in damp air heavy with the smell of organic decay, as fetid as a sewer. He knew he was in a swamp, a swamp that smelled like a charnel house. Many things had died there; many more things would.

Nearby, the buzzing and clicking of insects filled his ears, the sounds vaguely familiar but the rhythm somehow alien.

"What kind of water is this?" said a voice, Jak's voice, from somewhere near him.

Water splashed.

The sound of the halfling's voice helped center Cale, helped him climb the last few strides out of the darkness. Things became clearer.

He was not anywhere near the Lightless Lake. He was lying on his back in a bed of cold mud, covered in what he took to be a coarse blanket, or a shroud. He could not see because his eyes were closed, the lids caked shut with, scum, dirt, or blood. For the moment, he didn't try to open them. He didn't want to see what he thought they would reveal. He didn't want to know what his mind insisted he knew.

I'm not human, he thought, and the accusation hit him like a club. The simple truth of it left him empty. He thought of Tazi.

What would she say if she could see me now?

From Cale's right, Riven responded to Jak. Surprisingly, even the assassin's voice brought Cale some small comfort.

"It's the same water as anywhere, Fleet. Just . . . darker."

The creak of leather from Cale's right; Riven changing his stance.

"It's as thick as my mother's maple syrup," Jak said.

More splashing.

How long have we been here? Cale wondered.

"What is this place?" said another voice. "Where are we? The last thing I remember, we were watching an entire lake crash down on us. I thought we were dead."

It took Cale a moment to place the speaker—Magadon. The mind mage and guide from Starmantle. Cale had no recollection of the Lightless Lake crashing down on them.

"How many times will you ask the same question?" Riven said in a voice edged with tension. "You're the damned guide, Mags. *You* tell us where we are."

To that, Magadon said nothing, though Cale could hear him wading into the water.

Cale knew where they were—at least he thought he did—and he thought he knew how they had gotten there.

Jak spoke in a low voice: "Do you think we are? Dead, I mean?"

Riven scoffed. Cale could imagine his mocking sneer. He could also imagine the indignant glare Jak must have offered in response.

"You stuff that sneer," barked the halfling as he splashed through the water to get nearer to Riven. Jak's voice dripped venom. "You're right, though. Because if we *were* dead, you and I wouldn't end up in the same place, now would we?"

Riven chuckled darkly and said, "I wouldn't hang my sword belt on that, Fleet. You might think differently before this is all said and done."

Before this was all said and done. Cale did not even know what the *this* was. Slaadi in human form had murdered their ostensible master, a shadow adept named Vraggen, and taken a magical sapling tree—the Weave Tap—from a mysterious temple called the Fane of Shadows. Just before the slaadi had escaped, one of them, Azriim, had mentioned someone called the Sojourner, presumably their true master. That was all Cale knew, and his mind was too muddled to reason out the meaning of it all.

"The Wall of the Faithless," Jak said, still dogging the assassin. "That's the best you can hope for, Zhent. My guess—your afterlife is uglier than that. Much uglier."

"I wouldn't have it any other way," Riven responded,

and Cale heard the assassin's leather armor creak.

Jak replied with a *harrumph* and silence. The tension was as thick as the stink.

"The plants at least look familiar," Magadon said, in an obvious attempt to diffuse the situation. "But they're slightly different. Here. Look at this swamp flower . . . thicker roots, thinner stalks and leaves. The sky's different too. What in the multiverse is this place?" he asked again.

At that, Cale wiped away the substance caked on his eyelids—mud—opened his eyes, and looked up into a pitch black sky devoid of stars. Clusters of low, ashen clouds dotted the dark canopy, backlit by a dim, sourceless ochre light.

"The Plane of Shadow," he announced.

There was a moment's silence, followed by Jak's exclamation, "Cale! You're awake!"

The halfling splashed through a pool of shallow water to reach Cale's side. He knelt and helped Cale to sit up. Cale's muscles felt as though they had been beaten with warhammers.

"Trickster's toes," Jak said. "You're as cold as Beshaba's heart." Over his shoulder, he shouted to Riven, "Get him another blanket, Zhent."

When Cale smiled at Jak, the halfling's eyes went wide and he recoiled so hurriedly that he fell on his backside. His hand went to his mouth.

"Oh . . . oh, Cale."

Riven stepped closer to see, the request for the blanket forgotten, his lone eye focused on Cale's face.

"Dark," the assassin oathed.

Magadon, standing in ankle deep water and holding a gray flower in his hand, looked at Cale with some curiosity.

"Are you all right, Erevis?" the guide asked.

"I am," Cale replied, though the stares made Cale uncomfortable.

Still, he had been transformed and he knew how he

must look to them. He held up his arm and looked at the hand that the female slaad had bitten off, at the wrist that should have been a stump. The transformation had somehow regenerated it. He flexed the fingers. They felt normal, but his once pale skin had turned dusky gray, darker still on the regenerated hand. Wisps of shadows snaked at intervals from his fingertips and leaked from his pores. He was sheathed in shadows. Touching the darkness lightly with his normal hand he felt a slight resistance.

"You're covered in them," Jak said softly.

Riven kneeled on his haunches and studied Cale's face. "You've changed more in the time since we arrived here," the assassin said. "What's happened to you?" That last sounded more like an accusation than a question.

Cale had no ready answer.

"Your eyes," Magadon said. "The white's gone black. The pupils are yellow. They glow in this twilight. I can see them from here."

Cale managed a nod. The change in his eyes explained why he could see perfectly out to a bowshot's distance, despite the dimness of the plane. In fact, as his head cleared, he realized that each of his senses had grown sharper. He could hear Riven's breathing at ten paces, taste the subtle organic tang in the air, and smell the otherwise unnoticeable wisps of sulfur leaking from a nearby bubbling pool.

I'm not human.

The words rose unbeckoned from the back of his brain.

I'm a creature of shadow.

He pushed the words away.

"What's happened is what's happened," Cale said, looking meaningfully at Riven. "I'm still me."

Even to his own ears the words sounded like a lie. He unfolded himself and stood. Jak stood too, still staring at him.

Riven, rising and eyeing Cale doubtfully, said, "Are you?"

Unconsciously, the assassin reached for the onyx disc at his throat. In that gesture, Cale saw what Riven was wondering: Had the Shadowlord, their mutual deity, caused Cale's transformation? If so, Riven probably would perceive the transformation as a divine boon and be jealous of it.

"This wasn't him," Cale said, nodding at Riven's disc.

The assassin dropped his hand from the symbol.

Cale continued, "And you wouldn't want it even if it was."

Riven seemed to consider that before changing the subject.

"You're a shade, then. And you brought us here?"

Cale nodded and said, "I think so."

"You *think* so?" Riven asked, his voice edged with tension. "Can you take us back?"

Cale slowly shook his head and all three of his comrades visibly deflated. Even with all the new knowledge swirling in his brain, he didn't know how, or if he could return them to Faerûn. Whatever he had done back in the Fane to bring them there, he had done it unconsciously, out of an instinct for survival. He could not even remember it.

"The teleportation rods?" Cale asked.

Riven had taken two of the magical transport rods from the slaadi.

Jak perked up. So too did Magadon. But Riven gave a harsh laugh; to Cale, it sounded forced.

"First thing I tried," the assassin said. "They crumbled to dust in my hands."

He turned away, eyes hooded. Jak sagged. Magadon, stoic as ever, went back to his study of the flora.

Silence reigned. The realization lay heavy on all of them—they were trapped, at least for a time.

Magadon, with his psionic sensitivity, must have sensed their thoughts.

"Better here than drowned," he observed matter-of-factly, even as he continued studying the bog's flora.

No one disputed that logic.

Cale's eyes found Jak. The halfling held his gaze for only a moment before his expression filled with shame. He looked as though he might cry. Cale understood the reason. He knelt before Jak, put a hand on his shoulder and spoke in Lurienal, the halfling's native language.

"My choice, little man," Cale said. *"I would do it again."*

Jak looked away, eyes welling, but managed a nod. After a moment, he looked back at Cale and said, *"I would have done it for you too, Cale. Do you know that?"*

Cale smiled softly and replied, *"Of course I do. That's why I did it."*

He patted Jak's shoulder, eliciting a half smile from his friend, and stood. He turned a circle and looked, *really* looked around the Plane of Shadow for the first time.

A starless, moonless sky roofed a dreary landscape. Shades of black and gray predominated, as though the entirety of the plane had been coated in ash. Even Jak's ordinarily bright red hair appeared a dull rust color. The air was gauzy with shadows. Cale knew ten or more synonyms in nine languages for "darkness," and none of them adequately captured the brooding, oppressive gloom of the place.

The bog in which they stood extended in all directions to the limit of his vision. Steaming pools of stagnant water and mud dotted the lowlands. Stands of reeds and black-leafed trees not unlike Faerûnian cypresses grew in clusters along the edge of the ponds. Flotillas of dull gray flowers floated on the surface of the water. Clouds of birds, or perhaps bats, to judge from their wheeling, jerky motion, fluttered in the air above the trees. Black flies the size of coins teemed in the air.

"It changes over time," Magadon said.

Cale looked to the guide, met his white eyes with his own dark gaze, and asked, "What does?"

"The landscape," Magadon said. "It changes."

Cale could not keep the surprise from his face.

"What do you mean?"

"I haven't noticed that," Jak said, looking around at the swamp, and even Riven looked taken aback.

Magadon nodded, as though he had expected such a response, and said, "It's quite subtle." The guide pointed at a nearby cypress. "That stand of trees was over a stone's throw away yesterday—or however long ago it was that we arrived here.

"Dark," Jak oathed, wide-eyed. He stared at the ground under his feet as though it might swallow him at any moment. "What kind of place is this?"

"Why didn't you tell us this before, Mags?" Riven asked.

The guide shrugged and took a small bite of the plant he held in his hand. He spit it out almost instantly.

"Nothing to tell," Magadon said finally. "We cannot stop it, and we weren't moving until Erevis regained consciousness."

Cale eyed Magadon with new appreciation. The man noticed details. Cale liked that. But Cale noticed details too, and the guide's last words caused him concern.

"How long was I unconscious?" Cale asked.

Magadon shrugged again and said, "Hours. Days. Who can say in this? I can see only twenty paces. There are no stars, and if this place ever sees a sun, Drasek's a cloistered priest of Torm."

"Riven," Riven corrected absently.

Magadon gave a half-smile and continued, "We've seen a few animals, but I don't recognize any of them. So I cannot determine the passage of time from their activity cycle. We're in the dark. Literally. We were afraid to move you—you seemed almost catatonic—so we've remained here since we arrived."

Silence sat heavy while Cale digested that.

Jak began to pace a circle, kicking at the mud.

"But you're up now," he said, " and we've got to get out of here." He held his holy symbol in his hand flipped it between his fingers. "I tried divinations soon after we arrived, Cale. No answer."

Cale looked at him and asked, "What do you mean?"

Jak held up his holy symbol, a jeweled pendant.

"I mean divinations do not work here. The Trickster can't hear me. Or can't answer me. I'm. . . ."

Cale understood. Jak felt severed from his god.

The halfling began again to pace.

"It's not right here," he said. "I don't feel right." Jak stopped pacing, as though struck by a realization. He looked at Cale and asked, "Do you?"

Cale recognized the question behind the question but answered only with a non-committal grunt. Strange as it seemed, Cale felt better than he had in some time. The feeling brought him little comfort. He wondered again what he had become, that he could feel at home in such a godsforsaken plane. He reached for his own holy symbol before he remembered that the female slaad had devoured it along with his hand. Awkwardly, he rested his palm on his sword pommel. His sword; the sword that bled shadows. He wondered if it too had changed further upon its arrival in the Plane of Shadow. He resisted the urge to draw it.

"It's just another place," Riven said, seemingly as calm as the windless air. "Ease down, Fleet."

Apparently, the assassin too felt at home there. Either that or he hid is discomfort well.

"Ease down, little man," Cale seconded to Jak, to head off another exchange between the halfling and Riven. "We've been in worse places. Haven't we?"

Jak looked at him curiously and nodded.

"We'll get out of here too," Cale said. "It may just take some time." Cale looked to Magadon and made his voice sound normal. "How about a fire?"

"Tried," Magadon said, and nodded toward a pile of tinder not far from Cale. "The wood is saturated with this bog. It won't hold a flame. We tried to keep you warm with blankets, but. . . ."

Cale said, "A light then, at least. Jak, your bluelight wand."

"It's no good, Cale," Jak replied, shaking his head. "We tried it. I might as well have it covered in a sack."

"This place eats light," Magadon said.

Cale heard the tone of his comrades, saw their morose expressions, and realized that the gray of the plane had already infected their souls. Strange that it had not affected him. He supposed that made him a creature of the gloom.

"Pull it anyway, little man," he said to Jak. "It's better than nothing."

Jak shrugged and took his wand out of an inner pocket of his shirt. He spoke the command word and the tip glowed blue. The light did little to dispel the darkness.

"Listen to me," Cale said to all of them. "I brought us here and I will get us back. I just need some time to figure out—" to figure out what I am, he thought—"to figure out how." He looked at each in turn. "Well enough?"

Jak nodded. Riven said nothing, merely stared at Cale appraisingly. Magadon adjusted his pack and said, "Well enough."

"Now let's get the Nine Hells out of this bog," Cale said.

Jak brightened at that. Magadon grinned.

"Which way?" Jak asked, and held his wand above his head as though it would better pierce the twilight. It did not. "I can't see anything worthwhile in any direction."

Cale looked to Magadon and said, "You're our guide."

Magadon's pale eyes glowed in the twilight.

"I should have charged you more than three hundred gold," he said with a chuckle.

Cale could not quite bring himself to smile in response.

"Which way, Magadon?" Cale asked instead.

Magadon concentrated for a moment, and a nimbus of dim light flared around his head.

"That is north," he said when he opened his eyes, nodding in the direction behind Cale. "As good a direction as any. Follow me, and step where I step until we're clear of the bog."

With that, they geared up and Magadon set off. His

long strides devoured the distance. Tedium devoured the hours. More than once Magadon steered them away from a path that ended in a sinkhole or bog pit. Without the psionic woodsman to guide them, Cale had little doubt the swamp would have killed them all.

As they journeyed, Cale glimpsed small, furtive creatures at the edge of his vision, apparently drawn to Jak's light. They always darted away into hidden dens and burrows before Cale could clearly see them. Instead, he caught only flashes of twisted bodies, gangly legs, and malformed heads. He felt their eyes upon him as he passed. Calls like curses, alien screeches, chatters, and howls sounded in the twilight behind them. With Jak's bluelight wand cutting a dim path through the shadow, Cale imagined they must have stood out like a goblin in a gnome delve.

They walked the hours in silence. Throughout, the darkness was unrelenting. Shadows saturated them, clung to them like oil. Even their clothes seemed to be absorbing the pitch. Once blue cloaks faded to gray, green tunics to black. Moods too went from dark to darker. Cale saw in the transformation of their clothing an uncomfortable metaphor for his soul.

His soul—*villendem*, in Chondathan. He wondered if the transformation had stripped him of it.

No, he thought, and shook his head. I'm still myself.

But he wasn't himself, and something deep in his consciousness, some black, secret part of his brain, protested against his obstinate refusal to accept the truth. He fought down the feeling and put one foot in front of the other.

Later, Jak slipped beside him and said in a low tone, "I know what you said earlier, Cale, but I think this is worse than anywhere we've ever been. Even worse than when we were in the Abyss. That was evil through and through. You could feel it, so it was easy to keep yourself separate from it. This place, it seeps into your skin. I feel awash in it. It's almost . . ."

"Seductive," Cale finished for him.

Jak looked at him sharply, worry in his eyes.

"I was going to say, 'insidious.'" The halfling touched his arm and added, "Cale—"

"I know."

"Don't get comfortable here," Jak said. "Don't."

"I won't."

But Cale already was comfortable there, and that frightened him.

✦ ✦ ✦ ✦ ✦

Events were proceeding as Vhostym had foreseen. With his slaadi about their appointed task in the Underdark, he would hasten the Weave Tap's production of a second seed. For that, he would have to feed the artifact, fertilize it—and the Weave Tap benefited from only specialized kinds of fertilizer.

Just as Shar and Syluné embodied the dual aspect of the primordial universe that had spawned them, just as the Weave and Shadow Weave embodied the dual nature of magic on Toril, the Weave Tap embodied a dichotomous duality. Crafted with Shadow Magic, the Tap nevertheless reached its roots and limbs into both the Weave and the Shadow Weave; it existed simultaneously in both the Prime Material Plane and the Plane of Shadow. The Weave Tap, a living artifact, bridged the two sources of Toril's arcane energy, drawing power from both.

Vhostym found it fascinating, and was mildly chagrined that he had not thought to craft it himself.

To satisfy its dual nature, the Weave Tap required the life-force, the very magical natures, of both fiends and celestials. Vhostym long had kept plenty of the former in his pocket plane as spell component material, and he prepared to procure the first of the latter.

Like many of the chambers that honeycombed the underground realm of his pocket plane, Vhostym's summoning chamber was a spherical cyst of stone with no apparent ingress or egress. Engraved runes traced in platinum and gold covered the walls. A circular slab of polished granite floated in midair in the center of the chamber. Upon its face was etched a thaumaturgic circle.

The chamber was unlit, though Vhostym could see well enough. In fact, the magical darkness in the chamber was so complete that not even magical light sources could penetrate it—a necessary precaution when summoning celestials. Though not even the strongest of the celestials could approach Vhostym in power, their ability to generate and radiate light could prove painful unless Vhostym took precautions.

He floated around the slab, running his long, pale fingers along the etching, examining the lines for imperfections. As expected, he found none.

Vhostym took a moment to prepare a few defensive spells, warding himself against all but the most powerful magic and rendering his body impervious to physical attack. Ready, he moved his hands in complex gestures. Waves of arcane power gathered, went forth from his fingers, and coalesced above the granite slab. The lines of the thaumaturgic circle began to glow a soft, almost imperceptible, yellow.

When the power reached the necessary level, Vhostym spoke aloud an arcane phrase and felt a hole open in the walls between the planes. He called the name of the celestial being he sought to summon.

"Phaedriel," he pronounced.

Vhostym felt his magically augmented voice reach through the planes, find the deva, and try to pull the creature back to him. He felt the celestial's resistance, but it lasted only a moment before being overpowered by the force of Vhostym's calling.

A muted flash of pure white light flared in the midst of the summoning platform, forcing Vhostym to shield his eyes. Had he not prepared a spell ahead of time to mute it, the flash would have blinded him and charred his skin. When the spots from even that dim light cleared from before his eyes, Vhostym saw that his calling had been successful.

Phaedriel stood on the summoning platform, bound by the lines of power that went up from the floor. The tips of the deva's feathered wings, white and opalescent even in the darkness, touched the edge of the binding. Pale gold skin covered the celestial's perfectly proportioned, well-muscled body. A silver mace, powerfully magical, hung from the deva's belt. Piercing white eyes gazed out from over an aquiline nose and strong jaw. The smell of flowers filled the summoning chamber. The deva surveyed the space.

"What is this plane?" said Phaedriel, in the purest tenor voice that Vhostym had ever heard.

"You are on a plane of my own devising," Vhostym answered.

The celestial made no response, only fixed his eyes on Vhostym. A lesser being would have recoiled at the force emitted by those orbs, but Vhostym answered the deva's stare with one of his own.

"What type of creature are you?" the deva asked at last. "Neither Githyanki nor Githzerai, but . . . similar."

Vhostym replied, "I am nothing that you have encountered before, celestial. Nor will you encounter my kind again."

The deva heard the threat in that last and his brow furrowed.

"We are not enemies, creature," the celestial said.

He closed his eyes briefly and attempted to cast a spell, likely a divination or sending, but the casting failed, as Vhostym had known it would. The deva opened his eyes.

"Your binding prevents me the use of any magic," the deva observed.

Vhostym did not bother to reply.

"What do you want of me then, creature?" the deva asked.

Vhostym saw no reason to lie.

"I want all of you, celestial," he answered. "You will not leave this plane."

Positive energy, a manifestation of the celestial's anger, flared in a rosy-colored halo around the deva's bald head. His downy wings fluttered in agitation.

"Your confidence is unwarranted," the deva said.

Vhostym did not bother to correct the celestial's misapprehension.

"I will fight you," said the deva as he took up his mace.

"It will not avail you," replied Vhostym, waving a hand dismissively. "You could not harm me even if you were free of the binding."

"Allies will seek me," Phaedriel said. "They will avenge me should I come to harm."

"They will not find you," replied Vhostym. "And even if they could find you, they would dare not come."

Nothing short of a god would risk confrontation with Vhostym. In his time, he had single-handedly slain flights of dragons, annihilated entire faiths, left worlds in flame behind him. But he had been young then, and rash.

"You belong to me now, Phaedriel," Vhostym said. "But fear not. Others of your kind will join you. You will not die alone."

"Why?" the deva asked.

The radiance from his skin dimmed somewhat, and Vhostym almost smiled. He too had asked such questions once. Only after millennia of existence had he finally realized that the question had no meaning. The multiverse was infinite, unforgiving, and random. There was no *why*, not in the sense that the deva meant.

"Because I will it," he answered. "Will is the only why in the multiverse."

The deva's eyes narrowed and he clutched his mace tightly.

"You are mistaken," said the celestial.

Vhostym almost laughed, but instead said, "Am I? Where now is the god you serve? Where the planetar to whom you report? You think yourself a being of good, a servant of justice. Yet I tell you that there are no such things as good and justice. What is, is. In the multiverse, there is the will of the powerful and nothing more. Consider: If the multiverse was just, how could you be fated to this end?"

The deva stood up straight and fixed Vhostym with a steady gaze. Its radiance returned.

"You will not cause me to question my faith, creature."

Vhostym frowned, sad for the doctrinaire deva, and replied, "Then die a fool, Phaedriel."

The deva tensed, preparing for a fight, no doubt intent on expending his last breath in noble battle. Vhostym would give him no such chance.

The Sojourner moved his hands in a complex gesture and spoke words of power. His will flowed along those words, penetrated the binding, and entered the deva, attempting to dominate his mind. The celestial gritted his teeth and went rigid. Every sinew in his beautiful form was visible. He resisted admirably, but even the deva's will was no match for Vhostym's magic. The spell rooted in the celestial's mind. Phaedriel could still think for himself, but he could not resist obeying Vhostym's commands.

"Relax your body and remain still," Vhostym said.

The deva did just that.

Vhostym lowered the magical binding that encased the celestial and flew to the summoning platform. Gently, so as not to aggravate the pain in his bones, he lowered his feet to the granite slab.

"Shhh," Vhostym said, though Phaedriel had said nothing.

Vhostym placed his hands around the deva's head. Concentrating briefly, he made his mind into a knife and entered the celestial's mind.

The deva attempted to resist him, but his own psionic power was paltry compared to that of Vhostym. Systematically, Vhostym began to destroy the connections between the deva's mind and his body, allowing the celestial to live but preventing him from moving. It took only moments. Vhostym began to withdraw from Phaedriel's mind.

Before he got out, the deva asked in a small voice, *Will I experience pain?*

Vhostym answered truthfully.

Yes, he said.

CHAPTER 2

TREADING THE BLACK

With no sun by which to gauge the passage of time, Cale felt as though they had been splashing through the swamp forever. Time seemed to have frozen. There was no color, only fetid water and gloom. Cale recalled Magadon observing that the terrain actually moved. He wondered if, beyond the limits of their vision, the swamp was rearranging itself around them so they would never get free of it.

The guide stayed a full ten paces ahead, to ensure they'd avoid any pitfalls or other mundane hazards. His knucklebone eyes looked ghostly in Jak's bluelight. Mud caked all their cloaks and boots. Cale marveled at Magadon's pack, which was so large it looked as though he was carrying another person on his back. The guide must have been stronger than he appeared.

"We'll need food soon," Magadon called back.

Riven and Jak didn't even raise their heads in response, merely grunted in the affirmative. Cale too signaled his agreement, though he wasn't hungry. He simply wanted to engage in something ordinary, to take his mind off the plane, to take his mind off himself.

"It's taking longer than I had hoped to clear the bog," the guide continued. "So we must start rationing our supplies as of now. No one is to eat or drink anything native to this place unless it becomes absolutely necessary." He waited for them to catch up. "Let's inventory our stock. What do each of you have for food and water?"

"A few days of rations," Cale said. He squeezed the waterskins at his belt and added, "A skin-and-a-half of water."

He'd carried out of Starmantle only enough rations to get him to the Gulthmere and back. The starsphere and the book he had taken from the Fane of Shadows were the heaviest things in his pack.

"About the same," Riven said.

Magadon frowned, obviously troubled, and said, "I've got more than that, but not much more. We'll need—"

"Rations are not an issue," Jak interrupted. "I can conjure food and water with a spell. Anything I want, whenever we're hungry."

Magadon's raised eyebrows indicated both his surprise and pleasure.

"Jak, that's more useful than you know. I feared we'd have to drink the water here. Even after boiling . . ." He looked to Cale then continued, "Let's find a dry spot, make camp, and eat something conjured by our chef." He grinned at Jak. "With luck, we'll get out of the bog sometime tomorrow."

Cale agreed and they did exactly that.

"What do you need for your spell?" Magadon asked Jak, after setting up the two canvas tents he carried in his pack. The guide seemed to carry more in his backpack than would fit in the extradimensional space of a magical bag of holding.

"Just put that pot on the ground," Jak replied, indicating the large, beaten-metal cooking pot that Magadon carried with his gear. "And our waterskins too."

They piled the pot and their waterskins on the ground before Jak. The halfling held his holy symbol pendant over the pile and intoned a prayer to the Trickster. The pot filled with a thick, steaming stew. The waterskins swelled to capacity.

Magadon gave an appreciative whistle and said, "There's many times I could have used you in the bush, Jak." The guide knelt, dipped a finger into the stew, and tasted it. "Potato," he said with a smile. "And tasty."

Riven snorted irritably and glared at the halfling.

"Potato?" he grumbled. "Nine Hells, Fleet. You can make anything you want and you settle on potato stew? What about some meat?"

Jak bristled and pointed his pendant at Riven's chest.

"My mother made potato stew, Zhent," said the halfling. "Hot soup warms the soul, she used to say. Probably little help to you, seeing as how you're a soulless bastard. You're welcome to your rations, if you'd rather."

That last statement caused Riven to keep behind his teeth whatever retort he might have been considering. Cale grinned.

Smiling himself, Magadon removed several small, wooden bowls from his pack and used them to start serving the stew.

"Your mother was a wise woman, Jak," the guide said through his mirth, and gave the halfling the first steaming bowl of stew. "And you'll have to forgive Drasek for his words." He winked at the halfling and said, "He had no real mother, of course, being the spawn of ice and molasses. Which explains why he grew up to be cold and thick."

Cale laughed aloud.

Jak chuckled, eyed Riven with distrust, and said, "Slippery and dark, more like."

Riven scowled at the halfling, but nevertheless held out his hand for a stew bowl.

"That was a poor jest when you first made it years ago, Mags," the assassin said.

"Poor?" Magadon asked, and ignored Riven's outstretched hand in favor of Cale.

Cale sipped the thick soup. It was tasty.

Magadon continued, "That half-orc and his fellows would have pummeled you to gruel. That jest saved your life."

"Theirs, more likely," Riven said, and Magadon cocked his head to concede the point.

Jak, continuing to chuckle, said, "Cold and thick. That's good. Very good."

"That's enough, Fleet," Riven barked, but Cale heard the smile behind the words. "Now give me some of that godsdamned stew, Mags, before I pummel *you* to gruel."

The woodsman did, and for a time the camaraderie of the road and the warm food chased the shadows. But only for a time. After the meal, the weight of the plane and the chill of the swamp once again descended.

They huddled around Jak's bluelight wand saying nothing, suddenly exhausted. Magadon had selected a campsite within a stand of the brooding, cypresslike trees common to the swamp. To Cale, it felt like the trees were watching them, the leaves whispering evil words.

After a time, he said, "I'll take first watch. All of you, get some sleep."

❧ ❧ ❧ ❧ ❧

The next "day" seemed much like the one before—chilly, wet, and gloomy. They slogged alternately through knee deep, black water, soggy vegetation, and mud that stank like the worst of Selgaunt's sewers. Wisps of shadowy fog hovered over the land like dark tendrils squeezed from the saturated earth. Uncomfortably, they reminded Cale of the squirming tentacles from the Fane that had effected his transformation into a shade.

A few hours into the day's trek, Magadon said to them,

"The ground is rising and less saturated. We'll clear the swamp before this day is over. I'd wager on it."

"You never were a good gambler," Riven grumbled.

Magadon grinned.

For his part, Cale could see so no end to the bog in sight and felt no change in the ground. It just felt like the same mud. Still, he felt comfortable trusting Magadon's expertise and he continued to trek on.

Without warning, a wave of terror washed over Cale. His breath caught and he could hear his heart thumping in his ears. Sweat formed on his brow. To judge from the look of wide-eyed alarm on his comrade's faces, they all felt something similar.

The swamp fell silent around them. Even the ubiquitous flies had vanished.

Cale put his hand to his blade hilt and looked around, his gaze darting from pool, to reeds, to trees. He saw nothing amiss, except that each of his comrades had gone ashen. The feeling of terror lingered.

"What is this?" Magadon asked softly, his voice tense.

The guide unslung his ashwood bow, drew an arrow from his quiver, and scanned the swamp. Pools of black water stood to either side of them, steaming in the humidity. The dark trees of the swamp loomed like watchtowers.

Jak and Riven went back to back and drew their blades. Jak let out a sharp breath that sounded like a hiss. Magadon and Cale too closed ranks. Cale's hand stayed on his sword hilt but he did not draw. He looked around, but still saw nothing. He listened, but heard only the rapid respiration of his companions. The water around them remained still; too still. A blanket of shadowy mist pooled around their knees.

"There!" said Magadon, pointing his bow to the sky. "Above us."

Gazes followed the point of the woodsman's knocked arrow.

Against the backlit sky, one of the clouds, smaller than

the others and darker, slowly wheeled a circle. Even as they watched, it veered in their general direction.

"Trickster's toes," Jak oathed, squinting. "What is that?"

With his enhanced vision, Cale could see that what they were looking at was not a cloud at all. It was a pool of writhing shadows—semi transparent to his transformed eyes. Within it, he saw the source of their magically induced terror.

"Kill the light!" he hissed. "Now."

Jak could not have missed the urgency in Cale's voice. Asking no questions, the halfling spoke a word in his own tongue and the wand's glow ceased.

"We can't see more than fifteen paces, Cale," Riven growled, still eyeing the sky.

Cale knew, but their only hope was that the creature in the sky had not noticed them.

"Quiet," he ordered.

Nearby stood a cluster of thin-leafed, droopy-limbed trees—not the cypresses, but they would be enough to hide them.

"Those trees directly to our right," Cale said. "Go now. As fast and as quiet as you can."

They must have heard the alarm in his tone, for they sheathed their weapons and darted off without comment. The splashing water rang like a gong in Cale's ears. Twice Jak fell in the water, and each time Magadon and Cale pulled him back to his feet. Somehow, Cale seemed faster than usual. He actually had to slow down to not outpace his comrades. As he ran, he prayed to Mask that the huge creature soaring overhead would not notice them. He imagined its dark eyes boring into his back. He looked ahead to the trees, willed them all to run faster, sensed a space between the shadows, and—

—he felt a moment's disorientation, a transitory rush of air, and—

—he was there!

Cale stood in the copse, well ahead of his comrades.

Somehow, he had stepped instantly from one shadow to another, seemingly without passing through the intervening space.

Dark and empty! he thought.

He had no time to consider his newfound ability. He stepped out from under the cover of the tree's low boughs and beckoned his comrades on.

"Faster," he hissed.

They had stopped, dumbfounded at his sudden disappearance and reappearance so far in front of them. They again began to run in earnest.

The cloud circled above them, a giant, scaled vulture swathed in shadows. The creature began to descend.

Cale reached for his holy symbol, but realized that he didn't have one. Instead he put his hand to his blade hilt. He drew it a fingerwidth and hesitated. He had not yet drawn it in on the Plane of Shadow and he felt that to do so somehow would be to surrender something that he could not quite articulate. Reluctantly, he removed his hand.

His comrades, wet and winded, streamed into the copse and ducked under the sheltering boughs. There they waited, ankle deep in the soft earth, stink, and water. The leaves and darkness enshrouded them.

"Quiet," Cale whispered, then he listened and watched.

He willed the shadows around them to darken slightly and much to his surprise, they did.

Riven, standing beside him, whispered, "Bad?"

Cale nodded. It could not be worse. He looked out of the copse and saw nothing. The tree limbs obscured his vision, but he could not miss the creature should it come near.

Magadon touched the tip of his arrow to his head and it began to hum lightly. He re-knocked it.

"What is it?" the guide asked Cale.

The beat of huge pinions, like the wind that presaged a thunderstorm, drowned out anything Cale might have said in answer. The force of the wings rattled the trees under which they hid, and threw up a blinding mist of swamp water and clots of mud. A huge, sinuous form, still streaming the remnants of the shadows that previously had cloaked it, alit in the water forty paces from the copse and filled Cale's field of vision. Its body displaced so much water that the copse was flooded up to their knees.

Terror went before it.

Cale held his breath, heart racing. So too did his comrades. All of them stood perfectly still, both awed and terrified.

Jak finally managed a whisper: "Trickster's hairy toes."

Cale knew that his comrades probably could barely see the creature through the darkness and the trees. For his part, Cale caught only glimpses of it through the curtain of limbs, but. . . .

Dark and empty, its size!

Its wingspan could have shaded the whole of the Uskevren manse. Lustrous black scales as large as great shields covered its muscled form. When it moved, shadows played along its hide. The edges of its form appeared to merge with the darkness, melding with the shadows of the plane and making it difficult to determine where the actual body of the creature began and ended. In those shadows, Cale thought he saw the dark, shifting images of struggling bodies, of faces contorted in screams, of eyes agog with terror. His skin went gooseflesh. Somewhere in the back of his brain, he heard moans and wails. He pushed them back and focused on the creature. Cale caught a flash of ebon horns, of teeth longer than Jak was tall, and of merciless eyes that reflected no light.

Dragon, his mind registered. A dragon of shadows.

The creature beat its wings once, spraying water in all directions, and sniffed the air. Cale knew that if it caught their scent, they could never outrun it. They could only fight; fight and die.

It lowered its great horned head to the level of the

water and moved it from side to side, sniffing, searching. Its respiration sounded louder than a forge bellows. The shadows around it formed writhing bodies and contorted shapes before melding to sheathe the creature in gloom once again.

Cale expected the dragon to roar loud enough to deafen them all, but instead of a roar it spoke, and its sinister voice was the threatening whisper of a drawn sword.

"Lightbringers in my swamp," it said, still sniffing. Its eyes narrowed. "I smell your sweat. *Human* sweat."

Magadon's mental voice suddenly sounded in Cale's head, giving him a start.

We're linked, the guide projected.

Cale nodded. The link was a good idea, but it caused him to feel the fear pulsing along the telepathic channels that joined him to his friends. He tried to keep his own anxiety under control. Panic would not serve them.

It knows we're nearby, Riven projected softly, crouching silently to peer through the foliage. *I can barely see it.*

What is in the shadows around it? Jak asked.

Cale did not bother to answer. The dragon itself was terrifying enough.

Jak asked, *If it comes, then what?*

The halfling held his holy symbol in both hands. He hadn't bothered to bare his short sword. It was too paltry a weapon against a creature the size of the dragon.

Then we fight, Cale answered, with as much steel in his mental voice as he could muster. *There's nowhere to run.*

His comrades said nothing, but each of them shifted slightly. Magadon drew his arrow back another few fingers' breadth and took aim through the boughs.

The dragon continued to chuff after their scent, peering suspiciously at this or that copse of trees or stand of reeds.

Ready yourselves, Cale projected, though he did not know what any of them could do.

As quiet as a wraith, Riven drew his magical sabers. Cale closed his fist over his sword hilt. Jak edged closer to Cale.

The dragon, incredibly graceful for a creature so enormous, slid through the swamp toward them, sniffing, searching, its swinging tail and powerful forelegs propelling it through the muck. It reared back its long neck and looked in the direction of their copse. The pupils of its deep, violet eyes visibly dilated.

"I can hear your hearts beating," it said.

The dragon opened its mouth wide. Its inhalation sucked the air from the vicinity of the copse.

Cover! Cale mentally shouted.

But before any of them could move, the dragon expelled from its jaws a cloud of viscous shadows that washed over the copse, and soaked them for a moment in impenetrable darkness. Cale felt its effect immediately—the chill of the void, the pull of negative energy on his soul. Strangely, it seemed to have little effect on him. Jak and Magadon groaned as the dragon's breath stole some of their essence.

The cloud began to dissipate into greasy streamers, and Cale saw that Riven too seemed largely unaffected. Jak and Magadon, though ashen, remained on their feet and seemed still to have their wits. A rain of shriveled leaves and dry twigs fell from the trees around them.

Magadon's bow sang.

Jak's weakened voice rang out with the words of a spellcasting.

Riven lurched from the copse toward the dragon, wading through the water, blades bare and whirling.

The guide's psionically enhanced arrow hit the dragon in the throat below the hole of its mouth, but shattered harmlessly on its scales. A beam of white light streaked from Jak's outstretched palm, but the shadows surrounding the creature swallowed whatever effect the beam otherwise would have had.

Surrendering to the inevitable, Cale at last drew his blade and followed after Riven. He almost laughed, so absurd must they have looked, like fleas charging a dog.

From behind him, he heard Jak and Magadon following hard after, splashing through the mud and water. Jak began again to cast.

As Riven plowed through the muck, mud, and vegetation, he began to shout in the foul tongue he sometimes uttered in his sleep. Somehow his voice seemed more powerful, deeper, darker, as though amplified by the shadows. Cale could not fight down the nausea caused by the vile words. He coughed his midday meal into the waters of the swamp. Behind him, Jak and Magadon cried out in pain.

The shadows sheathing the dragon swirled into recognizable human forms, all of them covering their ears, though the dragon itself seemed unaffected by the utterance. As fast as a lightning strike, it lunged forward and clutched Riven in its foreclaw before the assassin could bring his blades to bear. Pinning the human's arms to his sides, the dragon picked Riven up out of the water and began to squeeze. Forms lurched forward from the shadows around the creature, arms outstretched, as though to embrace the assassin.

Cale could imagine the cracking ribs, the crushed organs. A bloody froth exploded from Riven's mouth but he continued to struggle to free his blades, all the while shouting in the vile tongue.

"You mouth the Black Speech, child," the dragon hissed, "but little understand the words. Hear this."

The creature held the dying Riven before its mouth and hissed into the assassin's face words so terrible, so awful to hear, that they made Cale dizzy. He staggered and kept his feet only by sheer force of will.

Behind him, Jak and Magadon fell to their knees, clutching their ears. Blood leaked from between their fingers, from their noses, from their eyes. The water around them reddened. They were dying.

Defiant even to the last, Riven answered the dragon with still more of the Black Speech. Somehow, the assassin's voice remained strong through the blood and pain. His eye still blazed.

Jak and Magadon, nearly senseless, collapsed into the mud.

Stop! Cale projected to Riven. *You're killing them!*

But the assassin could not hear, might not have understood, or did not care.

With his friends dying all around him, Cale made the only decision he could. He chose a spot on the dragon's spine at about the point where the roots of its wings sprouted from its back, took a step forward, and willed himself there.

He felt the momentary sensation of movement and found himself crouched atop a creature larger than a keep, and darker than a moonless midnight. Shadowy figures rose out of the dragon's dark cloak, reaching for him. Their hands passed through him, leaving him unharmed but afflicted with a feeling of profound sadness. He dropped to his knees to keep his balance.

The dragon must have felt his weight on its back. Still clutching Riven, whose body lay as limp as a rag doll in its claws, the creature snaked its head around. When its eyes fell on Cale, it uttered a low, threatening hiss. Fear almost paralyzed Cale.

Almost.

Able to maintain his position for only a moment as the creature beat its huge pinions, Cale did the only thing possible—took a two-handed reverse grip on his blade and plunged it as deeply into the dragon as it would go. The enchanted steel—Cale noted that the blade was nearly pitch black—split the dark scales and sank half its length into the mighty creature's flesh.

The dragon roared and lurched backward in a paroxysm of pain, and the shadows around it swirled in agitation. Cale would have oathed that he saw laughter in those dark faces. Shadowstuff streamed from the dragon's mouth and nostrils, and black blood poured from the slot in its back. The abrupt motion sent Cale careening from its back to fall to the earth, though he managed to pull his blade free and keep his grip on it as he fell. He hit the mud flat on his back. The impact blew the breath from his lungs. Though prone and gasping, he managed to keep his blade held defensively before him. He expected it would do little good.

The dragon flung the barely conscious Riven to the earth and whirled on Cale, sending water everywhere. Riven crashed down in a shallow pool and lay unmoving.

From Cale's position, the dragon appeared to be nothing more than an infinite wall of black scales, teeth, malevolent eyes, and writhing shadows. Still prone and unable to breathe, he held his sword defiantly before him. The black blade shimmered in the twilight.

The dragon reared back its head, a coiled snake ready to strike, opened its mouth so wide that Cale thought its teeth must go on forever, and—

Stopped.

Its eyes fixed on Cale's sword and widened. Its head turned to look upon Riven's form, then turned back to Cale and the sword. The darkness around the creature subsided.

Wisps of shadows twisted around the darkened blade. It had changed still more from what it had been back on Faerûn. The transformation of the weapon that had begun with Cale's splitting of the starsphere appeared to have advanced along with his own transformation into a shade.

"You bear the token," the dragon said in its whispery voice. "Weaveshear. After all the centuries . . . You are the First."

Cale made no response. What could he say? Instead, he slowly climbed to his feet and tried to regain his breath. As though from far, far away, he heard a hundred voices plead with him in a language he did not know he knew.

Free us, they begged.

Cale shook his head, kept the blade before him, and warily eyed the dragon. The beast's head swung around to look upon Riven.

"And that," the creature said, "therefore, can only be the Second."

The dragon's heavy gaze returned to Cale. It eyed him for a moment, considering. Cale saw reluctance there. He sensed an inner struggle.

The great beast lowered its head to the surface of the water as though bowing to royalty. The dragon's horns were longer than he was tall. Cale clearly saw that the wound in its back continued to leak blood.

Flabbergasted, Cale could think of nothing to say, nothing to do.

The huge reptile remained prostrate for only a heartbeat before rearing back its long neck and looking down on Cale.

"You and your companions will be allowed to live, First of the Five," said the dragon. "Furlinastis keeps his promises."

With that, the dragon uttered a single arcane word and stomped its left front foot in the mud. The wound on its back closed and a viridian glow illuminated the shadowy mist around its claw. The glow spread outward from the dragon's foot in all directions, crawling along the ground, water, and fog. Cale recoiled as the mist around his feet began to glow, but the effect caused him no pain. Instead it relieved his fatigue and healed the bruises on his back. It must have healed his companions too. Jak and Magadon each uttered a groan and climbed slowly to their feet, all the while staring, dazed, at the mountain of scales before them.

The glow dissipated and the dragon said, "The debt is paid."

It crouched, scales creaking, and prepared to take wing. The shadowy forms around the dragon reached desperate arms for Cale.

"Wait!" Cale said. He realized only after the word escaped him how absurd it was that he was making demands of a dragon. But questions were burning holes in his brain. "What promise are you talking about? To whom?

What debt? What of the . . . people who surround you?"

The dragon looked down on Cale with those unforgiving dark eyes and replied, "To answer your questions would be to break another promise. Find your answers elsewhere, First of Five."

Cale fought down his frustration. He was tired to his bones of being carried along a path that seemed predetermined, and about which he was utterly ignorant.

"At least tell me about this," he said, and held out the sword—Weaveshear, the dragon had called it.

"I will not, shade," the dragon replied, and made that last word sound like a curse. "Except to say that it is the weapon of the First in this age."

Cale thought about asking the dragon how they could escape the Shadow Deep but his pride caused him to reject the impulse. He would ask the creature nothing more, though by doing so he felt he was betraying the shadow creatures apparently bound to the dragon.

"Begone then," he said.

At that, the dragon's eyes narrowed and Cale wondered for a moment if he had gone too far. Wisps of shadow snaked from the reptile's nostrils. When the creature spoke, his voice was heavy with menace.

"Never return to my swamp, First of the Shadowlord. My debt is now paid. I will not forget the wound you gave me, paltry though it was. The next time we meet, an old promise will not protect you."

"Nor you," Cale said, and stared defiance into the creature's face. "Kesson Rel is not the strongest of the Shadowlord's servants."

The words came out of his mouth before he knew what he was saying, and even after, he did not know what he meant.

The dragon apparently did. It reared back its head and hissed.

Cale and showed the dragon contempt by turning his back to the reptile and walking over to check on Jak and Magadon.

He could feel the dragon's gaze on his back, as heavy as a hundredweight. The creature growled low, beat its wings, and leaped into the air over him. It flew so low over Cale's head that he could have touched its wingtips. The force of its passing nearly blew him over. Water lapped in its wake. Jak and Magadon watched it go, pale and wide-eyed.

"We're all right," Jak said when Cale reached them, and Magadon nodded in agreement.

Blood covered both of their faces, and each looked exhausted, but Cale took them at their word.

"I'm glad," he said.

Without another word, the three of them splashed their way over to Riven, who still lay on his back in the shallow pool. Cale feared the assassin to be dead.

He wasn't. He was staring vacantly up into the twilight sky with his one good eye, smiling. His grievous wounds appeared to have been healed by the dragon's spell, though he still visibly winced when he breathed.

Cale and Magadon shared a look.

"Drasek?" the guide asked.

The assassin didn't respond.

"He's lost his wits," Jak said. "Probably from speaking that Black Speech. I'll try a spell, but. . . ."

Riven smiled, and his expression lost its faraway character.

"Save your spell, Fleet," he said. "I've lost nothing. I've *found* something."

The assassin sat up and shook his head as though to clear it.

"What do you mean?" Cale asked, but thought he already knew the answer.

Riven smiled and said, "Watch."

The assassin spoke eldritch words and moved his hands in a complex gesture. As he did, he pulled wisps of shadow from the air and twisted them around his hands. When he touched his charged palms to his flesh, the wounds remaining on his chest closed entirely.

"Trickster's toes," Jak softly oathed. "Drasek Riven is a priest?"

"No," Riven replied cryptically, and left it at that.

Cale tried to keep the dismay from his face. Drasek Riven could heal himself by touch, perhaps he could cast spells. Cale had thought Mask would never favor Riven with spellcasting. That the Shadowlord had done so felt like a betrayal.

But the assassin had denied that he was a priest. Then what?

Riven appraised his hands the way a veteran campaigner might evaluate a new blade. When he looked at Cale, his one good eye fairly shone.

"He's given you something, *First* of Five, but now he's given his Second something too. The Dark Speech. This—" he held up his hands for Cale to see—"and still more."

Despite himself, Cale could not hold back a frown. He remembered the exhilaration he'd felt when he first had learned to cast spells, and imagined Riven must feel much the same now. But he also thought of a Sembian proverb: "Only a fool thinks a gift is free." Cale had learned that lesson well. No doubt Riven soon would too.

Cale scabbarded Weaveshear, slow enough so that Riven would get a good look at the transformed blade.

He stared into Riven's good eye and said, "Everything comes with a cost, Riven. Make certain you know the asking price."

Riven only sneered.

Cale said to Magadon, "Get him up. Let's get out of this swamp."

CHAPTER 3

DISCLOSURE

Gradually, Magadon led them out of the swamp. The muddy ground grew firmer, and the reeds, tall grasses, and cypresses gave way first to thorny undergrowth then to brooding stands of trees akin to willows, but darker-leaved, more ominous. It seemed that one moment they were surrounded by marsh, the next by trees. The transition from bog to forest was sudden enough to be eerie, almost as though the woods had walked to them.

And perhaps they did, Cale thought.

Leaving the bog behind did little to raise their flagging spirits. The trees of the forest seemed to glare down at them as they passed. Limbs reached out to snag clothes, and the rustle of the wind through the leaves seemed to promise violence. High above, bats wheeled in the canopy, feasting on the large, black flies and other insects that plagued the plane. Some other creature that Cale could never quite see, hidden high up in the trees, howled at them as they passed.

After a few hours of travel, Magadon came to a sudden halt, cocked his head, and asked, "Does this terrain seem familiar to any of you?"

To Cale, the whole of the plane seemed familiar—uncomfortably so—but he had assumed the feeling to be a result of his transformation.

"What? The trees?" Jak asked, holding his bluelight wand aloft. "I've never seen anything like them—or bats that big."

"No," Magadon replied, shaking his head. "I don't mean the particular trees. I mean the topography."

"Should it?" asked Cale.

"What are you getting at, Mags?" Riven growled.

Magadon grabbed a tree limb and yanked it downward. For a moment, Cale thought for certain that the tree would attack the guide in response.

"It's twisted here, dark," Magadon said, "but think about it. On Toril, the Moonmere was in a dried bog surrounded by a forest. The bog here, albeit larger and wetter than the one on Toril, is surrounded by this forest."

"And?" Riven prompted.

"A planar correspondence," Cale said, taking the guide's meaning right away.

He and Jak had once experienced something similar when they had been in the Abyss hunting the Lord of the Void.

Jak pulled his pipe and chewed the end, thinking.

Riven shifted his stance and took a swig from his waterskin. Above them, the howling creatures continued their harangue.

"All right," the assassin said after wiping his mouth with the back of his hand. "There's a correspondence. So?"

"So, Drasek," Magadon said, as though lecturing a

student, "if the correspondence holds, it suggests the lay of the land. It may mean that—"

"Starmantle is nearby," Cale said, finishing for the woodsman. "Or its equivalent here."

Magadon nodded, smiling.

"Burn me," Jak oathed, twirling his pipe. "That place was a pit on Toril. Here . . ."

He whistled and trailed off.

Cale eyed Magadon and said, "If you're right, and if there's a way out of this plane, a city seems as likely a place as any."

Before the guide could respond, Riven spat and stared at Cale with his one good eye.

"You're our way out, Cale. But until you accept that, I've got nothing better to do to pass the time. Show the way, Mags."

Magadon adjusted his pack and said, "Since the swamp was larger than its correspondent on Toril, we should expect the forest to be likewise. Two days and we should reach the plains. From there, three or four more days to reach whatever passes for Starmantle on this plane. Let's move."

Having a goal lent them speed, and they made rapid progress through the brooding woods.

That night, they made camp under the enshrouding boughs of a shadow-willow. They started a fire but the night remained chilly, the light still dim. Alien sounds filled the forest—squeals, roars, and the ubiquitous howling. Cale couldn't sleep. Despite the day's exertion, despite his fatigue, rest would not come. In his mind's eye, he kept seeing that dragon—that enormous, majestic, terrifying creature, enshrouded in souls—lowering its head in respect.

Looking up through a break in the leaves, he stared at the featureless black sky.

What have you done to me? he thought to Mask, but immediately answered his own question with: What have I done to myself?

Sephris had named him the First of Five. So too had the caretaker at the Fane of Shadows, and the shadow dragon. He didn't know what that meant. He felt exhilarated and disquieted all at once.

Riven and Jak slept nearby under one of Magadon's tents. Moving quietly and slowly so as not to wake them, Cale rolled over on his side and removed the starsphere from his pack. The map of the celestial heavens had started the whole recent chain of events. To his surprise, Cale saw that it had become a featureless orb of gray quartz, where before it had been an image of Toril's night sky, flecked with diamonds, emeralds, and other gemstones. He wondered if the sphere changed its appearance depending upon the plane in which it found itself. Perhaps it changed on each plane to show the time at which the Fane of Shadows would next appear there. If true, the blank sphere in his hands told Cale that the Fane never materialized on the Plane of Shadow. The Shadow Deep was the source of its magic, but it never manifested there. The Fane reserved its pollution for the realms of light.

For an instant, he felt a temptation to hurl the sphere into the woods, to leave it there forever, but he resisted. It had done what it was designed to do.

Two and two are four, he thought.

He slid it back into his pack, shaking his head. He could not figure it all out, but he decided then and there that he would keep the sphere for the purpose for which he had first intended: as a memento of his former master and lost friend, Thamalon Uskevren.

Knowledge you seek, said the caretaker in his head.

Find your answers elsewhere, the dragon answered.

He remembered the book.

He sat up from his bedroll, pulled the backpack onto his lap, and took out the large tome given to him by the caretaker. Its covers of black scale shimmered in the dim firelight, reminding him of the skin of the shadow dragon. Its fittings were of a dull gray metal he did not recognize and it felt warm to his touch, as though it was a living thing. He stared at the tome for a time, thinking. He felt the same hesitation about opening the book as he had felt about drawing Weaveshear. To do so felt like he was surrendering his will to events, and he would not—*he could not*—do that.

But he had already drawn the sword. And he had to know what lay within the book's covers.

He thought of opening it right there. He could see well enough with his new eyes to read in the dark, but he decided he would read it like the normal man he was, like he used to read Thamalon's books back in the library of Stormweather Towers.

Those times seemed far removed from him. Pangs of regret stabbed his heart. He missed the Old Owl more than ever, and Shamur, and Tazi. . . .

Shaking off the melancholy, he tucked the book under an armpit, rose, and walked over to the dimly burning fire. They had set the tents several paces away from the flames so as not to risk a stray ember igniting the canvas.

Magadon was seated on a log near the blaze and appeared to be meditating. Not wanting to disturb the guide, Cale said nothing, merely sat across from Magadon and stared at the scaled leather cover of the book. Jak and Riven continued to sleep soundly in their bedrolls. Riven's dreams did not seem to trouble him that night.

Just as Cale put his fingers to the corner of the book's cover and prepared to turn it open, Magadon opened his eyes and spoke.

"Unable to sleep?"

"No," Cale replied, and laid his hand flat on the cover, secretly relieved that he had not yet opened it.

He met the guide's knucklebone eyes, which reflected the flickering tongues of flame. Magadon shifted his legs and cleared his throat.

"I'm restless too," said the guide.

It didn't show.

"Why?" Cale asked.

The guide looked as though the question surprised him.

"I was thinking about Nestor," Magadon said.

It took Cale a moment to place the name: Nestor was the big fighter—actually a slaad—who had accompanied Magadon out of Starmantle.

"I wonder how the slaadi killed him," the guide continued. "I wonder when? How long did I walk with that demonic, hellspawned creature at my side, rather than my friend." He blew out a sigh. "Jak almost died because I failed to notice the change. Nestor's death pains me only a little, and I wonder why that is. It seems very far away now."

Cale understood that last statement. At the moment, everything that had happened on Toril seemed far away.

"It wasn't your fault," he said, and realized as he said it that he was not sure what he meant.

Magadon looked up, took in Cale's eyes, his skin, and asked, "No?"

Cale saw the guilt in that look, and understood it.

"No," said Cale. "You could not have known about him, or about . . . anything."

The guide nodded. To Cale, it looked as though a weight had been lifted from Magadon's shoulders. For the first time, Magadon seemed to notice what Cale held in his hand.

"That's the book from the Fane?" the guide asked.

"Yes," Cale said, and ran his fingers over the leather cover.

"You're going to read it?" Magadon asked.

Cale didn't look up when he said, "I don't know."

They sat in silence for a time. Cale had once more worked up the nerve to open it when Magadon spoke again.

"A close thing earlier," the woodsman said. "With the dragon, I mean."

"Yes." Cale didn't have to read minds to sense Magadon's internal struggle. He put the tome on the ground beside him and looked the guide in the face. "Why don't you say what you want to say, Magadon."

Magadon didn't bother to protest, merely gave an embarrassed smile.

"Damned if you're not direct, Erevis," he said. "I suppose I should pay you the same courtesy, shouldn't I?"

Cale made no answer.

The guide took a deep breath, looked Cale in the eyes, and said, "The Fane, the dragon, your skin, and your eyes. . . ." He paused a moment, braced himself as though he was about to dive into a cold lake, then said, "You are no longer a human being."

Cale went rigid, and he felt himself flush. Harsh words of denial rushed to his lips, but he kept them behind his teeth. He heard no judgment in Magadon's tone, more like . . . sympathy?

Cale stared and waited for the guide to continue. His yellow-eyed gaze must have discomfited Magadon, who looked off into the darkness.

"I did not say that as an accusation, Erevis."

"I know," Cale said.

"That's good." The woodsman threw a few stray twigs into the flames and replied, "I said it because we have that in common." He looked up into Cale's eyes. "I am not human either."

Cale could not keep the surprise from his voice.

"What?" he said, too loud. He looked over to Jak and Riven. The halfling stirred in his sleep, but neither he nor Riven roused. "What?" he said again, more softly.

Magadon smiled and said, "How do you think I came by these eyes?"

In truth, Cale hadn't thought overmuch about it.

"I suppose I thought it had something to do with your mental abilities. Or an accident of birth, possibly."

"An accident of birth?" Magadon's expression grew distant for a moment, thoughtful, and Cale saw a hardness in the line of his mouth. The guide stoked the fire with a length of wood while he spoke. Sparks flew into the twilight. "No, my birth was no accident." He looked up at Cale. "I am planetouched. Have you heard the word?"

Taken aback, Cale still managed a nod. He was familiar with the term. "Planetouched" was a word used to describe those who had the blood of an outer planar being in their ancestry. Those with celestial blood were *aasimar*, a word for which Cale had never been able to determine a linguistic origin. Those tainted with the blood of demons or devils were *tieflings* or *fey'ri*, both Elvish words. Those with elemental lords as ancestors were *genasi*, a word from ancient Calishite that literally meant "scion of the djinn."

"Few know this about me," Magadon continued. "With only a few precautions, I can pass for a normal man, though with unusual eyes. A normal . . . human."

Cale didn't try to respond.

"You wonder why I'm telling you this, don't you?" Magadon asked.

Cale's eyes narrowed and he asked, "Are you reading my mind, woodsman?"

"Just your face," Magadon replied with a chuckle. "And before I answer that question, you should hear everything. Well enough? There's a purpose to it."

"Well enough," Cale answered, intrigued.

"There are different types of planetouched," Magadon said.

Cale nodded. "I know. Which are you?"

"I am—well, here."

Magadon rose and came around the fire to Cale's side. He sat on his haunches, removed his wide-brimmed hat, and pulled his long, black hair back from his forehead.

"There," asked the guide, "do you see?"

Cale leaned in close. Just within Magadon's hairline, two protuberances of bone budded. Horns.

"You're a tiefling," Cale said softly.

Magadon nodded, let his hair fall back and donned his hat. He sat on a log nearer to Cale.

"I am, but . . ."

When the guide looked into Cale's eyes, Cale saw pain in his face, writ clear.

"It's worse than even that," Magadon continued.

The guide pushed back the left sleeve of his shirt, nearly to his shoulder. Cale saw that a tattoo adorned his bicep. No, not a tattoo—a birthmark unlike any Cale had seen before. It was in the form of a red hand with black nails, swathed in flames or mist. Pale, jagged scars crisscrossed the mark. Old scars.

Magadon was staring at him, reading his expression. He seemed relieved that Cale was not appalled.

"You do not recognize this symbol?" the guide asked.

"No," Cale replied, though the mark did somehow make him uneasy, a feeling reminiscent of the way Riven's use of the Black Speech made him feel. "But it's . . ."

"Disquieting," Magadon said, and lowered his sleeve. "It would be worse if you knew whose symbol it was." He stared into the fire and spoke in a quiet voice. "I will not speak here the name of that creature. But I will tell you that he is a diabolical, dark being of great power. Evil incarnate. Not a god, but . . . nearly so."

Cale felt the hair on his neck rise. The shadows around them seemed to grow deeper. The night sounds of the forest's animals went quiet, even the howlers. A cool wind sent the flames of the campfire flickering. The breeze seemed to whisper a name, a sinister, sibilant name, but it danced away before Cale could recognize it.

Magadon threw some more dried limbs onto the blaze and the flames picked up.

"You're descended from this being?" Cale asked.

Magadon gave a short, hard laugh and answered, "It is not a lineage of which I am proud."

"That is not what I meant."

"I know," Magadon said, nodding. "Forgive me. Speaking of him is difficult for me." The guide shook his head, as though to dispel thoughts best left undisturbed. "For his amusement, this creature took human form and raped my mother. I was the result. The descendant of a devil. I suspect he has many. By all the accounts that I've heard, his lust is matched only by his evil."

Magadon looked into Cale's face, which Cale kept free of judgment. Cale would judge no one, not then.

"Immediately after my birth," Magadon continued, "when my mother saw what she had brought forth, she exposed me, abandoned me to die in the forest. Afterward, she drowned herself in the Shining River."

Cale heard the bitterness in the guide's voice, bitterness softened only by regret at the mention of his mother's death.

"Is your mother alive, Erevis?" Magadon asked softly. "Your father?"

Cale shook his head. He had never known his mother, the man who had come closest to being his father had died a year past, and the god who had come to serve as a father of sorts seemed to have adopted a second son.

"Forgive me for asking," Magadon said, seemingly sensing Cale's pain.

"It's all right," Cale said, waving away the sting. "Continue."

Magadon cleared his throat and said, "I was abandoned. Before the cold could take me, a lame woodsman heard my wails and took me in. It was he who explained my origin to me, when I was old enough to understand it. It was he who taught me wood lore."

Cale struggled to imagine the burden Magadon carried—rejected by his mother, sired by a fiend. Cale's own past seemed ordinary by comparison.

"He always told me the truth," Magadon said absently. "I loved him for that."

"The woodsman?"

Magadon nodded.

"What was his name?"

Magadon smiled warmly.

"Father," he said, and Cale could see the guide's welling eyes reflecting the firelight.

Cale understood. He left Magadon alone with his memories for a time.

When the guide seemed ready again to speak, Cale asked, "Did your father also teach you how to . . . to use your mental powers?"

Magadon shook his head and stared into the fire.

"No," he said. "Psionics cannot be taught, Erevis. They are inborn, and I've developed them as I've aged. My mental powers I attribute to the bloodline of the rapist whose seed conceived me, as much as I do these horns. And like my horns, they've become more pronounced as I've aged. I'm changing too, you see."

Cale nodded. It seemed they were all changing.

Magadon looked into Cale's eyes and said, "Two fathers, Erevis. One a rapist archdevil, one a cripple with a noble spirit. Life is sometimes strange, is it not?"

Cale nodded and looked away into the distance. He could think of nothing to say, though he understood well what it was to serve two fathers. The silence stretched on.

At last, Cale said, "You were going to tell me why you were confiding in me. You had a purpose?"

"So I was and so I do," Magadon said, and adjusted his posture on the log. "Here it is: For years I struggled with what I was. *Devilspawn*, Erevis. How could I move past that?"

Cale looked at him from under his brows, genuinely curious, and asked, "How did you?"

"That's the question," Magadon whispered. He shook his head and smiled softly, as if amused by a private jest. "I pitied myself. You saw the scars on my birthmark. When I learned what it was, I tried to cut that mark from my flesh a dozen times, but always it returned."

He extended his arm and held his hand fully in the flames. Cale gave a start but Magadon's skin didn't char and the guide did not wince.

He looked into Cale's face and said, "Another gift from the rapist." He pulled his hand from the flames and looked at the unmarred skin. "Everywhere I turned, I was faced with my heritage. With each passing year, my flesh changed to show more and more of my devil sire. I fear how I may appear in my dotage."

He smiled, but Cale saw it was forced.

"So I couldn't move past it, Erevis," the guide said. "Not really." He flexed his unburned fingers. "It's part of me. It's part of what I am. When I accepted that, things became bearable. But—" and here he made a cutting gesture with his hand—"accepting the fact of my blood does not mean that I let it dictate the course of my life. The blood of an archdevil determines what I am in body; it does not determine the nature of my soul. And it's a soul that makes a man, Erevis. Do you see? Your transformation changed your skin, your eyes, but not your soul. You remain who you always were."

Cale heard Magadon's words, heard the echoes of his own protestations in them, but smiled in response only out of politeness. It was what Cale always had been—before the transformation as much as after—that gave him concern. Accepting his nature would not free him from what he feared; it would free *what* he feared, that part of himself that he kept closely tethered. Unlike Magadon, Cale had no good side to turn to.

He thought of Tazi; her smile, the smell of her skin. . . .

"Well?" Magadon pressed.

"I'll think about what you've said," Cale replied, to placate the guide.

Magadon nodded and said, "Fair enough."

They said nothing for a time. When the silence at last grew uncomfortable, Cale filled it by changing the subject.

"How did you come to know him?" he asked, and indicated Riven. "You seem hardly the type of man who would befriend a Zhentarim assassin."

Magadon's reply came quickly: "How did you?"

Cale took the point. Strange times made for strange alliances.

"Does he know?" Cale asked. "About your . . . heritage?"

Magadon shrugged and said, "I've never told him, but he may have learned of it. He has a way of doing that. Why do you ask?"

In truth, Cale did not know.

"Curiosity," he said, and left it at that.

The fire crackled, its smoke lost in the gloom of the forest.

"It's affecting him too," Magadon said at last. "Riven, I mean."

"What?"

"This place; what he's becoming."

Cale looked at Magadon sharply and asked, "What is he becoming?"

"I don't know," Magadon answered. "Neither does he. That's what makes him afraid."

Cale's doubt must have shown in his expression. To Cale, Riven seemed as calm and in control as ever. Magadon must have read his eyes—or his mind.

The guide said, "I know him better than you, Erevis. He has been your enemy, hasn't he?"

Cale nodded.

"You see him through those eyes," Magadon said. "But I've been in his head, and I see him through his own." Magadon paused before adding, "You two are very much alike."

Once, those words would have provoked a sharp denial, but not any more. Perhaps Cale and Riven were more alike than ever. Brothers in the faith if not the flesh. He looked at his regenerated hand and wondered again what he was becoming, or what he had already become. A shade, yes, but what else?

"Get some rest, Magadon," Cale said. "I'll keep watch for a while."

Magadon rose. and said, "Well enough." He hesitated, then extended his hand. "Call me Mags."

Cale took the tiefling's hand and looked into his white eyes.

"Mags it is."

The woodsman had laid down to sleep, pulling his hat down over his eyes. Cale looked down at the tome from the Fane of Shadows, picked it up, and after a moment's hesitation he flipped it open.

For a moment, he could not breathe.

A swatch of black cloth lay within its pages, formerly pressed between the cover and the first page. He stared at it a long while before brushing the silken mask with his fingertips.

A strange prologue, he thought, and placed what he knew to be his new holy symbol into his vest pocket.

Cale refused to admit to himself the comfort its presence brought him, the charge it sent through him.

He began to read, devouring the words as he once had done as a linguistics student back in Westgate. Written by several hands, alternatively in Thorass, Elvish, Infernal, and at least two tongues Cale did not recognize, the tome appeared to be a history of Shar, the Fane of Shadows as it manifested in several worlds, and the Weave Tap. As he read, he began to understand why Azriim—or Azriim's master, the Sojourner—had sought the artifact.

And with that understanding came fear.

CHAPTER 4

NURSING THE NIGHT

Vhostym uttered the words to a spell, waved his hand, and opened a dimensional portal through the smooth stone wall and into the nursery. The moment the aperture materialized, moans of pain hissed through the magical door, the steam of agony escaping a heated beaker. Vhostym tuned out the sounds, though he felt like moaning himself. His affliction grew worse daily, despite his spells and medicaments. His bones throbbed with pain. He imagined he could feel them putrefying within him, one at a time.

Pushing out of his mind an image of himself as a shapeless blob of flesh, Vhostym floated into the chamber.

The nursery opened wide around him, a circular cyst in the earth of his pocket plane. Forty-four paces in diameter, the polished walls of the perfectly spherical room gleamed in the dim green light of a single glowball. Lines of diamonds and amethysts glittered in alternating spiraling whorls inset into the walls—three thousand nine hundred and fifty nine of each stone. The amethysts, attuned to the shadow Weave, fairly hummed with channeled power; the diamonds, attuned to the Weave, sang at a slightly higher pitch. The sum of the stones, when combined with the one of the Weave Tap, equaled seven thousand nine hundred nineteen, the one thousandth prime number.

A number of power, Vhostym knew.

The gems, arcane spirals, and the Weave Tap combined to make the nursery a nexus of the Weave and the Shadow Weave, a place where the frayed edges of both lay exposed and sizzling. Fertile ground for arcana, so to speak; rich soil in which the Tap could grow.

And it had grown.

Suspended in midair by magic, in the exact center of the nursery, hung the living artifact. It had blossomed to three times the size it had been when his slaadi first brought it from the Fane of Shadows. With its long, thin limbs, snaking roots, and narrow trunk, to Vhostym it somehow looked feminine. He thought it sublimely beautiful and marveled that mere human priests—even those inspired by their goddess—could have crafted such an item.

Its glossy black bark pulsed with energy as it fed. Rings of soft, silver light periodically ran the length of its trunk, the pulse not unlike the greedy gulp of a magic-addicted drunkard. Even that mild silver illumination stung Vhostym's skin and caused him to blink back tears with each palpitation.

The limbs of the Weave Tap's mostly leafless canopy extended upward to grow into and out of the still living, twitching bodies of the semi-conscious, opalescent-skinned astral devas that Vhostym had suspended there. After bursting from the celestials' writhing forms, the Tap's limbs continued upward before melding with the warp of the Weave. Then it disappearing into nothingness toward the rounded, diamond-dotted ceiling. Similarly, the Tap's thick roots extended downward to penetrate the squirming bodies of the semi-conscious ghaele demons. Bursting from their malformed backs the roots invisibly enmeshed themselves in the weft of the Shadow Weave near the rounded floor, itself speckled with amethysts.

Vhostym ignored the pained moans of the creatures upon which the Tap fed. They were little more than sentient, pain-ridden husks. Living fertilizer, their nearly extinguished life-force had helped speed the Tap's growth. Already the artifact had produced one ripe seed. Soon, a second would be ready. And two was all Vhostym would need to realize his ambition.

He floated across the nursery to hover before the Tap. The blank, ivory eyes of the devas, and the thick, puss filled black orbs of the ghaele, stared at him unseeing, blind to all but their pain.

"Silence now," he said.

Vhostym cast a spell on the demons and devas that rendered them silent. Their mouths still moved in agony, but their verbalization no longer troubled his ears. He reached out and caressed the bole of the Tap with his frail hand. The warm bark felt more like supple leather than wood. He put his ear to the bark and sighed. A flash of the Tap's silver pulse set his eyes to watering and his skin to burning, but he endured. He looked with anticipation on the burgeoning seed, hanging alone from an otherwise bare, low-hanging limb. The seed was ovate, about the size of a fist, with throbbing black veins that crisscrossed its silver rind. In a sense, the seed was a metaphor, as was the Weave Tap itself. The priests of Shar had distilled an allegory of opposites down to a physical manifestation—a unique tree. Shar and Selûne; new moon and full moon. Shar and Mystra; Shadow Weave and Weave. Perhaps the perfect enmeshing of those opposites was the secret of the Tap's beauty and power. Of course, in the end the

Tap remained a creation inspired by Shar, and hence a tool designed to spite Mystra and Selûne.

On a whim, Vhostym had tried to contact the Tap psionically, but had received no response. He had sensed a lurking self-awareness, but the artifact's consciousness was so focused on its purpose—growing, tapping—that it could perceive nothing else.

He eyed the thin limbs of the Weave Tap and imagined them as they were meant to be: blossoming with leaves of power. When one of the tree's seeds was "planted" in a location of powerful magic, it would instantly root in the fabric of the magic there and pass the power thus gained along the net of the Weave and back to the Weave Tap, where Vhostym would be waiting to harness it.

He had chosen with care the locations at which he would seed the Weave. He had dismissed mythals outright. While the mantles of elven high magic *were* areas of highly concentrated power, they were also too conspicuous. Tapping a mythal would have immediately drawn the attention of Toril's most powerful high mages, and Mystra's Chosen as well, and it was too soon for that. Instead, he had opted to tap a form of mantle magic different from mythals, but nearly as powerful. Already his brood had taken the first Tap seed and journeyed to the location of the first such mantle, a one-time Netherese Enclave.

Eager to check on their progress, he concentrated briefly and sent his mind through the planes, across Faerûn and under it, until he touched Azriim's consciousness. During the first instant of contact, he sensed what Azriim sensed, but only dully, as though through a haze of mindwine.

He could smell the sour, organic reek of too many humans and other creatures crammed into too small a space. He heard the rising and falling murmur of a crowded street, and saw a web of catwalks, ladders, and ramshackle buildings sprouting like mushrooms from the walls of a mammoth cavern deep under the earth. If not for the mantle of magic that protected the city and spawned its guardians, the cavern would long ago have collapsed of its own weight.

Welcome to Skullport, Sojourner, projected Azriim, when Vhostym allowed his son to sense the psionic contact. *The arsehole of Faerûn.*

Vhostym went directly to the point and asked, *Have you located the provenience of the mantle?*

We continue to observe the activities of the Skulls, Azriim answered. *We believe the answer, if there is one, can be learned there. You are certain that another chamber survived the destruction?*

I am, Vhostym said. *And it will be near the main chamber. The mantle could not exist without a focus. It is there.*

Few knew that the mantle magic protecting Skullport was Netherese in origin. Still fewer had deduced—as had Vhostym— that a cavern entirely separate from the city itself must contain the magical focus of the mantle, the source from which the mantle emanated. It was in that focus that the seed of the Weave Tap was to be planted.

Vhostym suspected that the Skulls, Skullport's magical guardians, after whom the city had been named, had magically shrouded the chamber in which stood the mantle's focus. Accordingly, he had provided his brood with wands that would give them the ability to deal with any wards cast by the Skulls to disguise the mantle's origin. They had only to find its general locale.

Vhostym would have searched for it himself—after all, Skullport *was* underground—but his body was deteriorating, despite his spells. Besides, the Skulls would have immediately sensed his presence. Though he knew that he could destroy Skullport's guardians with relative ease, he was not yet ready for direct confrontation. The mantle could be damaged in the process, or worse, the Chosen drawn to the site of the conflict.

No, implanting Skullport's mantle with the seed of the Weave Tap required planning, stealth, and misdirection— Azriim's strengths. Vhostym would leave the implementation of that part of the plan to his eldest son. Azriim's reward for success would be transformation to gray.

Use the teleportation rods with caution, he projected to Azriim. *Be especially cautious before teleporting within Skullport. Teleporting from one location in the Underdark to another location in the Underdark can sometimes have unpredictable results.*

Azriim's mental voice, fat with insolence, replied, *Your concern touches us all.*

Vhostym resisted the urge to cause pain to his impudent son.

Continue your efforts, he instructed Azriim, then he broke off contact.

The rush of anger caused by Azriim's impertinence sent shooting pains along his thin body. He clutched his staff and mouthed the words to a spell that dulled his body's ability to feel pain. With effort, he calmed himself.

He already had waited centuries; he could wait another tenday, another month. His brood would find what he had sent them to find, and he would have the Crown of Flame before the end.

CHAPTER 5

STARMANTLE'S SHADOW

After everyone had awakened, Cale related what he'd learned of the Weave Tap from reading the tome. He didn't mention the silken mask he'd found within its pages, nor did he mention the fact that he'd slept perhaps two hours but no longer felt tired.

"So it's an artifact?" Jak asked, drawing thoughtfully on the pipe he always smoked upon waking.

Cale could only relate what he'd read, and didn't purport to understand it all.

"It is, but it's also a living thing," Cale said. "You saw it, little man. Shar's priesthood made it, or found and nurtured it, after the fall of Netheril as a way to spite Selûne and the newly-birthed Mystra. Its roots extend into the Shadow Weave, while its limbs reach into the Weave proper."

"The warp and weft of magic," Jak said from around his pipe stem.

Magadon sat cross-legged in the gloom with his fingers steepled under his chin. His wide-brimmed hat cast his face in darkness.

"What does it do?" asked the guide.

Riven coughed and spat—as much the assassin's morning ritual as Jak's smoking—and asked, "Why do we care?"

Jak blew smoke Riven's way and shook his head in disgust.

Cale chose to ignore Riven and looked at Magadon when he said, "It siphons the magic of the Weave, magnifies it, and makes that power usable by the mage who possesses the Tap."

"How?" Jak asked.

Cale shrugged and answered, "The tome did not specify the method."

"Those slaadi were no mages," Riven observed.

"No," Cale agreed. "But I'll wager their master, this 'Sojourner', is."

To that, Riven said nothing, merely studied his hands.

"If so, the Sojourner could be scrying us now," Magadon said, looking up into the starless sky.

Jak shook his head.

"I don't think so," the halfling said, and frowned at his pipe, which had apparently gone out. "Divinations do not seem to work in this place. At least mine don't. I'll wager he cannot scry us here. Besides, he may have no interest in us anymore. He might think we're dead at the bottom of the Moonmere. Why scry for the dead?"

The guide acknowledged Jak's point with a tilt of his head then asked, "What do we think this Sojourner wants to do with the power of the Weave Tap?"

Cale shrugged, chewed some trail tack, then said, "No way to know."

" 'Additional variables,' " Jak added, quoting Sephris,

the chosen of Oghma and ostensible madman who had prophesied their fate, albeit in mathematical riddles. The halfling tapped the ashes from his pipe and stuffed it back into his belt pouch. "Whatever it is, we can be sure it's not good." He glared at Riven. "And *that's* why we care, Zhent."

Riven scoffed, stretched, and said, "Speak for yourself, Fleet." He paused for a minute then nodded at the belt pouch into which Jak's pipe had vanished. "You have an extra one of those?"

Jak, eyebrows arched, asked, "What? A pipe?"

Riven nodded.

Jak nodded back, shared a perplexed look with Cale, then took his spare pipe—a plain, wooden-bowled affair— from a belt pouch. He tossed it to Riven along with an extra pipeweed tin and a tindertwig.

"Keep it. And that's good pipeweed from Mistledale," the halfling said. "Don't waste it."

Obviously familiar with the paraphernalia, Riven tamped, lit, and began to smoke without saying a word. Cale's astonishment must have shown on his face.

"You've never seen a man smoke?" Riven asked him.

"I've never seen *you* smoke," Cale answered.

Riven blew out a series of perfect smoke rings, gave a hard grin, and said, "And I've never seen a man with yellow eyes who can move from shadow to shadow. I guess this place is changing us all, Cale."

To that, Cale could only agree.

"We've got to get back," Jak said, "find those slaadi, and stop the Sojourner. No one else even knows what's happening."

"And no one else needs to know," Riven said from around the pipe. "Understood?"

Jak looked at the assassin as if he had turned green and asked, "What in the Hells are you talking about? Did the pipeweed go to your head that fast? We need help with this."

Riven drew on Jak's pipe, discharged the smoke from

his nose, and looked to Cale, who sighed and nodded.

"This is our fight, Jak," Cale said. "It's personal; it's been personal right from the start. *We* end it, no one else."

Jak's mouth hung open.

"*Our* fight!" the halfling said at last. "Dark and empty! This is big, Cale, bigger than us. That Tap is an artifact. We're talking about the Weave itself. This isn't some guild grudge we're settling. We need help. I know some people who . . ."

Cale stared at his friend and Jak grew quiet. Cale knew it was big, but he also knew it was *his*.

"We can do it, Jak."

Riven uttered something between a cough and a laugh.

The halfling turned from Cale, looked to Magadon, and asked, "You too?"

Magadon shrugged and made a show of reorganizing his giant pack while he said, "One of those slaadi killed Nestor, took his place, then nearly killed you. It's personal for me as well."

"You three aren't thinking right," Jak said, then mumbled, "Trickster's toes. Trickster's hairy toes."

At Jak's expression of dismay, Cale struggled to keep a straight face.

"We'll stop them, little man," Cale said. "We'll be enough."

"You better be right," Jak said, and obviously meant it.

Cale's mirth vanished. He had better be right, indeed.

Magadon stood, squirmed into his pack, and adjusted the straps.

"We can't stop anyone sitting here," said the guide. "Gear up. Let's move."

Cale stood and began to gather his gear.

The halfling touched the spot on his back where one of the slaadi, Dolgan, had run him through.

He shouldered his own pack with a grunt and said, "We do owe those damned slaadi some blood, don't we?"

"That we do," Cale answered with a smile.

He could see that the halfling was coming to terms with the decision.

"Now and again you say something that makes sense, Fleet," Riven said.

He put out his borrowed pipe, pocketed it, and pulled on his pack.

"You keep your words behind your teeth, Zhent," Jak replied. "And remember . . . that's *my* pipe."

❧ ❧ ❧ ❧ ❧

It took another two days, but at last the forest began to thin. By the time they broke for a midday repast on the second day, they were in the midst of endless plains that rose and fell like ocean swells. The tall grass, with thick, abrasive blades that looked like serrated daggers, reached to Jak's thighs. Only occasional copses of trees broke the flat monotony. Each tree was so gnarled it looked like it had twisted itself into knots trying to escape the soil. In truth, Jak had felt more comfortable in the brooding forest than he did in the plains. He felt exposed under the onyx sky. He could see little farther than a short stone's throw. There was nowhere to hide.

He held his holy symbol in a sweaty fist and his blue-light wand in the other. It seemed he had been sweating since the moment he arrived in that dark plane. He felt small, in a way that had nothing to do with his stature. When he considered the transformations of Riven and Cale, thought of the artifact, and saw in all of it the machinations of gods, he felt as though he were witnessing a myth in-the-making. It frightened him.

The stakes—albeit unknown—also frightened him. In the past, his adventures had been just that: adventures, and generally of interest only to him. But events had grown larger than the stuff of tavern tales. At that moment, Jak was pleased that he was nothing more than an obscure priest of a minor god.

He looked over at Cale, saw the dusky skin, the yellow eyes, the shadows that clung to him, and thought: Heroes have too much weight to carry.

"The correspondence seems to be holding," Magadon observed from his position out in front of them. The even tone of the woodsman's voice helped to relax Jak. Magadon seemed . . . steady somehow, like an old oak tree, like he always knew where he was and where he was going.

He was a seventeen too, Jak thought, recalling old Sephris.

Magadon went on, "If it continues, we should reach the Shadow equivalent of Starmantle in two or three days."

Assuming it's not moving away from us, Jak thought but nodded anyway.

The shifting terrain of the Shadow Deep made him feel like the land under him was a skiff floating on an endless, invisible sea. The thought made him queasy and he pushed it from his mind.

As the trek continued Jak tried several times to engage Cale in conversation, but each time Cale deflected the attempt with an inhospitable grunt. The halfling knew what that meant—Cale was thinking, planning.

Riven, for his part, seemed content to walk in silence, alone with the newfound power in his hands, which he continually examined as they traveled. Jak wondered uneasily what else Riven's hands could do, what else they had already done.

Late in the day it grew windy, then began to rain. Thick dollops of black water, whipped into sheets by a gusting wind, thumped against Jak's face as hard as sling bullets. Vermillion lightning ripped the sky into pieces. Deafening thunder pounded the earth. The storm was gorgeous and terrifying all at once, like the demon lord Cale and Jak had once fought.

Magadon called a halt and they camped under the eaves of a copse of something like elms. Jak made sure to create a beef stew with his spell that evening, to keep Riven's mouth shut. Though Magadon's weathered and oiled tents managed to keep the rain off of him, he struggled through only an hour or two of intermittent sleep.

The storm continued through the next day, but still they made good progress. Magadon refused to stop for the weather and Jak was glad. He wanted out of that plane and, if the theoretical city held the way out, he wanted to get there as soon as possible.

Sometime near the middle of that day, they reached their destination.

They stood atop a low rise, ineffectually shielding themselves against the wind and rain with their hats or the hoods of their sodden cloaks. A gently sloping, shallow valley extended before them. At its bottom, visible to Jak only in the lightning flashes, a ruined city erupted from the plain like a plague boil. The overgrown ruins covered as much acreage as did Selgaunt, perhaps more. Only the low, squat buildings in the city's densely-packed center had remained intact. Jak saw no people in the streets, no movement at all. It was eerie.

They stood looking at the ruins for a long while, as though assuring themselves that they were not looking upon an apparition. A pinpoint of golden light flashed from somewhere in the city's center, from amidst the low buildings, as though someone had briefly uncovered a bulls eye lantern.

Jak's breath caught, and he strained to see. He thought he might have imagined the light but it repeated again quickly. To him, that light, that *color*, bespoke one thing: a way home.

"Did you see that?" he shouted to Cale and Magadon over the wind.

Both nodded.

Magadon said, "That's the only natural looking light we've seen since we arrived."

"A way back?" Jak asked.

He couldn't keep hope from coloring his voice.

Magadon shrugged and said, "Possibly."

They squinted into the wind. The flash came again.

"A beacon, maybe?" Riven asked.

Cale drew Weaveshear and said, "Or maybe a lure. Either way, there's only one way to find out. Ready?"

Jak nodded and drew his short sword and dagger. Riven too drew his sabers, and Magadon his bow.

"Stay sharp," Cale said, starting down the rain-slicked grass of the valley.

Thunder boomed and another lightning flash illuminated the city. Jak caught a clear glimpse of toppled buildings, crumbling megaliths, and broken statues worn by the weather and pitted into anonymity. It looked as though the city had been destroyed in some unrecorded cataclysm. Sculptures perched atop the roofs of the small, single story buildings in the city's center, the only intact statuary in the ruins.

"The buildings in the center of town look odd," Jak observed. "Too small for a home. What do you make of them?"

Cale's voice was grim when he said, "Those are tombs."

Jak's skin went gooseflesh. There were a lot of them.

☙ ☙ ☙ ☙ ☙

Magadon led them into the ruined city, marking the path ahead with his bow. Cale walked beside the guide, coiled, Weaveshear in hand. Jak and Riven followed after, widely spaced, blades at the ready, eyes alert. Butterflies fluttered in Jak's gut. He couldn't keep his hands from shaking, causing the shadows cast by he and his companions in the blue light of his wand to dance on the ruins.

Crumbling, weed-overgrown buildings rose out of the darkness. Even in ruin, the structures managed to imply a sense of architectural majesty. Soaring arches, thick marble columns, and elaborately carved stonework were the rule. The city must have been beautiful to behold once.

Shards of bone stuck from the earth, most human-sized, but some gigantic. Cale simply stared at them and said nothing.

A broad, flagstone-paved avenue stretched before them, extending into darkness toward the crypts in the center of town. Weeds, tall grass, drab wildflowers, and even the occasional tree sprouted from between the cracked stones of the road. The ruins were old.

All but the cemetery, at least.

Jak felt uneasy, the way he did when unfriendly eyes were upon him, but he could not pinpoint a reason. He had an ominous sense of something lurking nearby, something malevolent.

Despite the continuing rain, the air felt clingy and thick, as though they were walking through a mass of invisible cobwebs. Jak could not help but hold his dagger before his face and try to part the air with it.

In silence, they trekked through the dead streets of a dead city. Riven and Magadon took the flanks, spreading out ten paces to the left and right, clearing buildings as they moved. Jak and Cale spaced themselves a few paces apart and walked down the broad road. Having descended into the valley, the ruins blocked their view of the necropolis so they could no longer see the occasionally flashing gold light. It didn't matter. They knew where to go. The road led directly to it.

Within a quarter hour, the rain lessened to something more moderate than a downpour, but lightning still flashed through the sky. Jak kept alert to Riven's side of the street—Jak's responsibility—but now and again stole a look at Cale. His friend's faraway gaze followed Magadon, but sometimes moved dully from here to there. Jak would never get used to those yellow eyes.

The halfling moved near Cale and asked in a sharp whisper, "What is it?"

Cale, who looked startled, said, "I don't know, Jak. I feel like I know this place somehow, like my mind is a palimpsest and the faded writing is now becoming visible."

Jak did not even know what a palimpsest was, but his skin went gooseflesh again.

"How would you know this place?" he asked. "The book from the Fane?"

Jak watched as Riven entered the crumbling entrance of what once might have been a shop. He exited a moment later, signaling that it was clear.

Cale shook his head again and replied, "I'm not cer—"

Riven froze and gave a sharp whistle that cut through the drumbeat of the rain. With rapidity and skill, the assassin climbed atop the building he had just exited. There, he crouched low on the flat roof and looked a block over, to a cluster of tall buildings, the domed tops of which Jak could just make out.

Cale and Jak signaled to Magadon. The guide left off his search of a building and hurried to Cale's and Jak's side.

"What is it?" he asked.

"Look," Jak said, and pointed in Riven's direction.

Beyond Riven's rooftop perch, a faint, icy blue glow rose just above the rooftops. Jak put its source perhaps a street or two away. Not the golden light they had seen in the center of town, but something else.

Riven kept his gaze on the source of the light and waved them over.

Jak, Cale, and Magadon ran to the base of the building—it was littered with decayed tables and broken ceramics—and they began to climb. Cale reached the top first and pulled Jak up the last bit. Magadon followed, struggling more with the climb but managing. All three reached the roof and crouched beside Riven. From there, they could see the cause of the glow.

"Burn me," Jak whispered.

Magadon knocked an arrow and drew it to his ear.

Two hundred paces away, hundreds of spirits, all women and young girls, streamed out of one of the tall, ruined buildings—formerly a temple, to judge from the partially collapsed metallic dome that capped its center.

In loose columns, the spirits advanced in their direction. They appeared to be walking, but their feet remained a fingerbreadth above the ground, and their robes of silvery samite rustled to a much gentler wind than the gusts that pulled at Jak's sodden cloak. Each bore a ghostly candle, and shielded it with her hands as though to protect it from the rain that was, in reality, passing through both candle and bearer. The candle flames were the source of the blue glow. Though they made no sound, their mouths moved in unison and Jak *felt* as though the ghosts were chanting or singing.

From beside Jak, Cale spoke in a distant voice: "The Summoners of the Sun. The last hope of Elgrin Fau."

Jak heard Cale's words but their import barely registered. He could not take his eyes from the processional of ghosts. Their silent, somber beauty hypnotized him. Though the spirits were walking the road below them, Jak felt no fear; he did not bother to reach for his holy symbol. Instead, he felt a deep sadness that went before the spirits like a wave. They wore the resigned expressions of the condemned, but held fast to their candles as though those flames were the only possibility of salvation.

Magadon's bowstring creaked and he prepared to let fly.

Cale put a hand on the guide's shoulder and whispered, "They can cause no harm, Magadon. Let them pass."

The woodsman hesitated for a moment before relaxing his bow.

The tide of ghosts continued toward the party then turned right exactly below them and headed up the street. They seemed oblivious to the companions. The women were all tall and slender, with light hair and fair skin. Their eyes were wide and slightly upturned at the corners, their earlobes unusually large and bedecked with several earrings. Jak thought them beautiful, surreal, and alien. He watched them as they passed by.

"Where are they going?" he asked, of no one in particular.

"East," Cale said. "To stand in the plains and pray for

the sun to rise again. They think they're still in their own world, but they are not. The sun never rises here." Cale's yellow eyes fixed on the women as they moved away. "They are the lingering memories of Elgrin Fau, Jak, once called the City of Silver."

The halfling stared at Cale with his mouth hanging open.

Magadon too looked at Cale with surprise in his white eyes.

Beside Cale, Riven nodded knowingly and said, "When Kesson Rel stole the sky, the inhabitants of Elgrin Fau began to perish. The darkness of this plane consumed thousands before it was sated. The survivors were long ago scattered to the planes."

The assassin's gaze swept the length and breadth of the ruins.

Jak tried to imagine the city, living, filled with people and light, but he could not. The Plane of Shadow had left it a dark husk. He thought of the tragedy represented there and a chill ran up his spine. He shared a look with Magadon, whose knucklebone eyes had grown thoughtful. Jak looked from Cale to Riven, Riven to Cale.

"How do you two know any of that?" he softly asked, and was not sure he wanted to know the answer.

"I saw it," Cale said, then he frowned and cocked his head. "Or perhaps I read it."

Riven looked at Cale curiously before answering, "I dreamed it."

Jak nodded as though he understood, but he did not. He simply could think of nothing to say. Things were too large for comment. When he looked at Cale he still saw his friend, but he saw something else too, something grander, something darker. A hero? For some reason, he thought of Sephris.

The First of Five, he thought, and wondered what that actually meant.

In respectful silence, they all watched the ghosts continue their hopeless trek east through the rain, to pray for a sun they would never again see. Cale gazed upon them wistfully.

When the spirits had vanished from sight, Magadon asked in a quiet voice, "Erevis, do you know if the flashing light we saw earlier is a way home?"

Cale, who had been lost in thought, came back to himself.

He shook his head and said softly, "I don't know, Mags. I wish I did. But . . . things are coming back to me."

"Back to you?" Jak asked. "What does that mean?"

Cale shrugged and said, "That's the only way I can explain it, little man."

Jak resolved in that instant to get Cale away from the Plane of Shadow at all hazards. The darkness there was sinking into Cale, soaking him. Jak didn't want to think about what would happen to his friend if he became saturated with it. He didn't want to think about what would happen to any of them. For the first time, Jak admitted—to himself at least—that he didn't want Cale to be this "First of Five." He didn't even want Cale to be a priest anymore. He wanted Cale to be Cale, his friend and nothing more.

Jak put a hand on Cale's forearm. The shadows that clung to Cale's person coiled defensively around the halfling's fingers.

"Let's keep moving," Jak said. "We need to find the source of that flashing light. It *is* a way out," he said, hoping that by saying it with certainty he would make it so.

As if in response to Jak's words, from their position atop the roof, they again caught the tantalizing flash of golden light from somewhere near the center of the crypts. They could not see its source, but the color reminded Jak of sunlight.

Lightning flashed, casting the city in vermillion.

"Jak's right," Magadon said, and jumped down from the edifice.

The rest followed, and together they headed through the rain and ruin for the center of town.

As they walked, Jak tried to take Cale's mind off of the ghosts and remind him of something ordinary, of their life before his transformation to shade.

"It was raining just like this last spring when I had a run of Tymora's own luck at the Scarlet Knave. Do you remember that? I must have won ten hands of Scales and Blades in a row. I lived well over the next tenday, my friend. I bought five new hats."

Cale smiled, but his eyes were distant when he replied, "I remember, Jak." After a pause, he softly added, "I remember a lot of things."

To that, Jak could say nothing, but he suddenly missed his hats a great deal. For a time they walked in silence.

At last, Cale looked down at him and said, "Little man, do you remember once, when you were talking about the life, and you said to me, 'This is only what we do, not what we are?'"

"I remember," Jak replied, "That's the truth, Cale."

Cale's mouth was a hard line when he said, "Not anymore."

Before Jak could protest, Riven interrupted them with a saber blade at each of their chests.

"You see?" the assassin said. "You two hens are too busy clucking to—"

With speed and strength that made Jak go wide-eyed, Cale batted Riven's left-hand saber aside, grabbed the assassin by the cloak, and yanked him in close.

The assassin let his blades fall slack and merely stared. Jak detected the beginnings of a smirk at the corners of Riven's mouth, though the assassin's breathing came fast.

Cale answered Riven's stare with one of his own. His yellow eyes flashed. Shadows spiraled around his head.

To his credit, Riven kept his voice level.

"If I was an enemy, Cale, you'd already be dead. It only pays to be fast if you see what's coming. Don't get sloppy. We both know that all of the dead in this city won't be as harmless as those ghosts. Stay sharp, just as you said.

You too, Fleet. Now—" and his eye narrowed—"put me down."

Cale's expression did not change, but he shoved the assassin away.

Riven kept his feet, chuckled, straightened his cloak, and turned away.

"Whoreson," Jak said to Riven's back.

"No, he's right," Cale said. "I'm losing focus. I feel like I'm in deep water, Jak."

The halfling felt the same way. He took a protective step closer to his friend as they continued on toward the crypts.

CHAPTER 6

THE DEAD OF NIGHT

The air grew darker as they neared the cemetery. It felt almost too thick to breathe, almost viscous. The buildings grew more and more blasted as they closed on the necropolis's perimeter wall. It looked to Jak as though the eye of an unimaginable storm had sat over the cemetery, leaving it in calm even while destroying the rest of the city.

Jak's bluelight wand illuminated little more than five paces. With each step, the sensation of being watched grew stronger in the halfling. The rain had grown colder.

Jak realized that the hairs on the back of his neck were standing on end. He took out his holy symbol and held it in the same hand as the bluelight wand.

"Strange to have a cemetery in the middle of town," Magadon observed.

"Originally, it was a commons," Cale replied over the rain. "In the final years, the inhabitants converted it to this. They wanted a cemetery within the walls, to keep their dead close. They thought that would keep them from rising. After the darkness had consumed them all, Kesson Rel returned and opened a gate in the midst of the graves. He wanted to taunt the dead with a means of escape that they could never avail themselves of."

Jak didn't bother to ask how Cale knew what he knew.

"A gate? he asked.

For a moment, Cale looked as though he had surprised himself.

He nodded and said, "Yes. The light is a gate. But I . . . I can't remember to where it leads."

Jak accepted that and kept moving.

Before them stood the low, crumbling stone wall of the cemetery. Jak felt as though that weatherworn wall demarcated more than merely the borders of the graveyard. Beyond the wall was a large expanse, overgrown with weeds, trees and tall grass, and dotted with densely-packed crypts and statuary.

They walked between two obelisks—the metal gate that once joined them lay twisted and broken nearby—and entered. It seemed to Jak that things went quieter the moment he passed through the gate.

To Jak's eye, all of the crypts appeared roughly similar—small, rectangular mausoleums of cut stone with pitched tops—though they varied in size and detail work. Most would have housed several dead, families perhaps. All had writing engraved into their face and tops, a jagged script that was faded and alien to Jak. Most had at least one statue of a winged woman on them, no doubt Elgrin Fau's patron goddess of the afterlife. Typically, she perched at the apex of the roof over the sealed door of the crypt, though she sometimes flanked the doors. Sometimes she cradled a body in her arms, and sometimes she was empty-handed.

Jak was amazed at the amount of resources the people of the city had committed to burial.

As they moved deeper into the graveyard, a fog began to form around their feet—a soup of gray mist and dark shadows. The rain slowed to a drizzle, then finally stopped. Even the thunder went quiet. The atmosphere seemed pensive, ominous.

Magadon called frequent halts, as though he saw or heard something, but then restarted the march. Jak heard nothing unusual, though his head felt muzzy. The wet must have been getting to him, but he forced himself forward.

The necropolis seemed to go on forever and fatigue gradually took its toll. Jak's legs hung from his hips like tree trunks. His vision began to grow blurry. How long had they been walking? He'd been too long on that dark plane and it was draining him.

In his dazed state, the halfling imagined deformed faces forming and dispersing in the wispy shadows that clung to their ankles and hid their feet. He shook his head frequently to clear it. The waist high shadow fog was everywhere. But hadn't it only been at his knees moments ago?

Jak couldn't see more than three paces in any direction. He was so tired that he felt as though the fog was clutching at him, turning him, forcing him to go only one way.

Magadon stopped, looked around at the crypts, and said in a whisper, "We're walking in circles." When his companions said nothing, the guide shook his head and said it again, more loudly. "We are walking in circles."

His voice sounded muted in the fog, deadened.

For a moment, it was as though no one other than Magadon could speak. It took several heartbeats for the guide's meaning to register with Jak. When it did, Jak could not fathom how the guide could have determined what he claimed. The crypts all looked the same to Jak, the trees, the grass. But Magadon knew what he knew.

At last, Cale asked in a dull voice, "Are you certain?"

"Yes," Magadon said, but then shook his head in confusion. "No."

"It's the shadows," Jak managed to say, and his tongue felt thick and unwieldy. "The fog."

Somehow the shadow fog had dulled their perception, had begun to siphon away their vitality.

The realization itself helped to clear Jak's head. It was as if a spell had been broken. His companions too seemed to recover. Gradually, each began to blink away the torpor and looked around with a more alert expression. The world suddenly came back to life and motion. Jak realized that the rain was still falling. It had never stopped! Thunder rolled in the distance. Jak felt as though he was awakening from a dream, or a three-night ale binge. He was so cold that his teeth were chattering.

"What in the Hells just happened?" Riven growled.

Though the magical effect of the shadow fog appeared to have diminished, the fog itself still enshrouded them. Jak's bluelight wand barely penetrated it. The tombs nearby faded into nothingness in its swirl of gray and ink. Tendrils of a deeper darkness ran through the mist and whirled around their legs and torsos like living things, pawing at their boots, steering them—

Steering them.

Jak took a step to his right and found that the shadows resisted him, then gently pulled him forward. His heart hammered.

"Light, Magadon!" he said over the rain. "Anything you have! Now!"

Jak didn't wait for the guide to respond. He quickly mouthed the words to a temporary light spell and focused it on the end of his bluelight wand. A globe of radiance took shape at the wand's tip. Magadon too acted quickly—almost simultaneously with the completion of Jak's spell—and a nimbus of white light flashed around the guide's head and a ball of white fire formed in the air above him, adding its own luminescence to that of Jak's spell.

The fog tendrils that had coiled around their bodies jerked backward from the sudden radiance, like a hand that had grasped a hot kettle. A palpable tremor rippled through the haze, and for a few heartbeats the light knifed through the otherwise impenetrable darkness and fog.

In that combined flash of light, Jak saw that the tendrils within the shadow fog were composed of a network of red and black veins, each as fine as a child's hair, each slowly pulsing. Just as that registered, a horrifying chorus of unearthly moans answered the light from behind them. The sound sent a chill down Jak's spine. He whirled around—

"Dark and empty!" he oathed.

Under cover of the fog and the mind-numbing spell, a host of dark figures had assembled behind them. They had gathered in an arc perhaps thirty paces away, some on the ground, others hovering in the air. Each was a roughly man-shaped outline of darkness, black as pitch, with coal red eyes that flared from the inky holes of their heads. A wave of cold went before them like a Deepwinter gale. Behind the assembled mass of undead, Jak could see more and more of the creatures rising from the mausoleums. They passed through the walls and roofs of the tombs as easily as if it was open air. It reminded Jak of black smoke issuing from chimneys. There had to be hundreds.

"Wraiths!" Cale said, brandishing Weaveshear.

Riven dropped into a fighting crouch beside him, sabers bare. Magadon knocked an arrow and drew. Jak knew that blades and arrows would be of little use against so many undead, so he did the only thing he could.

Before Magadon could fire, and before the wraiths could swarm forward, he leaped in front of his comrades, stared into the unholy eyes of the army of wraiths, and held forth his holy symbol.

"Back to your pits, creatures!" he commanded as he drew on the grace of the Trickster.

The power of Brandobaris suffused him and a dim luminescence flared from his jeweled pendant. For an instant, Jak felt more than mortal.

A symphony of hate-filled hisses answered his rebuke, but only a handful of the wraiths recoiled and fled back into their tombs. Among the rest, red eyes flared brighter and fixed their deadly gaze on Jak. Jak could feel their evil, their anger, washing over him like a chill wind. He kept his holy symbol in hand and continued to channel the Trickster's energy. Perhaps he could keep them from overwhelming him and his companions, at least for a time.

The dark army continued to assemble, like crows convening over a corpse. Red eyes burned hate into Jak. Dark bodies and darker souls strained against the divine resistance he offered through his holy symbol.

"Jak?" Magadon asked.

Straining against the wraiths, Jak could only offer a nod.

"Keep moving," Magadon said, backing deeper into the crypts while still holding his aim at the cloud of wraiths.

Riven and Cale followed the guide, with Jak bringing up the rear.

The moment Jak moved, the dark creatures moved with him, pressed against the power he was channeling. The strain of resisting the will of so many undead was wearing on him. He felt as if he was trying to hold a door shut against a hill giant. The glow from his holy symbol had diminished. He knew he could not last much longer.

"Cale!" he called in desperation, then remembered that Cale did not have his holy symbol. Without it, Cale could not affect undead.

But then Cale was beside him, *with* him, wearing a silken black mask.

"Right here, little man," Cale said, then he called out to the Shadowlord for power.

Jak had no time to consider how or when his friend had obtained a new holy symbol. Cale held Weaveshear before him like a talisman and the dark blade flared with ochre light.

"Back to your rest, dead of Elgrin Fau!" Cale commanded, in a voice not devoid of sympathy.

Again, the wraiths moaned, a few dissipated into nothingness, and another handful fled back to their crypts. But the bulk of them continued to advance. Still, Cale and Jak together managed at least to hold them at bay.

"Too many!" Cale called over his shoulder. "We can only slow them. Move. Move!"

Magadon fired an arrow into the mass of wraiths, then another. Jak couldn't tell if the shots had any effect on the incorporeal undead.

"Where to?" the guide asked.

"The gate," Jak said, looking over his shoulder. "There!"

He nodded in the direction of the center of the necropolis, where a flash of golden light temporarily blazed through the darkness.

Abruptly, Jak's light spell and Magadon's mental manifestation ended. Except for the dim light of Jak's bluelight wand, darkness again descended. Jak could see clearly only a few paces. The glowing coals of the wraiths' eyes behind them looked like the campfires of an army. They moaned and surged forward.

"Go now!" Cale shouted.

Magadon and Riven ran full out for the center of the cemetery, pushing their way through the fog that still resisted them. Cale and Jak followed as best they could while backstepping, continuing to slow the advance of the wraiths by channeling the power of their respective deities.

Through gritted teeth, Cale said to Jak, "They could break us if they pushed all at once."

Sweating and gasping, Jak replied, "But they aren't. Maybe they can't."

"Maybe," Cale said. Over his shoulder, he shouted to Magadon and Riven, "If they wanted to attack, they could have already. We're being herded. Stand ready."

"Are you certain?" Magadon said as he turned and fired an arrow, then another and another.

Cale could only nod, and Jak could only agree. The wraiths were holding back, waiting for a more opportune moment to attack.

Jak heard Riven spit, and heard the tell-tale whistle of the assassin's sabers whirling through the air.

"Something else wants the first bite, eh?" Riven chuckled darkly then added, "Whatever it is, it damned well better be hungry."

CHAPTER 7

Epiphany of the Self

They sped through the overgrown cemetery toward an unknown danger, trailed by a cloud of wraiths.

Another wraith emerged from each crypt they passed, as if their very presence summoned the creature from its tomb. Cale continued to hold forth Weaveshear. He managed to channel waves of the Shadowlord's power to keep the wraiths at bay even though he had pulled the mask from his face. Cale couldn't breathe easily with it on. Sweat soaked his tunic. He was exhausted. Beside Cale, Jak held his holy symbol before him. The halfling frequently stumbled, and Cale could see that he was wilting.

"I'm getting thin, Cale," Jak said, in a voice gone hoarse.

"Hold on, little man," Cale said. Over his

shoulder, he shouted, "Get us to the gate, Magadon! Hurry!"

Despite the rush of "memories" flooding Cale's consciousness, he no idea what to expect at the gate.

The guide nodded and picked up the pace. Cale and Jak struggled to keep up while backstepping. Together, they set up an invisible wall of resistance that prevented the wraiths from closing. But they could not hold it forever. Though the wraiths had not yet made a determined push, with each step they increased the pressure. More and more the creatures tested the limits of Cale and Jak's collective strength.

The shadow fog grew so tangibly thick around them that Cale felt like he was moving through water; or perhaps he was just exhausted. The wan glow of Jak's bluelight and the blazing eyes of the wraiths provided the only light.

"Here!" Magadon shouted.

"Dark!" Riven oathed.

Cale and Jak turned to see a wide declivity before them, swathed in a churning cloud of darkness. In the center of that cloud hulked a horror, the originator of the fog, the master of the wraiths. From the misshapen spheres of its huge body and head sprouted masses of black, rubbery tentacles, each as thick around as Jak's waist, and fifteen paces long. The tentacles reminded Cale of the tendrils that had transformed him into a shade back in the Fane.

A cluster of eight spiderlike eyes, as black and unforgiving as flecks of obsidian, looked out from over the creature's clacking, insectoid mandibles. The monster was spinning a pinwheel of shadow strands from its body into the fog the way a black widow spun her webs. Somehow Cale knew that the creature was a dark-weaver—the gatekeeper left behind by Kesson Rel. The wraiths—the dead of Elgrin Fau—were its thralls, and the shadowstuff was its tools.

The darkweaver sprawled atop a wide, oval platform of black-veined marble that sat in the center of the declivity.

Once a place for solemn ceremony, the platform had come to serve as the darkweaver's roost. Immediately behind the creature, two rune-encrusted obelisks rose from the platform, each as tall as a hill giant and as big around as the trunk of a mature elm. A curtain of translucent golden energy hung between the magical posts, sparking and sizzling like lightning. Occasionally, the energy coalesced into a bright gold wall and shot a flash of light into the dark sky—the source of the light they had seen from the city's outskirts.

This was the gate of Kesson Rel, Cale knew. The shadow sorcerer's final jest; the Chosen of Mask's final betrayal. Cale had no idea where it led—perhaps back to the world of Elgrin Fau, but perhaps not. Still, he knew it was a way out, and that was enough.

Cale needed to get out. Desperately. The longer he stayed on the Plane of Shadow, the more of its darkness sank into his skin and polluted his soul, further transforming him, filling his mind with memories that could not possibly be his own. He felt as if something was pushing around the edges of his mind, probing for weakness, trying to worm its way into his consciousness and overwhelm his identity. He held it back only by the dam of his will. And he couldn't hold it back forever, anymore than he could hold back the wraiths forever.

A cloud of shadows roiled around the darkweaver. It appeared as though the creature were swimming in waters of pitch. Its alien eyes fixed on them and its front tentacles squirmed in agitation, reminding Cale of a nest of giant snakes. It keened through its mandibles, the sound alien and menacing.

The wraiths responded as if that keen was a war horn summoning them to battle. As one they uttered a moan and threw themselves against the divine force channeled by Cale and Jak.

The two friends held for only an instant before their wall of resistance shattered with an audible crackle of energy. They staggered, pushed backward by the power backlash, while the dead of Elgrin Fau swarmed forward like a cloud of bats, red eyes seething.

Behind them, the darkweaver's mandibles began to churn. Its tentacles squirmed obscenely, but it didn't leave its position directly in front of the gate. It was Kesson Rel's guardian and it would not leave its charge.

"We make a stand here, then," said Riven above the rain, eerily calm. His sabers whirled as he watched the approaching wraiths. "Back to back. Nothing gets close and lives."

Magadon took a knee and set his bow to singing. Cale marveled at his rapidity. Arrow after arrow flew into the cloud of wraiths as they streaked forward. The head of each missile glowed white, charged by the power of Magadon's mind. Some flew harmlessly through the wraiths' insubstantial bodies, but others struck home, eliciting agonized moans from the undead. Jak, his face wan from the psychic war with the undead, drew his short sword and dagger and took a step nearer to Cale.

Cale spared a glance behind, at the gate behind the darkweaver. He knew that golden glow was their only hope. He hesitated, made up his mind, then grabbed Magadon and Riven by the cloaks.

"Not here!" he said. "We make for the gate. Mags, keep firing."

Cale knew that if they could cut their way through the darkweaver quickly, they might escape the wraiths and gain the gate. They needed only to hold the wraiths at bay for a bit longer.

Heedless of the poor footing afforded by the wet grass, the four pelted down the declivity, directly at the wriggling tentacles and black eyes of the darkweaver. Magadon came last, covering their retreat by firing into the swarm of wraiths.

Despite the dire situation, Cale felt a momentary flash of hope.

As they closed, two of the darkweaver's front tentacles rose before it and began to wave hypnotically.

In his head, Cale heard a soft, reasonable, but strangely-accented voice say, *Stop for moment, and place weapons at your feet. This be only a misunderstanding. You be not harmed if you stop now. Gate be by you used.*

Despite the poor syntax, Cale felt the magic in that command pull at his will. Weaveshear vibrated slightly in his hand, and Cale resisted the compulsion.

Jak didn't.

"A misunderstanding," the halfling said thoughtfully, slowing. "That makes sense."

He reduced his run to a jog and sheathed his blades. Nodding agreement, Magadon too lowered his weapon and slowed his pace. The wraiths moaned in anticipation, still speeding forward.

Cale and Riven slowed their own pace, nearly slipping on the rain-soaked grass. Jak and Magadon stopped all together, looking around with bemused expressions. Cale and Riven tried to pull them along, but they resisted.

"Move," Cale ordered the halfling.

"He'll let us use the gate," Jak said. "Ease down, Cale."

"Nine Hells!" Riven oathed. The assassin and Cale looked at the darkweaver to see its tentacles scrabbling up the declivity toward them. The squirming motion of those limbs made Cale want to vomit.

Riven looked past Magadon to the advancing cloud of wraiths. He took fistfuls of Magadon's cloak and shook him.

"Mags! It's a spell. Don't be a fool!"

But Magadon only stared vacantly and said, "It's a misunderstanding, Drasek. Put down your weapons. You'll see."

Riven's face twisted in disgust and he shoved the guide away. He fixed his gaze on Cale and asked the question with his eye.

Cale gave a nod; there was little else to do.

"This is where it ends," he said.

He pulled his holy symbol from his vest, wrapped it

around Weaveshear's hilt, and pushed Jak down behind him. Shadows streamed from Cale's flesh.

The halfling pulled at his cloak and said, "It's a misunderstanding, Cale. You can scabbard the steel."

Cale ignored the halfling and said to Riven, "I've got the wraiths and Jak."

"I've got Mags and that thing," Riven answered, nodding at the darkweaver.

"I'll hold them off as long as I can," Cale said, eyeing the advancing swarm. "You finish that abomination fast, and we might yet make the gate."

Riven only smiled.

They spaced themselves a pace or two apart, enough room to provide them some space to maneuver, but not enough to allow attacks from the rear.

Ready, the First and the Second of Mask awaited their foes.

The wraiths reached them first, swooping upon them like dark birds of prey, eyes burning. Cale stood in front of Jak and faced the onslaught, ducking, slashing, dodging, and stabbing. Each time Weaveshear struck the body of a wraith, a portion of the creature boiled away into wisps of foul, sulfurous smoke. The creatures were all around him. He could not help but strike one with each slash. Their moans of hate and pain filled his ears; the image of their red eyes burned itself into his brain.

"Cover me, Cale!" shouted Riven, as he darted out of the melee, dragging Magadon by the cloak. The assassin charged the darkweaver, saber blade whirling.

Ten pairs of red eyes followed Riven's back and started to give chase. Cale spun away from the wraiths near him and leaped in front of the would-be pursuers. He drove Weaveshear through one incorporeal body, then another. Both moaned, bleeding greasy black smoke, and retreated.

"Be quick, godsdamnit!" he shouted after Riven.

He would not be able to hold for long. As it was, he could not effectively keep the wraiths from Jak. Despite his best efforts, some flew past him after Riven and Magadon.

He was an island in an ocean of black. The wraiths attacked from all sides, from above, even emerging from the ground under his feet to attack from below. Their icy touch passed through his enchanted leather armor as though it did not exist and pulled at his life-force, chilling him to the bone. He managed to resist the pull of their touch time and again, and somehow knew that he could do so easily only because of what he had become. Still, the cold engendered by their fell touch was slowing him down.

He forced three wraiths back with a flurry of cross slashes from Weaveshear, then whirled around to check on Jak. A blanket of wraiths covered the halfling. Still deluded by the spell, Jak struck at them with his hand as if they were nothing more than annoying insects. But they were not, and each time they put their dark hands to the halfling's flesh, Jak grew a little paler, a little weaker.

Cale lunged at the wraiths attacking Jak, slashed the head from one—it vanished in a cloud of smoke—stabbed another through its chest. It too vanished, but another took its place. And another. There were too many.

Cale scooped Jak into his right arm and held him protectively against his body. The halfling was ice cold. With Jak in one arm, Cale knew that he would not be able to move effectively, but it was the only way he could protect his friend.

"Put down the steel, Cale," Jak said through chattering teeth. "This is a misunderstanding."

Cale ignored the halfling, brandished Weaveshear, and channeled the power of Mask through the blade.

"Down to the shadows," he said in a firm voice, his sympathy for the city's dead washed away by the heat of combat. Weaveshear pulsed forth a wave of divine power, amplified in power by Cale's anger. The wave obliterated a handful of wraiths; another handful fled the battle. But more took their place. He decided then and there that he would kill Jak himself before allowing the wraiths to drain the halfling's soul.

Desperate for another option, Cale stole a glance over his shoulder at Riven. The assassin wasn't faring much better. The darkweaver's tentacles had already walled in Riven and Magadon. Riven was unable to get close enough to strike at the creature's body. The huge appendages swung wildly at the assassin and guide, narrowly missing Riven but knocking Magadon to the ground. Riven answered with a flurry of saber slashes and yanked Magadon to his feet. Above them, still more wraiths hovered, awaiting an opportunity to attack.

Cale looked once more at the gate, the darkweaver, the wraiths, and realized that it was hopeless to fight. They were never going to reach the gate. If they persisted, they were all going to die. Riven wouldn't be able to finish the darkweaver before the wraiths had claimed them all.

"Hold as long as you can, Riven!" Cale shouted, not sure if the assassin could hear him. "I'll return."

With that, Cale did the only thing he could. Still clutching Jak, and not knowing whether his ability would work while carrying another, he tried to shadowstep as far away from the cemetery as he could.

For an instant he felt the strange sensation of rushing air and rapid motion, then he and the halfling materialized on an empty street somewhere in the middle of Elgrin Fau. Only the patter of the rain, Jak's chattering teeth, and the sound of Cale's breathing broke the silence of the street. He hadn't traveled as far as he'd hoped. His ability to shadowstep obviously enabled him to cover only so much distance. But they had escaped the wraiths.

Jak, still pale and weak, groaned, "Cale, what are you do—"

Cale shadowstepped again, still hoping to get outside the city—and he succeeded. He and Jak found themselves on the low ridge that overlooked the ruins of Elgrin Fau. From there, they couldn't see the cemetery, and the buildings below looked quiet in the rain.

Cale looked into the halfling's wan face and asked, "Are you all right? Jak?"

The halfling nodded, though his eyes were heavy with shame. Being removed from the necropolis seemed to have allowed him to shake the effects of the darkweaver's compulsion spell.

"I'm all right," he said. "I can heal myself. Go."

Cale thumped Jak on the shoulder and said, "Stay here. I'll be back."

He shadowstepped back into the city. Again, he materialized on an empty street. Hoping he wasn't too late, he took another step toward the cemetery, and materialized in the midst of a maelstrom.

Wraiths swirled everywhere and the darkweaver's tentacles thrashed about. Riven stood in the middle of it hacking wildly and shouting. Cale could see that the assassin was weakening. Riven's blows were wild; his speed a heartbeat slower. To Cale's left, Magadon lay on his back in the grass, barely visible through the crowd of wraiths that surrounded him and fed on his life-force.

Cale took the wraiths near Riven by surprise. Lunging forward and swinging Weaveshear in a wide arc, he sliced through three with a single swing. The stench from their dissipating bodies made him gag.

"Riven!" he shouted.

The assassin whirled on him, unleashing a vicious cross cut at Cale's throat with one of his sabers. Cale barely interposed Weaveshear in time to parry.

"Riven!"

Riven's good eye registered recognition. He grinned a mouthful of stained teeth.

"It isn't over yet!" the assassin shouted.

"We are leaving!" Cale countered.

Riven nodded, ducked under a swooping wraith, and split it open it as it passed. Cale impaled one, then another. Brandishing Weaveshear, he turned and channeled Mask's power at the wraiths surrounding Magadon.

"Away, darkspawn!" he commanded.

Four wraiths withered before the onslaught of divine might, leaving behind only moans and wisps of dark smoke. A tentacle wrapped around Cale's ankle and pulled him from his feet. Riven hacked it off with two swings of his sabers. It squirmed near them in a paroxysm of pain, spitting black blood and wisps of shadow. Cale jumped to his feet and bounded forward. He grabbed the groaning Magadon, clasped Riven by the forearm, uttered a prayer to Mask, and tried to shadowstep.

It worked, even with his two comrades. They found themselves standing in the rain on a quiet side street, surrounded by ruins. The only sound was that of their labored breathing. Before Riven or Magadon could speak, Cale shadowstepped again, and the three comrades appeared near Jak on the ridge overlooking the city.

For a time, they all sat there in the grass, in the rain, and said nothing. Even Riven, who moments before had seemed lost in the adrenaline rush of combat, seemed to have deflated.

In the distance, the golden light of the gate again flashed, a tantalizing reminder of a way out. Cale stared at it, thought, and made up his mind.

"Regroup," he said. "After we've recovered, we go again."

Incredulous expressions looked out from pale faces.

He explained with half the truth. "We know where the gate is now. We know what's guarding it. We can prepare and get through."

The rest of the truth was that he *had* to get through.

Magadon said, "You said that you don't know where it leads, Erevis. A divination to determine—"

Cale cut him off with a wave of his hand and a shake of his head.

"Divinations do not work here, Mags. Besides, wherever it leads, anywhere is better than here."

"Cale . . ." Jak began.

"We go again!" Cale snapped, and instantly regretted it.

Jak recoiled. He struggled to keep the hurt from his eyes.

"All right," the halfling said, voice thick with emotion. "We go again."

He climbed unsteadily to his feet, and Cale had to control the urge to go over and help him stand.

Riven's voice sounded from behind Cale, "No."

Cale's grip on Weaveshear tightened as he turned to the assassin.

Riven's good eye took in the blade, took in Cale's expression, and narrowed dangerously. Even Riven's ordinarily sallow face looked pale from the wraiths' attacks. He still held a saber in each hand. He raised one and pointed it at Jak and Magadon.

"Look at them, Cale. They can't go through that again. Fleet can barely stand. There are too many. You got us out of there—" he nodded back at the city—"and you're going to get us out of here."

His gaze took in all of the plains.

"We can do it," Jak said, but Cale heard the lie in the halfling's voice.

He chose to ignore it. He had to escape.

Cale said to Riven, "We're going back."

Riven shook his head and took two steps nearer to Cale, until they stood nose to nose.

"No, we're not," the assassin said. "Listen to what you're saying, Cale. You're desperate to get out of here, even more than Fleet. Why is that?"

Because I'm afraid of what's happening to me, Cale thought but did not say. He felt himself transforming into a man like Sephris Dwendon—seeing things that others did not, hearing a god in his brain, going mad.

Instead, he said, "Take one step back, Zhent. Now."

Riven's good eye narrowed to a slit, as though he was considering the seriousness of the threat. He took a step back but continued to face Cale.

"You're ready to sacrifice me, yourself, fine," said the assassin. "But Fleet? That transformation darkened more than your skin, Cale. I'm not sure you're even a man anymore."

That hit too close to the mark. Cale remembered his thought, born in the heat of battle, that he would kill Jak rather than let the wraiths take him. Hot with rage, he grabbed Riven by the cloak and pulled him close.

"No," Cale hissed. "I'm not just a man. Not anymore. I am the First of the Shadowlord." He stared Riven in the face. "And that's what bothers you, isn't it, *Second*?"

Riven's good eye flashed and his nostrils flared. Cale could feel the tension in the assassin's body.

"Among other things," Riven said, his voice low and predatory.

Cale released the assassin's cloak, took one step back, and drummed his fingers on Weaveshear's hilt. Wisps of shadow trailed around his face.

"And?" he asked, daring Riven with his eyes to further escalate the exchange.

Riven tightened his grip on his sabers, but before the assassin's snarl could form into a coherent reply, Magadon jumped to his feet and interposed himself between them.

"That's enough!" the guide said. He looked into Cale's eyes, then into Riven's. "Back off, Drasek. Erevis. Just . . . back off."

The assassin continued to stare daggers into Cale, but he did as Magadon requested. Cale's own ire vanished as quickly as it had risen. He just felt tired. He slumped, leaned on his blade.

Magadon turned angrily on Riven and growled, "You. You keep pushing and pushing, though you see his struggle and understand it full well. Stop it. Besides, he's as human as me, and probably more than you."

Cale appreciated what Magadon was trying to do, even if it was not entirely correct. Riven would have none of it.

"I'm pushing for a reason," the assassin said as he sheathed his sabers. He looked into Cale's face. "And he's not human. He was hit by wraiths too, same as you and me. Look at him. Unscathed. He's no more human than your father."

Magadon glanced up sharply at that. Had he been

closer, Cale would have punched the assassin in the face for salting the wound of Magadon's heritage.

"What did you say?" Magadon said, his voice eerily calm.

"I've known you the better of ten years, Mags," the assassin said. "I know what you are."

Magadon said through gritted teeth, "And I know what you are, Riven."

The assassin waved a hand dismissively and said, "I've never tried to hide it." He looked past Magadon to Cale. "Like I said, you're our way out of here, Cale. Not the gate. *Stop fighting it.*"

"You said that before, Zhent," said Cale, glaring, "and it's still the same nonsense."

"Not so," Riven sneered. "I've seen it, Cale, dreamed it. You're the only way we're getting out of here. And you're the reason we're still here. You're still hanging on to what you were. You're changed. *We're* changed. You keep saying it with words, but not feeling it. Let it go. Stop fighting."

Cale simply stared. He could frame no reply, because there was no reply to be made. Deep down, in that secret part of his brain that he kept walled off, he knew that Riven spoke the truth. Cale had been fighting it, and fighting it hard since the moment he'd opened his eyes to see a starless sky. He was not human. He never would be again. He'd told himself as much, had seen it in Jak's haunted eyes, heard Magadon state it across a fire, but he'd held it at bay with the wall of his will, kept the reality of it from infecting his psyche. And that wall was crumbling.

Tears started to form in his eyes—whether from frustration, fatigue, fear, or some combination of all of them, he didn't know—but he blinked them back. He wouldn't give Riven the satisfaction.

The assassin stared at him, waiting.

"Cale?" Jak asked tentatively.

He'd voluntarily transformed his body to save Jak, but had fought the transformation of his soul. He couldn't fight it any longer. He was too tired, and he was a shade. A monster.

What had he done to himself?

Weaveshear fell from numb fingers. His legs went weak. He fell to his knees and turned his face to the ground. He would have screamed his anger into the night, but he couldn't muster the strength to shout. Instead, he simply sat there and let the rain wash over him. After a moment, he raised his gaze and looked upon Riven. The assassin returned his look, expressionless, and nodded.

Cale nodded back. Staring at Riven all the while, Cale made a conscious decision, steeled himself, and surrendered to what he had become.

He thought he could hear Mask laughing.

Darkness entered him, enveloped him, a cocoon of night.

Knowledge flooded Cale—the full scope of his abilities as a shade. He knew then that his body resisted magic, that he could form animated duplicates of himself out of shadowstuff, could turn invisible in darkness, could travel between worlds. He saved them from the destruction of the Fane when his instincts tapped those powers. Having embraced it, he knew he could do it at will.

He was the Divine Agent of Mask, the Champion of the Shadowlord. He knew the names of the others who served Mask in a similar capacity: Drasek Riven, Kesson Rel, Avner of Hartsvale. . . . Proxies, Chosen, Agents, Seraphs—they had many titles. But among them all, Cale was the First and Riven the Second. It was Cale and Riven who would retrieve for the Shadowlord what he had lost.

Groaning, Cale gripped his head between his hands and tried to prevent his skull from exploding under the pressure of the influx of knowledge.

He knew in that instant that Riven was right. Cale *was* their way out. The irony was that Cale could not have escaped the Shadow until he surrendered to it. He knew that Mask had planned it that way. Mask planned everything that way.

Time passed, he didn't know how long, and gradually his head ceased pounding. He sat on his knees in the grass. Around him, everything stood quiet except the patter of the rain. It would never wash him clean, he knew. Not anymore.

Thazienne. . . .

A touch on his arm. He looked over and saw Jak, concern writ clear in the halfling's green eyes.

In Luirenal, the halfling said, *"It doesn't matter, Cale. I'm your friend. I'll always be your friend."*

It did matter, but Jak's simple words brought Cale more comfort than anything else could have. He even managed a smile.

"I know. Thank you, Jak." He cleared his throat and said, "Earlier, when I snapped at you—"

Jak waved it away.

"Forgotten," he said.

Cale nodded, patted the halfling's arm. Still a little lightheaded, he leaned on Jak and climbed to his feet. He took a deep breath and looked to Riven and Magadon.

"Riven was right," he said. "I know how to get us back to Faerûn."

Riven looked only mildly smug. Magadon looked both pleased and alarmed.

"How?" the guide asked, hope in his voice.

"I'm going to shift us there," Cale replied. "But first we need to have a conversation. I've been considering something for a time. We need to handle it before we leave this place." He looked an apologetic glance at the halfling. "Jak, stay here."

"What?" the halfling asked in surprise. "Why?"

"Trust me," Cale said.

He offered a smile. It was better if Jak knew nothing of what Cale was about to propose.

The halfling looked perplexed, and maybe a little hurt, but he nodded anyway.

❧ ❧ ❧ ❧ ❧

Jak tried to hide his frown as Cale steered Riven and Magadon out of easy earshot. The halfling knew that Cale must have a good reason to exclude him—likely due to a discussion of what Cale sometimes referred to as "methods"—but that lessened the sting only a little. Besides, Jak wished Cale had spoken to him about it beforehand. Jak didn't need to be sheltered from hard choices, not anymore. His views on what was acceptable had changed since his torture at the hands of the slaad.

Merely recollecting that agony made his eyes water. He still bore the scars of slaad claws on his chest and on his soul. He supposed he always would.

But in the aftermath of that pain he had come to realize that sometimes—but *only* sometimes—principle must give way to pragmatism. It was a hard lesson, but a true one. Otherwise, the slaadi and those like them would always win.

Sometimes good people have to do hard things, he thought, recollecting Cale's words to him on that rainy night outside of Selgaunt.

He knew the words stank of a rationalization, but he knew too that they were true. The truth was just so ugly that it sometimes needed to be rationalized.

He wondered what hard things his three companions were discussing just then. He wondered if his old friend Sephris would still consider him a seventeen.

He pulled his pipe, quickly gave up trying to light it in the rain, and instead twirled it in his fingers; a nervous habit. He eyed his comrades sidelong, trying not to listen, but unable to keep himself from watching.

Cale spoke softly but earnestly, gesturing often with pointed fingers and clenched fists. At first Magadon looked confused, but after a time the guide nodded slowly and said something in reply to Cale. Riven took a step back, as though Cale was threatening him, and shook his head. His voice rose in anger.

"No," the assassin said. "That's madness."

Cale shot a concerned glance at Jak and replied to the

assassin in an intense whisper. Shadows bled from his hands and exposed skin, as if his intensity was squeezing darkness from his pores. In a thoughtful tone, Magadon too said something to Riven, evidently reinforcing Cale's point.

Riven shook his head again, but less forcefully. He looked at Cale with narrowed eyes and asked a question. Cale didn't blink, and Jak heard his reply clearly over the rain:

"You already know why."

At that, Riven showed his signature sneer, but Jak saw the insincerity of it. If he hadn't known better, Jak would have sworn he saw fear in Riven's eye.

Magadon put his hand on the assassin's shoulder and offered him comforting words. Riven glared at him, brushed his hand aside, and said something in a sharp tone. Magadon frowned and took a step back.

Cale spoke to Magadon in a language Jak did not understand. Magadon answered in the same tongue, but slowly.

For a moment, Magadon, Cale, and Riven simply looked at each other. Riven said something and nodded. To Jak, the assassin's tone sounded as final as a funeral dirge.

"Do it," Cale said to the guide, loud enough for Jak to hear.

Magadon visibly gulped but nodded. He put his fingers to his temple and closed his eyes. A halo of white light formed around his head. The glow expanded, and moved to encapsulate Riven. While it glowed, Magadon spoke softly to the assassin. Then the guide nodded at Cale, who added something further, again speaking in a strange language. Throughout, Riven said nothing. Abruptly, the light flared out.

For an instant, a veiled look came over Riven's face but quickly vanished.

What in the Nine Hells just happened? Jak wondered.

Cale caught Jak's eye and smiled softly—an insincere smile—before nodding at Magadon.

Riven said, "What are you doing?"

Cale responded softly. Magadon then asked something and Cale nodded. The guide hesitated for a moment, put his fingertips to the side of his head and closed his eyes. A moment later, a nimbus of angry red energy formed around his skull. It flared brightly. Another such halo formed around Riven's head. The assassin gripped his skull in his palms, groaned, and collapsed. Cale said something in a terse manner to Magadon, and another red nimbus formed around Cale's head. He too groaned and collapsed to the ground. Magadon took a deep breath, then screamed in pain and fell to the dirt himself.

All three lay on the ground unmoving.

Jak couldn't help himself; he ran over and knelt first at Cale's side. To his relief, the tall man was breathing.

"Erevis," he said, shaking Cale gently. "Cale."

Cale's yellow eyes fluttered open and Jak forced himself to stare into them. Cale blinked and groaned, obviously disoriented. When his eyes regained their focus, he sat up, shook his head, and climbed to his feet. Magadon and Riven both were rubbing their temples, groaning, and struggling to sit up.

"What happened?" Jak asked, even though he knew he shouldn't.

A curious expression crossed Cale's face, and Jak thought he might have been struggling for words.

Finally, Cale said, "Precautions, little man. Let's leave it at that."

To that, Jak said nothing. Cale obviously wanted Jak ignorant of what had transpired. Jak hoped his friend knew what he was doing.

With nothing else to do, Jak removed his holy symbol and uttered prayers of healing over each of his companions. Even Riven, perhaps still too disoriented to protest, accepted the spell. The warm energy flowed through Jak and into his comrades. It seemed to bring each of them back to themselves, at least somewhat.

None of them spoke of what had just transpired. To Jak, each of them looked at though they had just awakened from a deep sleep.

☙ ☙ ☙ ☙ ☙

When Cale had drained the last of his waterskin and recovered himself as fully as seemed possible, he looked around, eyed his friends, and said to them, "Let's leave this place."

Jak said, "We're just waiting for you to tell us how, my friend."

Cale didn't bother to explain that he had an intuitive feel for the overlap between Toril and the Plane of Shadow.

Instead, he simply said, "Watch."

He concentrated for a moment, attuning himself to the correspondence between the two planes. When he had his mental hands around the connection, he opened his eyes and traced a glowing, vertical green line in the air with his forefinger. At any moment in time, he knew, the Plane of Shadow and Toril were separated by a planar barrier as thin as the cutting edge of an elven thinblade. Cale could slice open that barrier at will.

Putting his palms together and making a knife of his hands, he poked them through the center of the glowing line and drew them apart, as though he was parting draperies from before a window in Stormweather Towers's great hall. The line expanded after his hands to become a rectangular curtain of ochre light hanging in the air—a gate back to Toril.

The appearance of the gate evoked a grin from Jak.

"After all this," the halfling said, shaking his head, "and it was just that easy."

Cale didn't bother to tell his friend that it hadn't been easy at all, that the transformation back in the Fane had changed his body, but it was only a short time ago that the place had transformed his soul.

Instead, he nodded at the portal and said to Jak, "That's home. You're the first, little man."

Jak hesitated for only an instant. He beat his hat on his thigh to free it of mud, donned it with verve, smiled broadly, and hopped through the gate.

Magadon followed.

"Well done, Cale," he said, and stepped through, bow held at his side.

Before Riven stepped into the gate, the assassin stopped and looked Cale in the face.

"I had to do it, Cale," the assassin said. "I'd seen it."

"Maybe," Cale said.

Riven frowned, then said, "*You're* the First, Cale." He nodded at the gate. "And that's not home anymore. Not for us."

"Go through, Riven," Cale said.

Just as the assassin was about to step through, something registered with Cale. He grabbed Riven by the arm.

"The teleportation rods," he said. "They didn't crumble to dust, did they?"

Riven looked him in the eye and replied, "We had to go through this, Cale. I know what I saw. You had to be our way out."

In his mind, Cale heard Sephris say, *Two and two are four.*

"We all could have died," Cale said.

Riven shrugged.

"Where are the rods now?"

"I threw them in the bog," the assassin said with a smile, "the moment I understood the vision."

"Afraid you couldn't have resisted temptation?" Cale asked.

Riven grinned.

Cale released Riven's arm and said, "Go through."

Riven did.

Cale lingered for a moment in the glow of the gate and spared one last glance around the Shadow Deep. Its darkness seemed familiar to him, comforting, like the companionship of an old friend. Its gloom felt more protective than oppressive. He knew that Riven had spoken the truth. The gate to Toril did not lead home, not for him, not anymore.

But for a moment at least, he would turn his back on the darkness.

He stepped through the portal. It felt like slipping into warm water.

CHAPTER 8

THE CITY OF SKULLS

An immense, complicated network of caverns and tunnels honeycombed the rock below Faerûn's surface, stretching for leagues in all directions—the world below the world, the sunless expanse of the Underdark. To Azriim, it felt much the same as the Sojourner's pocket plane, itself simply a pinched-off portion of the Underdark.

In the endless night of that oppressive realm, a quarter-league below the city of Waterdeep, Skullport squatted in an immense L-shaped cavern carved from the rock by the slow but inexorable flow of the dark waters of the Sargauth, the underground river that fed Skullport a steady diet of ships and fresh water. The unsupported vault of the cavern's soaring but stalactite-dotted ceiling would have collapsed of its own weight long ago if not for the mantle magic that supported it.

Even in his current, vulgar form, Azriim could feel the subtle currents of magic moving through the still, dank air of the city. The mantle's magic touched everything, and it remained powerful, even after the death of its creators many centuries before.

Millennia earlier, Azriim knew, the cavern in which Skullport stood had been part of a much larger complex of caverns used by Netherese arcanists for magical experimentation—Sargauth Enclave, it was called, or so the Sojourner had explained to Azriim. It was the Netherese who first crafted the magical mantle that blanketed the caverns, an attempt by the human arcanists to secure the safety of their new city and to mimic the highest achievement of elven high magic, the mythal. But when the most powerful of the Netherese archwizards, Karsus, temporarily unraveled the Weave in a failed bid to achieve godhood, the enclave's mantle temporarily ceased to function. Those few heartbeats during which magic was dead in Faerûn were as catastrophic to Sargauth Enclave as they were to the rest of the Empire of Netheril. Most of the caverns in which the enclave had stood, no longer buttressed by the magic of the mantle, collapsed in a hail of stone, crushing hundreds.

But a few caverns, by sheer happenstance, suffered only partial collapses. Centuries later, in one such cavern, Skullport squirmed from the corpse of the ruined Netherese outpost like an infestation of maggots. There it crouched, flourishing in the darkness and damp, a great fungus hiding in the shadows.

Bordered on three sides by trade tunnels stretching away into the Underdark, and on one side by an underground bay formed by the dark, pooling waters of the Sargauth, Skullport gradually grew into an important trade link in the chain of the Underdark's unsteady economy. Beings of all races came to the Port of Skulls to trade in wares and flesh.

With limited space in which to build, the city's inhabitants filled the cavern's **L**-shaped floor and grew upward. Dilapidated homes, shops, and vice-dens—most built of salvaged shipping lumber washed down to the Sargauth by the currents of the surface sea—hugged the walls and ceilings of the cavern like lichen, or lay stacked one upon another, layer after layer, like a human child's blocks. The roof of a brothel might be the floor of the eatery built above it.

An intricate network of catwalks, recycled ships' rigging, tightropes, swings, and unstable bridges connected the buildings that stood above floor level. Strung from structure to structure, or spiked to the stalactites that pointed down from the vaulted ceiling like spear tips, the "hemp highway" made for an effective, if precarious set of airborne streets.

To Azriim, looking up from the floor, the hemp highway resembled the web of an insane spider, vibrating with the movement of hundreds of struggling flies going about their business. With a frequency bordering on clockwork—at least once every twelve hours or so—someone would fall to a screaming, splattering death on the streets below. Sometimes a bridge or catwalk gave out, but just as often it was a creditor's or enforcer's patience that finally came to a vciolent end.

Without fail, the moment the corpse hit the street Skullport's residents stripped it of valuables as quickly and efficiently as a swarm of fire ants stripped the flesh from anything unfortunate enough to cross its path. Azriim found it amusing.

He and his broodmates had been in the city long enough even to have learned the vernacular and the less-than-sensible geography. Skullport's natives—skulkers, they called themselves—conceptually divided the city into three distinct sections: the Port, which was nearest the bay; the Trade Lanes, which straddled the **L**-shaped center of the cavern; and the Heart, the darkest and most dangerous area of the city, which stood in the bulb-shaped terminus of the cavern. Each of those sections was further subdivided into subsections to reflect the vertical elevation: lower, middle, and upper. Over the past tenday or so, Azriim learned that the nomenclature was inexact, and that what one person might call the Upper Trade Lanes, another might call the Middle Port. No matter. The city was the same everywhere, whether walking a rickety bridge through a forest of stalactites in the Upper Heart, or elbowing through the crowd of illithids and drow in the Lower Trade Lanes. It was dark, lit only by torches, candles, lanterns, and dim glowballs. And it stank of decayed corpses, wet garbage, and rotting fish.

At every level, the narrow streets and walkways teemed with all manner of hard-eyed creatures: houseless drow mercenaries, white-eyed derro savants, inscrutable illithids, fierce orcs, chattering gnolls, and much worse. Violence was common and bloody, even in public streets, so weapons, wands, fangs, and claws were always bare.

Azriim loved the chaos.

Coffles of slaves, the true coin of Skullport's realm, were as ubiquitous on the lower levels as the drug dens, prostitutes, and muggings. They stood in huddled groups, vacant-eyed and hopeless, awaiting their fates—humans, dwarves, goblins, elves, and creatures Azriim did not recognize. Some would end up as laborers, some as test subjects for chirurgeons, some as food. And even after death, those who were not consumed would continue to work. Zombie laborers were commonplace, especially on the docks. Shambling and stinking, they loaded and unloaded cargo from the many ships that called at the piers of the Port of Skulls.

Unable to help himself, Azriim grinned his mouthful of perfect teeth (even in his current form, he refused to adopt foul teeth or show any eyes other than his natural blue and brown orbs), reveling in the degeneracy of the place. He savored its barely controlled chaos the way he might a fine meal. His only complaint was the filth and the stink. Skullport was the boil on the arse of the world, and it stank accordingly. He would never get his clothes clean. He had not yet been able even to keep them dry. A slow but steady drip of brownish, mineral-laden water fell from the ceiling above, causing the whole city to swell with moisture, and giving the stifling air a mineral tang.

With so many creatures packed into so small a space, the tension was palpable, a temperamental beast that lurked behind every transaction, every word, face, and gesture, waiting to erupt. But for the presence of the Skulls, Azriim knew, the city would long before have devolved into a bloodbath.

Thinking of the Skulls erased his smile and brought a frown to the thick-lipped, doughy face he wore. Skullport's ostensible rulers were almost comically absurd—flying, glowing skulls of all things—but they managed to keep the city under control and the flow of trade continuous. The Skulls kept the violence of the city manageable through the careful, but seemingly chaotic, application of power. Not enough to wreak mass destruction, but just enough to instill the fear of an ugly death. Their spellcraft was paltry compared to the Sojourner's, of course, but still powerful enough to keep the populace from running amok.

To Skullport's citizens, the Skulls were enigmatic, even mystical. To Azriim, they were nothing more than what they were.

When Sargauth Enclave collapsed, the mantle supporting the caverns had absorbed the consciousnesses of thirteen of the mightiest Netherese arcanists killed in the destruction. They later rose from the ruins as the Skulls, the creatures that had given the city its name. For Azriim, the Skulls held no awe. They were simply another obstacle to be overcome on his way to transformation into gray.

Since arriving via a portal in Waterdeep—innumerable portals in Faerûn ended in Skullport—Azriim, Dolgan, and Serrin had remained inconspicuous in the city by changing forms and lodgings frequently.

Throughout, they had painstakingly studied the movement and behavior of the Skulls. They noted the time it took the creatures to respond to street fights in various parts of the city, and the frequency with which they were seen in certain locations. From that, they had deduced the general direction of the Skulls' hidden lair, not far up the winding western tunnels that led into the wilds of the Underdark. Azriim was confident that somewhere in a cavern off of those tunnels, hidden by time, fallen rock, and the Skull's magic, unbeknownst to all but the Skulls themselves, stood another cavern that had survived the destruction of Sargauth Enclave. The Sojourner had assured him of as much, and that made it so.

It was in that hidden cavern, that second surviving remnant of Sargauth Enclave, that the Skulls laired. And it was there that Azriim would find the focus for Skullport's mantle, there that he must plant the seed of the Weave Tap. Since their arrival in the city, Azriim had kept the seed in magical stasis, held within the small, invisible, extradimensional space created by the magical ring on his finger. He could release the seed with a shake of his hand and a mental command.

But first things first, he reminded himself. With practiced ease, he regained his smile. He suspected it looked like more of a grimace in his current form.

Azriim walked—plodded, really—the packed earth avenues of the Lower Port, threading his way through the crowds and trailing his mark: a thin, pot-bellied, tonsured human named Thyld, who walked with a limp and wore stained, threadbare brown robes. Azriim had been trailing Thyld for over a tenday, learning the human's habits, his haunts, and his tastes. Azriim felt as though he'd learned as much about the human as there was to know. Thyld was a "collector" for the Kraken Society, an organization perceived by the factions in Skullport to be a legitimate broker of information. The human had contacts among most of the important power groups in the city, in places both high and low. In addition, Thyld ran a lucrative side business, unbeknownst to his Kraken Society superiors, selling some choice bits of information to interested parties in the city. That made him ideal for Azriim's purposes, which was unfortunate for Thyld.

To further his plan, Azriim would "borrow" Thyld for a time, use his contacts, and trade on the Kraken Society's legitimacy. Then, when all of the variables were in place, he and his broodmates would locate the hidden chamber, lure the Skulls away, and plant the seed of the Weave Tap.

Ahead, the open plaza of the Slavers Market was thronged with an auction day crowd. Shouted bids rang loudly in the dank air. Dozens of torches on tall posts illuminated the plaza and sent smoke curling through the caliginous air toward the ceiling. Two chained ogres in filth, flab, and worn leather tunics stood on a raised wooden platform while a middle-aged human with an elaborate mustache, fat-puckered arms, and a bright red tunic stood before them and managed the shouted bids carrying from the crowd. Near the platform, a line of chained slaves—one of them an attractive human female—awaited their turn on the block. The irony of slavery in Skullport was that few of the slaves were actually put to work in the city. The great slave market simply provided the venue for purchasing and selling. The slaves themselves were typically shipped out into the darker corners of Faerûn and the Underdark.

Beyond the plaza stood the docks, and ships of all sorts lined the piers, from Calishite slave-schooners to Luskan clippers. Most arrived via the many gates that dotted various areas of the Sargauth's channel. Some made the journey from the surface seas via an intricate, secret network of magical locks and hoists. Crates, bags, and urns of goods lay neatly stacked in piles along the docks. The calls of sailors and goblin dockhands occasionally penetrated through the noise of the auction to reach Azriim's ears.

Azriim's magic sense suddenly caused the back of his throat to tingle and drew his eye upward.

There, high above the plaza, watching the auction and wharves with its inscrutable, eyeless stare, floated one of the Skulls. A dim orange nimbus surrounded it, and its gaze moved slowly hither and yon, seeing all.

Azriim willed himself to be unobtrusive.

Without warning, the Skull swooped down from its high perch and whizzed low over the crowd, trailing a tail of orange light. A gasp went up, fingers pointed, eyes went wide, and the auctioneer fell quiet. Many people fled the plaza, hunched over and terrified. The Skull swooped out wide, turned a half circle, and sped back toward the crowd. Azriim feared he might have been discovered, but no. The Skull stopped directly in front of a thin human male dressed in an ill-fitting gray tunic and leather breeches. A sword hung from his belt but his hand stayed well clear of it. When the human stared into those empty eye sockets, he visibly shook. He licked his lips nervously. The people and creatures around him cleared away, leaving him alone with the Skull.

An anticipatory hush fell over the crowd. The auctioneer seemed frozen with his jiggling arm held aloft, about to accept a final bid for one of the ogres. Like Azriim, the audience knew what was coming—slaughter or slapstick. Either way, an amusing spectacle in Skullport.

The Skull's jaw did not move when it spoke.

"You are a pilferer of trivial things," it pronounced, loud enough to be heard throughout the plaza. The man shook his head and started to protest, but the Skull went on, "Thieves are not tolerated in the Market. Speak now the name of the favored hound of the third son of the fourth high arcanist to rule Iolaum or face immediate punishment."

The accused thief's face flushed red to his ears. Fear paralyzed him, though he looked like he wanted nothing more than to run.

"Wh-what do you mean?" he stammered. "I . . . I didn't steal nothing. I don't know any arcaners."

"Incorrect," said the Skull.

At that dire pronouncement, the thief must have sensed the fullness of his danger. He finally managed to break free of his fear-induced paralysis and turned to run. Even if there had been somewhere to go, he was too late. The Skull spoke a series of arcane words and a green beam fired from its eyes. It struck the man in the back, swallowed his scream, and instantly reduced him to a pile of fine dust. A handful of silver coins, scattered in the soot, was all that remained of the offender.

"Retrieve your stolen property," the Skull announced to no one in particular, and began to fly off. As it rose back toward the top of the cavern, it gave its pronouncement. "Thievery shall not be tolerated at auction, nor time with eggs, lest they be hatched. Heed well."

For a moment, no one moved and all was silent. Then a laugh sounded, and another, followed at last by the low murmur of a satisfied audience discussing the show. A mad scramble ensued, with several skulkers grabbing for the silver. Within moments, the voice of the fat auctioneer rose, the auction resumed, and the first of the ogres went into bondage.

Disintegrated for a handful of silver, Azriim thought. *That* was the power of the Skulls, the studied but unpredictable application of discipline that kept the populace respectful and the chaos manageable. Smiling, Azriim relocated Thyld amidst the crowd and continued to follow him through the plaza.

At first, Azriim thought Thyld was heading for the Murkspan, a somber stone arch bridge that reached across Sargauth Bay to set its far footings in the dark earth of Skull Island where stood the crenellated walls and fortress tower of the Iron Ring, the master slavers of Skullport. All slave ships docked at Skull Island to brand and inventory their cargo in the fortress before it could be sold in the plaza. The Ring took its cut of all trade in flesh.

But Thyld turned left and knifed through the crowd, steering wide of a group of illithids, and headed for the fish market.

Azriim followed at a distance, weaving his way through the coffles of slaves for whom buyers would soon bid. Whips cracked; slaves moaned and cried. Would-be buyers poked and prodded the merchandise.

Though Azriim had no sympathy, as such, for the humans and other fodder destined to toil and die in the dark of Skullport, he could imagine few fates for himself worse than a life spent in bondage. Even the relatively moderate boundaries put on his existence by the Sojourner drove him to near madness. While it was true that the Sojourner treated Azriim and his broodmates well, that only made them well-treated servants. Thinking such thoughts boiled up the strange emotional dichotomy he always felt when he considered his "father"—an admixture of love and hate, fear and respect.

He controlled his emotions by reminding himself that he would have his freedom, and be transformed into a gray, when he had assisted the Sojourner in obtaining the Crown of Flame. Azriim didn't know what the Crown of Flame was, nor what the Sojourner intended to do with it, but he knew it must be a mighty artifact indeed to be so desired by his father.

Thyld made a straight path through the fish market and headed down a narrow street lined with rickety taverns and shops. The smell of bad food and the shouts and laughter of patrons boiled from the shutterless windows.

Ignoring the fishermen who lined the street hawking the long, pale fish of the Sargauth, Azriim followed Thyld. The fishermen ignored him too. Azriim took the form of a muscular duergar slaver, complete with a whipblade, a scarred face, and a hard scowl. No one seemed to find him worth more than a first glance. Though he missed the grace of his preferred half-drow form, he deemed the duergar shape less obtrusive. Drow, he had learned, were obsessed with House affiliations, especially recently, when rumors in Skullport told of a drow civil war. Azriim had no time to waste with explanations to every passing drow of his seeming "Houselessness." He did miss the comfort of his usual fine attire, though. The coarse tunic and trousers he wore in his duergar guise made even his dwarven flesh chafe.

He eyed a passing illithid with two troll thralls in tow. The flayer's face tentacles twitched. No doubt he had just received some psionic contact. The towering trolls—green-skinned walls of teeth, claws, and muscle—eyed him with the slack expression of the psionically dominated.

Azriim feigned fear as he passed, though were he in his natural form, his own claws and teeth could have torn apart both trolls and illithid alike. He found himself wondering what illithid brain might taste like if the tide was turned on the brain-eating creature. The temptation to make psionic contact with the mind flayer almost over-came him, but he resisted it. The Sojourner would not be pleased if he took unnecessary risks. His task was to lo-cate the source of the mantle. He kept his focus on Thyld.

The human made a right and turned down a narrow alley. Having learned the man's habits, Azriim knew that Thyld was heading to Aryn's House, a brothel and hostelry, to "seed the soil," as Thyld called it, by paying his informants. Thyld had three spies among the girls at Aryn's. After paying the doxies their tenday stipend, and providing bonuses for any especially useful information they may have gleaned from their patrons, he would move on to the next location. Azriim knew them all.

Are you prepared? Azriim projected to Dolgan.

His broodmate's mental voice answered immediately, *We await you at the storehouse. Everything is ready.*

Dolgan had secured a room in an isolated storehouse along the docks and Azriim had carefully memorized the look and feel of the space. In order to use his teleportation rod, he needed to have a clear mental image of his desired destination.

He picked up his pace and closed on Thyld.

Though the Sojourner had warned Azriim against ca-sual use of the teleportation rod while in the Underdark, Azriim had little choice but to utilize it. Unfortunately, in order for the rod to transport Thyld, the human had to be either willing or unconscious. The former was unlikely and the latter presented a problem. Azriim could not simply knock Thyld out on the street and steal him away. Witnesses to the human's vanishing—and the consequent rumors that would quickly circulate through the city—would defeat the whole purpose of Azriim's plan. Accordingly, he needed to be somewhat more creative.

Moving quickly, he came up behind Thyld.

"Out of the way, human," he grumbled, in his coarse dwarf's voice, and bumped into Thyld as he passed him by.

As he did, Azriim mentally channeled arcane energy through his hand and into Thyld, turning the human invisible. Azriim could still see Thyld, of course; his vision was that keen.

Though Thyld could see himself, and thus did not know that he was enspelled, it would be only a moment or two before he began bumping into passersby and deduced that something was amiss. Azriim had to act quickly.

He feigned dropping something in the street and bent over to retrieve it. Thyld walked by him, still oblivious to the fact of his invisibility. The moment the human passed by him, Azriim surreptitiously palmed a coin with one hand and with the other removed from a leather tube on his thigh one of the handful of wands given him by the Sojourner. Made of carved ivory, and inscribed with many arcane symbols, the wand fired a beam that would transmogrify the target into any creature or object Azriim desired.

While still purporting to be searching the packed earth road for the fictitious item he'd seemingly dropped, Azriim surreptitiously pointed the wand at Thyld and whispered the words, "Cave shrimp."

The thin yellow beam struck the invisible Thyld in the back. He was able to utter only the beginnings of a scream before his form shrank and shrank, down to that of a tiny shrimp. A passing mercenary spent a moment looking confused by the sourceless, choked-off scream, but quickly went about his business.

"There it is!" Azriim exclaimed, hopping forward two paces and retrieving Thyld-the-shrimp.

The tiny creature squirmed in his fist. With his other hand Azriim held up the coin he'd palmed, brought it to his eye, and smiled as though he'd just picked it up. None of the other passersby looked twice.

Still smiling, but for a different reason, Azriim walked a few paces down a dark side alley. When he thought no one was observing, he willed himself invisible. Still holding the squirming Thyld in his hand he waited for the human-shrimp to become incapacitated from lack of air.

I have him, he sent to Dolgan. *I will be along presently.*

Dolgan projected an acknowledgment.

Azriim pulled out his teleportation rod while Thyld's struggles grew fainter and fainter. When they stopped entirely, he deftly manipulated the rod and transported himself to the storehouse.

Serrin and Dolgan awaited him there. Serrin, in the form of a dark-haired human corsair, wore high boots, a falchion, an earring, pantaloons, and a blue silken shirt. Azriim envied him the silk. Dolgan had taken the form of a thin, balding drunk, dressed only in dirty trousers and a homespun tunic pitted with holes. His potbelly looked as though it hid a melon.

The small office stood empty but for a desk and a high-backed chair. Three large wax candles sat atop the desk and provided the only light. A coil of fine rope sat beside them.

Azriim threw Thyld-the-shrimp onto the chair and pulled another wand from the leather tube at his thigh. Made from duskwood and capped with an opal, the wand dispelled magical spells and effects.

Hoping that Thyld had not already died—but only because it would be inconvenient otherwise—Azriim pointed the wand at the Thyld-shrimp and caused it to dispel the human's transformation. The shrimp burst, grew, and gave birth to a human, a human who was not breathing.

Had Azriim not had such distaste for expletives, he would have cursed.

"Uh oh," Dolgan said, and bent over Thyld. He grabbed the human by his receding chin and turned his head back and forth. He looked back to Azriim and said, "He's dead, I think."

The big slaad sounded indifferent.

"I can see that," Azriim snapped, and crossed his arms over his broad chest. "Help him."

Dolgan frowned, dumbfounded. "How?"

"I don't—"

Thyld inhaled sharply and deeply, a long breath that rattled with phlegm.

The slaadi shared a look of mild surprise, and Dolgan looked vaguely disappointed.

"Secure him," Azriim, smiling, said to Dolgan. "And take off his robe."

Dolgan asked no questions. He stripped off the human's robe and cast it at Azriim's feet, then used the coil of rope to tie the still-unconscious and only semi-dressed Thyld to the chair. They waited. After a few moments, the human began to groan. In short order, his eyes fluttered open.

To his credit, Thyld took in his situation and managed to not look panicked. He didn't even struggle against the bonds, possibly because he appeared to be the prisoner of a drunk, a sailor, and a badly dressed duergar.

Having gathered his wits and some of his dignity, the human eyed them coolly, each in turn.

"How dare you attack me in the street! Do you know who I am?" he asked, in a nasally, imperious tone. "And who I serve?"

Azriim "tsked" at the bound human and said, "Poor grammar is the sign of a lazy mind. Of course I know who you are and *whom* you serve. That is the very point." He gave a hard smile and let that sink in. "But you do not yet know who we are. Allow me to make introductions."

At Azriim's mental command the slaadi all began to

change. Their ridiculous manling forms grew bulky, leathery green skin formed tightly over powerful musculatures, clothing stretched and tore, mouths exploded with fangs, and claws burst from fingertips. Thyld's eyes went wide and he began to struggle against his ropes, but managed only a mild rocking of the chair. His mouth hung open but no words came forth. A string of spittle hung between his lips like one of the hemp highway's rope bridges.

Azriim felt more at ease in his natural form than in that of the duergar. He flexed his claws, ran his tongue over his fangs. When he reached out his mental senses to touch Thyld's mind psionically, he tasted the human's terror. He worried that Thyld might begin to yell out for help.

"If you begin to shout, I will use this claw—" Azriim held up his forefinger—"to sever your vocal cords."

Then you will answer my questions this way, he projected. *Do you understand?*

Thyld looked so fearful that Azriim was concerned that the human might become incoherent. No doubt Dolgan's hungry presence did little to make the man feel at ease. The big slaad stood behind the bound Thyld, drooling and shifting from foot to foot with excitement. Dolgan was so intoxicated with Thyld's fear, so eager for Thyld's blood, that he had sank his upper fangs into his lower lip hard enough to draw his own black blood, which mingled with his spit.

We understand each other now, I think, Azriim projected soothingly. *And I'd go so far as to say that we're on familiar terms. Friends almost.*

"What do you want?" Thyld said, looking from Azriim to Dolgan and back to Azriim.

Azriim let his mental voice drop to a suitably menacing tone.

I require that you answer some questions, Thyld. Without expletives, and without lies. If you tell a falsehood, I'll know. If you curse, or otherwise give voice to vulgarity, I will punish you.

Thyld seemed unable to speak. Sweat dotted his high brow. At last he gave a sharp nod.

You are an agent of the Kraken Society, Azriim projected, and nodded at a small tattoo inked onto Thyld's bare chest—a purple squid in a red field. *In addition, unbeknownst to your superiors, you sell information on the side to the various factions in Skullport.*

The human did not deny it, simply stared wide-eyed and breathed hard.

Azriim continued, *That fact need never leave this room. But it happens that I am in possession of information that would be of interest to Zstulkk Ssarmn and possibly the Xanathar. Who are your contacts within those organizations?*

He held up a clawed hand to forestall any protests that Thyld might have offered. Azriim already knew that those organizations were nearly at war—the fact was integral to his plans. Ssarmn, the yuan-ti slaver, and the Xanathar, the beholder crime lord and slaver, had been quietly murdering one another's operatives for months. They needed only an additional spark to turn their campfire of a conflict into a conflagration.

Thyld shifted uncomfortably in his bonds. Azriim could see the human's mind racing, desperately seeking for a way out of his current straits.

"I can provide you an introduction," Thyld offered. "My contacts are accustomed to speaking only with me."

Azriim smiled a mouthful of fangs, which disconcerted Thyld.

I understand, but I must contact them directly, Thyld, without the intervention of you or the Kraken Society.

When Thyld seemed still to hesitate, Azriim dispensed with the niceties.

Listen carefully: If you do not tell me the names of your contacts now, I will torture you until you do.

At the mention of torture, Azriim sensed a flash of agitation from Serrin.

It seemed to take Thyld a moment to understand the

importance of Azriim's words. When he did, he began to shake. So too did Dolgan, but out of a different sentiment all together.

Azriim continued, *If you tell me what I want to know, you will be paid handsomely.*

That was a lie, of course. But like all lies, it came easy to Azriim.

Three times Thyld opened his mouth to speak and each time nothing but a squeak emerged. Finally, Dolgan clapped him on the back of the head. His claws scratched open the human's scalp. Thyld squealed and bled.

"There," Dolgan said in his guttural tone, after licking his fingers clean. "At least something other than a squeak is coming out. Now answer the question, creature."

Thyld blurted a reply, "Kexen the slaver, for Ssarmn, and Ahmaergo the dwarf for the Xanathar. Both have ways of sending information up the hierarchy. Both will pay you well."

Azriim knew the names. With only slight effort he would be able to locate and set up meets with each of them. He fixed Thyld with a stare. The human recoiled as much as his bonds allowed. The stink of fear leaked from his pores.

"When are you due to report back to your superiors in the Kraken Society?" Azriim asked.

The human hesitated, apparently sensing the danger that lurked behind that question.

"Ten cycles," he said at last.

Cycles. Skullport's skulkers had dwelled in the dark for so long that they no longer divided twenty-four hours into day and night, but instead into two twelve-hour cycles. Azriim would have five days before Thyld's superiors noticed his absence. Time enough.

The human must have mistook Azriim's thoughtful silence as something more foreboding.

"Th-that's the truth," Thyld stammered.

Azriim waved a hand dismissively, his mind still on how to move his plan forward. A Xanathar caravan was arriving through a magical portal within the next six hours.

That should do, Azriim thought.

"What are you going to do with me?" Thyld asked, the trepidation in his voice evident.

Azriim ignored the human, eyed his broodmates, and silently asked the question. They could spare Thyld, he knew, and merely keep him prisoner for the time it took for their plot to unfold. In another five or six days, it would all be finished and the seed of the Weave Tap planted. After that, it could not be undone, and whether Thyld was alive or dead would be irrelevant.

Serrin answered his look with a predictably efficient response.

We should not leave him alive. If he is found, or escapes, it would compromise our efforts.

Dolgan licked his lips and nodded, eyeing the crown of Thyld's head hungrily all the while.

Azriim too nodded. He had been thinking much the same thing. Leaving Thyld alive would entail taking an unnecessary risk. Azriim enjoyed risks, but only when they brought him a thrill. He saw no thrill in sparing Thyld.

With his mind made up, he leaned in close to Thyld—the proximity of his fangs and eyes sent the human into a virtual paroxysm of terror. Azriim studied the human's face with care, took one last look at his build, and began to change. His squat dwarf frame lengthened, his head narrowed, and his build slimmed. In moments, he looked very much like Thyld, complete with a weak chin and potbelly.

Seeing that, the human slumped in his chair.

"You're not going to let me live," he said.

"You're not going to let me live," Azriim parroted, adjusting his vocal cords to approximate Thyld's tone. "No, I fear not. But if it dulls the pain any, I will need your robe." He eyed the rag at his feet with distaste before adding, "Unfortunately."

The human said nothing, merely hung his head in resignation.

We should not leave a body, Dolgan projected, with eagerness in his tone.

Azriim knew that too. Though he preferred brains almost exclusively, they would need to devour Thyld's entire body. He sighed and took out the wand that transmogrified one creature into another. He looked to his broodmates.

Alive or dead for the feast? Azriim asked.

Alive, Dolgan responded quickly.

Azriim nodded. He would use a silence spell to mask the human's screams. He took a deep breath.

"What are you hungry for?" he asked his broodmates.

Thyld began to weep.

❧ ❧ ❧ ❧ ❧

Dolgan had requested that Thyld be turned into an ogre before they ate him, bones, hair, flesh, and all. Azriim shook his head as he walked. The big slaad's tastes were sometimes inexplicable. After cleaning up and retaking Thyld's form, Azriim exited the storehouse and made the rounds of Thyld's appointments. Hungry for more sensation, and intoxicated with the aftereffect of consuming Thyld-the-ogre's brain—Azriim had taken that choice morsel for himself—he bedded two of Thyld's whore-spies at Aryn's before paying them their stipend.

Shapechanging had its benefits, he thought.

Later, he would set up meets with Kexen and Ahmaergo. But first, he and his broodmates had a Xanathar caravan to intercept.

CHAPTER 9

SENSELESS MASSACRE, SENSIBLY DONE

Azriim, Serrin, and Dolgan crouched amidst a grouping of thick stalagmites and waited. There was no sound except the quiet, anticipatory respiration of the slaadi, and the steady, monotonous drone of dripping water from somewhere near the high ceiling.

Azriim shifted his weight from one clawed foot to the other. The stone floor of the chamber felt damp under his hind claws. The dank, stale air slicked his leathery hide—the closest he could come to perspiring while in his natural state. He felt a bit awkward in his own skin. Of late, he'd been more comfortable as a humanoid, particularly when he took his preferred half-drow form. He attributed the feeling to the enjoyment he took in humanoid fashions, humanoid females, and to the pleasure he took in the sensitivity of humanoid skin. In slaad form, he wore not high fashion, but only a leather belt with pouches, a canvas satchel, and a thigh-tube for his wands. And his slaad skin was not sensitive but tough, coarsened to withstand the seething chaotic energies of the Plane of Limbo. In his natural form, he could hardly have felt the playful brush of a humanoid female's fingertips.

He pushed such things from his mind. Violence needed doing, and soon.

Though the darkness was as black as demon's blood, Azriim and his broodmates could see out to a spearcast as well as if they were on the surface of Faerûn under a noon sun. The cavern in which they waited was fifty paces wide, perhaps two hundred paces long, and tall enough that Azriim could not have touched the lowest-hanging stalactite had he been standing on Dolgan's broad shoulders. The floor, which otherwise would have been covered completely in stalagmites and uneven patches of cracked stone, had been cleared down the center of the cavern and worn smooth by the passage of many feet. It looked much like someone had hacked a cart road from the forest of stalagmites, which was probably not far from the truth.

The only apparent ingress and egress into the cavern was an archway in the southern wall that opened onto one of the innumerable, winding tertiary tunnels that forked off of a main tradeway leading back to Skullport. But Azriim knew better than to believe first looks. There was another way into the cavern, he knew. Or at least there would be soon.

Along the north wall, opposite the opening that led back to the trade tunnel, a band of exposed rose hematite traced a rough, horseshoe-shaped arch in the otherwise unremarkable stone. The tines of the horseshoe started near the floor, ten paces apart, and met to form the top of the arch halfway up the wall of the chamber. It looked as if an unsteady hand had attempted to draw a huge doorway, an observation that also was not far from the truth.

In Azriim's magic sensing sight, the lines of hematite glowed a soft red, indicating a latent dweomer.

Azriim knew that the hematite arch was a real doorway, the endpoint of a magical one-way portal that had its beginning thousands of miles away in a dirty storehouse on the outskirts of Hillsfar. He had learned of its existence after much investigation, a bit of torture, and two murders. Apparently, the Xanathar had reached an agreement with the First Lord of Hillsfar regarding the use of the portal: demi-humans, and other undesirables in Hillsfar, were escorted by Xanathar agents from the First Lord's dungeons to Skullport's slave pens and were never seen again on the surface of Faerûn. Azriim had to acknowledge the arrangement to be good business. The Xanathar received slaves that he could sell and the First Lord relieved himself of all trace of certain undesirable prisoners. The slave shipments came through on the eighth of every tenday—that very day—sometime between the fifth and tenth hour of the second cycle.

At first it had surprised Azriim to learn that the Xanathar did not post guards near the portal and typically didn't send a team to meet the agents that came through. He had thought that such a valuable, permanent means of cross-continent transport would have been heavily guarded, but after thinking about it he saw the Xanathar's wisdom. Posting guards in the tunnels, or sending escort teams out of Skullport, would only have drawn unwanted attention from the Eye's rivals in the city—namely Zstulkk Ssarmn. It would have been only a matter of time before the beholder would have had to fight a war in order to hold on to the gate.

No, secrecy was the best option. Rivals couldn't take something about which they were ignorant. Of course, even the strictest secrecy could be compromised if one knew where to look.

And what to look like, Azriim thought with a smile.

Beside him, Dolgan was growing restless. Unfortunately, Azriim and his broodmates had already been waiting impatiently for over two hours. Dolgan had the hardest time with the wait. He wanted violence, and wanted it soon. The big slaad shifted irritably from foot to foot, chewing his lower lip and emitting a low growl with each movement. His claws made an annoying scrabbling sound on the stone floor of the cavern.

"Be still," Azriim ordered. Unless something unforeseen had occurred in Hillsfar, he knew that the Xanathar caravan would be coming through soon. "The time is near."

"That is what you said an hour ago," Dolgan muttered.

The big slaad stopped shuffling his feet and instead began to rock on his heels. Azriim tried to ignore his lumbering broodmate.

Beside Dolgan, with one clawed hand on a stalagmite and the other loosely holding a falchion, Serrin stared holes into the hematite archway. As always, Azriim's smaller broodmate was focused only on carrying out the task. Serrin was efficient, Azriim acknowledged, but he lacked verve, he lacked style. Still, he had his uses.

Unlike Serrin, Azriim and Dolgan bore no weapons. They would rely on their magical abilities, and if it came to it, their claws.

As if in answer to Dolgan's impatience, the hematite lines of the archway began to glow more brightly in Azriim's vision—latent magic turning patent. At first he thought he might have been imagining the change, but as the glow intensified he knew the gate was opening.

"They are coming," he said.

"I see it," Serrin replied softly.

Azriim spoke an arcane word and caused a wall of silence to form at the mouth of the tertiary tunnel behind them. Sound traveled far in the Underdark, and he did not want the din of battle to travel up to the tradeway and attract the curiosity of any passing creatures.

The outline of the archway began to pulse, glowing like embers even to ordinary vision. A low hum, probably inaudible to humans, emanated from the stone. Like a spreading bloodstain, the red glow expanded from the hematite border lines and started to fill the space in the interior of the arch. Soon, the whole of the arch was blazing red.

Dolgan grew so excited that he began to drool. Azriim scowled and took a step away from his broodmate to avoid getting spittle on his feet. Quickly, he recited the word to another spell and cast himself and his broodmates in a concealing darkness that even magical light could not easily penetrate, though the slaadi could see through it clearly. From the inventory of wands provided to him by the Sojourner, he withdrew a thin, birch taper capped with a narrow diamond.

Once we begin, Azriim projected to his broodmates, while eyeing the shining portal, *we have not longer than a two hundred count to finish it.*

His broodmates signaled their understanding.

Any longer than that, Azriim knew, and they would be risking intervention by the Skulls. While Skullport's rulers rarely patrolled that far out of the city, they could sense powerful magic at work and likely would appear to quell a magical disturbance near a tradeway.

And just such a disturbance would soon occur, Azriim thought. He had no doubt of how he and his broodmates would fare if they were cornered by Skullport's rulers. One, perhaps two Skulls would be destroyed. But he and his broodmates would be slain or forced to flee. More importantly, the Sojourner would not be pleased. . . .

The hum coming from the portal took a lower pitch and the red arch flared blindingly bright. Even within their magical darkness, the slaadi shaded their eyes with their forearms. The stone within the arch looked to Azriim as red and viscous as melted ore. The entire cavern was cast in crimson. Far back in the stone, shadows took shape, wavering images distorted by distance and magic. Muted voices sounded.

Within moments, the glow diminished and the shadows within the arch grew sharper, larger, and took on shape and color. The voices grew more distinct.

The shimmering portal began to give birth, squeezing men and carts from the wall of glowing stone. The travelers' voices echoed off the walls of the cavern.

"Mind that!"

"Stay close!"

Armor clinked; boots thumped.

Eight men emerged first. Four wore red tabards, chain mail, and red plumed helmets—Hillsfarian guardsmen, no doubt. The other four were clad in plate mail and hard looks—likely returning Xanathar agents. The Hillsfarian guards held bare swords in one hand and glowing sunrods aloft in the other. The Xanathar's agents bore cocked and loaded crossbows. Their eyes and their crossbow sights swept across the chamber, passing over and past the darkness-cloaked slaadi.

Wait for all of them to come through, Azriim projected, sensing the eagerness of his broodmates.

Moving quickly and saying little, the eight men formed a protective arc of flesh and steel before the still-glowing archway while the rest of the caravan began to follow them through. Two creaking wagons emerged, each pulled by two giant, surefooted, subterranean lizards as large as ponies. The wagons, tightly crammed with slaves—chained elves, half-elves, and dwarves mostly—were little more than wheeled cages with an attached driver's bench. The slaves wore the hopeless expressions of the damned. They must have sensed that the underground hell they'd just entered was to be their final stop. A fat teamster drove each of the slave wagons, guiding, prodding, and cursing at the lizards, which answered with hisses and flicked tongues.

After the slave wagons were through, six more crossbow-armed guards stepped through the portal and flanked them to either side, eyeing with wary gazes both the shadows of the cavern and the forty or so demi-human slaves destined to toil and die in Skullport's darkness. The slave wagons and guards moved forward to make room while two more wagons began to emerge through the still glowing portal.

These last two wagons, each also pulled by a pair of giant lizards and manned by a single driver, piqued Azriim's curiosity. He craned his neck to see.

Both were built of duskwood, completely enclosed, and visibly locked at the rear door. They looked like giant chests on wheels. Several more armed men accompanied those wagons, including, at the rear, a huge man whose enameled black armor sported on the breastplate a great eye, surrounded by eight smaller, lidless eyes: the symbol of the Xanathar.

Azriim silently "tsked" the armored man's weather-worn overcloak and unshined boots. He decided then and there that the human was a poor dresser and no doubt would go unmissed when he died.

With the emergence of the two enclosed wagons, the portal began to dim, fading first to rose, and finally dying to nothing more than a wall.

That is all of them, Serrin said without a hint of eagerness.

Beside Azriim, Dolgan's respiration came fast and hard.

The armored human moved up and down the assembled caravan and barked orders in oddly accented Common. Men stiffened at his passage, lizards snarled, and slaves averted their gaze or cowered.

The caravan, clustered together like wine grapes, prepared to move out.

Azriim played out the anticipation just a moment longer, then—

Now, he projected, and began his mental count to two hundred.

As one, the slaadi stepped out from behind the stalagmites. Azriim pointed the Sojourner's wand at the armored human, spoke the arcane word of command, and discharged a searing stroke of lightning from the diamond tip. The bolt hit the human squarely in the breastplate, drove him backward five paces, knocked him prone, and left him belly-up and smoking on the floor. The energy arced to another nearby guard, blew out his eyes before killing him then arced to another, and another, sending each into a spasmodic, burning death. Finally, no doubt drawn by the iron of the cage, the lightning bolt found its way into one of the slave wagons and alternated from one to another of the wretched demi-human slaves, sparing all of them a life of servitude by painfully killing each in turn.

Before the stunned guards could effectively respond— before they could do more than utter shouts of warning, scan the darkness for their attackers, and wildly fire a few crossbow bolts—Dolgan and Serrin called upon their innate magical abilities and fired fist-sized balls of fire from their outstretched claws. Both of the fireballs struck the cavern's floor in the midst of the bunched caravan and exploded into gorgeous spheres of heat and flame. The screams of the humans were lost in the explosion as the fireballs roasted the caravanners and giant lizards alive, incinerated the surviving slaves in their cages, and knocked over, but did not set aflame, the two enclosed wagons. The temporary inferno dried the damp from Azriim's skin, for which he was grateful.

Hold, Azriim projected to his broodmates, and took a moment to survey the destruction. He had not yet reached a mental count of ten. The attack had gone as smoothly as he had hoped.

The heavy, sweet scent of cooked human flesh filled his nostrils. Black smoke churned from corpse and wagon alike, pooling around the stalactites above. Nothing was moving. Men, weapons, and animals lay cast about the chamber floor like so much flotsam. Except for the crackle of a few small fires—one of the slave wagon wheels and several of the corpses were burning cheerily—all was quiet. Scavengers would begin to arrive soon, Azriim knew, attracted by the stink of dead flesh. The Skulls too might soon arrive, attracted by the expended magic.

Ensure that they are all dead, Azriim said to his broodmates.

Serrin and Dolgan bounded out of hiding and down into the carnage.

And eat nothing, Azriim added for Dolgan's benefit.

The big slaad slouched with disappointment but did as he was told.

Serrin and Dolgan moved from corpse to corpse, stabbing or slicing the throats of any of the guards, teamsters, or slaves that did not seem suitably charred. Dolgan sometimes patted one of the human's heads, as if to apologize for not eating the brains.

Azriim followed his broodmates to the slaughter at a more leisurely pace. He savored the ease with which they had dispatched the caravan nearly as much as he savored the feeling that his plan was coming together. The Sojourner would be pleased. The transformation to gray would be Azriim's reward.

He picked his way through the dead and wreckage to one of the enclosed wagons. The fact that it had not burned suggested that it was warded with magical protections. With a grunt, he pulled the lock from its setting and tore the rear door from its hinges. The slab of wood exploded with a blue flash, sending a jolt of power through Azriim's body: a magical trap. He nearly cursed, more annoyed than injured—though his hands did sting—and tossed the door atop two corpses that lay nearby. He knelt down on his haunches and looked inside.

Within the wagon, thrown into disarray by the explosions, lay swords, several staffs, a scroll belt stuffed full, several gem-tipped wands wrapped in cloth, and three chests. One of the chests had broken open and was bleeding platinum. Azriim called upon his innate ability to detect dweomers and saw that most everything in the wagon except the currency was magical. A hurried examination of the second sealed wagon revealed much the same. Both were stuffed full with magic items and wealth destined for the Xanathar. Some of the agents carried magical goods as well, Azriim saw. Most such items had survived the inferno.

The beholder would not leave unavenged the loss of so many men and so much magical treasure.

Azriim could not contain his grin. The situation couldn't have been better.

Assist me, he projected to Serrin and Dolgan, who had finished their macabre task. *We are taking it all.*

CHAPTER 10

RETURN TO STARMANTLE

After stepping through the gate, Cale, Riven, Jak, and Magadon found themselves standing in the midst of a stand of towering elms, blinking in the light of the midday sun. Compared to the gloom of the Plane of Shadow, the light of Toril's sun was nearly blinding. Here and there, the sun's rays cut through the elms' canopy in a shower of beams.

And hit Cale like crossbow bolts.

His exposed skin felt as if it were being stabbed with sewing needles. His senses too felt duller, his hearing less keen, and his sight less sharp. While his skin was still dusky, the protective sheath of shadows was gone. He had known that while he stood in the light, his shade abilities would be lost to him. He hadn't known that he would feel somehow less substantial. Faerûn's sun melted a part of him away, as surely as if he were made of ice.

Gritting his teeth at the pain caused him by the light, Cale threw the hood of his cloak over his face. Only then did he notice that his regenerated hand was gone. He stared at the stump of his wrist, not quite shocked, but simply uncomprehending. He felt the memory of his hand as though it still sprouted from the end of his wrist, but it was not there.

Surreptitiously, so as not to draw attention from his comrades, he moved his hand into the darkness cast by the bole of an elm. He felt a tingling in his forearm and within those shadows, his hand rematerialized. He flexed the fingers, twisted the wrist, and it felt normal. He moved his arm back into the light, felt a sharp stab of pain in his wrist, and his hand again disappeared. He moved it back and forth for a moment, enduring the dichotomous sensation, and marveling at the appearance and disappearance of flesh and bone on the end of his wrist.

Was it flesh and bone? he wondered.

He realized in that instant that he was half-a-man whether he stood in light or shadow. The transformation into a shade had taken something of his soul but given him back his flesh; when the sun re-lit his soul it took a tithe of flesh as recompense.

Fitting, he thought, and immediately chided himself.

He recognized in his thoughts the beginnings of self-pity. Words floated to the front of his mind, something his favorite language teacher once had said to him back in Westgate, when Cale had thought his life a hard one: "Self-pity is an indulgence for artists and noblemen. Don't spend any more time with it than you must. Hear what it says, learn from it if you can, then move on."

Cale prepared himself to do just that. He was both shade and man. And a man could not stand forever in the shadows.

With that, he braced himself, threw back his hood, and endured the pain caused him by the sun. He welcomed it the way an Ilmaterite welcomed suffering—a way of purifying the soul through the pains of the body. The sun would be the instrument of Cale's agony, and the instrument of his purification.

"Cale! We're home!" Jak said. "You did it." The halfling fairly capered about the undergrowth. He stopped and stared at Cale, apparently noticing his discomfort for the first time. His smile faded. "Are you all right?"

Cale, keeping his stump hidden by the sleeve of his cloak, nodded and said, "I'm all right, little man."

Jak recaptured his smile.

"Good," he said, then he let himself fall backward onto the grass. He spread his arms and legs out wide and soaked up the sun. He inhaled deeply the fragrance of the air. "Smell that? The air here reminds me of my family's farm in Mistledale. Have you ever been to the Dalelands, Cale? I'll take you sometime. You can try my mother's cooking."

Cale nodded, though he could imagine Jak's mother's expression upon seeing a yellow-eyed, shadow-wrapped creature walk through her door.

Magadon stood ten or so paces away with his eyes closed and the palm of one hand pressed against the bole of an elm. He looked as though he was drawing strength from it. He held his bow in his other hand. The guide must have felt Cale's gaze. He opened his eyes, looked over to Cale, and smiled softly.

"This elm is over ninety winters old. It has seen much in that time." He studied Cale closely, cocked his head to the side, and said, "Your eyes appear normal now."

Cale was surprised and pleased, but knew that the man behind those eyes was far from normal.

"Nothing has changed," he said, "at least not really."

Cale knew that the moment he stepped back into darkness or shadow, he would again look like the creature he was.

"No?" Magadon asked, looking at Cale's sleeve, at his wrist.

Jak sat up and followed Magadon's gaze. Riven looked on with interest as well.

Cale stared at Magadon for a moment before blowing out a sigh. The woodsman missed nothing. As though unveiling a shameful secret, Cale held up his arm and pulled back his sleeve to reveal the stump.

"Your hand!" Jak exclaimed and leaped to his feet.

Cale debated with himself for a moment before saying, "Yes, but watch." He put his stump into shadow. His hand, with its slightly duskier skin, reappeared. Streams of shadows took shape around it. "It's there in darkness or shadow, gone in the light."

"Like bad dreams," Jak whispered, before blushing in embarrassment at his words. "Sorry," he said.

Riven wore a hard expression that Cale couldn't quite read. Before Cale could figure it out, the assassin looked away, pulled his borrowed pipe, tamped, and lit.

"There's an idea," Jak said softly. Still eyeing Cale's wrist, he pulled out his own pipe. To Riven, Jak said, "You, Zhent, cannot come with us to Mistledale, since you're an ungrateful bastard who insulted my mother's potato soup."

"I insulted *your* potato soup," Riven answered, smiling around the stem of his pipe.

While his friends were thus engaged, Cale let his sleeve fall back over his stump. He looked out of the copse and into the sun. His eyes stung and began to tear up.

He turned back and asked Magadon, "Where are we, Mags?"

"We're home, Cale," Jak said as he struck a tindertwig and lit. From around his pipe stem he said, "And burn me if I ever want to go back to that place. No offense, Cale."

Cale caught Riven's sidelong glance. This isn't home anymore, the assassin's eye said, and we'll be going back to the Plane of Shadow soon enough.

Cale offered Jak a half smile and said, "No offense taken, little man."

"I might be able to offer a bit more specificity than Jak," Magadon said with a grin.

The guide patted the elm near him as though it was a pet, and walked past Cale out of the shade of the copse and into the full light of the sun. He took off his hat, shaded his eyes, and looked across the plains.

"We are on the southern plains between the Gulthmere and Starmantle," Magadon said. "We're two days away from the city."

"How long were we gone?" Cale asked.

Magadon shrugged and answered, "No way to know that."

To Jak and Riven, both smoking away like chimneys, Cale said, "Take a few moments, then gear up. We need to move."

He knew that Azriim and the rest of the slaadi would not have been idle. Cale would spend the travel time back to Starmantle thinking of a way to track them down.

❧ ❧ ❧ ❧ ❧

Within hours they had reached the southern road out of Starmantle. A day and a half later and they had arrived at the city itself. By then, Cale had become almost inured to the pricks of pain caused him by the sun. Almost.

As always, the gates of Starmantle were thrown open and the spear-armed guards hardly noted them as they passed inside, except to smirk at their filth. Glares from Cale and Riven wiped the guards' smiles away.

The city's wide streets appeared much as Cale and his companions had left them—crowded with men, horses, humanoids, wagons, and stink—a stark contrast from the dark, desolate ruins of Elgrin Fau. The row of temples still loomed over the cityscape, supervising the sin with a knowing wink. Starmantle had not changed.

But they had. The Plane of Shadow had changed them all. Cale looked at their clothes, all faded to shades of gray and black, and knew that each of them had left more than the color of their clothes behind in the darkness.

Riven peeled off his dirt-caked cloak and tucked it under his arm.

"Where and when are we meeting?" asked the assassin.

Jak stuck a finger in his chest.

"Where do you think you're going, Zhent?" the halfling asked. "We ought to stick together."

Riven flashed his stained teeth. "You're welcome to accompany me," Riven answered. "I need to tend my gear, get cleaned up, take a meal, then take a whore. Food and flesh, Fleet. What else is there?"

Jak looked mildly shocked and said, "Pipeweed, philosophy, religion, friendship . . . lots of things, Riven."

Riven offered a sincere, "Bah," as he watched a stray dog sniff its way along the street. Cale would have sworn he saw caring in Riven's face, but when the assassin looked up, his face was as hard as usual.

"What about you, Cale?" Riven asked. "Mags? Either of you interested?"

Cale hadn't engaged the services a prostitute since he'd left the entirety of his feelings for Thazienne Uskevren scribed on a piece of paper back in Stormweather Towers, though he had felt the drive often enough. Self denial was another form of cleansing pain, he decided, and resolved that he would not surrender to his needs just then.

"No," he said, and left it at that.

"Well enough," Riven said. "Mags?"

The guide doffed his cap, pushed his hair back, and shook his head.

"I think not. I'll gear us up for the next—" The guide stopped in mid-sentence and looked to Cale. "Where are we going next?"

Cale did not yet have an answer, but he thought he had a means that might help them find out.

"I'm still thinking," he said. "I hope to know by tonight."

"Let me know when you know," the guide said, "so I

can equip us appropriately. Meantime, I'll procure the necessities."

Cale nodded. For a moment, he debated with himself.

Finally, he said to the guide, "Magadon, I feel like I owe it to you to say this . . ." He took a deep breath. "If you want to, if this is too much for too little, now is the time to walk away. I hope that you won't, but I want you to know there's an out. No shame and no hard feelings."

Cale regretted saying the words almost the moment he uttered them.

A brief look of hurt and surprise flashed across Magadon's face, but the guide recovered his composure quickly, fixed his knucklebone eyes on Cale, and offered a grin.

"What do I look like," he asked, "a Zhent assassin for hire?"

Riven scoffed.

Magadon continued, "We're long past three hundred pieces of gold, Erevis. I'll be seeing this through, if you please."

Cale couldn't help but smile, both relieved and chagrined. In less than a tenday, he'd come to count on the guide's solid presence. He thumped Magadon on the shoulder.

"Good," Cale said. "Mags, I didn't mean—"

"I know what you meant," Magadon said. "It's appreciated but unnecessary. You remember our conversation back on the Plane of Shadow?"

Cale nodded.

"So do I," Magadon said, and left it at that.

Riven scoffed again and said, "There's your friendship, Fleet, as sweet as a turnip, ain't it?" The assassin looked to Cale. "If you're done with the orders now, Cale, I'll be finding my flesh."

To all of them, Cale said, "We meet at the Ninth Hell, around the tenth hour tonight. We'll take our rest and . . . recreation today, but tomorrow we start again. In the meantime, stay clear of the Underworld."

Cale didn't want any of them bumping into Dreeve and

what remained of the gnoll's pack. If the creature had returned to Starmantle, he probably still held a grudge.

Cale seized each of them with his eyes before offering his last bit of advice: "And remember that the slaadi are shapechangers. They could be anywhere and anyone. Walk lightly, and stay sharp."

Each gave a serious nod, then Riven set off for his whore and Mags for his gear.

Cale, looking forward to the darkness of a common room and the warmth of a meal, started in the direction of the Ninth Hell before he realized that Jak had lingered behind. He looked back and saw the halfling, with a wistful expression, watching Riven move through the crowd. Jak noticed Cale's gaze on him, flushed with embarrassment, and jogged to catch up.

"What is it?" Cale asked.

"Nothing," Jak said, but his eyes found the road. "Food sounds good, is all."

"We can get a meal at—" Realization dawned.

Still staring at the ground, Jak wore an embarrassed grin. His cheeks flushed as red as an apple.

"The touch of a woman's hand doesn't sound bad, either, eh?" Cale asked.

Jak looked chagrined but did not deny it.

"What was it your fat uncle always said?"

Jak looked up but didn't make eye contact as he replied, "A man's work merits a man's reward. Of course, he was talking about meals, not . . . other things."

Cale knew that, but the principle was the same.

"You can still catch up," he said, nodding after Riven. "I'll see you at the inn."

Jak ran off like a bowshot.

❂   ❂   ❂   ❂   ❂

Despite its dire name, the Ninth Hell Inn and Eatery was well-tended, well-built, and well-run. The paunchy innkeeper, wearing a food-stained apron and sporting a lazy eye and thinning brown hair, greeted Cale with an insincere smile wanting for several teeth. Cale gave him a nod of welcome while he surveyed the common room out of professional habit: a single hearth with a low fire, eleven round tables with stools, windows on three sides, and a stairway leading up to the rooms. A handful of other patrons sat the inn's tables—tan-faced day laborers on midday repast, mostly. No one and nothing dangerous.

Assuming things were as they appeared.

As he stepped out from behind the bar, the innkeeper 's nose wrinkled a bit at Cale's roadworn attire, but he quickly recaptured the hospitable look innate to the brotherhood of innkeepers. Thankfully, he seemed unbothered by Cale's dusky skin. Cale had feared that his transformed appearance would cause him to stand out as clearly as an orc in a dwarfhold, but in truth, he probably looked like nothing more than a dark-skinned southerner. Like Magadon, he could pass for human with only a little work.

"A meal, a room, and a bath for the road weary traveler," the innkeeper said. "I'll see to it immediately."

Cale couldn't help but smile at the man's effusiveness.

"Two rooms," Cale corrected. "Adjacent. I have three comrades. The rest is right."

He handed over to the innkeeper eight gold fivestars. He still didn't have any local currency.

"Sembian, eh?" the innkeeper said, eying the coins.

Cale made no reply.

"Hmm, then," the innkeeper continued, frowning. "Two rooms it shall be. Top of the stairs, last two doors on the left, then. I'll see to it that a washbasin finds its way to your room. Meantime, sit where you will and I'll have food brought."

"Thank you," Cale said.

The innkeeper wiped his hands on his apron and extended one.

"Call me Crovin, or Crove if you prefer. I'll answer to either."

Cale took the man's palm in his right hand.

"Crove," he acknowledged, but did not offer his own name.

"Hmm. Very well, then," Crovin said, frowning still deeper.

He walked back toward the taproom.

Cale found an isolated table to the right of the hearth and eased into a seat. Afternoon sun poured in through the open shutters of the common room's windows, but Cale's table was comfortably cast in shadow. With an insignificant exercise of his will, he increased the intensity of the shadows around his table, creating a cocoon of darkness in which he could relax.

In moments, a thin young woman with her long sandy hair pulled into a horsetail brought him a meal of mutton stew, bread, and a creamy cheese made from goat's milk. Absently, he thanked her and began to eat. The fare was good, but his mind remained on the slaadi: finding them and killing them. He had an idea of how to do the former, and he'd never needed instruction on the latter.

The heat he felt when he considered the slaadi surprised him. Jak burned with desire to stop the Sojourner and his slaadi in order to save innocents. Though Cale understood the sentiment, he knew that saving innocents didn't motivate him, at least not primarily. The slaadi had tortured Ren, murdered other Uskevren house guards, nearly killed Jak, taken Cale's hand, and indirectly stolen his humanity. *That* motivated him—revenge.

Or justice, he thought, trying to prettify it.

He found it telling that in ancient Thorass, the words for revenge and justice, *charorin* and *chororin*, shared a common linguistic origin, distinguished only by a difference in vowels. That was the fine line between the two concepts—vowels. Fortunately, Cale was not interested in distinguishing them. He cared not at all which of the two he was after, so long as at the end of it the slaadi and the Sojourner ended up dead. And if doing so saved innocents and served Mask—and Cale knew that it would accomplish at least the latter, he just couldn't see how—then so much the better.

He swirled his ale. It felt good to put a name to his anger: *chororin*, he decided to name it. Justice: for Ren, for Jak, and for himself. He coiled his anger, his need for *chororin*, into a tight ball and placed it close to his heart. It would be his compass, the new sphere about which his universe would turn until the slaadi and their master were all dead.

He thought of something Riven had said to him back in Selgaunt: *You be Mask's tool, Cale. I'll be his weapon.*

Cale would be a weapon too. And it was time to sharpen his edge.

He flagged the barmaid as she passed by. She smiled down at him, the tired smile of a tired woman. He removed a platinum coin from his belt pouch and handed it to her. Her eyes went wide.

"Please see to it that a few extra ewers of clean water are placed in my room," he said.

She slipped the coin into her bodice.

"Uh, um ... Of course, sir," she stammered, then bustled off.

Cale took some time to savor the last of his cheese and stew. After gulping down the ale, he headed upstairs to his room to hunt slaad.

He opened the last door on the left to reveal a small room that smelled faintly of stale sweat and the smoke from poor-quality pipeweed. A straw-stuffed mattress sat against one wall under the room's only window, while a chair, chamber pot, and a rickety wooden table stood against the wall to Cale's right. Atop the table sat a ceramic washbasin, three tin ewers of water, and a clay oil lamp. Cloak pegs stuck out of the wall like fingers. Cale doffed his filthy attire. Stripping down to only tunic, vest, breeches, and weapons belt, he hung the rest on the pegs.

Cale crossed the floor and pulled the shutters closed, sealing out most of the sun and the sounds from the street below. But for the grid of light cast on the floor through the shutter slats, darkness cloaked the room. He willed it darker still, and darker it grew.

To fully prepare himself before casting the powerful divination he was contemplating, he donned his mask and sat cross-legged on the floor. He regulated his breathing, offered a prayer to Mask, and focused his mind on one thing: Azriim. In his mind's eye, Cale pictured the slaad in both his natural form and in his half-drow form. He imagined the slaad's mismatched eyes, one brown and one blue, the asymmetry seemingly always present irrespective of the form Azriim took.

Cale let the darkness embrace him, as soft as a feather bed. He pulled out the need for *chororin* and let it feed his intensity, until the image of Azriim in both of his known forms had burned itself into Cale's brain. When that image felt as sharp in his mind as the edge of a hornblade, he rose and went to the table. Intuitively, he knew what to do.

Cale filled the washbasin with the water from one of the ewers. He whispered a word of power, spiraled his regenerated hand in the dark air, and came away with his fingers enmeshed with a cats-cradle of reified threads of shadow. He held his hand over the basin and let the liquid shadows slip from his fingers to coil in the water. He unsheathed one of his daggers and without even a wince, opened the palm of the same hand. He held the slash over the basin and let his blood drip into the water. In the darkness, the crimson fluid looked black, as black as his thoughts. The wound bled for only a few heartbeats before the regenerative properties of his flesh sealed the gash. With his dagger blade he stirred them all together—water, shadows, and blood—all the while praying to Mask to consecrate the brew.

When the surface of the water became as black and reflective as polished obsidian, he knew the Shadowlord had answered. He stared at the mirrorlike surface of the water, seeing his masked face reflected there, and whispered the words to a spell that allowed him to scry a person or thing that he mentally selected, wherever they were. He imagined Azriim.

Cale's reflection vanished from the surface of the basin. Points of dim ochre light lit the water like distant embers in the deep. Cale felt the intangible threads of magical power scouring Faerûn, searching for the slaad, searching . . .

Nothing. The light within the basin dimmed and died.

"Damn it," he softly cursed.

Cale leaned back in the chair and took a breath to calm himself. He knew that a variety of factors could prevent the success of the spell, including magical protections or simple bad luck, so he was not alarmed. Since Azriim couldn't know or suspect that Cale was looking for him, he believed that sooner or later his spell would take.

He cut his palm again and recast the spell. Again no success. He repeated the process again and again, growing more and more frustrated with each attempt, until the basin contained as much of his blood as it did water, and the harsh light leaking through the shutter slats had faded to evening's twilight. Still nothing.

"I'll find you," he promised the slaad—promised himself.

Distantly, Cale recognized the beginnings of obsession, but ignored it and cast the spell again.

Sometime later, hours perhaps, the door to the room opened and Jak entered, bathed, shaved, fed, and bedded. Light streamed in from a lantern in the hallway. Cale blinked in the sudden brightness but barely spared the halfling a glance.

"Cale?" Jak asked in a concerned voice, his silhouette framed in the door by the lantern. "Dark, man! It's pitch in here. Did you even eat?"

"Yes," Cale replied.

"Cale . . ."

"Not now, Jak," Cale replied, focusing on the basin.

He put Jak out of his mind, concentrated, and cast again. The image of the slaad's eyes was imprinted on his brain. He focused . . .

There!

In the depths of the basin, a light sparkled. He fixated on it, willed the spell to follow it.

"Cale?" Jak asked.

A wavering image took shape in the water. He saw a gray-skinned, grizzled dwarf walking a torchlit street. Decrepit buildings made of scrap wood lined a packed earth road. At first, Cale thought the spell might have gone awry, but when the dwarf turned and Cale saw the perfect teeth and the eyes—one blue and one brown—he knew his spell had located Azriim. He tried to contain his exultation and keep the spell focused.

He couldn't hear the sounds around Azriim, but he could see the surroundings. Shadowy buildings, creatures, and people moved in and out of the spell's field of vision. Most of the people and creatures appeared to be running. Several were shouting and pointing.

"Where are Riven and Mags?" Cale asked the halfling.

"Next door," Jak answered.

"Get them. And all three of you get in here," Cale said. "Right now. I've found them."

Jak took Cale's meaning right way. The halfling ran to the room next door and pounded on the door. Cale heard muffled voices and boot stomps. Magadon, Jak, and Riven piled into his room, shutting the door behind them.

"It's pitch black in here," Magadon said. "What are you doing, Cale?"

"Scrying for the slaadi," Jak answered. "He's got them."

"You've got them?" Magadon asked, excitement in his voice.

Cale nodded and beckoned them over, saying, "Look for yourself."

His three comrades gathered behind and around him, and stared into the bowl.

Azriim walked the dark street beside a gray haired, balding human with a giant pot belly.

"But . . ." Magadon started to protest, then the dwarf's eyes became clear.

"Dark and empty," Riven breathed. "That's him. That's his eyes, Mags, and no mistaking. The bald one must be one of the other slaadi."

"Where are they?" Jak asked, standing on tiptoes to see into the bowl.

Cale shook his head. From what they'd seen, Azriim could have been walking the nighttime streets of any city in Faerûn. He needed more information. He concentrated, working to expand the field of vision afforded him by the spell.

The vista spread out. People and creatures of all sorts—gnolls, orcs, even drow—crowded the streets around Azriim and the pot-bellied human. A coffle of nearly naked slaves stood in the background. A troll shambled by. They were all looking up at something.

"What in the name of the goddess . . . ?" said Magadon.

With an effort of will, Cale moved the scrying eye to view the object of attention. The spell dispelled the moment they focused on it, but in that single instant they all saw it well enough: a glowing skull floating amidst a backdrop of rope bridges and catwalks.

Riven's sharp intake of breath rang loud in the quiet of the room. Cale sat back in the chair, his mind racing.

"Burn me," said Jak.

Magadon looked from one face to another. "What? What is it?"

"Skullport," Cale said, turning to face his comrades.

The guide's face showed recognition.

"Skullport?" Magadon blew out a soft whistle, looked to Riven, then to Jak, and asked, "What I've heard . . . Is it as bad as that?"

"Likely worse," Riven said. "Imagine Waterdeep is a sieve. The Lords of Waterdeep shake their city and the worst of the residents fall down to Skullport, there to join the worst the Underdark has to offer."

"You've been there?" Magadon asked Riven.

The assassin nodded, his face thoughtful.

"Once, a long time ago," the assassin said, his voice low. "Slaves . . . drugs . . . life is worth coppers. The worst things you can imagine, those things you can buy cheap. It's the things you won't even consider until you see them that cost the real coin." He shared a glance with Cale then eyed Jak meaningfully. "If we're going there, we need to understand that it ain't nice. And we can't try to fix it and make it so. Understood? Fleet? Cale?"

Jak pulled out his pipe, tamped, and lit. The tindertwig gave their faces an eerie cast. The smell of pipeweed, rich and deep, filled the room.

"I hear you," the halfling said.

"Is that new leaf?" Magadon asked absently.

Jak raised his eyebrows and looked impressed.

"It is. Bought it today."

"I purchased some new gear for us," Magadon said, still in that same thoughtful tone. "New cloaks, boots, road tack. . . ."

Riven ignored all that and said, "You enter Skullport knowing what you want. You get it, then you leave. As fast as possible. And no one crosses the Skulls. I've seen what they can do."

Jak blew a cloud of smoke up into Riven's face and grumbled, "I said I understood."

Riven inhaled Jak's exhaled smoke and blew it back at the halfling.

"Good," the assassin replied. "If things go ugly there because you can't keep your conscience in your—"

"Enough," Cale said, standing and interposing himself between Jak and Riven. "We know what we want in Skullport. We're hunting slaadi. The question is, how do we get there?"

Cale knew that Skullport was somewhere below Waterdeep, Faerûn's largest city, over half a continent away.

Jak shrugged, drew in some smoke, then said, "Magic?"

Riven scoffed and took out his borrowed pipe.

"You have something better to offer?" the halfling asked.

Riven lit, inhaled, then replied, "No. The way we—the way *I* used before won't be available. We need another way."

Magadon used one of his own tindertwigs to light the wick of the oil lamp on the table. Shadows sprung up on the walls. Cale realized then how cognizant he had become of the presence or absence of darkness and shadows. He also knew that in darkness he could use his own power to instantaneously transport himself, and possibly his comrades, from the shadows in Starmantle to the shadows in Skullport. Not shadowstepping, but teleporting. Still, something caused him to hesitate. He remembered: Long ago, he had overheard something about the dangers of teleporting into and out of the Underdark. Stories of men materializing half in and half out of solid rock, screaming in agony for the last few heartbeats of their lives. He didn't want to risk that with his comrades. If there was no other way, he could go alone. . . .

"I know a way," Magadon said. His pale eyes glowed in the lamplight. "But it's four days away, even moving quickly."

Cale barely acknowledged the relief he felt at Magadon's pronouncement.

"Four days is too much time," he said. "But I may be able to get us there sooner. What's your way?"

Magadon looked at Cale with raised eyebrows and asked, "How can you get us there sooner?"

Cale indicated his skin, the shadows leaking from his fingertips, and said, "With this. I can teleport us there if you can describe the location to me."

Magadon nodded and said, "I can do better."

Before Cale could ask what he meant, Riven asked, "Then why not teleport us all the way to Skullport?"

"Something I heard once," Cale replied. "I think teleporting that deep underground is dangerous."

"I've heard that too," Jak said, nodding and blowing a smoke ring.

Riven seemed to accept that. No doubt he'd heard something similar.

Magadon said, "The way I know is dangerous too."

Shaking his head, Cale replied, "Not as much."

He said it as a statement, but there was enough of a question in it that Magadon smiled.

"We'll see," the guide said. "The guardian can send us anywhere we want to go, provided there's water at the destination."

All of them knew that Skullport sat on the shore of an underground harbor.

"Guardian?" Jak said from around his pipe stem.

"Describe your route, Mags," Cale said.

"A Crossroads," Magadon said, as though that explained it all.

Cale had no idea what the guide meant.

"Explain," said Riven, echoing Cale's thoughts.

The guide shrugged and frowned, seemingly surprised that none of his three comrades showed any recognition.

"Faerûn is crosshatched with secret ways," he said. "Druids call them the Hidden Paths, but most know them as Crossroads and Backroads. They are not quite portals, they're more like . . . folds in the world. A tunnel of one step that carries you through a space of a hundred leagues. Take a step onto a Backroad in Selgaunt and instantly find yourself outside of Arabel. Does that make sense?"

Riven's narrowed eye and furrowed brow said, "No."

Cale wasn't quite sure he understood either.

"So you're saying these Crossroads are all over?" Jak asked. "Only, we can't see them?"

Magadon smiled and said, "Not quite, Jak. The *Backroads* are everywhere, or at least most everywhere. The Crossroads are the access points, where the Backroads intersect our perception of the world. It is there that we can enter the Backroads. And no, most people don't see them."

Jak shook his head, obviously still confused.

Cale too was uncertain. He had never in all his travels heard of anything resembling the phenomenon Magadon was describing. Perhaps comprehending the nature of the Hidden Paths had something to do with Magadon's psionic abilities. He suspected Magadon's careful choice of the phrase, "our perception of the world," went to the core of the issue.

"Where do they come from?" Cale asked.

The guide scratched his nose and shook his head.

"The Hidden Paths are part of the nature of creation, Erevis. They did not come from anything. They just are and have always been."

Cale digested that.

"And one leads to Skullport?" he asked at last.

Magadon nodded and said, "They lead everywhere."

Riven took a long draw on his pipe.

"How did you come to know about these things?" the assassin asked.

Magadon gave his best Drasek Riven sneer and tapped his temple.

"I looked for them, Drasek. And I'm willing to see." His voice grew colder when he said to the assassin, "It's surprising the things you can see when you're willing."

Riven offered his own sneer in return.

Cale doubted that it was that simple. Still, Magadon had not yet led them astray; he knew he could trust the guide and his judgment.

"You mentioned a guardian?" he said.

"Indeed. The fey keep the Crossroads, and each Crossroad has a single guardian. We'll have to bargain our way past. Sometimes the guardians are . . . temperamental."

"What in the Nine Hells does that mean?" Jak asked.

"You'll see," Magadon replied.

Cale took his cloak from the peg on which it hung and said, "I can only teleport us at night. Gather your gear. We leave as soon as we're equipped."

"Can you teleport with a boat too?" the guide asked

Cale. "We'll need a boat. Big enough for the four of us."

Cale nodded.

"A boat?" Jak asked.

Magadon grinned, a feral smile, and said, "You'll see."

"You say that a lot," Jak said.

Cale looked to Jak and said, "Little man, can you get us a boat at this hour?"

Jak exhaled a cloud of smoke, snapped his fingers, and snuffed his pipe.

"Easy. You'll see," he said, smiling at Mags. "Meet me at the docks in a half hour."

CHAPTER 11

Running the River

Even by night, Starmantle's harbor bustled with activity. Laborers and ships' crews—some composed of humans, some not—unloaded crates of cargo by torchlight and glowball and stacked them high. Cale could imagine the illicit contents of many of the crates. Starmantle traded in vice as much as legitimate goods, the same as any other city of the Inner Sea.

The shouts of the sailors carried along the shore through the salt-tinged night air. Laughter, smoke, torchlight, and shouts carried from the open windows of the many dockside taverns. Pedestrians walked the wharves in small groups: revelers, sailors, whores, pimps, and worse.

Cale felt at home there in the night, surrounded by sin.

He stood with Jak, Riven, and Magadon on

the rocky shore of an out-of-the-way inlet, down the shoreline and east of Starmantle's main harbor. Small wooden piers and docks, large enough only for small fishing craft, dotted the shoreline there. Jak led them to one such pier, a rickety wooden construct that extended a long dagger toss into the bay. There, tethered with thick hemp rope, several small rowboats floated in the gently lapping water.

The breeze off the sea smelled fresh and clean. As he had when he'd been aboard *Foamrider*, Cale felt the water pull at his spirit.

"That's it," Jak said and gestured at one of the rowboats near them, "on the left side of the dock."

Cale eyed the boat doubtfully. Even with his limited exposure to the sea, he could see it was a creaky tub, with rusty fittings, splintering oars, and no less than ten seasons of wear on its hull. Worn fishing nets lay piled aft. A coiled rope affixed to a rusty anchor lay fore. On the positive side, the boat was big enough that they could all fit in it. It also appeared to float . . . sort of.

"Did you pay for that, Fleet?" Riven asked.

"Of course I paid for it, Zhent. If Cale wanted it stolen, he'd have asked you to get it."

Riven gave a hard smile and replied, "No. He would have asked me to do it if he wanted the owner dead and the boat burned to ash. And after selling you that, the owner deserves no less."

"It floats," Jak grumbled. "Now let's just get in the damned thing."

"I'll row," Magadon said.

They all walked down the wood-planked pier. Jak lowered himself into the small boat and took a seat on the rear bench. Still sneering, Riven hopped into the boat and sat beside the halfling. Jak scooted away from him and looked in the opposite direction.

Before getting in, Cale asked Magadon, "Are you sure this is going to do? We're not going to be on the open sea, are we?"

"This will do," replied the guide. He nodded for Cale to get in. "And we won't be on the sea at all."

Cale nodded, climbed into the boat, and sat fore. Magadon, after unmooring the small craft from the pier, came last and sat on the middle bench, facing aft toward Jak and Riven.

The guide took the oars and over his back, Magadon said to Cale, "Allow me to get a feel for it before you . . . move us."

Cale replied, "You say when you're ready."

As Magadon rowed them out into the bay, Cale looked up into the clear night sky, alit with stars. The starlight reflected off the surface of the water, reminding him of the basin he had used to track Azriim to Skullport, of the starsphere that he still carried in his pack. The transformation of his soul had begun with the stars, he knew, had been foreordained thousands of years earlier when the makers of the starsphere had captured in magical crystal the periodic appearances in Faerûn of the Fane of Shadows.

Somehow, he thought that everything would end with the stars too.

Two and two are four, he thought, and let his fingertips crease the water.

The oars thumped in their settings as Magadon rowed them out a bowshot and turned the boat sharply hither and yon, finally spinning it in a tight circle.

"Well enough," the guide said, seemingly comfortable with the boat. "This is the best we have, so we'll make do. Are you ready, Erevis?"

Cale pulled his gaze from the sky and nodded.

Magadon reached back and gripped Cale's forearm.

"Be at ease," he said, and Cale felt Magadon's mind reach for his. "This is where we need to go."

Motes of silver light formed before Magadon's eyes, flared, and floated over to surround Cale's head. In his mind's eye, Cale saw the image Magadon had transmitted, as clear a "memory" as if Cale had seen it himself: a wild river—the Wet River—racing northward from a long lake, coursing through a jagged canyon, and finally spilling over a high cliff to empty itself, in a torrent of foam and violence, into the Dragonmere.

Towering maples lined the river's winding course, ancient watchmen guarding the waterway and giving the river the appearance of a processional. There was no sign of human habitation. The area looked untouched and untraveled, pristine.

The silver motes winked out but the memory of the place remained fixed in Cale's mind.

How strange the mind works, Cale thought.

He caught an inkling of something that had happened back on the Plane of Shadow. But before he could recall it, it dissipated like a puff of smoke.

"Can you see it?" Magadon asked.

"I can," Cale replied. "How did you do it?"

Magadon said, "Simple really. I transferred a memory of something that I had seen to you, as though you had seen it. That can go both ways. I can use a modified mind-link to take something that you've seen, or even to see through your eyes."

"That's why no one likes you, Mags," Riven said.

Cale gave a half smile, feeling a strange sense of having done that all before.

"Didn't you already tell me that?" he asked Magadon.

The guide looked at him curiously, started to speak, stopped, then said, "I don't . . . I don't think so."

Cale shook his head, meanwhile storing what Magadon had told him in the back of his mind.

"Ready yourselves," he said to all of them.

With an exercise of will, Cale drew the shadows about the boat until darkness cloaked them like a shroud.

"I can't see," Jak said, and his voice was small in the darkness.

Cale pictured the location in his mind and transported them from the darkness of Starmantle's bay to the darkness of the Wet River canyon. He didn't feel any sensation of motion, though he heard Jak gasp.

When he let the shadows begin to dissipate, it was plain that they were elsewhere. Sound filled their ears: the slow croak of frogs, the chirps of crickets and cicadas, and the steady rush of the river. Maples loomed over them, blotting out the stars. Behind the maples rose the steep, boulder-strewn sides of a rocky canyon. The boat was moving, careening sideways in a moderate current.

"Help me get it to shore!" Magadon shouted. "The current gets fast very quickly."

While the guide skillfully plied the oars, Cale, Jak, and Riven used their hands to help paddle. Together, they pulled the craft out of the current and steered it into the shallows. There, Magadon hopped out and pulled the craft onto a stony beach.

Breathing hard, they all exited the boat and sank to the ground.

When he'd caught his breath, Magadon said to Cale, "We covered over twenty leagues in a heartbeat. Well done."

Cale caught Riven's frown, but chose to ignore it.

"We'll camp here," Magadon said, indicating a knoll under the leaves of a maple. "With the dawn, we start downriver for the Dragon's Jaws."

Jak and Riven stared at the guide.

"The falls are called the Dragon's Jaws," Magadon explained. He cocked his head. "If you listen with care, you can hear them even from here."

With his darkness-enhanced senses, Cale could hear them quite clearly. In the distance sounded the dull roar and boom of thundering water. In his mind's eye, he could see the falls: a raging river cutting a jagged gash in the wall of a high cliff. The gash looked vaguely like jaws snapping shut.

Magadon looked at Riven and Jak and said, "The falls at the Jaws descend two bowshots or more before crashing into the Dragonmere. The mist is as thick as an autumn fog; the roar as loud as the bellows of a hundred ogres. It's wondrous to see."

"Wondrous?" Jak said, while he stuffed his pipe. "Trickster's toes! Two bowshots is a long drop, Magadon."

Riven said nothing.

"The Jaws are the location of the Crossroad," the guide said. "More precisely, the Jaws *are* the Crossroad."

When Cale and Jak looked a question at him, Magadon said, "You'll see tomorrow. Save your questions until then. I need to prepare tonight."

Since Magadon seemed disinclined to speak further about it, Cale let it drop.

After they had pitched their tents and Magadon had gotten a campfire going, Cale volunteered to take the first watch. He would need to pray to the Shadowlord at midnight anyway.

"There is no need for that here," Magadon said, and nodded up at the maples. "This place is already being watched."

Cale followed Magadon's glance to the canopy above. He saw nothing there and heard only the wind through the leaves, the rush of the river, and the distant boom of the Dragon's Jaws. Still, he took the guide at his word, shrugged, and lay down to sleep.

He awakened at midnight, as always. Sitting up from his bedroll, he saw Magadon sitting near the river, keeping vigil and whispering to its waters. The guide's words were lost to the rush of the current and the song of the crickets.

Cale looked to the other side of the fire and saw that Riven was not in his tent. He sat up fully and scanned the campsite. His vision allowed him to see clearly in the darkness and he spotted Riven right away. The assassin sat in the deeper darkness against the bole of one of the maples. He had his legs partially drawn up and rested the back of his palms on his knees. His eyes were closed.

He was praying, Cale realized, and the understanding made him uncomfortable.

With effort, he put it out of his mind. So as not to disturb either Magadon or Riven, Cale quietly donned his mask and prayed to the Shadowlord. His patron answered; power filled his brain, the words to prayers that would unlock magic.

Afterward, he lay back down to sleep. By then, Riven was back in his bedroll, sleeping.

Magadon awakened him just as the false dawn began to lighten the sky above the canyon. Together, they roused Jak and Riven. Jak lit his pipe; Riven's coughs sounded loud off the canyon's rocks.

While they gathered their gear, Magadon explained the situation: "The guardian is a river fey, and will only appear if we brave the current near the Jaws while the sun is rising. I had hoped to win his favor last night. He did not answer, but we shall soon see if I succeeded."

"Near the Jaws," Jak muttered, and lost his pipe from between his teeth. "Dark," he said, retrieving it and dusting the dirt from the stem.

"You're right to be concerned," the guide said. "Once in that current, there is no getting out. We must convince the guardian to allow us passage, or we'll go over the falls."

Between his coughs, Riven managed a hard laugh. Cale and Jak shared a look.

"How do we do that?" Cale asked, his voice and mood serious.

Magadon shrugged, and as he finished loading his pack he said, "Fey are fickle. Some days, one thing will work, someday another. But *something* will work. We need only find what it is."

Cale wondered if he should reconsider his decision not to transport them all directly to Skullport.

Magadon must have sensed his hesitation.

"All we can do is try, Erevis."

"Try and die," Riven said, as he pulled on his pack.

"Maybe," Magadon acknowledged.

Jak pocketed his pipe and threw his pack in the boat.

"You've got nothing better, Zhent," the halfling said to Riven. "I trust Magadon's judgment."

Riven glared at Jak then turned back to the guide.

"How often have you made this passage, Mags?" he asked.

Magadon hesitated a moment then answered, "Once."

"Still trust his judgment, Fleet?" said Riven, laughing.

Jak looked concerned but said nothing.

"Can you do it, Magadon?" Cale asked, looking the guide in the eyes.

Magadon's brow furrowed and he said, "It will take all of us. But yes, I think so."

That was good enough for Cale.

"Then let's go," he said, and thumped Magadon on the shoulder.

They piled into the boat and Magadon pushed them off. After climbing in and taking his seat on the middle bench, he linked their minds.

This way, he projected, *we can communicate unheard by the fey.*

Just as the current seized them and sent them speeding down the river, Magadon looked meaningfully at Riven and Cale.

"Violence and threats cannot avail us with the guardian," said the guide, "so do not offer any. Provide it with what it asks, and it will grant us passage."

Cale and Riven acknowledged Magadon's words with a nod. As the sun's light began to peek over the canyon and brighten the sky, Cale resisted the urge to draw up his cloak hood. His skin stung, but he endured. His hand vanished and he drew the sleeve of his cloak over the stump. He would abide the light, though he knew that the sun would prevent him from using any of the abilities granted him by his transformation. If they went over the Dragon's Jaws, he would not be able to save them from drowning. But he *would* face death with his friends, in the sun, unhooded, and with open eyes.

Currents of nervousness and anticipation traveled

along the telepathic lines that connected them. None were sure that it would work.

Nothing for it now, Cale thought, and held on.

The current accelerated rapidly and sent them hurtling down the river. Magadon used the oars not for propulsion but to help steer the boat, since it had no tiller. While he worked, he began to sing in a language that Cale had never before heard, but that somehow stirred him, calling to mind moonlit nights, forested glades, and quiet revelry. The guide's voice was a mellow baritone, and the song used the river's rush as a counterpoint to its melody.

Cale looked to the back of the boat, to Riven. The assassin clutched the side of the vessel with one hand and the bench he shared with Jak in the other. Dark circles painted the skin under his eyes.

In a mental voice only Riven could hear, Cale projected, *Dreams?*

Riven looked up sharply, furrowed his brow, and shook his head.

No. I haven't dreamed since we came back from the Plane of Shadow.

Cale considered that as the boat scraped against a rock and began to pick up still more speed. Magadon continued to sing the song of summoning, even as his mental voice cursed the rocks and current.

Perhaps he's through with you? Cale said to Riven, but doubted it.

Riven knew whom Cale meant by "he." The assassin's eye narrowed and fixed on Cale.

I don't want him to be through with me, First of Five.

Cale heard the venom in Riven's mental voice and understood the feelings well. He had seen them in Riven before. When both Cale and Riven had served the Righteous Man in the Night Knives, Riven had been second to Cale. And in serving Mask, Riven was second again. Cale knew that a man in that position might do anything, might *give* anything. He recalled the assassin's prayers of the night before and wondered what Riven had asked of Mask, and what the Shadowlord had given and taken. For reasons he could not explain, Cale felt pity for Riven. The assassin was as caught up in the schemes of the Shadowlord as Cale, but he had no one to keep him grounded. Riven didn't have someone like Jak. Cale decided that he would try to give the assassin some ballast.

Listen to me, Riven, Cale said, in as brotherly a tone as he could muster. *You give yourself over fully to Mask and you'll be stepping off a cliff bigger than anything we'll be seeing today. Keep yourself.*

Riven answered with only a frown and a turned head.

Cale stared at him for a moment then shook his head. He had done what he could.

Magadon ceased his singing and Cale noticed for the first time that another voice had taken up the tune, a wondrous voice, an otherworldly, sing-song tenor. Cale scanned the churning river ahead and behind but could not see a source; it appeared to come from the rush of the waves itself. The words and the voice sent a charge of energy through Cale and he had to force himself to not stand in the boat. Where Magadon's version of the song had called to mind a majestic forest under the stars, the same words, sung in a different voice, had come to evoke an image of roaring waves, leaping fish, and the thrill of the hunt.

Remain still and non-threatening, Magadon projected to them, then he called aloud, "We hear your song, guardian, and beseech you to show yourself."

"White water," Jak shouted over the singing from his bench in the rear, pointing past Cale to the river ahead. Magadon cringed at the halfling's shout and the guardian's song faltered.

No shouting, the guide admonished.

Cale turned to see rapids around the next bend in the river. Rocks poked through the river's surface, causing swirls, little whirlpools, and foam. The water roared around them, roiling and splashing. A host of small cascades awaited them ahead, culminating in the distance in the torrent that spilled over the Dragon's Jaws. Cale dug his fingertips into the gunwales and tried to keep from spilling over the side as the boat began to lurch.

"We humbly request your presence, Guardian," Magadon said.

"I've been here all along, woodsman," said a voice from beside the boat, "at least for those with eyes to see. And please do not shout on my river, half-a-man."

Cale looked to the side of the boat and his breath caught. Rising halfway out of the roiling water to swim beside the boat was the guardian fey. Though roughly humanoid in stature—at least from the waist up—it looked to be composed of the river water itself. In its shimmering, liquid shape, Cale could make out the watery outline of long, unkept hair, laughing eyes, and a smiling mouth. Though Cale could see no means of propulsion—the creature appeared to have no body below its manifested torso—the fey darted around the boat, gliding through the water with the ease and rapidity of a hummingbird in the air. The creature looked each of them over; an appraising glance. It lingered longest near the bow, eyeing Cale.

What's happening? Cale asked Magadon.

Do nothing, replied the woodsman, and grunted as he managed the boat through the increasingly powerful current. *It is observing.*

At last, the fey again took up station beside Magadon.

"You keep unusual company, woodsman," the fey said. "And sing out of tune. And confuse many of the lyrics. And befoul the Sylvan tongue. I am deeply offended."

The fey crossed his arms over his chest and looked away, still somehow keeping pace with the boat as it careened along in the current.

Keeping one eye on the rapids and one eye on the river fey, Magadon said, "I am but a simple guide, as you suggest. Forgive my mistreatment of your tongue."

He pulled the oars hard back as the boat tumbled down a small cascade. Cale's stomach raced up his throat.

"We've come to petition you for access to the Crossroads," Magadon said, struggling to keep his tone even. "We wish to journey to Skullport."

The fey's gaze darkened. It looked at Cale doubtfully.

"You seek the Sargauth then," it said. "Dark waters, those."

More rocks, Mags, Cale projected. *Big ones.*

Ahead, the river accelerated. The water boiled around huge, jagged rocks.

I see them, the guide projected back. *Hold on tight.*

The fey watched with amusement as Magadon tried to steer the boat away from the rocks.

"Beware now," the fey said and giggled, the sound like rain tinkling on metal.

The creature's body slammed into a rock, exploding into a shower of drops and mist, then instantly reformed on the other side, still grinning.

After passing the rocks, the full force of rapids seized them. Cale felt as if a hand had taken hold of the keel of the boat and thrown it forward. Foam churned, water roiled, and the boat thumped again and again against more rocks hidden just below the surface. Cale's teeth rattled in his head and his cloak was sodden. Throughout, the fey somehow swam along beside them, just out of arm's reach, smiling benignly.

"The Sargauth," Magadon said, breathing hard and trying to keep the boat from breaking into pieces. "Yes. Will you grant us passage?"

The boat slammed so hard into a rock that Cale thought for certain they had staved a side. The craft spun off the stone and rotated ninety degrees. Magadon righted them with effort. A dip, another. Water swamped the bow. Cale was soaked. The boat hit another rock, tumbled down another cascade. From the rear, Jak shouted, bounced high in the air, and would have gone overboard but for Riven's reflexes. The assassin grabbed the halfling by the cloak and yanked him back into the boat.

"Hang on godsdamnit, Fleet!" the assassin said.

Over the roar of the river, the fey frowned, waggled a translucent finger at the assassin, and said, "No. I think I shall not grant you passage. You and your friends wield words as though they were weapons. I remain offended."

Ahead, Cale could hear the roar of the falls. It was growing louder. The river bed was dropping by steps; cascade after cascade. The maple trees and canyon walls around them were blurs. The boat bobbed through the water like a child's toy. Cale knew that the mad rush down the waterway ended in a fall that none of them could survive.

Be quick, Magadon, Cale projected to the guide.

He held on as the bow crashed down another cascade and nearly unseated him. They had a thirty count, no longer.

"Guardian," Magadon shouted, and Cale felt the guide's desperation travel along the telepathic channels. "Please, what can we do to gain passage?"

Ahead a spearcast, Cale saw the Dragon's Jaws. It looked just as it had in Magadon's mental image: the river's current had carved a great U-shaped channel through the cliff face. Foaming water roared through the channel and vanished from sight, falling into the thick mist formed from the water slamming into the Dragonmere far below. Jagged boulders jutted from the waters before the Jaws.

"The falls!" Jak shouted from behind.

The fey made a show of thinking.

"You've offended me with words, woodsman. Now you must amuse me with them. Or surprise me. Or astonish me." He waved a watery hand and said, "Begin."

The four comrades shared a look.

Try something! Riven projected.

Cale watched with dread as they neared the Jaws. The river surged, nearly capsizing the boat. They all four uttered a collective shout.

"Magadon!" the halfling called.

"I am born of a devil," the guide blurted.

The fey raised his eyebrows, laughed, and clapped his hands.

"Wonderful! Which one?"

The boat slammed into a rock, nearly sending Cale over the bow. They were taking on water.

"What?" Magadon shouted, doing everything he could to slow their approach to the falls.

"Which devil?" asked the fey. "Name your sire—or mother, as the case may be."

Cale saw Magadon's resistance, felt it in his mind. Cale didn't know if he wanted the woodsman to speak his father's name or keep it behind his teeth. He understood Magadon's struggle. Speaking the name of his demonic father—something Magadon was loathe to do—would have felt to the guide like surrender, like the way Cale had felt back on the Plane of Shadow when he'd drawn Weaveshear for the first time.

"Tell the thing what it wants to hear, Mags!" Riven said. His good eye was wide, eyeing the approaching falls. "It's just a name."

The fey's gaze fixed on Riven and hardened.

"The shadow of the shade speaks at last." It indicated Cale, looked back to Riven, and said, "You *are* merely his shadow, are you not?"

Riven's eye narrowed. His mouth set into a hard line. Despite the upset of the boat, one of his hands went for a blade. His anger was palpable through the mindlink, overriding the group's collective trepidation at the onrushing Jaws.

"Mephistopheles!" Magadon shouted, and the word made Cale's stomach churn worse than the river. "Mephistopheles is my blood sire."

The fey seemed unperturbed by the foul name.

"Excellent!" the creature said to Magadon. "A base word but well said!"

"You want to hear words of power, you little pissdrip?" Riven growled from the back of the boat. "Then hear this."

Do not! Cale ordered, but it was too late.

Riven spat a stream of corruption in the tongue he sometimes used as a weapon. Cale, Jak, and Magadon doubled over in pain upon hearing the words, but the fey only squinted as though he was facing the wind in a rainstorm. After Riven had spewed the sentence, he looked surprised to see that the fey had not disintegrated.

The fey, seeing Riven was done, clapped his hands lightly.

"Foully told, but well said." It turned to Jak and said, "Now you, little bedraggled half-man. The pissdrip has yet to hear from you."

Jak, his eyes still watering from the obscenity mouthed by Riven, could not take his gaze from the river.

Say something, Fleet, Riven projected.

You keep your mouth closed, Zhent! Jak shot back with heat, and glared at Riven.

Little man. . . . Cale prompted.

"Come now," said the fey. "Confess."

At that Jak gave the creature a sharp look, then looked to Cale. Cale gave him a reassuring nod and the halfling nodded back and turned to the fey.

Barely audible over the roar of the approaching falls, Jak said, "I'm afraid of what is happening."

The fey grinned.

"Well done, half-a-man! Well done indeed! I'd ask what in particular frightens you, but I know it is everything." The creature spun around to face Cale, and pointing past him to the onrushing falls said, "Time is short, shade. What do you have to say to me?"

The roar of the water was loud in Cale's ears. He struggled to find something to say, something the fey would not have heard before. Nothing. He could not think above the roar of the Jaws.

Hurry, Cale, Riven prompted.

" 'Ware," the fey blithely cautioned.

They all saw it too late. The boat crashed into a jagged rock jutting a handbreadth above the waterline. It split the side of the little craft and sent Cale tumbling into the river. He heard the shouts of his comrades for only an instant before he went under. His single good hand clutched for something, anything, but managed to take hold of only a broken bit of the boat's hull. Not enough to keep him afloat.

He felt as if a giant's hand pressed him to the riverbed and held him submerged. The water was not deep. His back scraped against the rocky bottom and he could still see sunlight cascading through the rough water. But he couldn't gain purchase to push himself to the top. The current rolled him, twisted him, twirled him like a dry leaf in a gale.

And above it all, even underwater, he could hear the dull, foreboding rush of the Dragon's Jaws.

In his head, he heard the fey say, *Speak, shade, or all is lost. Already your friends are drowning, though the woodsman swims strong and even now tries to save them.*

Cale's breath was failing. He didn't even have the sense to feel much surprise at the fact that the fey could communicate telepathically. He reached for the surface and felt his hand broach the water, feeling the sun's sting on his flesh for only a moment before the current pushed him back down. The falls were near. His breath was gone. A flurry of incoherent images flashed through his mind: Riven leading a religious service, the Fane of Shadows, a twin spire built on an island and reaching for a starry sky, a laughing mask stepping from Shar's shadow to stab at Cyric, the Plane of Shadow, the ruins of Elgrin Fau.

The ruins of Elgrin Fau. . . .

He hoped the fey was still listening.

Over six thousand years ago, he projected to the fey, *on a world now forgotten, Kesson Rel the Dark, first Chosen of the Shadowlord, angry at his forced exile from Elgrin Fau, banished the whole of the city into the Plane of Shadow. The inhabitants thought he had stolen the sun, but he had stolen only them. He lingers still in the darkest places of the*

Shadow Deep, feeding his malice. One day, I will find him and avenge his betrayal.

For a heartbeat, everything fell silent. Cale blew out the last of his breath in a stream of bubbles. A sudden roar filled his ears, impossibly loud. He felt himself falling, going through the Dragon's Jaws and down into oblivion.

Your travels will lead down dark paths, said the fey in his head. *Journey well, shade.*

CHAPTER 12

PLOTTING

Kexen sat alone at a small table in the Pour House Inn and Tavern. Under his sleeve, Sessa, one of Zstulkk's sets of eyes, coiled tightly around his forearm. The noise and smoke agitated the serpent, and it slithered irritably around Kexen's arm. Kexen stayed still and calm. Zstulkk's familiars had been known, on rare occasions, to bite their bearers.

An image of his body, bloated and purple from cave viper venom, floated through Kexen's mind. He pushed it away with effort. Everyone in Zstulkk Ssarmn's slaving organization knew that the yuan-ti saw through the eyes of his pet serpents. Bites occurred only when Zstulkk was displeased with what he saw through the serpent, or when the operative was captured and in possession of incriminating information. Kexen would give his employer no cause for displeasure, and had no intention of being captured by anyone—ever.

Tallow candles scattered around the common room provided the only light, sending greasy, swirling spires of smoke ceilingward. The stifling air smelled of unbathed sailors, the cheap body-fragrance of whores, and a wretched, dried-fungus incense that Felwer, the one-armed proprietor, insisted on burning in a ceramic incense tray behind the bar. Felwer always told anyone who would listen that the incense attracted whores and repelled cats. The innkeeper had an affinity for the former and an inexplicable phobia for the latter. Felwer even kept a dog to keep the cats at bay: a grizzled old bitch named Retha, who typically did nothing except lay before the hearth and leak piss on the floor.

The shouts of passing street vendors, selling cured rothé meat and pickled mushrooms, carried through the irregularly-shaped holes in the wall that served as the Pour House's windows. Kexen's rickety table, cobbled together from salvaged wood from ruined ships, seemed ready to tip at the slightest bump and spill the tankard of mushroom ale that sat untouched atop it. He would not have cared. The swill smelled like urine and probably tasted worse; he'd bought it only to keep Felwer from fretting.

Bleary-eyed, grinning sailors of various races thronged the common room, all either drunk already or well on their way. The professional girls circled the sailors like perfumed sharks that smelled blood in the water. Kexen had already made his own disinterest plain to an insistent, would-be skulker courtesan who looked haggard even in the dim light of the house's candles. Sessa would have bit her had Kexen not pushed her away. The courtesan moved on with an indignant huff to sit on the lap of a gigantic half-orc sailor, probably a pirate.

Bawdy songs erupted at intervals from a group of dark-skinned Calishite sailors who sat on the other side of the common room. Gaming for coppers went on at several tables and in every corner: *sava*, scales and blades, roll-the-bones, and king's ransom. Shouts of glee or moans of despair went up from time to time, depending upon the roll of the dice or the draw of the deck.

Kexen smiled. He understood well what it was to lose a month's pay on a throw of the dice or a hand of cards. He had long ago served his time crewing a slaver, squandering his pay in dives like the Pour House—but not anymore. As a rising member of Zstulkk Ssarmn's organization, he was accustomed to finer surroundings. All he wanted was to complete his business with Thyld and get back to his residence in the Middle Heart.

A patient man by nature, Kexen continued to wait without fidgeting, staring through the smoky air at the curtain of strung oyster shells that served as the main door of the Pour House. Thyld was due presently.

Kexen and Thyld had a longstanding relationship. Thyld, a member of the Kraken Society and hence a man with considerable contacts, sold pertinent information to Kexen on the side, and occasionally acted as a middleman between Zstulkk Ssarmn's organization and third parties in need of certain services. It was the latter that Kexen expected. It just annoyed him to have to meet at the Pour House. For reasons inexplicable to Kexen, Thyld had chosen that time to hold their meet in the Lower Port tavern.

Kexen shifted in his chair—taking care not to upset either the rickety table or the even less stable cave viper affixed to his arm—and adjusted the two cocked and loaded magical hand crossbows he wore on his hips. He had taken them from the corpse of a drow mercenary he'd put down a year earlier. The open-bottom holsters, flexibly affixed to his weapon belt, permitted easy aiming and firing while still holstered, even under a table. The bolts carried a quick acting paralytic he'd purchased from a duergar herbalist. A professional precaution. The cutlass on his hip could serve too, if necessary.

Obviously, Kexen thought it unlikely that Thyld meant him harm, else he would not have come alone. In truth,

Thyld was naught but a scrawny skulker done well. Still, Kexen preferred to be overcautious rather than under-breathing. Operatives of the Xanathar knew Kexen to be a member of Zstulkk's organization. With a war in the offing between the yuan-ti slaver and the beholder crime lord, an overzealous servant of the Xanathar could decide to make a name by trying to put Kexen down. Best to be prepared. In Skullport, it always paid to be prudent.

Still, it made him uncomfortable that Thyld was late. It smelled ever-so-slightly of a set-up. Typically, Thyld was nothing if not punctual. He decided to give the ferret-nosed fool another hundred count and he would leave. He was busy with Zstulkk's business—a Luskan caravel filled with flesh was due in port within hours, and he needed to process the stock. He had only scant time to waste with Thyld.

As if summoned by Kexen's thoughts, the sea-shell curtain parted and there stood Thyld, balding head, nervous eyes, potbelly and all. Behind him lurked another man, tall and muscular, with a huge axe strapped across his back.

Kexen breathed easier. It was no set-up.

Thyld looked around the common room and Kexen hailed him with a raised hand—the hand attached to the arm free of a serpent. Thyld nodded his oversized head and waded his skinny body through the sea of sailors and whores. The large man followed, eyeing the sailors coldly.

Kexen figured the big man was an Amnian, possibly a ship's captain to judge from his bearing. He wore a threatening scowl and a dark cloak interlaced with silver thread.

Thyld slid into the chair opposite Kexen. He looked a bit different somehow but Kexen couldn't quite place the change. The big Amnian sank into the chair beside Thyld, bumping the table and nearly toppling Kexen's tankard. Thyld showed surprisingly quick reflexes in snatching the ale before it tipped.

"Kexen," Thyld said with his typical brisk nod. "This is . . . a client."

Thyld indicated the big man, who nodded.

"*Potential* client," Kexen corrected automatically. "Zstulkk takes only the highest paying jobs."

"Of course," Thyld acceded with a bow of his misshapen head. "This *potential* client needs goods moved and protected. I recommended Zstulkk, which naturally brought me to you."

"Naturally," Sessa hissed as she slithered down Kexen's forearm, head first.

The viper, concealed by Kexen's sleeve, went unnoticed by either Thyld or the Amnian. Her hissing voice was so quiet Kexen only barely heard her himself.

Kexen looked in the mustachioed face of the Amnian and asked, "Nature of the goods?"

"Where did you get that shirt?" asked Thyld, studying Kexen's overshirt.

He reached out a hand to touch the cuff and Sessa tensed.

Taken aback, Kexen looked curiously at Thyld, then at the black sleeves of the wool shirt he wore.

"Don't touch it," he said, and withdrew his arm. "What in the Hells kind of question is that?"

Thyld stiffened, frowned, and wagged a finger at Kexen.

"I've recently sworn off the use of expletives," he said. "Please refrain in my presence."

Never a man of quick temper, Kexen resisted the urge to shoot Thyld in the belly and walk away. Business was business.

"Very well," Kexen said to Thyld. He looked at the Amnian and asked again, "Nature of the goods?"

Sessa poked her head out from under Kexen's cuff, apparently to allow Zstulkk a better view of Thyld. Neither of the humans noticed the serpent and it quickly withdrew into the shirt sleeve.

"Highly magical," the big man replied to Kexen, with a curious sidelong look at Thyld. His voice was deep but had the lazy diction of a dullard. "Let us leave it at that."

Kexen nodded, unsurprised. Most of his clients were secretive about their wares. He didn't need, and typically didn't want to know what it was his men were guarding.

"Very well," said Kexen. "How many wagons will you need?"

After a thoughtful pause, the man replied, "Only one."

Kexen raised his eyebrows, looked to Thyld, and said, "You understand that I don't arrange transport unless the fee, in addition to expenses for the manpower, is in excess of a thousand gold?"

"We understand," Thyld replied with a smile.

His teeth, Kexen noted, were perfect; he had never noticed that before.

Thyld continued, "The cargo is extremely valuable and my companion here understands and accepts your minimum. He would want not fewer than twenty-five experienced men with substantial magical support. The latter is critical."

The Amnian nodded agreement.

Kexen raised his eyebrows and nodded. Whatever was in that wagon must be valuable indeed. Sessa gently coiled around his forearm, as though content.

"Costly," Kexen said. "Location?"

The big man shifted in his chair, shared a look with Thyld, and said, "A meet with a buyer two leagues into the northern tunnels of the Underdark."

Kexen ran some calculations through his head. The wilds of the Underdark were dangerous territory. He would need to hire experienced men, probably Underdark natives.

"Four thousand gold," he said, and quickly added, "and I do not haggle."

Sessa rested her head on his wrist.

The Amnian frowned, but Kexen could see the thoughts behind his eyes. The cargo was valuable, that much was obvious, and there were few organizations in Skullport with the manpower and expertise to provide the kind of protection Thyld and the Amnian had requested. Kexen sat in silence, waiting for the Amnian to draw the obvious conclusion.

"When can you have arrangements completed?" Thyld asked.

Kexen considered the question then said, "I'll let you know. But not longer than twelve cycles."

Thyld's eyes flashed excitement, and Kexen wondered what stake the skulker had in the cargo.

"Done," the Amnian said, and thumped his fist on the unsteady table, again nearly sending Kexen's beer to the floor.

Irritated with the sudden movement, Sessa hissed and her tongue flicked Kexen's arm. He kept it perfectly still. The two men across the table from him seemed not to have heard the serpent.

Thyld smiled and asked of Kexen, "I'll take my usual finder's fee?"

Kexen waved a dismissive hand and replied, "Of course."

"You can leave word for me here," the Amnian said. "I'll provide the wagon and pack lizards. You provide the men."

Kexen rose from the table, nodded at each of Thyld and the Amnian, and said, "I'm pleased we've reached an agreement. Expect to hear from me soon."

The Amnian nodded and Thyld smiled a mouthful of perfect teeth.

❧ ❧ ❧ ❧ ❧

A few cycles later, still dressed in Thyld's flabby, dirt-encrusted skin, Azriim stood unobtrusively to the side of a narrow Lower Trade Lane street and awaited Ahmaergo. The so-called "Horned Dwarf," a high-ranking member of the Xanathar's organization, had insisted on meeting Thyld in the open street. A symptom of the dwarf's well-known paranoia, Azriim assumed.

Azriim patted and pinched disgustedly at Thyld's pot-belly as he watched the slaves, sailors, and malnourished skulkers materialize out of the darkness and walk past. A squad of street sweepers hustled by, collecting the rothé dung and worse that littered Skullport's streets. No one seemed to notice Thyld, so unremarkable a being was the human.

What a pathetic life the man had led, Azriim thought. I did him a favor by eating his head.

A gang of six bugbear slave overseers emerged from a nearby street, each garbed in a leather jack, a series of piercings, and armed with a whip and axe. Laughing and talking loudly in their guttural tongue, they stomped in Azriim's direction. Their muscular, fur-covered bodies stank of alcohol and pent-up violence. Their bloodshot eyes promised a quick end to any who got in their way.

Like the rest of the skulkers on the street, Azriim-as-Thyld scurried out of their path. Though it galled him, Azriim avoided eye-contact and feigned fear until the savage, ill-dressed creatures passed him by.

Thyld's rag of a cloak, moist from the ever-damp air, chafed Azriim's skin. The irritation of his borrowed flesh mirrored his irritability of mind. He was bored. For a moment, he toyed with the idea of casting away his carefully planned ruse and simply attacking the Skulls outright. After all, he and his broodmates had deduced the general area in which must lay the Skulls' hidden lair, and there too must be the origin of Skullport's mantle.

He smiled at the thought but dismissed the idea. The Sojourner had instructed him to avoid alerting the Skulls until the seed was planted, and Azriim always obeyed the Sojourner, albeit grudgingly. Besides, the Skulls actually were formidable foes.

Azriim recognized the root of his boredom: things had gone too easily. He felt no challenge, and hence no thrill. He and his broodmates had surveilled the Skulls for over a tenday and located the vicinity of their lair, all the while avoiding notice. They had eliminated Thyld and Azriim had clandestinely stolen his skin and identity. They had annihilated a Xanathar caravan in under a ten count. And they had put an additional spark to the embers of a brewing gang war, embers that would turn into a wildfire after Azriim's meeting with Ahmaergo.

All too easy, he thought with a sigh. Even Dolgan could have planned it.

He adjusted the sling satchel he wore over his shoulder. Within were some of the magical items he'd taken from the slaughtered Xanathar caravan—fodder to feed Ahmaergo's ire. He put his back to the warped wooden wall of a brothel, and reminded himself that success in planting the seeds of the Weave Tap would result in his transformation to gray.

Above him, the windows of the brothel leaked giggles, growls, and playful screams. The faint smell of rotted flesh carried through the dark streets and filled his nostrils. Something nearby had died recently. Had he been in his own form, Azriim would have been able to pinpoint the source and the nature of the corpse. His senses in human form, however, were much too dull for such fine work.

Except for the tactile sense, Azriim reminded himself. Human skin was an unequalled medium for transmitting the pleasure of touch. Perhaps after his meeting with Ahmaergo, he would visit the brothel himself.

A few glowballs, seemingly in the possession of no one—escapees, no doubt, from one the city's glowball dealers—floated randomly down the narrow street. Otherwise, all was cloaked in the gloom of the Underdark. In the distance, the faint voice of a caller announced the hour. Dogs and cats scrounged the shadows of garbage-strewn streets. A gang of skulkers, scrawny adolescents all, lingered at the mouth of a nearby alley, whispering amongst themselves and sifting through a pile of trash. Most would eventually be rounded up by the Iron Ring and sold as slaves, Azriim knew, if the streets didn't claim them first.

The brothel against which Azriim leaned sat sandwiched

between a cooper's workshop and the Black Pot Inn. A black pot hung eponymously over the door of the dilapidated building. Smoke billowed out of the Black Pot's windows and Azriim caught the tantalizing tang of mistleaf. He resolved that if Ahmaergo did not soon show, he would take a meal at the inn and enjoy the smoke-saturated air. No doubt Thyld's body would feel the effects of the drug quickly.

Just as he was about to give up on the dwarf and head into the inn, Ahmaergo stomped into view. He appeared to be alone. Azriim grimaced, both because he would not yet get to enjoy the mistleaf haze and because the dwarf dressed like an idiot. Azriim was amazed that such a dolt could have risen so far within the Xanathar's organization.

Ahmaergo wore a bright yellow shirt with gaudy, embroidered cuffs, a wide black belt, black pantaloons, and enough jewelry to fill a wyrmling's hoard. A breastplate peeked from under the shirt, a helmet sprouting two horns sat atop his stewpot head, and a huge axe hung across his back. A large iron ring swimming with keys hung from Ahmaergo's belt—an indication of his profession as a slave trader.

Azriim surreptitiously attuned his vision to see dweomers and saw that the dwarf's armor, axe, horned helmet, two beard rings, and one of his front teeth all glowed red.

Though unfortunately dressed, Ahmaergo was powerfully built. The horned dwarf cut a swath through the street traffic by the sheer force of his reputation and physicality. Skulkers cleared a path for him more quickly than they had for the bugbears. The dwarf's heavy gaze looked out from under his thicket of brows, took in Azriim, those skulkers in the immediate vicinity, the layout of the buildings, the rooftops, and the catwalks overhead. Apparently satisfied with what he saw, the dwarf brushed past Azriim toward a nearby alley.

"Follow, Thyld," Ahmaergo ordered.

His voice sounded like stones grating against stones, and his key ring jangled.

Azriim fell in behind the dwarf.

The moment they got off the street and into the deeper darkness of the alley, Ahmaergo whirled on Azriim, took him in two ham hands, and smashed him up against the alley wall. Startled rats scurried past Azriim's feet and his breath went out of his lungs. Ribs cracked, but the rapid healing of his kind began to reknit them instantly. Ahmaergo punched him hard in the stomach. Azriim doubled over in agony, temporarily unable to breathe.

By the time he recovered himself, Ahmaergo had unslung his axe and had the shining head spike pointed at Azriim's chest.

"You've been in contact with that dog, Kexen, who serves that snake, Ssarmn," the dwarf spat, and pressed the tip of the head spike into Azriim's chest. "You trying to game me squid?"

Azriim took that last to be a derogatory reference to Thyld's membership in the Kraken Society.

"No ... game," Azriim replied, feigning fear and breathlessness.

The dwarf's gaze darkened.

"Anyone crosses Ahmaergo, that anyone decorates this axe with his blood."

With effort, Azriim resisted the temptation to smack Ahmaergo for referring to himself in the third person—a personal peeve of Azriim's. At least the dwarf didn't make casual use of expletives.

"I did meet with Kexen on a matter unrelated to you or the Xanathar," Azriim said. "But during that meeting he asked me if I could locate a buyer for certain magical goods."

Ahmaergo managed to keep his crenellated face expressionless, but Azriim sensed the sudden tension in his body. For days, Skullport's underworld had been abuzz with news of an ambushed Xanathar caravan and its store of magical goods. The Xanathar, Azriim knew, was eager to avenge the attack and needed only the slightest nudge to move against Ssarmn.

"Continue," the dwarf commanded. "And be truthful. If Ahmaergo does not like your story, he can have your corpse questioned almost as easily as your living body."

Azriim let his eyes show concern, though he felt an almost uncontrollable compulsion to gut Ahmaergo.

"Here is evidence of the truth, Ahmaergo," Azriim said.

He unslung the satchel bag at his shoulder, and the head spike of the axe pressed more firmly into his chest.

"Slowly," Ahmaergo said, his voice low and dangerous.

Azriim nodded and reached into the satchel. From within, he slowly withdrew four garnet-tipped wooden wands wrapped in leather oilcloth. The appearance of the magical devices had the desired effect. Ahmaergo lowered his axe and seized them from Azriim's hand.

"How did you get these?" he asked.

Azriim kept the smile from his lips. "I had a contact arrange the purchase from Kexen. These wands are from among those items for which he asked me to find a buyer. It seems he has many more. When I heard about the . . . unfortunate events that befell one of the Xanathar's caravans, I purchased only these, declined further dealings with Kexen, and resolved to inform you."

"Ssarmn," Ahmaergo hissed.

"Indeed," Azriim said. "And there is still more, Ahmaergo." He adopted the mien of Thyld-the-businessman. "We need only discuss my price first."

The horned dwarf was notoriously cheap, but he surprised Azriim by saying, "Name it."

"Four thousand in gold coins," Azriim said. "Waterdhavian mintage."

That amount was the exact fee that Kexen had charged Azriim and Dolgan to provide an armed escort for the bait caravan. Azriim enjoyed the symmetry.

"Very well," Ahmaergo said. "But if this is a set-up, Thyld, or if you tell me a half-truth . . . death will not come quickly."

Azriim feigned the appropriate amount of fear while saying, "If I wanted to set you up, I would have employed a middleman to convey this information."

Ahmaergo tilted his head to concede the point. He also put the wands in an inner pocket of his shirt. Apparently, the dwarf meant to keep them.

Azriim closed his satchel bag and went on, "I have learned that Kexen has arranged for a heavily armed troop of over twenty men and mages to escort a caravan into the northern caves of the Underdark within the next eight cycles." Azriim and Dolgan were still negotiating the exact time with Kexen. "The remainder of the magical goods are to be in that caravan. I believe he used another agent to arrange a meeting with a buyer."

The creases in Ahmaergo's brow deepened to chasms.

"Twenty you say, eh?" He reslung his axe. "You stick down the time and tell me immediately. I know those tunnels. That caravan won't get more than a quarter league into those tunnels before I kill them all."

Azriim had to hold back a smile. He knew the tunnels too, and thought he guessed the likely spot that Ahmaergo would set up the ambush.

"I expected nothing less, Ahmaergo," he said.

CHAPTER 13

In the Deep

Cale came back to himself in darkness, floating on his back in water as black and cold as a devil's heart. The weight of his gear threatened to pull him under. While not a strong swimmer he managed, sputtering, to right himself and stay afloat. His skin was clammy and tingled with gooseflesh. His breath sounded loud in his own ears. He knew he had to get out of the cold water quickly or it would suck the body heat from him. The last thing he remembered he had been rolling, tumbling, falling forever over the Dragon's Jaws—and he found himself somewhere else, with his head above water. A gentle current propelled him slowly downstream.

A vast, winding tunnel loomed over him and ran before and behind as far as he could see. The wide, curving ribbon of the river in which he swam tracked the tunnel's course, its water still and foreboding. Sharp-tipped stalactites hung from the ceiling, a crowd of pointed fingers accusing the river of something unspeakable. Water dripped from many of the stalactites to *plop*, with ominous echoes, into the water. Phosphorescent orange lichen clung in sporadic patches to the crannies of the rough wall and ceiling. The plants cast little light and Cale could see in the otherwise pitch darkness only because of his transformed vision. Jagged rocks and stalagmites littered the narrow riverbanks to either side. Smaller side caves too dotted the riverbanks, holes in the walls of the river's channel that led off into darkness. Some caves were large enough for an ogre, some were small enough to accommodate only a halfling. Some had been worked, others were natural. Bats fluttered overhead. The damp air carried a mineral tang.

The Underdark, Cale realized.

He was half a league under Faerûn's surface in a world that never saw the sun. He felt comfortable with the darkness, but uncomfortable with the comfort. And the realization that the world literally hung over his head gave him a sense of oppression that he could not shake.

"Jak," he called, and his voice echoed loudly in the tunnel, reverberating down the river's course as if there were ten of him. He winced, and more softly called, "Magadon. Riven?"

"Here," Magadon responded, from somewhere to Cale's right. A soft splashing sounded. "I've got Riven. He's alive, but nearly drowned."

With effort, Cale paddled himself around and saw the guide's head bobbing above the water a stone's throw behind him. Magadon had an arm wrapped around the unconscious Riven's throat and used his other hand to help keep them both afloat.

"Jak?" Cale asked.

"I don't see him," Magadon answered.

Cale spun around, kicked himself as high out of the

water as he could, and scanned the dark surface. The halfling was nowhere to be seen.

"Jak!" Cale called.

He swam through the water between him and Magadon, spreading his arms out wide, waving them under the water, increasingly concerned. He swallowed several mouthfuls of river water; it tasted like iron.

"Jak! Little man!"

Cale's hand brushed up against a small form floating just under the water. He grabbed the halfling by the hair and pulled him to the surface. Jak's eyes were closed; his face pale. Cale couldn't tell if he was breathing. He wrapped an arm around him and held his head out of the water.

"I've got him, Mags," said Cale. "But he looks nearly drowned too." He scanned the riverbank. "That beach to our right, the one with the clear spot between the tall boulders. See it?"

"I see it," Magadon said.

For the first time it occurred to Cale that Magadon appeared to see well in darkness too. Another gift from his fiendish father, Cale supposed.

A dim white luminescence flared on the beach between the boulders—Magadon's psionic power manifesting. Pale lizards scrabbled out of the sudden light, and bats fluttered in agitation above.

"Get Jak to shore," Magadon said. "I'll bring Riven."

With Jak in his arms, Cale shadowstepped from the water to the beach.

Behind him, Magadon swam for the shore, dragging the unconscious Riven and grunting as he splashed through the water.

Cale laid Jak down on his back on the beach, just at the perimeter of Magadon's psionic light, and tapped the halfling's cheeks. No response. Cale pulled his soaked mask from his pocket, laid his regenerated hand on Jak's chest, and whispered the words to a healing spell. Still nothing.

"Mags. . . ."

"Turn him around, hold him upright, and squeeze his chest," Magadon called, still swimming. "His lungs are filled with water."

Cale nodded, picked the halfling up from under his armpits, adjusted his hold, and squeezed his ribcage.

"Jak!"

The halfling lay limp in Cale's grasp. He squeezed again.

With shocking suddenness, the halfling spasmed back to life, coughed up a stomachful of river water, then immediately vomited his partially-digested rations from breakfast. Cale couldn't help but smile. He lowered Jak, still coughing, to the ground.

Cale knelt beside him, put a hand on his shoulder, and asked, "Are you all right?"

Jak coughed a bit more and dry heaved before the fit passed.

He groaned and managed a weak, "I'm all right. Thanks."

Cale nodded, thinking that Jak still looked pale.

By the time Magadon neared the shore, Riven had already regained consciousness.

"I can swim, godsdamnit," said Riven, sputtering. "I don't need to be ca—"

The assassin inhaled a mouthful of water, sending him off into a fit of coughing and cursing.

"Keep your mouth closed," Magadon ordered.

The guide continued to swim to shore until they reached the shallows and could wade. There, he helped Riven get his feet under him and the two stumbled onto the beach.

"You look like all Nine Hells," Riven said to Jak.

The halfling was too tired to respond.

With all of them safely on the black sand beach, they sagged to the ground and lay there for a time, saying nothing, with Faerûn for a ceiling and a score of stone points aimed at their chests.

"We convinced the river fey," Magadon said at last, with a touch too much disbelief.

"You sound surprised," Cale said.

Magadon shook his head, sat up, and wrung out his hat. Somehow, he had managed to keep it, though he had lost his oversized backpack to the river.

"Not surprised, just . . . pleased. What did you tell him?" the guide asked Cale.

"What I plan to do someday," Cale answered.

Magadon accepted that without further questions.

Once Jak was more or less recovered, he looked around with interest. He took in the tunnel, the river, and the darkness.

"The Underdark, eh?" he said, and reached for his pipe. He frowned when he found it and the pipeweed sodden. "You have any dry leaf, Zhent?" he asked Riven.

"You ought not smoke, Jak," Magadon admonished.

The halfling waved the guide's advice aside and said, "I'm guilty of a handful of vices, Magadon. I'll not let a little river water keep me from my favorite."

Magadon said nothing and Riven tossed Jak his tin.

Jak popped it open and smiled when he saw that the interior was still dry. The halfling tamped the pipe and tried to light it, but the river had left his tindertwigs soaked. Cale smiled at Jak's forlorn expression.

"That's Tymora looking out for you, Jak," said Magadon. "Smoke later."

"First thing I get when we get to Skullport," the halfling said, "is a tindertwig."

He tossed the dry tin of pipeweed back to Riven, who absently snatched it from the air.

Riven climbed to his feet and wrung out his cloak and gear as much as he could.

"We follow the river's current," the assassin said. "It empties into the harbor outside Skullport. The cavern containing the city is not far."

They all nodded but no one else stood. Cale gave Jak and Magadon a short time more to recover themselves before climbing to his feet.

"Ready?" he asked and extended a hand to Jak.

"Ready," Jak answered.

He took Cale's hand and pulled himself up.

Magadon rose, checked his blades, inventoried his gear not lost to the river, and nodded.

The City of Skulls and the slaadi awaited.

☉ ☉ ☉ ☉ ☉

Following Riven's lead, they picked their way between the sharp rocks along the riverbank's black sand beaches for what felt to Jak like hours. The phosphorescent lichen provided just enough light to travel by, albeit slowly. Throughout, the halfling alternated his gaze between the water and the cave mouths that opened in the wall of the tunnel. Both the water and caves were black and quiet, as though they hid dark secrets. They made Jak nervous.

"They're just holes Fleet," Riven said, "and ordinary river water. In truth, I'm surprised we've seen no ships. There are invisible, intangible portals all along the river, each made visible and operational by a unique magical phrase. That's how most of the slave ships arrive and leave."

Jak noticed that Riven's voice dropped slightly when he said the word "slave." The halfling wondered but did not ask if the assassin had been crewman or cargo the last time he'd set foot in the City of Skulls. Riven offered nothing more, and they continued onward.

After a time the river and the riverbanks began to widen. From ahead, carrying down the tunnel, Jak caught the faint sound of voices and activity. A short time later, its source still hidden behind a curve in the passage, Jak saw a soft orange glow reflecting off the black water ahead: flickering firelight, rather than the steady, dimmer orange phosphorescence of the ubiquitous lichen.

Riven stopped and turned around to face them, as though he had just made up his mind about something.

"We're nearly there, now," said the assassin. "Remember what I said. We keep a light tread here. Do not attract the attention of the Skulls. I've seen what they can do." He looked hard at Jak and Cale. "You're going to see things here. . . ." He trailed off, shook his head and stated, "You cannot right what's wrong with this place. Understood?"

Cale and Jak shared a look but both nodded. Jak wondered what Skullport could offer that he had not seen before. He supposed he would know soon enough.

Seemingly satisfied, Riven turned and led them forward.

While they walked, Jak fell in beside Cale and whispered, "I've never seen the Zhent so agitated."

He watched the assassin's back—the tension visible there—and wondered again what had happened to Riven in Skullport.

Softly, Cale replied, "Me either."

Jak heard something odd in Cale's voice, something like guilt.

He looked up at his friend and asked, "What is it?"

Cale rested his shadow-birthed hand on his sword hilt and gave Jak a forced smile.

"Nothing, little man. Just thinking."

Before Jak could press further, he noticed something unusual about Cale's sword. Fine wisps of shadow clung to Weaveshear's scabbard, leaking through the leather and swirling around the hilt.

"Your blade," Jak said, a bit more sharply than he had intended.

Riven and Magadon heard Jak's exclamation and turned to look. Cale looked at the blade, at each of them, and nodded.

"It's been like this from the start and it's getting worse as we get closer to the city. It's the magic here, I think. It's attracted to it, as though it wants to be unsheathed."

Riven's eye narrowed in a way that Jak did not like.

"If that steel draws the Skulls' attention, *First* of Five," the assassin warned, "this little dance is going to end early."

Jak thought much the same thing.

"Then let's just stay smart," the halfling said. "We

tread lightly and keep our steel in our scabbards until we find the slaadi."

"It's nothing more than shadows," Cale added. "It won't draw anyone's attention."

Riven said nothing, only turned on his heel and continued on.

Cale, Jak, and Magadon followed.

After only a short distance more, the tunnel through which the Sargauth flowed opened without warning onto a breathtaking cavern that formed an underwater bay as large as many surface lakes. Delicate, natural stone spires rose out of the still water to merge with stalactites hanging from the ceiling—and those melded, majestic pillars of stone were the only visible support for the cavern. Jak didn't need the stonelore of a dwarf to know that magic must have buttressed the cavern. Otherwise, it would have long ago collapsed of its own weight. He looked at the shadows still clinging to Cale's blade and thought that Weaveshear must have been responding to the presence of that supportive magic.

Perhaps that was the very magic the slaadi intended to drain with the Weave Tap? Jak wondered. He didn't care to think what might happen if the slaadi succeeded. The whole cavern would collapse, crushing everyone.

In the center of the dark bay stood a rocky island adorned with a brooding fortress of gray stone. Orc and human guards patrolled the parapets. Torches hung from the walls, casting the pockmarked stone in shadow. The dark windows looked like mouths open and screaming. Looking at that fortress gave Jak gooseflesh.

"Skull Island" Riven said, following Jak's gaze. "Fortress of the Iron Ring, the master slavers of Skullport. All slaves in the city start there for . . . for treatment. Not our problem, Fleet."

Jak nodded, but thought he heard in Riven's low tone a promise: Not *yet* our problem. Yet again he wondered what had happened to Riven in the Port of Skulls.

A thick stone arch spanned the water, reaching across

the bay from the edge of Skull Island to disappear around the curve in the tunnel. Torches burned at even intervals across the bridge. A few fishermen—two of whom were goblins—sat on the edge of the span with their lines lowered into the dark water. Several coffles of slaves shambled across its length toward Skull Island harried all the while by savage, whip-wielding bugbears.

Seeing the poor slaves and imagining what awaited them in the Iron Ring's Tower caused Jak's gorge to rise.

Perhaps the slaadi *should* succeed, he thought. The destruction of Skullport might be a blessing for Faerûn.

"This way," Riven said, leading them onward.

They continued to hug the bank, drawing closer and closer to the darkest hole in Faerûn. They passed several small fishing boats tethered to rocks, posts, and makeshift docks. They also passed several fishermen—mostly goblins and thin humans in tatters. No one spoke to them and they spoke to no one, though all eyed them with suspicious, furtive gazes.

At some point, the black sand beach gave way to a packed earth path that hugged the cavern's wall. They walked single file.

Skullport's piers came into view first: twenty or so timeworn wooden quays that jutted into the waters of the bay. Each sat on stout wooden posts that Jak thought must surely once have been masts. Ships floated in perhaps half of the berths. Jak noted a longship, several clippers, a wide-bottomed river barge, even a schooner from the Inner Sea. Lanterns and glowballs hung from the gunwales of many of the ships. Shadowy figures, their identities lost in the darkness, unloaded crates and people from the holds. Heavier cargo was lifted out with rope and a block and tackle attached to wooden posts near the berth. Goblin deckhands swarmed the wharves shoreside, carrying crates, rope, and urns off the ships to waiting lizard-pulled wagons. Armed overseers shepherded, monitored, and sometimes whipped the living cargo that emerged from the holds.

Most of the slaves were human, though Jak saw elves, dwarves, and even a few gnomes. He also saw many women and a few terrified children. The sight nearly undid him. He had to stop walking. He bent at the waist, hands on his hips, and took a series of deep breaths. He did not think he could keep down the vomit.

"Keep yourself in one piece, Fleet," Riven growled.

"Shut your hole," Cale said, and placed his hand on Jak's shoulder. "Look at it all, little man. Look at it and remember. We'll come back one day. I promise. And when we do we'll visit the Iron Ring."

Jak heard in Cale's voice the same steel he'd heard when Cale had faced off Vraggen under the Twisted Elm. Violence lurked in that tone; righteous fury. Jak had no doubt that Cale intended to return, that he *would* return.

The thought somehow made the scene a little less abominable, but only a little. He patted Cale's hand in gratitude, recovered himself, and looked at it, remembered it. He signaled to Riven that he was ready to move on.

The path widened into a road that ran along the wharves. A vast cavern opened off of the bay and retreated into the bedrock of the Underdark. To Jak, it looked like the open mouth and twisting gullet of a beast, more a Dragon's Jaws than the falls along the Dragon Coast could ever aspire to. Within it, covering it like the black rot, stood the City of Skulls, an amazing hodgepodge of dilapidated buildings. Many were stacked atop each other; others clung precariously to the cavern's walls.

A bewildering array of rope bridges, swings, and wooden planks hung between the upper buildings and extended back into the cavern, the highest of which stood a bowshot above the cavern's floor. Busy with a steady stream of foot traffic, they vibrated like spiderwebs.

On the cavern floor between the wharves and the city itself stood a great market. There, illithids, duergar, trolls, ogres, orcs, and the worst of humankind bought and sold the unfortunate creatures who stood atop the tall selling blocks. Bids carried to Jak's ears and an excited hum electrified the still air.

They would have to walk through the slave market to get into the city.

Jak felt lightheaded. Cale fell in beside him.

"Find the strength, little man," Cale said. "I need you here. Don't surrender to this place. And don't give Riven the satisfaction."

Jak managed a nod. He was clutching his holy symbol so tightly it was digging into the flesh of his palm.

"The city is unguarded?" Magadon asked Riven, obviously trying to distract Jak. "We can just walk in from the wilds of the Underdark?"

Riven nodded toward the stalactite-dotted ceiling and replied, "It's not unguarded, Mags."

Jak looked to the ceiling. There, high above the wharves and the market day crowd, nearly hidden in the stalactites, floated a softly glowing Skull. Its empty eyeholes moved back and forth over the market, over the wharves, over them, seeing all. Jak felt the weight of its gaze like a physical blow. Involuntarily, he quailed.

Cale took him by the arm and pulled him along. Weaveshear continued to leak darkness, but the Skull seemed to take no notice.

"Don't stare, Fleet," Riven said to Jak, then turned to Magadon. "Even if it was unguarded, Mags, what would it matter? The worst of the Underdark is welcomed here, not fenced out."

To that, Magadon said nothing.

Together, the four comrades picked their way along the wharves, dodging the filthy goblin deckhands, bugbear overseers, and slaves. The ringing clang of chains was everywhere, and slaves were everywhere. With an effort of will, Jak resisted the impulse to comfort the captives and kill their sadistic overseers.

When Jak saw that animated corpses worked beside the goblins and sailors to unload some of the cargo, his knees again went weak. The stink of their rotting corpses revived his nausea. Cale steadied him.

"It's too much, Cale," he said softly.

"No, it's not," Cale replied.

They made their way into the market. The smell of sweat, rot, and decaying fish filled Jak's nostrils. Torches and glowballs illuminated the horror. And the sounds. . . .

Jak tried to filter out the hopeless groans and screams of the many slaves, the ring of chains, the eager snarls of the hungry buyers, and the shouted bids of the would-be purchasers. The market was as much an eatery as a labor pool. Jak saw an illithid—right out in public—immobilize an enspelled teenaged boy and begin to burrow its facial tentacles into his skull. He could not bear it.

"Cale," he said between gritted teeth, averting his eyes.

"Straight through, Riven," Cale said, still pulling Jak along at a near jog. "Get us to a room."

Riven looked back and nodded. His one eye fixed on Jak and the halfling was surprised to see in his gaze not contempt but understanding. For a reason he could not explain, Jak felt comforted.

Riven led them into the maze of narrow streets and alleys that was Skullport proper. Leaving behind the relative openness of the market plaza, Jak felt as if he were walking down the gullet of a beast. While the port and its markets had been relatively well-lit to show the merchandise, farther into Skullport pedestrians and shopkeepers had to provide their own light—at least those who wanted it. Only an occasional torch or glowball lifted the darkness. People, creatures, stink, and trash thronged the narrow thoroughfares.

Jak started to pull his bluelight wand from his pocket but Cale stopped him.

"No light," Cale said. "It would be like carrying a beacon here."

Riven nodded agreement, though Jak knew the assassin couldn't see well in the poorly-lit streets. Jak's halfling blood allowed him to see well enough in darkness, but the black still caused him to feel isolated. They moved deeper and deeper into the city. The halfling felt as though he was swimming underwater, discovering what lay ahead only when it was already dangerously near, and instantly losing to the darkness everything that passed behind.

Side by side, Riven and Cale shouldered their way through orcs, ogres, sailors, whores, even a pair of trolls. Open sewers yawned like burst boils in the streets, churning out vileness. Great shaggy rothé, the cows of the Underdark, lowed from their pens.

Eventually they found themselves outside of a ramshackle inn. Riven seemed to know it. A rusty anchor hung from hooks over the crooked door. Jak assumed the "Rusty Anchor" to be the name of the place.

Riven turned and was about to say something when a bearded old man in tattered breeches, covered in nothing but dirt from the waist up, stepped out of the street crowd and lunged at Cale, arms outstretched. Cale had a hand on his throat and Weaveshear at his belly before the old man touched him. The sword leaked darkness. The old man paid it no heed. Jak checked above them. There was no sign of the Skulls, and no sign of interest from the passersby on the catwalks.

The old man's eyes were wild.

"There's a hole in the sun," he said to Cale intently, spraying spittle. "A dark hole in the sun. Do you see it?"

Cale took him gently by the shoulders and moved him away. The man stumbled and fell in with the other street traffic, still babbling.

"He's mad," Magadon observed.

Cale nodded but seemed thoughtful.

"Cale seems to attract those sorts," Riven said without a smile. "I'll get a room."

Cale said, "We move every twenty-four hours, Riven.

Like you said, we maintain a soft footprint. No pattern. We'll try finding them first. If that doesn't work. . . ."

"We'll let them find us," Riven finished, and entered the inn.

Jak, Magadon, and Cale waited in the street, tense and still damp from their time in the Sargauth.

Riven soon returned, having procured their lodging.

When they entered the wood-floored common room, Jak barely noticed the corpulent innkeeper, the wolf-eyed patrons, the barmaids, the smoke, and the whores. He made straight for the stairs, straight for their room, and it was only after he got behind a closed door that he felt like he could breathe. After he recovered himself he realized he'd forgotten to buy a tindertwig, but he didn't care.

CHAPTER 14

CHANCE ENCOUNTERS

Though Cale had no reason to suspect that Azriim or the other slaadi knew that he and his comrades were in Skullport, he thought it prudent to ward each of them with a spell that would prevent them from being easily scried. He also sought to minimize the times they appeared together on the street or in public. Accordingly, they took their dinner—salted fungus, a stew sprinkled with rothé meat, and cellar-cooled mushroom ale—in pairs, each protected by a magical ward that Cale and Jak would have to periodically renew.

Cale took his meal with Riven. They needed to plan.

Sweating patrons thronged the Rusty Anchor's common room. Cale hadn't seen quite such a pack of rogues since his days in Westgate. To a man, all of the patrons wore sharp steel and hard looks: duergar slavers, human and half-orc sailors, mercenaries, even the goblin laborers squawking over a game of dice looked seasoned. No doubt Skullport had long ago culled the weak from the flock.

The pungent smoke from the dried fungus that substituted for pipeweed in Skullport cloaked the room in a thin, brown haze. From time to time, Cale caught an acrid whiff of crushed mistleaf, a powerful narcotic, wafting up from the basement.

Professional women were as ubiquitous as the smoke, all of them wearing alluring smiles and scant clothing. Cale and Riven had already made their disinterest plain. A steady stream of paired men and women moved up and down the small staircase that led to the Anchor's dark basement, where the women plied their trade.

Apparently, the Anchor was inn, brothel, and drug den all in one. The rooms upstairs provided lodging for travelers. The rooms in the basement were home to courtesans, mistleaf sellers, and their respective clients.

The boisterous crowd—drinking, smoking, whoring, eating, and gaming—created a tumult so loud that Cale and Riven had to sit close just to hear one another. That was well, Cale figured. The raucousness ensured that they would not stand out and would not be overheard.

"We're here," Riven said. "So what's the play?"

Cale held his tongue as a dark-eyed barmaid placed full tankards of ale on the table before them. Her black hair and high cheekbones reminded him of Tazi.

"Thank you," Cale said to her, loud enough to be heard above the raucousness.

She looked at him as though she had never before heard the words. Under her gaze, for a reason he could not explain, he felt keenly conscious and vaguely ashamed of his transformed flesh. She was attractive, he saw, even with a sheen of sweat coating her face and tired circles painting the skin under her eyes. She started to say something but thought better of it. Behind her, a patron shouted for another round. She gave a smile that barely moved her mouth, nodded to acknowledge Cale's gratitude, and walked away. Cale admired the sway of her hips as she moved between the tables, thinking again of how much she reminded him of Tazi.

He shook his head as he turned back to Riven, back to business. Riven wanted the play. Unfortunately, they had little information upon which to operate. They knew the slaadi were in Skullport for a reason related to the Weave Tap—no doubt they hoped to drain the magic of the Skulls, or perhaps the magic that supported the cavern itself. But Cale didn't know exactly how or when the slaadi were going to do it. He would not be able to attempt to scry Azriim until midnight, when he again prayed to Mask for power.

They had no answers, only questions, only uncertainties. So the play would be the same in Skullport as it would be anywhere else.

"Turn angler, find a long-tongue who knows something," Cale said, easily falling back into the cant of the professional. "We know Azriim has taken the form of a duergar and a half-drow. Start there."

Riven took a draw on his ale.

"Neither of those are exactly rare here," he replied.

Cale could only agree. Duergar and drow were as common in Skullport as the damp.

"The slaadi are staying low, Riven," he said, his thoughts solidifying as he spoke. "That's why Azriim is changing forms. Whatever they're planning, it's big enough that they want to give no sign beforehand and leave no trail afterward. If you don't have any luck quickly, we'll make ourselves obvious and try to draw them out."

Riven's one-eyed gaze was piercing and he did not smile.

"Still Cale the clever, eh?"

Cale made no reply, instead took a drink of his ale. He looked across the table and realized that he had slowly, as slowly as the southern movement of the Great Glacier, come to rely on Riven. The realization made him uneasy.

To hide his discomfort, he said, "Just be quick."

Riven sneered, nodded, and slammed down the rest of his ale. He started to rise—

And from the other side of the common room, Cale heard a deep voice proclaim over the tumult, "Once a whore, always a whore."

A bout of harsh laughter followed. Cale turned in his chair to see a muscular man, bristling with steel and covered in leather, pull the dark-haired barmaid onto his lap.

"Come here," the man said.

The four comrades who shared the man's table smiled stupidly at the sport. They too wore leather jacks, swords, and daggers. Cale made the lot as mercenaries.

Fighting off the sellsword's groping hands, the barmaid forced an insincere smile and squirmed to free herself. Cale couldn't hear her over the patrons, but read her lips when she spoke.

"Let me go," she said, and her eyes featured an edge that Cale did not miss. "I'm working."

The man grinned, jiggled her breast and gave it a squeeze, hard enough to elicit a wince.

"Oh, you're working all right," he bellowed, and his comrades joined him in laughter. "I've got a job for you."

With impressive suddenness, the barmaid slammed the heel of her shoe onto the big mercenary's boot, smashing his toes. He howled with pain, clutched at his foot, and she leaped to her feet and started to scramble away.

Before she could get out of arms' reach, the mercenary, still red-faced with pain, lashed out with his other hand and grabbed a handful of her hair. Jerking her backward, he nearly pulled her from her feet. She squealed with pain and fell to the floor before him.

"You sneaky little bitch!" he roared. "You stay just like that."

He stood and reached for the laces of his trousers.

Cale jumped to his feet. He was conscious of shadows leaking from his fingertips.

"Do not," Riven hissed, and grabbed his wrist. "She's just a tavern wench. If this escalates. . . ."

Cale took Riven's point—if a fight escalated too far, it could draw the Skulls—but he would not stand idly by while the woman was assaulted.

Before he could say a word, the mercenary noticed him. Cale was grateful for it. The big sellsword left off undressing and pointed a finger and hard look at Cale.

"Something you want to say, scarecrow?" the big man asked.

All eyes turned to Cale. The common room went as silent as a tomb. Even the goblins left off their game. Mindful of Riven's point, Cale kept his eyes on the barmaid and tried to diffuse the situation.

"My tankard is empty, woman," he said to her. "A refill, if you please."

The woman, still on her knees with her hair in the mercenary's grasp, looked at him as though he were mad.

"She'll fill it when I'm done with her," the mercenary said, his heavy brow knotting.

He shook her by the hair and she screamed in pain. No one laughed except for the mercenary's four tablemates, and their laughter was far from mirthful. Everyone else seemed to be waiting.

Cale's gaze narrowed. He found that he had taken a step toward the mercenaries' table. Several of the patrons began to whisper behind their hands.

"I'm thirsty *now*," he said, and despite Riven's admonition, he let a note of challenge creep into his tone.

The mercenary caught it. He flung the barmaid to the floor and straightened his tunic. He stood a hand shorter than Cale, but had a third-again Cale's bulk. He rested his hands on the hilts of the daggers at his belt. The four comrades that shared the sellsword's table smiled and ribbed each other.

Cale took their measure with an eye long trained in

evaluating professionals: the four at the table he deemed nothing more than inexperienced pups. If their lead dog went down, they'd skulk away with their tails between their legs. The big man, on the other hand, wore his blades with comfort. But Cale figured the man's intimidating size had kept him out of more fights than his skill had won.

As though echoing his thoughts, Riven said in a low tone, "You put the oaf down quick and it's over. Those four will never draw steel."

"You say something, boy?" the big man asked Riven.

Cale could imagine, even if he couldn't see, Riven's sneer.

"I'll leave him to you," Riven said softly. "But I'm tempted now."

The mercenary fixed his gaze on Cale and said in a voice fat with threatened violence, "When I'm done with her, is what I said."

Free from the mercenary's clutches, the barmaid climbed to her feet and adjusted her dress, avoiding eye contact with the sellsword.

"Bitch," the mercenary said again.

She ignored him, stepped into the space between the two men, and walked for Cale. Cale admired her dignity.

"Coming now, sir," she said. "A tankard of ale, you said?"

With her back to the mercenary, her eyes and expression told Cale to let it go. No doubt the sellsword had a reputation in the Rusty Anchor. Instead of disabusing her of the man's relative competence, Cale calmed himself and decided to give the mercenary a chance to walk away.

"It appears you're done," Cale said.

He turned and sat at the table, showing the mercenaries his back. Riven looked past him while the barmaid hurried over, thumped into their table in her haste, and picked up Cale's tankard. She nearly spilled it in surprise when she realized that it was full.

"He's dangerous," she hissed at them.

Riven sneered, but Cale said nothing, only listened.

From behind, he heard the scrape of wooden chairs being pushed back. An anticipatory sussurance ran around the common room. There was no city watch there, Cale knew, and even the innkeeper was nowhere to be seen; he was probably semi-conscious in the drug den downstairs.

"We ain't finished, scarecrow," said the mercenary.

Cale sighed. He had seen idiots like that sellsword in countless taverns in Westgate and Selgaunt—fool kings of a few slat boards and a greasy table who picked fights with strangers in an effort to secure their kingdoms.

"Oh, gods," the woman said in a whisper. "Don't get hurt on my account."

Cale and Riven shared a look. It wasn't Cale who would get hurt.

"Here they come," Riven said, and Cale sensed the dangerous quiet in the assassin's tone.

"Leave it to me," Cale said.

He rose, turned, and stepped away from the table. Cale put himself in front of the barmaid.

The big mercenary snaked his way through the tables and enthralled patrons, and stalked toward Cale, scowling. Cale gave no ground, and soon they stood face to face. The sellsword's four comrades stayed a few paces behind, still wearing idiot smiles.

"When I'm done with her, I said," the mercenary said. His breath stank of sour ale; his clothes of mistleaf. He looked past Cale to the barmaid and said, "I'm not through with you, whore."

"I'm no more a whore than you are a man," she said.

Cale enjoyed the rush of anger visible on the sellsword's face. He allowed shadows to swirl around him and stared into the mercenary's scarred face.

"Apologize," Cale said.

The mercenary's eyes narrowed. His bravado seemed unaffected by the wisps of shadows swirling around Cale.

"What did you say, scarecrow?"

"To her," Cale said, staring down into the man's face. "Apologize. Now."

The mercenary licked his lips. He seemed taken aback by Cale's calm.

"If the next words that come out of your mouth aren't an apology," Cale said, "things will turn out badly."

The mercenary responded with arrogance and a sneer, the latter a poor, distant cousin to Riven's perfected expression of disdain.

"You think you can—"

Fueled by his shadow-enhanced speed and strength, Cale drove his palm into the underside of the mercenary's jaw before the man said another word. Teeth snapped shut on the man's tongue and a spray of blood exploded from his mouth. The man staggered backward, but still managed to lash out a weak punch with his other hand. Cale caught him by the forearm, yanked him forward and slammed his hand down on the table near Riven. The man punched Cale in the back of the head—a weak blow—while Cale drew a dagger and with it nailed the man's palm to the wood.

While the mercenary was still screaming, Cale yanked the dagger free, elbowed him hard in the face, and stuck the dagger at his throat.

"Apologize to her," he commanded. "Now."

Bleeding from mouth and hand, breathing like a bellows, the mercenary glared hate at Cale through eyes watery with pain. His unwounded hand floated near one of his daggers. Cale pricked his neck.

"You're done here," Cale said. "You can walk out, or be carried."

The man stared at him, and must have seen his resolve.

After an additional moment of hesitation, he muttered to the barmaid, "Sorry."

She was too shocked to respond.

"Is that acceptable?" Cale asked her over his shoulder.

She offered a nod, eyes wide.

"You made a mistake, is all," Cale said, trying to offer

the man some dignity. "You've been drinking. But now you're leaving. You and your friends."

Behind him, he heard Riven begin to chuckle.

The mercenary's four comrades grumbled and moved a step closer. Hands went to hilts, but Cale saw the lack of resolve in their eyes.

Riven stopped chuckling.

"I wouldn't," the assassin said to them. "Or five get carried out."

They backed off. Cale pushed the big mercenary toward them.

The big man staggered into his comrades, shook off their assistance, wiped his bloody mouth, and cradled his pierced hand. Mumbling half-hearted threats and curses, the five sellswords walked out of the Anchor. Cale and Riven watched them go.

The instant they exited, the common room resumed its normal pulse.

"Dead in the dirt," Riven said to Cale, shaking his head with disapproval. "That's my rule when I pull steel."

"Not mine," said Cale.

He sat, and the barmaid, visibly shaking, started to clear his tankard.

"I-I'll get you another," she said in a quavering voice.

Cale touched her hand—it was warm and soft—and guided the tankard to the table.

"It's still full," he reminded her. "Did he hurt you?"

She looked down at the mercenary's blood that stained the table.

"I've had worse," she said.

Cale didn't doubt it.

"What's your name?" he asked.

He realized he was still touching her hand, and let her go. She looked him in the eye and Cale saw strength there, and pain.

"Varra," she said. "Thank you for . . . that."

Cale nodded an acknowledgment. He thought her name a nice one.

"When do you go home, Varra?"

Her gaze narrowed and she flushed.

"What? Why do you ask? What that oaf said—It's not true of me, not anymore. I'm not—"

It took Cale a moment to understand her meaning. When he did, he felt his own ears flush. "That's not what I meant," he said, waving a hand. "I meant that I would escort you home."

He saw that she didn't understand his offer.

"Men like that,"—he nodded at the door through which the mercenaries had exited—"might try to find some dignity by revenging themselves on you."

When she understood his meaning, her eyes softened, but she still said, "They won't. And an escort will not be necessary."

"They're not coming back, Cale," Riven said.

Cale ignored the assassin.

"I know it is not necessary, Varra," he replied, impressed with her diction and dignity. He sensed an education in her background, or at least an educated mentor. "But I'd prefer to do so even still."

She held his gaze for a moment, as though measuring his intentions. The moment stretched.

"Very well," she said at last, and walked away.

Riven, having watched the whole exchange, favored Cale with his signature sneer then said, "I wonder if the Shadowlord knows that his First is as soft as an old woman."

Cale gave the assassin a stare.

Riven chuckled in response.

"Well, while you do *that*," the assassin said, nodding at Varra, "I'll get to work."

❖ ❖ ❖ ❖ ❖

Cale walked beside Varra, following her lead while he kept his eyes and ears alert for any sign of the mercenaries. Like Riven, Cale thought it unlikely that the men would return, but he'd been wrong before.

Fortunately, the sellswords didn't show themselves, though orcs, drunken sailors, bugbears, and slaves marched past. Diseased, reed-thin men and women—human, goblin, and even orc—lingered in alleys or lurked in sewer mouths, coughing, smoking, watching them with the dull eyes of the damned. Voices and the tread of boots carried from the bouncing catwalks and bridges strung high above them. Cale had to adjust his technique to evaluate danger in three dimensions. He found it discomfiting.

Cale hadn't bothered to disguise himself against discovery by Azriim and the other slaadi. He would have to rely on the darkness and crowds to give him anonymity. A disguise would have required an explanation to Varra, and might have dissuaded her from allowing him to escort her. And Cale felt a strange attraction to the woman. Souls akin, perhaps.

Varra used no torch or candle, instead choosing roundabout routes lit by lichen, glowballs, and torches. She seemed unafraid of the street, and Cale knew enough not to attribute her fearlessness to his presence. He admired her mettle. In truth, he admired her.

They walked in silence for a time.

"I told you it was unnecessary," she said after a while. "Those men won't be back. It's happened before."

Cale only nodded.

"It's not far now," she said, filling the silence between them.

Cale, who spoke nine languages, found himself somewhat at a loss for words. Except for Thazienne and Shamur Uskevren, he had not had much interaction with women in recent years.

"How long have you lived here?" he finally managed.

She gave a soft little laugh and said, "A long while." She looked at him sidelong as they walked. "How long have you been here? No. *Why* are you here? You don't belong here. I can see that. You're friend might, but you don't."

"He's not my friend," Cale replied, though he was not

so sure. "We just . . . understand each other. And work together. Why are you here?"

It was clear to Cale that Varra didn't belong in Skullport either.

She smiled fully, an expression that illuminated her face, and said, "You first."

"Business," Cale replied. To ensure that she didn't take him for a slaver or worse, he added, "I'm looking for someone."

"Aren't we all," she said, but otherwise had the sense to ask nothing more. Cale appreciated that.

"And you?" Cale asked.

She waved a delicate hand in the air and said, "Where else would I go?"

Cale could think of nothing to say to that.

"Where are you from?" she asked.

To his surprise, Cale thought first of the Plane of Shadow but he immediately righted his thinking.

"Westgate," he replied. Her face showed no recognition. Surprised, he wondered if she had been born in Skullport. "A large city overlooking the sea," he explained. "Far from here."

He put his hand to Weaveshear's hilt as two ogres plodded by. Only their stink proved offensive.

"It's sunny in Westgate, I expect?" Varra said.

Cale supposed it was, at least sometimes. Of course, he had done most of his work in the night.

"Yes," he replied.

Her expression grew wistful, even as she absently stepped over a body that was either drunk or dead.

"I haven't seen the sun in . . . a long time," she said.

Again Cale found himself with no words. The silence sat between them as they passed one rundown, rickety building after another, and one rundown, rickety human being after another.

After a while, he asked, "Why do you stay?"

She gave that same quick laugh then said, "I was born far away, too far to easily return." Her voice dropped and she added, "I've nowhere else to go. This is my home now."

Before Cale could respond, she pointed to a dilapidated, moisture-swollen flophouse leaning dangerously against the cavern's wall. A rothé pen stood to its right; a fungus garden to its left. Unlike most of the structures in Skullport, another building was not built atop the flophouse, though Cale could see movement in some of the caves and recesses higher up the cavern wall.

"That's it," she said. She stopped and turned to face him. "Thank you for the escort."

Cale thought again how pretty she was, how beautiful she might have been with appropriate food, dress, and a softer life under the sun. Tempting though it was, he knew he could not help her with those things, at least not just then. He had other, more pressing business.

"My pleasure, lady," he said.

He gave his best bow, smiled, and turned to leave. She caught his cloak sleeve.

"I have a fire pit inside," she said, with only a hint of self-consciousness. "It's warm. I share lodging with two other women, but they're probably still . . . out."

At that moment, under Varra's gaze, Cale didn't need a fire pit to warm him. He felt an inexplicably powerful compulsion to take Varra in his arms and it almost overcame his better judgment. Almost. He smiled at her and gently took her hand. It was soft and feminine, despite the harshness of her work. He noticed for the first time that only a few shadows were leaking from his flesh. It was as if she kept his darker nature at bay.

"This is not a good time," he said. "I have something important that I must see through to the end."

A coffle of slaves trudged past, chains ringing. Cale noticed a ragged looking human staring at him, all the while wearing a crazed smile. The human looked familiar, perhaps the same madman who had accosted him on the street when they had first arrived in the city.

Varra pulled him back to himself by touching his cheek

and staring into his eyes. She smiled, the first smile he had seen that touched her eyes. Seeing her face light up like that, he almost changed his mind.

"A man of secrets," she said. "But with a darkness about you that is plain."

Cale could not deny it.

She held her smile and said, "Does the man of secrets have a name?"

Cale flushed, feeling the fool. He had failed even to introduce himself. He started to say his name but quickly caught himself.

"Vasen Coriver," he said, making her one of the only people still living on Faerûn who knew his given name.

One less secret, he thought.

She withdrew her hand from his and brushed a stray hair from her face.

"Vasen," she repeated. "I like that. Well, Vasen, will we see each other again?"

He answered her honestly, "I don't know."

She seemed to accept that, though her smile faltered.

"I think we will" she said, "But until then *relain il nes baergis.* "

Cale had never before heard the language.

"What does that mean?" he asked.

She winked at him and said, "I'll tell you when I see you next."

Without another word, she turned and walked into the flophouse.

Cale could do nothing but watch her go, thinking how important the briefest of encounters sometimes felt, and how he had a new reason to stop the Sojourner and his slaadi.

❧　❧　❧　❧　❧

At first, Azriim did not believe his eyes—his *own* eyes, which he retained despite being in the form of Thyld. He peered through the darkness at the two humans. Was it possible? Awkward in Thyld's pathetic skin, he picked his way through the slaves and other street traffic to draw closer to the pair of humans. He eyed the male.

The height, the bald head . . . it could only be him.

Azriim drew in a sharp breath, and flexed his hands as though they were his natural claws.

Though Azriim could not imagine how, not more than a block away stood what looked like the priest of Mask, Erevis Cale. The same Erevis Cale who had followed Azriim and his broodmates all the way to the Fane of Shadows, who had wounded Azriim, killed Elura, and whom Azriim had thought drowned at the bottom of the Lightless Lake.

Azriim stared at Cale, afraid to move, thinking that if he did the image of the priest must reveal itself as an apparition conjured by his imagination and boredom.

For the first time, he noticed that the dusky skin was not a play of the dim light. He saw too the shadows that flared at intervals from Cale's skin like black fire. That took him aback at first, causing him to doubt what he saw, but then he took its meaning. He was indeed looking upon Cale, and Cale was a shade. The priest had undergone the transformation that Vraggen had sought for himself. That transformation had somehow allowed Cale to survive the dissolution of the Fane. And there he was. Azriim wondered if any of Cale's comrades had also survived. Certainly Serrin would be interested in reacquainting himself with the one-eyed assassin.

Azriim smiled and almost laughed aloud. The boredom that had until then afflicted him vanished. Cale had tracked him to Skullport. A hundred questions ran through his mind—most importantly, *how*?—but he pushed them all aside. It was enough that he had a challenge.

As though feeling Azriim's stare, Cale looked away from the human female who stood near him and made eye contact with Azriim. Azriim looked away quickly, though he could not contain his grin.

When Cale looked away, Azriim withdrew into the darkness and softly whispered an arcane word. His body wavered for an instant and he knew that he had become invisible to onlookers.

Azriim reached out his consciousness and established contact.

I have news, he projected.

He sensed curiosity from Dolgan and Serrin. Both were preparing the final stages of Azriim's plan.

Erevis Cale, the priest of Mask, is here, he said.

Silence. It was as though Serrin and Dolgan had broken the connection.

Serrin recovered himself first.

Are you certain? he asked. *What of his companion, the one-eyed assassin?*

Azriim fought down his irritation with the question and answered, *Of course, I'm certain. I'm looking upon him even now. I do not know of his companions.*

We should kill him, Serrin offered.

Obviously, Azriim answered again, though he had begun to conceptualize a way in which he could first use Cale to further his plan. *But with some style, of course.*

Dolgan seemed at least to have gathered his wits.

How can he be here? asked the big slaad. *How could he have known?*

To that, Azriim had no certain answer though he suspected scrying.

Impossible to say, Dolgan, he replied, though he remembered that Dolgan had named Cale as relentless. Azriim realized that his broodmate could not have been more correct. *As a precaution, immediately take a new form and from this point onward, maintain a ward against scrying on your person.*

They projected acquiescence.

What will you do? Serrin asked.

Follow him, Azriim replied. *In the meantime, proceed with the preparations.*

He cut off the link with his broodmates and grudgingly

reached out across Faerûn for the Sojourner. When he located him, he indicated his mental presence and waited for his father to allow him contact.

Azriim? the Sojourner asked. *You are agitated.*

Azriim did not waste words: *The priest of Mask followed us here.*

For a moment, the Sojourner did not respond, then: *His companions?*

Unknown.

If I attempt to scry him to determine whether his comrades live, he may sense it. Has he seen you?

Of course not, Azriim snapped. *We have taken precautions.*

He will attempt to scry you, said the Sojourner. *He has no other course. Keep defensive wards in place henceforth, and avoid contact.*

Azriim ground his teeth, finding the activity unsatisfying without fangs, and asked, *Avoid contact? We should be allowed to kill him.*

Azriim felt the Sojourner's mental presence lightly scouring his brain, causing him an itch behind his eyes.

You wish to kill him because his presence offends your pride, the Sojourner said. *You consider him a challenge worthy enough that you will take satisfaction in his death.*

Azriim didn't bother to deny it, though the Sojourner's pedantic tone irked him.

The Sojourner continued, *You would do this despite my admonition to you that pridefulness in excess is self-destructive?*

Azriim did not bother to deny that either.

His father said nothing for a time, then, *Very well. Kill him. Perhaps the lesson may be learned another way.*

With that, the Sojourner cut the mental connection.

Azriim fumed over his father's condescension but kept his attention on Cale.

The human left off the female and walked past the invisible slaad. Azriim fell into step behind him. He toyed with the idea of attacking Cale, taking him by surprise, killing him on the street, and taking his form, but dismissed the idea. The Sojourner's disappointed tone had rankled him. He would swallow his pride and observe.

For a time.

CHAPTER 15

OLD DOGS

After only three days—after only six *cycles*, Jak corrected himself—the halfling could mostly tolerate the sights, sounds, and smells of the city. He still felt weak-kneed when he saw the hapless and hopeless slaves being whipped, zombie laborers carting goods, or illithids feeding on brains, but he managed at least to keep down his meals and banish the nightmares.

Throughout the cycles, Cale periodically had tried to scry Azriim, but to no avail. Jak wasn't sure whether he should take the failure as Beshaba's own luck or something more foreboding. Cale offered no opinion on the matter, though he seemed thoughtful. Jak put it out of his mind. If the slaadi had known Jak and his friends were in Skullport, they would have already attacked.

While Cale tried to magically locate the slaadi,

Riven had taken the mundane approach. He put out inquiries but learned only that Skullport's underworld was tittering with the expectation of a gang war between two rival slaving organizations, one run by a beholder crime lord and the other by a yuan-ti slaver. After two cycles of questioning, bribing, and threatening, Riven had been able to learn nothing about the slaadi.

"It's too tight here," the assassin told them across the table of an inn. Jak had forgotten the name of the place already. Frustration tinged the assassin's voice. "No one is talking."

Cale considered that.

"Then we need get obvious," he said.

Jak knew what that meant. They would make themselves apparent—and make themselves targets—hoping to draw the slaadi out.

Riven looked across the table and asked, "You're certain?"

"We've got nothing else," Cale replied, nodding.

Thereafter, as they moved to a different inn every two cycles, they all four traveled together rather than moving in more circumspect pairs. Accustomed to "quiet work," Jak felt they might as well have had a royal herald announcing their presence in Skullport. Each time they moved, the halfling eyed with suspicion everyone they passed on the street, certain that each skulker was a slaad in disguise.

Cycles passed, and they moved from inn to inn. Skullport seemed to have as many inns as a stray dog had fleas, and all of them were the same: rundown drug-dens filled with whores, bad food, and swill that passed for ale. Jak began to lose hope. Perhaps the slaadi had already left the city?

Then Riven got a lead.

"This man named Thyld purports to have information on a duergar with unusual eyes," Riven said.

They sat around a small table in their filthy, windowless room.

"You looked into him?" Cale asked.

Riven nodded and said, "Of course. He's a well known information broker in the city, associated with a group called the Kraken Society. He looks legitimate."

"When?" Cale asked.

"Later this cycle," said Riven. "I go alone. At a place called the Crate and Dock."

Cale rubbed his chin, thinking.

After a time, he said, "This is all we have, so we go. But it smells wrong. Treat it that way."

"I always do," replied Riven.

Cale stood and said, "Let's get a room in another inn closer to the Crate and Dock. Mags and I will back you up. You read the broker, and let us know through Mags. We'll improvise after that."

"Improvise?" Riven asked with a smile.

Cale shrugged and said only, "Let's go."

Walking through the darkness, Jak held his holy symbol in one hand and kept his other on the hilt of his short sword, his wont when traversing Skullport's streets. He stayed near Cale, who he knew could see better in the dark than anyone else they might meet, a fact from which he refused to draw any conclusions. Cale was still a man, he reminded himself, and still his friend.

They stalked the narrow, dimly-lit avenues past ogres, lizard-pulled carts, stray rothé, gangs of kobolds, and other beasts for which Jak didn't even have a name. Slaves, rolling cages lit with torches, bugbear overseers holding like clubs shanks of an unknown meat, nervous goblins, and dead-eyed zombies all shared the road. The stink and sounds wafted out of the darkness like nightmares. Jak kept his eyes alert and his blade at the ready.

From ahead, the pained yelp of a wounded animal sounded above the general murmur of the city street. About fifteen paces in front of them, a grizzled female hound dragging a visibly broken hind leg pelted as best it could out of the doorway of a tavern and into the street. It stumbled as it ran, yelping with pain each time its broken leg touched the packed-earth road. A faded wooden sign hung outside the tavern. On it was the name of the place, written in phosphorescent lichen that the innkeeper must have tended to daily. The Pour House, it read.

A giant of a pirate, covered in a coarse beard, a chain shirt, and sharp steel, burst through the shell curtain doorway of the Pour House and stormed after the dog, stomping and cursing it in a gruff voice. Two other similarly armed men stumbled out of the tavern behind the pirate, smiling and watching with eager eyes. A one-armed elderly man raced through the door after them, gesticulating wildly with his one arm. Jak deemed him the innkeeper, to judge from his apron. The two sailors grabbed him by his shirt and prevented him from getting past.

"You leave her be," cried the old man at the huge pirate, barely holding back tears. "Leave her alone!"

With a surprising demonstration of dexterity, the old tavernkeeper managed to slip the two sailors' grasp and squirm past them, but before he could take a step, they grabbed him by the shirt and pulled him backward to land hard on his rump.

"Leave her alone!" the old man shouted again, trying to rise.

"Shut up," the sailors said, and used their boots to hold him down.

"Mongrel bitch!" the big pirate shouted, and attempted to stomp on the scrabbling hound. He missed, but only just. The dog, whimpering with pain, tongue lolling, gave up trying to escape on its broken leg, and instead rolled over on its back in the dirty street and showed his belly to the pirate—a sign of submission.

Jak saw Magadon put a restraining hand on Riven. Riven batted it away, his eye hard and cold.

"She meant no harm," the old man said, and again tried to stand. "Don't you hurt her, Ergis! She's old is all."

The pirate, Ergis, still looming over the submissive dog, turned and glared at the tavernkeeper. The old man quailed. To judge from Ergis's musculature, the coarse hair that covered his arms, and the feral eyes, Jak deemed the pirate to be orcspawn, not more than two generations removed. A savage lot.

"It pissed on my boot," Ergis growled, and lifted his leg to show a leather boot stained dark. "My *new* boot. I'm going to kill the mongrel and stew it in your own pot, Felwer."

At that, the old man summoned up his courage and cried out a protest. The two sailors laughed and stomped on him with their boots.

"Kill it, Captain," encouraged one of the sailors.

Ergis turned back to the dog and raised his shiny black boot high. The dog, too tired or too pained to move, just lay there, tail wagging uncertainly.

Just as Jak prepared to charge the pirate, just as Cale pulled Weaveshear half its length from its scabbard, a sliver of balanced steel spun through the air and stuck in the half-orc's calf. The pirate screamed in surprise and pain, hopped on his unwounded leg, and clutched at the throwing dagger stuck in the meat of his leg. Blood poured from the wound. The dog rolled over onto his belly, crawled away a bit, then stopped and licked at its wounded leg.

All eyes turned to the thrower: Riven. Jak had never even seen the assassin draw a blade.

Dark but he's fast! thought the halfling.

Already Riven held another throwing dagger in his right hand. His eye was an emotionless hole but anger visibly tensed his entire body.

"You touch that dog, whoreson, and the next one finds your eye," the assassin said, his voice as gelid as an ice storm. To his comrades, Riven softly stated out of the side of his mouth, "The dog is my problem. Remain here."

Without waiting for a response, without taking his eyes from the half-orc, Riven stalked forward with a purpose.

Magadon broke the surprised silence between the three by softly saying, "He's always been soft for dogs. I still don't know why."

Jak couldn't imagine Riven being soft for anything, but there he was, championing an old bitch on the streets of Skullport. He eyed the passersby—a slaver, a trio of drow, four humans, and a halfling that looked shockingly similar to Jak's dead Uncle Cob. At first, Jak feared that one of the shapeshifting slaadi had read his mind and taken a form familiar to him, but he saw no malice in the halfling's dancing eyes. Before Jak could hail him, the halfling shot him a rakish grin and vanished into the darkness. The other passersby too spared only a quick glance at the brewing confrontation before moving on. Either everyone in Skullport took care to mind their own affairs, or violence was so common in the streets that it scarcely warranted notice.

"You're a dead man, human," Ergis promised.

He jerked the throwing dagger from his calf with only a slight wince. The hole continued to bleed freely, but the half-orc seemed not to care.

"First you, then the dog," he promised.

Keeping his weight primarily on his unwounded leg, Ergis tossed Riven's dagger to the ground, burying its point in the street, and drew his oversized cutlass. Armed, he shot Riven a fierce grin that showed his orc's canines. His two companions drew their own blades, gave the tavernkeeper one last kick each, and hopped forward onto the street to stand beside their captain.

At that, Jak started to pull his own blade but both Cale and Magadon stopped him with a hand to either shoulder.

"There's three of them," Jak protested.

"This is the way he wants it, little man," Cale said.

Magadon nodded and said, "Not going to matter."

Jak hesitated for a moment then let his hand fall off the hilt of his blade.

Despite three opponents armed with larger blades, Riven didn't break stride. He walked toward them with a throwing dagger in his hand and blood on his mind.

"This is your last chance to walk away," Riven said.

The pirates shared a grin.

"Ain't no walking away from this," the half-orc said.

"I'm going to cut him, Captain," said the thinner of the two sailors.

The sailor faked a lunge at Riven. He stuck out his tongue and leered.

Cale, standing beside Jak, said, "All three have been drinking. Riven will take the one who spoke first, just to make a point, then the other. The half-orc he'll save for last."

From behind, the sailors the tavernkeeper climbed to his feet.

Patting his thighs with his one good arm, he called to the dog, "Here, girl. Here, Retha."

Hearing that, the old dog clambered unsteadily to her feet and started to limp toward the tavernkeeper, whimpering all the while. Ergis did not take his bestial eyes off Riven, but the thinner of the two smaller pirates drew back his leg as though to kick at the dog.

Riven's dagger flashed and embedded itself in the man's throat. The pirate clutched futilely for the blade and didn't even manage a gurgle before he fell over dead. Only a slight trickle of blood squeezed from around the buried blade.

The dog limped to its master.

"Dirty bastard," said the other pirate, though he didn't charge, and Jak heard the doubt in his voice.

"He'll be next," Cale said from beside Jak.

Riven said not a word, only continued to advance. He was not visibly armed.

When the assassin got within two strides, the smaller pirate lunged at him drunkenly, crosscutting with his cutlass at Riven's throat. Riven ducked under the blade, leaped in close, arm-locked the sailor's sword arm, and wrenched it at the elbow. While the sailor squealed, Riven slammed the crown of his head into the man's nose. Blood sprayed. With his other hand Riven drew a punch dagger from a sheath on the back of his belt.

Jak marveled at the assassin's fluidity.

Beside Jak, Cale called the combat as though he and Riven were one and the same.

"Lung, lung, heart," he said, and Riven did exactly that with the punch dagger, penetrating between the links of the sailor's light chain mail shirt.

The sailor sagged. His mouth opened, but no sound emerged.

Moving quickly, the assassin spun the dying sailor around and stabbed the awl point of the punch dagger into the base of his skull.

"Brain," Cale said.

Magadon uttered a low whistle.

Blood soaked the front of the sailor's tunic. His eyes were open but his body was already dead. Riven kept him upright with a hand on his shoulder and the dagger stuck in his head like some bloody marionette.

The entire exchange had taken less than five heartbeats.

"Now the half-orc," said Cale.

Jak looked to Cale and remembered then the words that Cale had said to him many times before: *Only an assassin knows an assassin.* His friend—his *best* friend—was separated from Drasek Riven by no more than the edge of a blade, if that.

With nothing but ice in his expression, Riven put his foot into the back of the corpse and shoved it at Ergis. The body collapsed in a heap at the half-orc's booted feet. The pirate's feral eyes showed fear.

"I'm leaving," the half-orc said, and took a single step backward. He lowered his blade and held up his other hand. "All right?"

He looked past Riven to Cale, Jak, and Magadon as though for support.

"I'm sorry, Felwer," he said to the innkeeper. "I won't be back." To Riven, he said, "Umberlee's arse, man. It's just a dog."

Riven eyed Ergis with a gaze devoid of emotion. He

ominously tapped the blade of the bloody punch dagger against his palm. He looked back at the wounded dog, which was licking the dirty hands of the innkeeper and whining.

Jak saw a ripple of anger run the length of Riven's body.

The assassin turned back to Ergis and said, in a tone so low that Jak could barely hear him, "And you're just a number. There ain't no walking away from this, *Captain*."

The half-orc paled, turned, and ran. But he couldn't move quickly on his wounded calf.

Riven bounded after him, would have closed on him, but Cale's voice stopped the assassin cold.

"Let him go," Cale ordered.

Hearing those words, Jak almost grinned in relief. Cale and Riven might be separated by only a blade's edge, but that edge was keen and clear. Cale showed mercy. Riven did not.

The assassin stopped his pursuit but did not otherwise acknowledge that he had heard Cale. Ergis vanished into the darkness of the street. For a moment, Riven simply stood with his back to them, a bloody punch dagger in his fist, anger written clear in the bunch of his back. After a moment, he turned, picked up his daggers, and stalked over to the innkeeper and the wounded hound. With surprising gentleness, the assassin knelt, let the dog sniff his hand and scratched it behind the ears.

"The gods smile on you," said the innkeeper, taking Riven's other hand.

Jak caught Riven's sneer.

The assassin muttered words under his breath, entwined shadows around his fingers, and touched them to the dog. The little hound yelped as its leg bone twisted back into place and reknit.

Riven gave the dog one last pat, stood and said to the innkeeper in a cool tone, "Gods smile on the strong, granther. Go back inside and mind your dog."

The old man's thankful smile grew uncertain. Visibly confused, he turned and walked back into the tavern, trailing his hound.

Riven spun on his heel and marched up to Cale, still holding the punch dagger, still wearing that emotionless expression. Cale gave no ground and shadows leaked from his skin.

"Don't ever tell me what to do, Cale," Riven said.

Cale's eyes narrowed.

"Then don't make me. You made your point." He nodded at the two corpses cooling in the street and added, "The dog was safe."

Riven replied, "You save whores, I save bitches, and we both let someone walk away. Those are bad habits, Cale."

The shadows around Cale's head and hands intensified.

"Those are *my* habits," he replied. "You don't like them, walk away. And don't *ever* call her a whore again in my presence."

Riven's eye narrowed and his voice lowered.

"Softness for women is another of your bad habits, *First of Five*."

Jak had no idea what woman they were talking about and he dared not ask, at least not just then.

Cale answered with a cold stare and colder silence. For a moment, they stood there glaring into each other's faces, priest and assassin, saying nothing, saying everything.

Magadon broke the tension.

"Let's get to where we're going and get off the street," the guide said, eyeing the passersby.

Jak realized that he had been holding his breath. He blew it out. Cale and Riven could go from working as smoothly together as interlocking cogs one moment, to grating against one another like flint and steel the next. The constant underlying tension was exhausting to Jak.

"A good idea," Riven said. "And this may as well be where we're going." He indicated the Pour House. "Likely the old man will give us free room and board. Meantime, I've got to get ready for my meet."

With that, he spun on his heel and walked away.

Cale stared daggers into Riven's back as the assassin walked away.

As they passed through the curtain of seashells that served as the doorway of the Pour House, Jak looked back to see several skinny humans in tattered clothing emerge from nearby alleys and begin to strip the dead sailors of valuables like a pack of dogs stripping a kill of meat.

The moment Cale and Magadon had procured a room from the innkeeper—Riven had been right; the old man insisted on providing them free lodging—Cale said to him, "Little man, stay here for this. We'll be back within two hours. Mags, you're with me."

❂ ❂ ❂ ❂ ❂

From a rope bridge suspended a dagger's throw above the street, Azriim had watched the confrontation between Cale and the one-eyed assassin. He hadn't been aboble to hear their words, but he could see the genuine tension between them, and could sense the latent anger.

When the assassin stalked off and Cale and his comrades entered the inn, Azriim sped off down the hemp highway. Azriim-as-Thyld had arranged a meeting with the assassin within the half hour. After the confronation with Cale, he knew the assassin would come alone.

CHAPTER 16

NEW TRICKS

Azriim watched the one-eyed assassin stalk into the common room of the Crate and Dock. The human moved with a grace, a predatory sinuousness, that reminded Azriim of his broodmate Serrin. The human's efficiency too—at least to judge from the fight with the sailors in the street—was also reminiscent of Serrin. No wonder Azriim's broodmate hated the human so. Serrin and Azriim had nearly come to blows over Serrin's insistence that he be allowed to attend the meeting with the human. Azriim had refused, concerned that his broodmate's hostility for the assassin would have shown through even a changed form. Instead, he'd stationed Dolgan on the street outside, in the big slaad's habitual form of a street drunk, and left Serrin back at the storehouse.

Anything unusual? Azriim projected to his broodmate.

He was alone, Dolgan responded.

Dressed in a non-descript gray cloak over leathers, the human wore his sabers—magical sabers, Azriim saw—with practiced ease. The assassin's one eye quickly swept the candlelit, hazy common room, and the dozen or so laborers sitting at the worn tables—the Crate and Dock was a favored eatery of dock laborers. When he spotted Azriim, in the form of Thyld, the human's eye narrowed.

Rather than sit at the table in the center of the common room that Azriim had chosen, the human nodded Azriim over and sat at another table in a dark corner, one with a view of the rest of the space. Azriim smiled as he rose. The human was choosing the battlefield, in case Azriim had set him up, and forcing Azriim to put his back to the door.

Limping along as Thyld, Azriim crossed the common room and slid into the chair opposite the assassin. For the meeting, Azriim grudgingly had changed his eye color to match Thyld's dull brown.

"Speak," the assassin said. "You know what I want to hear."

Azriim placed his hands on the table and interlaced his fingers.

"First, my price," he said, playing his part.

"If what you offer is of value to me, you'll be treated well," the assassin said with a sneer. "If what you offer is lies, you'll be treated quite differently."

Azriim rubbed the back of his neck, making a show of worried consideration, then said, "Very well. You wanted to know about a duergar with eyes of two different colors. Here is what I know. Without embellishment, of course."

Azriim began to tell the assassin a fiction about the duergar slaver and his two human companions who had hired a troop of armed guards to escort a caravan into the northern tunnels of the Underdark. Apparently, they were transporting valuable cargo.

As he spoke his lies, Azriim thought all the while

of how the appearance of Cale and his comrades in the midst of a slaver gang war would only increase the likelihood of a rapid and overwhelming response by the Skulls. It was beautiful really. The timing could not have been better.

❖ ❖ ❖ ❖ ❖

Cale and Magadon cowled their faces with the hoods of their cloaks and used side streets to approach the Crate and Dock. Cale would have preferred to have included Jak, but as much as possible he wanted to spare the halfling the sights of Skullport. He knew the vileness of the city affected Jak more than the rest of them. Skullport was combination slave pen, slaughterhouse, charnel pit, and general store. Even Cale found it hard to stomach.

Across the street from the front door of the Crate and Dock, Cale and Magadon lurked in an alley so narrow that Cale could have held his arms outstretched and touched both sides. The air smelled of urine, vomit, and the general musty odor that permeated all of Skullport. An open sewer a dagger toss away emitted an unspeakable stink. A few street torches near the eatery's door provided the only light in the immediate vicinity.

Drow, serpent men, orcs, and worse stalked by, dragging slaves and speaking quietly in their alien tongues. Periodically, the muffled roar of a crowd sounded from within a large stone building down the street, outside of which a crowd milled. Cale figured the place to be some kind of fighting arena. The smell of cooking meat carried from somewhere on the hemp highway high above.

Do you make that drunk? Cale projected to Magadon.

Down a bit, on their side of the street, an unshaven drunk lay against the wall of what looked to be a brewery, his dirty shirt too small to cover his fat belly, his double chin pressed into his chest. Passersby stepped over him, on him, and occasionally spat at him.

Magadon peered into the darkness. Cale knew the

guide couldn't see as well as he could in the pitch darkness, despite his demonic heritage.

I see him, Magadon said.

He's not drunk, Cale said.

Cale had noted the man the instant he'd scanned the street, and had been watching him since. With regularity, the apparent drunk looked up from under hooded eyes and surveyed the street. He was watching the entrance to the Crate and Dock. Likely, he worked for the person with whom Riven was meeting.

One of the slaadi? Magadon asked. *Or just a lookout for Riven's contact?*

Cale shook his head. He had no way to know without closing to use a divination spell, but that would risk his being noticed. He could have turned himself invisible to approach the drunk, but he remembered well the fight in the alley back in Selgaunt when Azriim had seen and captured an invisible Jak. From that, he assumed that the slaadi—if the drunk was indeed a shapechanged slaad—could see invisible creatures. He didn't want to tip his presence.

"Mags, link us to Riven," he said.

The guide nodded and closed his eyes. After a moment, Cale felt as though another window had been opened in the room of his mind.

Riven? he projected.

A pause.

I hear you, the assassin responded. *Didn't expect to, after our little disagreement. Think I'm untrustworthy, First of Five?*

Cale ignored Riven's venom and asked, *What's your assessment?*

Another pause. Likely the assassin's attention was focused on whatever the contact was telling him.

Eyes are normal, Riven finally answered, his tone more moderated. *He looks right and talks the talk. But he offers too much for too little. He's either stupid or one of our slaadi.*

Hearing that, Magadon shifted on his feet. Cale too felt

adrenaline charge his muscles. He doubted stupidity to be the explanation.

Keep him talking, Cale said to Riven. To Magadon, he projected, *Back in Starmantle you said you could put yourself behind someone's eyes and see what they see.*

Magadon nodded, immediately grasping Cale's point.

The slaad or Riven? Magadon asked.

The slaad, answered Cale.

I can do that, the guide answered. *But I need to see the target first, to plant the first hook. After that, he can be anywhere.* He paused, then added, *Also, he might sense the mental intrusion.*

Cale nodded. They would have to take that chance.

How long can you maintain it?

Magadon answered, *As long as I wish, though it will drain me somewhat. The connection is latent and requires little mental energy until I activate it to see what the target sees. Each time I activate it, though, we again risk him sensing my presence.*

This is a waste of time, Riven said. *Let's just put him down right now.*

Cale shook his head, though he knew Riven couldn't see him.

No, he answered. *He's only one of the three slaadi. Another may be out here in the street. We need to learn their play and put all of them down at once. Stopping them doesn't necessarily stop the Sojourner.*

Riven fell silent, though Cale could sense his irritation through the mental connection.

Cale thought about having Magadon connect to the drunk down the street but decided against it. If the drunk was a slaad, he was not the leader. The leader would be the one talking to Riven.

Riven, Cale projected, *we need to see the one you're talking with. Hear what he says and walk out with him. If he detects Magadon's psionic attack, you'll get your chance then. If that happens, Mags and I will take the watchman out on the street.*

Riven projected acquiescence and the connection went quiet.

❧ ❧ ❧ ❧ ❧

Riven stared across the table, hearing what the false human was saying, wondering what the slaadi were planning, and fighting down the desire to draw steel. Despite his inner turmoil, he had no trouble keeping his expression neutral, even vaguely friendly. Riven had so often sat across tables from men he intended to kill that he had long ago mastered the ability to keep his face expressionless even while choosing between blade, garrote, or poison. No moral crisis ever rose from Riven's conscience to trouble his expression. For him, murder was business. For him, *everything* was business. The critical point was that he be on the winning side in the end.

Unlike his comrades, he felt little personal animosity toward the slaadi. In truth, he probably felt more antipathy toward Cale—the *First* of Five—than he did the slaadi. Riven wanted to put down the slaadi only because letting them live offended his professional pride.

And because the Shadowlord seemed to want it.

The slaad was just finishing describing to Riven the route the caravan would take through the northern tunnels of the Underdark.

"When?" Riven asked.

"The third hour of the cycle after next," responded the slaad.

Riven nodded, giving the appearance of being satisfied.

"This duergar has earned your ire?" asked the slaad.

Riven stared into the slaad's eyes, wondering if there was not an offer there. The slaad's gaze revealed nothing. Riven shook his head.

"No," he said. "This is a business matter. And like all matters of business, I care only for coming out of it better than how I came in." He paused while the slaad nodded sagely, then added, "For that, I always make sure that I end up on the winning side."

The slaad stopped nodding and gazed at him curiously. "I see. . . ."

"I'm pleased you do," Riven said, and offered no further explanation. He leaned back in his chair, reached into one of his belt pouches, and withdrew one of the small diamonds he had brought with him from Selgaunt.

"This is equitable, I assume?" he said.

The slaad mumbled agreement, scooped the gem into his palm, and pocketed it in his worn robe without even an appraising glance. If Riven hadn't already been certain, the slaad's nonchalance regarding payment would have solidified Riven's opinion that he was not dealing with an ordinary human information broker.

"This business is complete, then," said the slaad, rising to his feet.

He smiled down at Riven, a disingenuous gesture, and the assassin noted his perfect teeth.

Not hardly, thought Riven, but he only offered a nod.

"Luck to you with this duergar," the slaad said. "I've heard he's quite the killer."

Riven waved a hand dismissively and took a drink from his ale.

The slaad's ears flushed red with anger but to his credit, he managed to keep an agreeable smile pasted on his face.

"I'll take my leave, then," said the slaad, his voice tight.

Riven let him walk a few paces away before he stood.

"I believe I'll be leaving too," he said. "Hold a moment."

The slaad, looking uncomfortable at the prospect of the assassin's company, waited for Riven to catch up. As they walked for the door, Riven casually kept a hand on one of his sabers. He eyed the slaad's back sidelong, located the kidneys, and wondered whether the creature would sense Magadon's psionic attack.

We're coming out, he projected to Cale and Magadon.

Be ready, Cale answered back. *If he responds to the attack, he's your responsibility.*

Riven didn't bother with an answer. He didn't require instruction from Cale. He understood his responsibilities—*all* of his responsibilities—full well.

Riven and the slaad exited the inn and the assassin quickly surveyed the nearby street traffic, rooftops, and catwalks above. Nothing unusual. In the darkness, he didn't see Cale and Magadon, and he didn't see the drunk. A rothé-pulled wagon piled high with dried mushrooms was stopped in the street near them, its gray-skinned gnome owner pulling at the rothé's bridle. The creature lowed in agitation, shook its shaggy mane, but did not budge. A group of drunk half-orcs peppered the gnome with laughter and curses. From down the street, a crowd in one of Skullport's many fighting dens let loose an approving shout.

Now, Magadon projected.

Riven knew that somewhere nearby, Magadon was insinuating himself into the slaad's mind.

I'm in, Magadon said.

The slaad spun around to face Riven.

Reflexively, Riven's grip on his saber hilt tightened, though he kept his face expressionless

"Louts," the slaad said, indicating the half-orcs. "Listen to them curse. They have the intelligence of rocks."

Riven let his grip on his saber relax.

He sneered at the slaad, hoping it was Azriim, nodded agreement, and said, "It's in the breeding. Half-bloods are often a stupid lot."

❧ ❧ ❧ ❧ ❧

Cale and Magadon took a different route back to the Pour House than the assassin, in case the slaadi decided to follow Riven. After the assassin arrived, all three of them met Jak. Sitting in the quiet darkness of their room, Riven explained to them what the slaad had told him. Cale took it all in, thinking.

"They want us to attack them?" Jak asked.

The halfling took a draw on his pipe and blew it out.

"Or the whole caravan," Magadon said. "Or at least to follow it out of the city."

"The latter seems the most likely to me," Cale said. "But there's no way to be certain."

"What's the play, Cale?" Riven asked, taking a draw on his own pipe.

Cale, pacing the floor with his hands clasped behind his back, spoke his thoughts aloud: "Whatever they're planning," he said, "they plan to do it around the third hour of next cycle. Agreed?"

Heads nodded agreement and Cale continued, "So, we're either part of their plan somehow or they want us well out of the way. It doesn't matter which. With Magadon's connection to the slaadi, we can figure out where they are at any time. So we observe and improvise. If they're with the caravan, fine. If they're somewhere else, that's fine too. Wherever they are, we follow them and put a stop to whatever they're planning. Then we put a stop to them."

Riven blew out a smoke ring, smiled, and said, "You seem to have grown fond of improvisation, Cale. Leads to surprises."

Cale said nothing, for there was nothing to say. Improvisation was all they had.

CHAPTER 17

HUNTING

Twice during the cycle, Cale asked Magadon to open the link between the guide and the slaad. Each time, Magadon's peculiar gaze went vacant as the psionic contact allowed him to see through the eyes of the targeted creature. Based on Magadon's description of the surroundings, the slaad appeared to be in some kind of storehouse or office with his two brethren, one in the form of a huge Amnian, the other in the form of a Sword Coast pirate. They were talking, but Magadon couldn't hear their words.

"Our slaad does all the talking," Magadon reported. "The others listen. I see the gray-eyed slaad—he's the corsair with the falchion ... goatee. Looks a bit like Riven. The Amnian's face is slack. He looks like a dullard."

Cale looked to Riven and said, "Gray-eyes is our friend from the barn outside of Selgaunt."

"I remember him," Riven said.

Jak, seated in the room's sole chair with his feet up on the small table and his hands interlaced behind his head, said, "We owe that one."

One of his hands went to his chest where the gray-eyed slaad had torn it open.

"We owe them all, little man," Cale agreed, nodding. "The Amnian I make as Dolgan. He's big and stupid no matter his form."

Twice Cale had almost killed Dolgan. He would be sure to finish the work next time they met.

Jak said, "That leaves only Azriim. We're seeing through his eyes."

Cale nodded, imagining the slaad's brown and blue orbs. He was pleased they had tagged Azriim with Magadon's power. From what he'd seen, Cale deemed Azriim the leader, the most cunning, and hence the most valuable. Whatever happened, Azriim would be at the heart of it.

Magadon sat up straight and said, "Gray-eyes is leaving."

"Without Azriim?" Cale asked.

Magadon nodded and said, "He's getting instructions."

Cale wished again that Magadon's ability allowed him to hear what the slaadi were saying.

He thought for a time, then said, "End it, Mags. We've got a connection with Azriim. We'll call on it as needed. This is too risky."

Though Azriim had shown no sign up till then of having detected Magadon's presence, Cale didn't want to press his good fortune by prolonging the connection. He would keep all the contacts short, just long enough to get a feel for the slaadi's location and activities. Tymora sometimes smiled on the foolish, he knew, but she more often favored the circumspect.

More importantly, Cale could see that maintaining the mental link for even a short time was draining to the guide. Magadon's skin was pale, his knucklebone eyes sunken, and from the way he rubbed his brow, Cale thought he probably had a severe ache in his temples. But not once did the guide complain. Cale's respect for him grew all the more.

Magadon held the connection for a moment longer, then cut off contact with an audible sigh. He blinked rapidly and his eyes came back to life.

"Check him every half hour," Cale said to the guide, patting him on the back. "The time is getting close. We don't want them to have too much of a head start."

The guide exhaled, massaging his brow, and nodded.

Geared up and ready, they continued to wait in their room, increasingly restive. Time passed, and Magadon's periodic checks revealed the two remaining slaadi doing little. Riven paced their small room like a caged animal.

"We could move on them right now," the assassin said to Cale. "You could shadowstep us to that storehouse."

Cale shook his head, not bothering to explain his reasoning.

"Delay is foolish," Riven snapped. "By the time we move, we may find them in the midst of thirty hired swords. Then what? *Your* decision to wait will have put us all at risk, Cale."

Cale understood that, but simply killing the slaadi was not enough. He wanted vengeance, justice, *chororin*. For that, he would need to find the Sojourner, who had put all of it into motion, and stop him, *kill* him.

Instead of arguing with the assassin, he said, "You're welcome to stay behind."

Riven stopped pacing and his eye flashed. He stared at Cale for a moment before nodding at the pocket in which Cale kept his mask, his holy symbol.

"You'd like that, wouldn't you, First of Five?" the assassin asked. "No one to vie for his favor, eh?"

Cale answered Riven's stare with one of his own.

"His favor has nothing to do with it," he replied. "His *favor* got me this." He held up his regenerated hand, swathed in shadows. "This is about you doing it my way or not at all. Your choice to stay, Zhent. Nobody is holding you here. You can walk away anytime."

Riven held Cale's gaze for a moment before giving a mirthless smile through his goatee.

"I think I'll stay around," said the assassin, "for now."

He started pacing anew.

Jak and Cale shared a look. Jak's green eyes said, *I don't trust him.* For his part, Cale attributed Riven's mood to the irritability that had plagued the assassin since arriving in Skullport, and his impatience for action. Cale too was irritable, which explained his own overly harsh response to Riven's challenge.

"They're moving," Magadon said.

Cale and Jak jumped to their feet. Riven whirled on the guide and took three steps toward him.

"Where?" all three asked in unison.

Magadon held up a hand to forestall further questions. His eyes showed only whites.

"Exiting the storehouse. I cannot tell where they are. Heading along the street . . . carts . . . slaves . . ."

"No landmarks?" Cale asked.

Magadon shook his head and replied, "Still haven't seen the harbor. I think they're in the Lower Trade Lanes, heading north or east. Lots of street traffic . . . brothels, taverns, shacks, a glassblower's workshop . . ." He was quiet for a time then said, "The buildings are getting more and more decrepit, even for Skullport."

Magadon continued to describe the surroundings, hoping that one of them would note something with which they were familiar.

"Do you see any brewer's shops?" Riven asked. "Lots of goblins? Kobolds?"

Magadon shook his head and said, "No . . . wait, yes! A lot of untapped ale casks stacked outside of several buildings. And there are more goblins than usual."

Riven said, "They're in the northern Trade Lanes, in the slum warrens near Cart City. They're heading toward the Underdark tunnels that lead north out of the city."

"You're sure?" Cale asked.

Riven nodded and replied, "That's consistent with what the slaad described to me back at the Crate and Dock."

"Wagons . . . lizard pens . . ." the guide continued.

"Hold him for a while longer," Cale said to the guide. "We need to be sure."

Magadon nodded, his eyes still showing only whites. They waited.

"They're reaching the end of the cavern," Magadon said. "Tunnels ahead. Lots of torches and lanterns . . . goblin runners. It's a caravan assembly point but I only see one closed wagon. There are many heavily armed duergar, and four in no armor. I don't see the gray-eyed slaad."

"Cut if off, Mags," Cale said.

"Wait . . ." Magadon said. "The unarmored duergar are gathered around Azriim. To judge from his hands and perspective, it looks as though Azriim is in the form of a duergar himself, or something similarly short. He's handing them wands. He's looking toward a tunnel, gesturing. I think they're preparing to move out."

"Cut it now, Magadon," Cale ordered. "We know enough."

The guide nodded distantly and shook his head as though to clear it. Exhaling heavily, his eyes returned to normal. He looked exhausted.

Cale patted Magadon on the shoulder while he said to Riven, "That must be the caravan they described to you."

"Agreed," Riven replied. "Two of the three slaadi are there, along with the squad of duergar."

"Where then is the gray-eyed slaad?" Cale asked of no one in particular.

Magadon shook his head. Riven shrugged.

Jak already had pocketed his pipe and pulled on his pack.

"I still don't get it," said the halfling. "The slaadi are *with* the caravan, but they want us to attack it?"

"An ambush?" Magadon offered.

"Possibly," Cale replied, "but I'd wager it's more complicated than that. Remember that they can teleport away anytime, if they're willing to risk it. They might just be with the wagon to make it look believable, planning to get out of there when we appear."

Magadon tilted his head, conceding the point.

"Either way," Cale continued, "baiting us to attack the caravan is only a ploy, not the real play. So we follow it and them, hidden, but hold our steel until I say otherwise. There's something else going on here."

Magadon stood and shouldered his pack. Riven did the same. Cale looked to the assassin.

"You know the way to the area Magadon described?" he asked.

"I've been there," Riven answered softly.

"Then we're following you," Cale said. "Mags, when we get close, you take us to the tunnel the caravan is heading down. Let's move."

☙ ☙ ☙ ☙ ☙

They sprinted through the torchlit streets of Skullport, dodging carts and slaves, mercenaries and mages, bugbears and orcs. With Magadon running easily beside him, Riven led them north through the brewing district—rich with the acrid smoke of distilleries and fermentation casks—and through the slums—rich with the stink of filth, sewage, and rotting garbage—until they reached a flat, open area of Skullport dotted with rothé pens, coopers' shops, large tents, wheelwrights, and other services related to caravannering.

Smoking torches on tall iron stands lit the area as brightly as a surface city street at night. The hemp highway did not reach that far north, and the ceiling soared away into the darkness above. To Cale, the area appeared to be the mirror image of Skullport's wharves, but with wagons and carts instead of ships, teamsters instead of sailors, and dark tunnels instead of dark water.

"Cart City," Riven said, over his shoulder.

Cale saw where the area had gotten its name. The

place was thronged with beasts, wagons, carts, humans, and various humanoids, all busily loading and unloading goods and slaves for transport in caravans. Cale did not care to ponder the dark destinations to which the slaves would be taken.

Squads of kobold and goblin laborers flitted frenetically through the area, carrying rope, barking orders, herding rothé and pack lizards. The sulfuric smell of forge smoke and the heavy pungency of animal dung filled the air. The voices of the mass of caravanners merged into an indistinguishable murmur that rose toward the ceiling like smoke.

Jak elbowed Cale and pointed to the ceiling far above. There, framed by stalactites as thin as spears, two glowing Skulls supervised the area from on high, preventing the nascent chaos from erupting into violence. Cale felt the incredible weight of their gazes as they passed over him, the pull of Weaveshear at his waist, and a brief flash of concern that the magic in the blade would draw the Skulls' attention as surely as a lodestone drew iron shavings. But it did not, and Cale and his companions continued on, unmolested by Skullport's guardians.

To their right, a caravan of eight carts was assembling, the carts forming up, the teamsters yoking a recalcitrant pack lizard or two. A score or so of armed orc and hobgoblin guards eyed them coolly. A large hobgoblin in a chain shirt aimed a crossbow in Cale's direction, smiling a mouthful of pointed teeth. Cale slowed and stared. The hobgoblin lowered the weapon, offered Cale a hard smile, a mock salute, and shared a laugh with the other guards.

Meanwhile, Magadon and Riven pushed and elbowed their way through and around the street traffic, hurrying toward the looming, sloping face of Skullport's northern wall. The guide seemed to know exactly where he was going. Jak and Cale trailed after them.

They stopped in the middle of a packed earth road, twenty or so paces before the rough stone facade of the cavern's wall. The street traffic broke around them like a wave.

Ordinarily, the fact that Skullport existed in a huge cavern was easy to forget. The city was so large and the darkness so thick that Cale had not seen a wall or ceiling in cycles. But standing before the craggy face of the city's northern border, he remembered that Skullport existed at the whim of the gods of the earth and stone, in a fragile bubble nearly a league below the surface. He thought it likely that if Azriim and the other slaadi succeeded with whatever they were planning, Skullport's bubble would burst.

And Varra would suffer the same fate as the city.

"Which way, Mags?" Cale asked. "Riven?"

Ten or more large cave mouths opened at ground level in the cavern's wall, each easily large enough to allow a cart's passage. In fact, the last wagon of a caravan was vanishing down the leftmost tunnel at that very moment.

Riven shook his head.

"The slaad wasn't specific enough," said the assassin. "I don't know which tunnel."

Stepping forward out of the heaviest of the traffic, Magadon knelt on his haunches and stroked his chin, looking from one tunnel to the next, as if searching his memory. Wheel ruts scored the packed earth in front of each tunnel, and Cale couldn't tell them apart. Innumerable smaller tunnels opened at all heights along the rough rock face but Cale ignored them as impassable for a cart. Bats and stirges wheeled in the air above.

"This way," Magadon said, standing and nodding in the direction of the third tunnel from the left.

"You're certain?" Cale asked.

"Yes," the guide said, and that was good enough for Cale.

But apparently not for Riven.

"Let's make certain," the assassin said. He grabbed a passing goblin laborer by the scruff of its homespun shirt and lifted it from the ground. The creature squeaked in agitation, legs flailing.

"Quiet," Riven ordered it.

The goblin ceased squeaking and instead hissed at Riven through its stained fangs.

"Puts me down, human," it said in a high-pitched voice, its Common rough and awkward, "or I'll finds you asleep and cuts out your other eye."

Riven scowled and the creature recoiled. The assassin produced three gold pieces from his pouch and flashed them before the goblin's eyes. The creature grabbed at the coins but Riven pulled them out of reach.

"What's it you wants, one-eye?" the goblin asked.

Cale looked around to see whether they had drawn attention. To his alarm, he saw that one of the Skulls had moved nearer to them to observe. It floated above them, its empty gaze seeing everything.

"Riven. . . ." Cale said, gesturing toward the ceiling.

Riven's gaze followed Cale's. Seeing the Skull, he slowly lowered the goblin to the ground, but kept his grip on its shirt.

"These are yours," Riven said to the creature, again flashing the coin while eyeing the Skull sidelong, "when you tell me what I want to know."

A cunning look came across the goblin's red-skinned face. It rubbed its hands together greedily.

"Asks me, hole-in-face."

Riven said, "Less than half an hour ago, a single wagon went into the tunnels. It had a score or more of gray dwarves as guards."

The goblin nodded and said, "Me sees that one."

"Which tunnel?" Riven asked, giving the goblin a shake.

"You gives more," the goblin replied.

Riven's gaze went hard.

"I'll give you two more," he said.

The creature smiled in satisfaction, and licked its lips. Riven took out two more coins and held them before the goblin's face.

"And I'll drive each of these through your eyes and into your braincase, you little vermin. Speak, now."

The goblin's eyes went wide.

"That one," it said, and pointed toward the tunnel that Magadon had indicated.

Riven released it and flung the coins into the crowd. The creature let out a shriek and scrabbled after the gold.

Above, the Skull turned away from them and floated back to its high perch.

"Wanted to be sure, Mags," Riven said to the guide, by way of apology.

"Keep moving," Cale said, and they hurried down the tunnel, all the while under the watchful gaze of the Skulls.

❧ ❧ ❧ ❧ ❧

The stink of the duergar drove Azriim to distraction. He thought they must bathe once per month, at best. And their clothing! He wondered how anyone could long tolerate the coarse mushroom-fiber tunics and lizard-skin leather trousers they wore. Even their armor, while obviously well-crafted, looked boxy and inelegant.

He consoled himself with the knowledge that soon all of the gray dwarves would be dead. He hadn't even bothered to remember their leader's name, only that the foul creature was an ally of Kexen and served Zstulkk Ssarmn. In fact, the whole clan of duergar to which the guards belonged had pledged its service to the yuan-ti slaver.

Pulled by two of the sure-footed, pony-sized cave lizards endemic to the Underdark, the lone wagon in the caravan rumbled its way north through the twisting but smooth-floored tunnel. Stalactites hung from the low ceiling, and ledges and curtains of stone marked the walls. Phosphorescent lichen lit the road ahead. Water dripped from the ceiling to pool in the recesses of the floor, natural cisterns to quench the thirst of travelers.

Thirty-three duergar—including Azriim in the form of a duergar—guarded the enclosed cart. Dim glowballs hung in rope nests from the sides of the wagon, bouncing with each bump in the road, lighting the caravan like a beacon. Within the cart lay the bait: the magical items Azriim and his broodmates had stolen from the Xanathar.

Four of the gray dwarf warriors walked point perhaps thirty paces in front of the cart, crossbows cocked and loaded. The remainder of the duergar warriors stomped loudly along beside, before, and behind the cart, axes and hammers bare, scowls visible even through their beards. The four duergar mages, each armed with a wand provided to them by Azriim (and taken from the Xanathar's stash; Azriim enjoyed the irony), moved amongst them.

Dolgan, in the form of the Amnian ship's captain who had commissioned the caravan, paced along beside the cart, looking as dull-witted as usual. Azriim lingered near the rear of the troop, eyeing the walls above and listening for noise from behind. He knew where Ahmaergo had set up the ambush—less than an hour's travel ahead—but he couldn't be certain how, when, or where Cale and his companions might appear. As best he could, he wanted to time their appearance with that of the dwarf's ambush. With a combat between two of the most powerful, influential factions in Skullport taking place in a main trade tunnel not far from the city, and with ample magic use occurring, Azriim thought it a virtual certainty that the Skulls would appear in force. By his estimation, Skullport's guardians would appear quickly once the combat began in earnest. He simply wanted Cale and his companions to find themselves in the middle of the hell storm. Watching them die would have been a joy. But alas, it would not be. Azriim and his broodmates would remain on the battlefield only until the Skulls began to show.

Smiling, he reached out with his consciousness, connected to Dolgan, and continued through the tunnel ahead, until he felt contact with Serrin.

❧   ❧   ❧   ❧   ❧

Serrin, dressed in the flesh of one Maxil, a human male warrior in service to the Xanathar and late of Skullport, crouched with his "comrades" in the darkness of one of the many narrow side tunnels that opened off a main cavern. An entire network of thin, winding tunnels intersected in the large, open cavern that Ahmaergo the dwarf called the killing field. It was in that cave that Ahmaergo intended to ambush the caravan.

The dwarf had assembled a sizeable force of mercenaries, mages, and even four trolls. All were protected with wards cast by priests of Bane allied with the Xanathar. The dwarf's force waited in hiding in multiple separate groups near the mouths of several of the side tunnels. When the trap was sprung, they would catch the caravan in a crossfire of quarrels and spells.

Or at least that is what Ahmaergo planned. Serrin would have none of it, of course. He and his broodmates would manipulate the would-be ambush to make it unfold as they wished. Afterward, they would use their rods—in Serrin's case, a replacement rod provided by the Sojourner—to teleport away.

He shared his tunnel with six men armored in mail hauberks and armed with crossbows and swords. A gnome mage stood with them, an illusionist, and his glamour had rendered them all invisible. A troll hulked at the mouth of the cave, its respiration as loud as a bellows, the stink from its green, warty skin as foul as a sewer.

"Demons' teeth," whispered one of the warriors near Serrin, looking down the main tunnel from which the caravan would approach. "I'd just as soon get this thing going apace."

Playing his part, Serrin offered a disingenuous nod.

"Aye. Move your arses, boys," he whispered to the empty tunnel, "and let's get to it."

The soldier thumped him on the shoulder at the same moment that Serrin felt the familiar tingle of psionic contact at the base of his brain—Azriim. He gave no outward sign of the contact.

Is the dwarf's force in position? projected Azriim.

They are, Serrin answered, *and I am with them.*

Notify Dolgan before the ambush is sprung, Azriim said. *Dolgan?*

I'll alert the caravan when Serrin alerts me, Dolgan replied.

Azriim's satisfaction was palpable even as he sent, *The attack must not be allowed to take the caravan by surprise. Once it begins, draw out the battle as long as possible, and ensure that magic is cast in abundance. We make for the provenience of the mantle when the Skulls begin to appear.*

Understood, Serrin answered, and Dolgan too projected an acknowledgment.

What of Cale and his companions? Serrin asked before Azriim broke contact.

Serrin wished to see the one-eyed assassin die, and die slowly, for what the human had done to him back in the farmhouse outside of Selgaunt.

I will backtrack down the tunnel to ensure that Cale and the others do not miss the festivities, Azriim replied. *Remain ready.*

❧ ❧ ❧ ❧ ❧

Azriim cut off contact with Serrin. Satisfied that all was in order with his plan, he gradually let himself lag behind the caravan. The duergar didn't seem to notice his absence, and when he reached a satisfactory distance away from the rear guard, he whispered an arcane word to render himself invisible. He knew that Cale and his companions had not preceded him down the tunnel. In his guise as Thyld, Azriim hadn't told the assassin which tunnel exactly the duergar caravan would take. Accordingly, the humans could only have watched the northern tunnels and followed after.

Pleased with himself for covering all contingencies, Azriim shifted form from duergar to slaad and prowled back down the tunnel.

⊛ ⊛ ⊛ ⊛ ⊛

Cale, Riven, Magadon, and Jak sped down the tunnel. The floor was smoothed, presumably to allow easy passage for carts, but they still had to skirt occasional stands of stalagmites and pools of still water. Mindlinked by Magadon, they traveled in near silence, brushing over the rock of the Underdark without even a rustle, the only sound that of their respiration and the occasional flutter of startled bats. Cale kept his hearing, heightened when he was in darkness, attuned to the passage ahead.

They traveled without light, fearful that luminescence would betray them to the duergar guards. Cale knew it must have been difficult for Riven to see by only the faint luminescence of the orange lichen, but the assassin kept up the pace and did not complain.

They traveled for nearly half an hour and still saw no sign of the slaadi, or the caravan. Magadon stopped twice to examine the tunnel for signs of passage, but the hard rock floor didn't allow him to confirm that the caravan— that *any* caravan—had recently passed through.

It cannot be far, Magadon said. *It will be moving much more slowly than us.*

Cale nodded and swallowed his concern that they may have picked the wrong tunnel. Magadon had never yet led them astray. If the guide said they were in the right tunnel, then they were in the right tunnel.

Make certain, Mags, Riven said.

Magadon looked to Cale and Cale nodded, ignoring Riven's frown.

The guide put his fingers to his temples and a corona of white light flared around his head. His eyes rolled back in his head as he made contact with Azriim and looked through the slaad's eyes.

The guide stiffened; his intake of breath was as sharp as a keen blade.

"What is it?" Cale said.

With visible effort, Magadon relaxed.

"The caravan did pass this way," he said, a bit overloud, and pointed up the tunnel.

Before Cale could ask a question, Magadon projected, *Azriim is looking upon us right now. Do not turn around.*

❂   ❂   ❂   ❂   ❂

Invisible, Azriim crouched on a ledge slightly up on the wall of the tunnel and eyed the four humans. Until just moments before, he had not yet known whether the woodsman was a psionicist or a mage. But the telltale nimbus of white light that had just flared around the human's head bespoke the manifestation of psionic power. Azriim imagined that the taste of the woodsman's brain would be particularly sweet, flavored as it was with the spice of mental magic.

He grinned, and almost laughed aloud. The priest of Mask certainly had assembled a ragtag group of fools to follow him across and under Faerûn. Had any of them understood the scope of the Sojourner's power, they would have long ago curled up in a dark hole to hide.

No matter, he thought. Soon, they will all die in the dark.

He licked his lips, eyeing the back of Erevis Cale's bald head while the woodsman confirmed for them that the caravan had traveled up the corridor. They had followed along behind the duergar, just as Azriim had expected.

I have located the humans, Azriim projected to his broodmates.

Absently, he pawed at the teleportation rod in his hand.

Dolgan and Serrin projected an acknowledgment.

Of Serrin, Azriim asked, *Do you see the lights from the caravan yet?*

Not yet, responded his broodmate.

But the caravan is getting near to the ambush point, Dolgan added.

Azriim allowed himself to feel satisfied. Everything

was working out exactly as he had foreseen. Certainly the Sojourner would reward him.

Serrin's voice sounded in his head, *Perhaps you should kill one now?*

Azriim flexed his claws, powerfully tempted. He could reach Cale in a single step, and could tear the human's head from his shoulders with but one swipe.

❧ ❧ ❧ ❧ ❧

Despite Magadon's admonition, Cale tensed. The shadows around his skin swirled, animated by his agitation. Beside him, Riven's hand drifted to his saber hilts. Jak's breath came faster.

Where? Cale asked.

"The caravan is not far," Magadon continued. *On a ledge on your sword arm side, perhaps ten paces back the way we came. In slaad form. He holds the teleportation rod in his hand.*

Cale's mind churned.

Kill him now, Riven said.

Cale considered it, and soon gave in.

Follow my play, he projected.

"The caravan could not have come this way," Cale said to Jak with affected frustration in his tone. "If it had, we'd have already caught up to it."

Jak looked startled for an instant, but quickly took to the play. The halfling shook his head and let anger creep into his eyes.

"The Hells it didn't," Jak spat back as he drew his short sword, offering Cale an excuse to unsheathe his own blade. "You keep questioning our competence. I've had enough. If you think the caravan didn't come this way, then go back the way we came. You won't find it down another tunnel."

Cale pulled Weaveshear, pointed its tip at Jak's chest, then at Magadon.

"You're both out your shares. And only our past friendship

is saving your life, halfling." He gave Jak a final scowl and turned to Riven. "Riven, you're with me."

Jak made an obscene gesture.

Cale answered him with a glare, and he and Riven turned to stalk back up the tunnel. Cale saw the ledge immediately, imagined Azriim crouched atop it.

He's looking at you, Magadon projected.

You tell me if he moves, Cale answered, still holding Weaveshear bare. The blade, sheathed in shadows, seemed to want to pull him toward the ledge.

Riven rested his hands on his sabers as they walked.

Three paces . . . five . . . seven . . . and they were right next to the ledge. Cale could almost feel the weight of Azriim's gaze. His hands were sweating.

We go on my mark, he said to Riven.

❀ ❀ ❀ ❀ ❀

Azriim could have reached out and touched Cale. He tensed the thick muscles of his thighs, imagined a pounce, but fought down the impulse to kill. He wanted to draw Cale and his companions into the battle with the caravan. Their presence there would increase the intensity of the combat, drawing the Skulls to the site even sooner.

To his broodmates, he projected, *No, I will not kill one. We must get the caravan to the ambush point and begin the combat. The humans will hear it and rush ahead. They can die there.*

His broodmates projected an acknowledgement.

Serrin said, *I see the lights from the caravan now. It is near. The dwarf's forces are preparing.*

Azriim smiled, mouthed a "good-bye" at Cale, and began to activate his teleportation rod.

❀ ❀ ❀ ❀ ❀

Now! Cale projected, and sprung into motion.

He spun toward the ledge and leveled Weaveshear in

a cross cut designed to take Azriim's head, even as Riven whipped free both sabers and lunged at the ledge with the points stabbing low.

They hit nothing.

"Gone," Magadon said aloud. "Teleported out."

"Blast," Riven said.

Frustrated, Cale slammed Weaveshear back into his scabbard.

Magadon said, "He's . . . he's back near the caravan. I can see it ahead. I think he's changing form back into a duergar."

"Cut it, Mags," Cale said. "Let's keep moving. We're close to that caravan now."

CHAPTER 18

THE CARAVAN

The duergar on point whistled for a halt and the caravan creaked to a stop. Two of the gray dwarves who had been on point were jogging back to the main body of the caravan, their armor and weapons clanking. Dolgan, Azriim (who had just returned from the rear), and the duergar leader stepped forward to meet them.

"A large open cavern is just ahead," one of the two dwarves said in Undercommon. Scars crisscrossed the gnarled duergar's bald head, and dirt caked his beard. "It's flat as an orog's head and riddled with side tunnels. Ideal for an ambush."

The duergar leader, his dusky skin pockmarked with the scars of a past disease, turned to Azriim and said, "I know that cavern. It'll take the wagon a hundred count to cross it, and that's pushing the lizard. We should scout it out first."

The duergar leader looked to Dolgan, who the slaadi had represented to them as the client paying their wages. "That cavern's the equivalent of an exposed valley on the surface. Very vulnerable to attack from the heights, or in this case, from all sides. We should be cautious."

Dolgan nodded, but unwilling to respond without Azriim's prompting, he projected to his broodmate, *What do I answer?*

Instead of responding to Dolgan directly, Azriim sniffed, pulled his beard, and shook his axe.

"Bah! If you're concerned, the mages can prepare wards for as many of the men as possible." Azriim-the-duergar looked to Dolgan and added, "We cross quickly, with axes ready."

Make a show of considering it, Azriim projected, *then agree. Have the mages cast protective wards on the men. It will make the combat last longer anyway.*

Dolgan did exactly as he was told, and when the duergar mages had cast a variety of protective wards on many of their guardsmen, the caravan again moved out. They were heading directly into the cavern, where Ahmaergo's ambush awaited.

Here we come, Dolgan projected to Serrin.

❧ ❧ ❧ ❧ ❧

When the caravan had crossed half the cavern the ambush was sprung.

Enjoy, Serrin projected to his broodmates.

From four of the side tunnels that opened onto the main cavern, crossbow bolts whizzed. Most skittered harmlessly on the stone floor or thumped off of sturdy duergar armor, but a few found homes in flesh. One sank into Dolgan's shoulder. He grunted and jerked it free, his flesh regenerating the damage almost immediately. Two bolts sank into the pack lizard, causing the creature to rear up and roar in pain. Its sudden movement caused the wagon to lurch forward.

"Ambush!" Dolgan shouted, barely able to contain a grin, partially because of the pain he felt in his shoulder, and partially because Azriim's plan was working well.

He answered the crossbow fire with a trio of magical bolts fired from his wand into the mouth of a side tunnel, where he saw shadowy figures cowering.

True to Kexen's representation that they were veterans, the duergar guardsmen reacted quickly. The mages ducked behind the lurching wagon and began to mouth the words to still more powerful protective wards. The warriors jumped behind the wagon or fell prone, plying their own crossbows.

Shouts and bestial roars erupted from the side tunnels. Huge, lumbering figures formed out of the darkness and loped forward, their great strides eating up the distance.

"Trolls," shouted the duergar in Undercommon, and those nearest the onrushing trolls leaped to their feet.

Calling upon the magical attributes native to their race, several of the duergar grew to twice their normal size, nearly matching the onrushing trolls in stature. Several others vanished from sight, masked by invisibility spells.

Dolgan watched with satisfaction as the combat began to unfold. A force of a score or more human warriors poured from the tunnels, following the charging trolls.

Beams of green energy and swarms of magical darts arced over the onrushing humans and trolls to slam into the duergar force, all fired by Xanathar mages emerging from the mouths of the side tunnels.

"Use your wands!" Dolgan shouted at the duergar mages. "These are Xanathar troops!"

The duergar mages, some of them protected by visible fields of magical force, leveled the wands Azriim had provided to them, and fired lightning bolts into the charging forces. Men screamed, stumbled, and fell. Their comrades leaped over them, still charging.

Duergar warriors met the charge, returning to visibility at the instant their hammers crushed the heads of some of the Xanathar's troops. A fierce melee began halfway between the side tunnels and the caravan. Hammers and axes rose and fell, and swords and shields cut and bashed. Men and dwarves alike screamed in rage and pain.

A globe of brilliant light flared to life, illuminating the cavern, limning the violence. The light-sensitive duergar recoiled and shielded their eyes, temporarily blinded. Trolls and human warriors took the opportunity to press the attack against the gray dwarves, forcing them back with a fierce onslaught. Thinking quickly, one of the duergar mages dispelled the light's sustaining magic, and the dim luminescence of the Underdark again took hold.

Near Dolgan, Azriim plied his own wands, alternately firing lightning and a transmogrifying beam at anything that moved: duergar, human, or troll. Dolgan did likewise. They didn't care which side won the fight, only that it continued for a time and involved powerful magic.

The combat quickly turned into a series of pitched battles scattered all across the cavern floor, with mages and archers supporting from a distance. Spells and counterspells flew. Lightning bolts sizzled from the wands of the duergar mages, leaving a spray of stone splinters, burned flesh, and screams in their wake. Xanathar mages answered, and fireballs blossomed in spherical infernos all over the cavern. Some exploded near the cart, roasting the pack lizard, two duergar, and setting the cart aflame. Giant spiders summoned by the duergar mages prowled the battlefield, pouncing on the wounded and dying.

Wedges of multi-colored magical force ripped through the air, knocking warriors from their feet. Beams of green and red energy laced across the cavern. Globes of darkness formed and were dispelled. Walls of ice and fire appeared from nowhere to burn and freeze. Waves of magic turned stone to mud, set flesh melting and flowing like water.

Throughout, roaring trolls and shambling spiders

rampaged across the battlefield, claws and fangs dripping blood and shreds of flesh. Duergar axes and hammers rose and fell as the doughty dwarves fought in isolated groups of two and three. Sword and shield clashed in answer. Archers patrolled the perimeter of the melee, picking targets. Their crossbows twanged again and again. Quarrels sprouted from the flesh of combatants with the suddenness of lightning strikes. Ahmaergo himself stomped through the battlefield, wielding his huge axe and bellowing challenges in the name of the Xanathar.

This ought to serve to draw the Skulls, Dolgan projected to Azriim.

Even as he completed the thought, a series of magical bolts seared into his flesh. He grinned, reveling in the exquisiteness of the pain.

And Cale and his companions as well, Azriim answered, discharging a lightning bolt into a troll. *It's nearly time to take our leave. Be ready Serrin. You know the location.*

❧ ❧ ❧ ❧ ❧

From ahead, Cale heard the shouts of men and the clash of metal.

"A battle?" Magadon said.

"A big one, to judge from the sound," Jak said.

All four of the comrades readied blades, holy symbols, and bows.

"We move quickly and quietly," Cale said. "No one gets involved except on my say-so." He looked pointedly at Riven as he said that last. The assassin made no response and Cale decided to take the silence as agreement. "The slaadi want us caught up in this, and that's reason enough to stay out," Cale continued. "Mark the slaadi as quickly as you can. Mags, I'm going to need you to show me what Azriim sees, so stand ready."

The guide nodded.

"Let's move," Cale said.

Hurrying through the darkness, the four approached

the scene of battle. Cale intensified the darkness around them slightly as they drew closer. From the tunnel ahead came the flash of fireballs and lightning. Metal rang on metal. Sounds echoed down the corridor: men shouting, beasts roaring, and stone cracking. It sounded as though the ceiling was falling down.

Stay out of it, Cale reminded them again, and all of them nodded, even Riven. Crouching low and hugging the wall, they hurried forward.

Before them opened a wide, open cavern. All around it, a battle roiled. Trolls, men, and duergar fought in pockets, fierce little battles of horrible violence. Hammers, swords, shouts, curses, and roars rose toward the ceiling. Corpses lay scattered across the cavern like so much driftwood.

The caravan's wagon lay on its side, burning. The pack lizard lay on its side too, still yoked to the wagon and hissing in pain, crossbow bolts protruding from its charred flesh. Magical energies arced across the cavern from the side tunnels, the casters hidden by darkness and distance. Duergar mages answered with shots from their wands or spells of their own. The amount of magic flying in the cavern caused the hairs on Cale's arms to stand. Weaveshear fairly hummed in his grasp, bleeding shadows.

"Follow me," Cale said.

He darted off to the side of the cavern a good distance away from the combat. There, Cale saw a protruding ledge of rock sticking out of the stone about eight paces up on the wall. It would offer a good view of the battle, and some small cover from the missile fire and spells.

"There," he said, pointing.

The others nodded and they raced to the wall and began to climb. Behind them, a troll roared in pain. A ricocheting lightning bolt ripped into the wall near them, sending splinters of stone spraying. They reached the ledge, breathing hard, and crouched low.

"Trickster's toes," Jak said. "This is chaos."

"Find the slaadi," Cale said, scouring the battlefield for any telltale sign of their quarry.

He saw only indistinguishable duergar, mercenaries, and trolls.

"I can't see well enough to find anything," Riven growled.

"There!" Jak said.

Cale followed the halfling's pointing finger and saw a large fat human and a duergar slipping toward the far side of the cavern.

Could be them, Magadon projected. *I can confirm.*

Cale replied, *Do it.*

Motes of light flared around the guide's head and his eyes rolled back in their sockets. For a moment, Magadon said nothing and Cale, Jak, and Riven waited in anticipation. Below them, the battle raged, reaching still greater heights of violence.

"It is Azriim," Magadon said.

"Stay with him," Cale said. "When they leave, we follow."

"Leave?" asked Jak.

Cale nodded. He thought he understood the slaadi's play.

"The slaadi engineered this entire battle," he said. "And now that it's going full on, they're backing out of it. It's a distraction."

"Who are they trying to distract?" Riven asked. "Us?"

Cale shrugged, but before he could form a reply, an orange luminescence formed at the mouth of the main tunnel that led back toward Skullport. It grew brighter and brighter, as if someone or something carrying a giant torch were moving closer to the cavern.

"What is that?" Jak asked.

"Find a hole," Riven said, "and stay low. This is bad."

Cale and Jak shared a look. Weaveshear fairly shook in Cale's hand. The shadows around the blade whirled as if in excitement.

The luminescence grew brighter still and the combatants in the chamber seemed to notice it for the first time. Duergar, troll, and human backed away from each other.

Weapons were lowered, and gazes turned toward the tunnel mouth.

Cale pulled down Magadon, who was still connected to Azriim, and willed the darkness around them to deepen.

A murmur of curiosity ran through the chamber, and quickly turned to one of concern, then fear. The combatants saw what was coming. Cale and his companions, off to the side of the tunnel mouth, could not yet see the source of the light.

Stay with Azriim, Cale projected to Magadon. *No matter what occurs.*

"Goddess," Magadon oathed.

Through Azriim's eyes, he too saw what was coming.

A voice louder than a thunderclap and deeper than the Moonsea shook stalactites from the ceiling as it pronounced, *"Cease!"*

Other than the moans of the wounded and dying, an eerie silence reigned.

"The Skulls," Riven said softly, as six glowing human skulls whizzed in through the tunnel and rapidly circled the battlefield.

All eyes followed Skullport's enigmatic guardians. Duergar, man, and troll visibly cowered under the inscrutable gaze of the Skulls. Finished with their flyover, the Skulls positioned themselves around the combatants, fencing most of them in. A nervous rustle ran through the chamber. Some of the casters and crossbowmen outside of the ring of Skulls began to back away down the side tunnels.

Cale and his companions were outside the circle. Cale sensed the power in the room, as did Weaveshear, to judge from its hungry vibrations. With six of the Skulls present in the chamber, and presuming that five or six of them were still lurking about in Skullport, as Cale thought typical, most all of the guardians were accounted for.

It was then that it hit him.

"Dark and empty," he whispered.

Azriim and the slaadi had arranged the battle for one

purpose: to draw the Skulls away from the city, or away from something else. But what?

Again the booming voice: *"Warfare in a main thoroughfare of the city of Skullport jeopardizes trade and is in direct contravention to our standing edict! Also, rat scales offer unique numerary opportunities! Most foul! Most foul, indeed!"*

The Skull then went on for several more heartbeats in a language that Cale could not understand, though the tone was unmistakably hostile.

The combatants shared confused looks, but none dared move.

The Skull reverted back to Common, saying, *"For all of the foregoing reasons, Ssarmn and the Xanathar shall be individually disciplined and each of you shall be exterminated."*

It seemed to take a moment for the import of the pronouncement to settle in. When it did, the duergar and humans tentatively raised their weapons. The trolls snarled defiance.

And the Skulls began to kill.

As one, the six Skulls unleashed their awesome magical power. Arcane energies slammed indiscriminately into the encircled forces—fire, ice, lightning, and a hail of stones. Waves of warping magical force ran amok among the duergar. Bolts of amber energy pierced shield, armor, and finally flesh. Men screamed, twisted into shapeless forms, burned, froze, and died.

The mages and crossbowmen poured out of the side tunnels in a panic, like rats fleeing a sinking ship. Two Skulls pursued them. Somehow the city's guardians had ambushed the would-be ambushers. Cale finally counted a total of eight Skulls in the chamber.

In the smoke and flashing lights, Cale could no longer see Azriim and the other slaad.

"Mags?" Cale asked.

Riven grabbed Cale's cloak and said, "We need to get out of here, Cale. Now! No one is going to leave here alive."

Cale heard the urgency in Riven's voice but shook him off.

He looked at Magadon and asked, "Mags?"

"I've got him still," replied the guide. "He's taking out his teleportation rod."

Cale said, "Wherever they go, get a look and give it to me. I'm taking us after them."

Magadon nodded.

"We're leaving, Riven," said Cale. "Well enough?"

The assassin backed off and gave a soft nod, his single eye wide and staring at the Skulls.

In the cavern below, the combatants appeared to have put aside their differences and fought together to survive. Warhammers flew toward the Skulls, crossbow bolts, beams of energy, lightning bolts, and fireballs. The impact of weapons and spells jolted Skullport's guardians, but seemed to do little actual damage, until one of the Skulls fluttered in the air like a wounded bird and sank to the cavern floor. A duergar smashed it with his hammer. A cheer went up.

The duergar standing over the slain Skull took a yellow beam in his chest, screamed, and turned inside out, spraying gore.

The remaining Skulls, unperturbed by their fallen brother, floated across the cavern, unleashing power and death wherever they moved. Duergar, trolls, and humans formed groups and rushed the Skulls. Duergar and Xanathar mages fired everything they had at the Skulls—wand and spell. Huge stalactites broke from the ceiling and crashed on the cavern's floor. One of them crushed a second Skull and buried a group of duergar.

"That's it!" Magadon said. "They've moved. All three of them. They're in a smooth walled tunnel, still in the Underdark but not in Skullport. Something is wrong with one of them." The guide held out a hand. "Here. I can show it to you."

Cale reached out and clasped Magadon's arm.

"Cover!" Riven shouted.

Before Cale could respond, an explosion of fire rocked the ledge. An inferno of heat and light engulfed the entire face of the wall and he lost his grip on Magadon. Vaguely, he heard Jak, Riven, and the guide scream, then he heard the dull thud of flesh slamming into rock. The force from the blast flattened Cale against the ledge, stealing his breath. Only mildly stunned, he looked up a moment later to find his clothes smoking but his flesh unharmed. Weaveshear, sheathed in shadows, vibrated in his hand.

Magadon and Jak lay near him, off to the side, their flesh charred, their clothes aflame. But both of them were blinking, both of them were conscious. They were looking past Cale, wide-eyed. Jak tried to say something but no sound emerged. Cale turned his head to find himself face to face with the glowing visage of a Skull.

❧ ❧ ❧ ❧ ❧

Azriim materialized in the tunnel to the sound of screams—Dolgan's screams. The big slaad's hind claw had materialized up to the ankle in the stone of the cavern's floor. It looked as if stone jaws had clamped shut on his broodmate's foot.

Azriim pocketed his teleportation rod and shook his head in irritation—not because he was concerned with Dolgan's pain, but because time was of the essence and Dolgan's plight would slow them down. He had known an errant teleport to be a possibility of using the rods in the Underdark, but had decided to run the risk. In truth, he'd had no choice. He needed to get to the provenience while the Skulls were distracted with the battle in the north tunnels. He did not have a lot of time.

Still wailing, Dolgan pulled at his extremity as though he might jerk it from the stone. His claws dug bloody grooves in the flesh of his exposed calf, but the stone did not release its grip.

Azriim knew the effort to be futile. The hind claw could

not be pulled free. The substance of his broodmate's foot had melded with the stone. There was only one way to get him loose.

"Silence, fool," Azriim commanded, concerned that his broodmate's wails might be heard by any remaining Skulls.

When Dolgan showed no sign of having understood, Azriim willed a globe of silence to surround them, and all sound died.

Serrin, standing beside Dolgan and eyeing the big slaad's extremity with emotionless gray eyes, projected, *Transform yourself into a smaller shape.*

Dolgan looked up sharply and grinned through his pain. Drool ran from the corners of his mouth. He closed his eyes for a moment and began to change, his large human form shrinking down into that of a gnome.

As Azriim had known, the transformation did not free his foot.

It did not work, Dolgan said through clenched teeth.

Azriim could not tell if the big slaad was smiling with pleasure or grimacing with pain.

We can see that, Serrin answered.

Dolgan's eyes watered with the agony.

It is painful, he said.

Azriim sighed.

Of course it is, he replied. They had to move, so to Serrin he projected, *Chop it off.*

Dolgan's eyes went wide.

What? Do not!

Serrin did not show surprise, though his eyes narrowed. He hefted his falchion.

It is the only way, Azriim said to Dolgan. *Be grateful that Serrin carries a blade, else you would have to chew your way through your own leg.*

But—

Otherwise, Azriim continued, *we will have to leave you behind to starve.*

Dolgan stared at Azriim for a moment before his

expression dropped. The big slaad looked to Serrin, then the falchion, and Azriim saw acceptance in his eyes.

Do it, then, Dolgan projected.

Serrin didn't hesitate. He raised his blade high. Dolgan, still in gnome form, held up a small, gnarled hand.

Don't do it all in one swing, he projected, warming to events. *And make certain it's painful.*

☻ ☻ ☻ ☻ ☻

Cale climbed to his feet, Weaveshear in hand.

The Skull pronounced something in a tongue that Cale did not understand, though the ominous tone was clear.

Cale said, "I don't understand" and began to back off toward Jak and Magadon.

The Skull moved with him and spoke sharply in the same tongue. Before Cale could utter another reply, the Skull's eyes flared and a green ray fired from the sockets. Cale, trying but failing to sidestep the beam, instinctively brandished Weaveshear before him.

To his shock, the shadows around the sword swallowed the beam. The blade grew hot in his hand and began to shake. He felt the power contained within it, sensed its desire to be released. With nothing else for it, he pointed Weaveshear's tip at the Skull.

The green beam, interspersed with hair-fine threads of shadowstuff, blazed forth. It hit the surprised Skull between its eyes, and for a moment the creature shook violently, as if it was about to blow apart.

But it did not, and instead the Skull cocked itself curiously to the side and eyed the blade. It spoke a long string of phrases, each in a different language. Cale understood almost nothing, catching only one word that he knew: *coluk,* a Turmish verb meaning, "to absorb."

Behind the Skull, the battle raged on. Fire and lightning lit the cavern. The stone was awash in magical energy and blood. The Skull before Cale uttered a piercing, keening wail. A second Skull engaged in the battle turned sharply at the sound. It turned from the battle and veered toward the ledge.

Cale's heart hammered in his chest. He could not manage two Skulls.

Still holding Weaveshear between himself and the Skull, he moved nearer to Jak and Magadon, knelt, and grabbed the halfling by the cloak.

"Get up, Jak," he hissed. "Mags . . . up. Now."

With Cale's help, his two stunned companions climbed to their feet, still smoking and dazed from the fireball. The second Skull was nearly to the ledge. The first kept its impassive gaze fixed squarely on Cale.

"Riven!" Cale called, not seeing the assassin.

"Here," Riven's voice called from behind them and to their right.

Cale glanced over his shoulder to see Riven crouched against the wall, his one eye fixed on the Skull. He held throwing daggers in each hand—paltry weapons against so formidable a foe. His clothes were blackened, but he looked generally unharmed by the fireball.

"We're leaving," Cale said, speaking as much to the Skull as to his comrades. "*We're leaving*," he said again, but in Turmish, hoping the Skull would understand.

The Skull softly muttered something in reply. The second Skull was nearly there.

Pulling Magadon and Jak along, Cale backed toward Riven.

Mags, he projected, *show me where the slaadi went.*

The Skull began to mouth arcane words. The second Skull fell in beside it and joined its incantation. Cale feared that Weaveshear would not be able to absorb whatever was coming next.

Put your hand on me, Riven! Cale projected. *Mags, now!*

Riven grabbed a fistful of Cale's cloak as a mental image formed in Cale's brain: a smooth walled cavern with a formation of stalagmites on the right and a shallow pool. While Cale knew that teleporting in the Underdark presented danger, he had no choice. He drew the shadows around him as quickly as he could and willed them to move to the cavern—willed them to move that instant.

The Skulls' dead eyes stared holes into Cale. Their power gathered, and Cale summoned power of his own.

With alarming suddenness, a wave of incredible magical force exploded outward from the Skulls.

Cale closed his eyes against the impact. He felt a flutter in his gut, and everything went black.

CHAPTER 19

SOWING

Cale materialized in a ready crouch, Weaveshear in hand. He took a quick scan of the tunnel. It extended in both directions to the limits of his darkvision. Clusters of stalagmites stood at intervals on the uneven floor, and stalactites hung from the ceiling like drips of stone. A still pool was along the wall to the right, its dark water smeared with a gray fungal growth that floated on top. Cale had no sense of how far they were from either Skullport of the battle they'd just fled. He found the feeling disorienting, isolating.

The tunnel was silent but for their breathing. The slaadi were nowhere in sight.

"Where are we?" Jak asked.

"Somewhere in the Underdark," Cale replied. "Light, little man. Mags, find them."

Beside Cale, Jak struck a sunrod on the rocky

ground. The thin shaft of alchemically treated metal rang softly off the stone and began to glow more brightly than a torch. It would last an hour or so. Jak held it aloft, illuminating the tunnel for all of them. Though Cale had not needed the sunrod to see, he welcomed its dim luminescence for the shadows it cast.

Magadon's knucklebone eyes took in the surroundings, and scoured the floor.

"Blood," the guide said.

He moved to a splotch of dark matter on the floor. Cale followed the guide's gaze and saw a large smear of black blood, intermixed with chunks of flesh and a shard of bone. The stone floor near the remains looked malformed, as though it might have melted and been reformed.

Magadon put his fingers to the blood, studied it. He rubbed the flesh between two fingers.

"Slaadi," he said. "And still damp. One of them was wounded here."

He wiped his fingers clean on his trousers.

"Which way, Mags?" Cale asked, trying to keep his voice calm.

He knew they had only moments to stop the slaadi, and they could ill afford to get the direction wrong.

Magadon studied the floor near the blood while Cale silently implored him to hurry. The guide brushed his fingers along the stone as if communing with it. He moved across the stone, stopping here and there to examine the floor more carefully.

"What is it?" Jak asked.

Magadon replied, "Scratches from their hind claws. Very faint. They must have transformed back to their natural forms." He stood and nodded down the tunnel. "They went that way."

Cale exhaled and thumped him on the shoulder.

"Let's go," he said.

They sped down the tunnel. Magadon ran at Cale's side, while Jak and Riven brought up the rear. Weaveshear still vibrated in Cale's hand and continued leaking shadows.

Not more than two hundred paces later they found a wide corridor that opened off the tunnel. Unlike the rough, natural walls of the cave, the corridor had a finished floor lined with marble. It looked like a road, or some kind of processional. It curved after a short distance, and from around the curve emanated a soft orange glow.

Weapons and holy symbols ready, Cale led them forward.

The corridor went on for only a short time after the curve before it ended, as though cut off with a knife, and opened onto a breathtaking panorama.

"Trickster's hairy toes," Jak oathed.

Cale could only agree.

They stood at the edge of the corridor, in an opening halfway up a sheer cavern wall that was easily as tall as three bowshots. A great circular cavern stretched before and below them, nearly as large as the one that contained Skullport. Within the cavern lay ruins. Toppled buildings of gray granite, impossibly thin towers of stone carved from stalactites, and collapsed temples of white marble littered the cavern's floor in a chaotic jumble. Their stone skeletons obscured the otherwise mathematically precise web of wide roads and broad avenues that once had connected the districts of the city. The ruins reminded Cale of Elgrin Fau, but instead of a necropolis of intact tombs, only one structure remained whole.

In the center of the cavern, glowing orange with power, towered an immense spire of rough gray stone like the finger of a god. It appeared unworked but for a covered cupola of metal that capped its top. Open archways yawned in the cupola, one on each of the four sides of the spire, and all of them leaking orange light. It was impossible to see within.

Tumors of clear crystal bulged here and there from the stone of the spire. A thin strip of protruding crystal, like wire around a sword hilt, wound a path from the base of the tower to a platform before the near archway in the cupola. It took Cale a moment to realize that the crystalline spiral was either a stairway or a ramp.

A beam of orange light as thick around as an ogre emanated from the tower through a hole in the top of the cupola. The orange beam shot toward the ceiling and cast the entire cavern in soft orange luminescence. The light caused Cale to squint with minor discomfort but didn't burn like the sun, steal his powers like daylight, or take his hand as a tithe.

When the beam reached the ceiling, it spread out and dispersed into ten thinner beams that wove amongst the stalactites like veins. In turn, each of those separated into ten still thinner beams, and so on until the threads became so tiny as to be invisible. The entire chamber was roofed by a lattice of power, and Cale had no doubt that the lattice extended its invisible grasp into Skullport's chamber, buttressing the stone, preventing it from collapsing of its own weight. They must have been nearer to Skullport than he'd thought.

"That tower is the hidden chamber where the Skulls lair," Cale said, realizing the truth even as the words passed his lips. "It must be the source of their power. Azriim has lured the Skulls away from their secret chamber and the source lays exposed. He wants to use the Weave Tap to somehow drain the tower and the web of energy . . . perhaps even destroy it."

Jak let out a long, low whistle. Riven and Magadon remained silent.

Cale realized that if Azriim was successful, it would result in a catastrophe for Skullport—a catastrophe for Varra.

"We can't let it happen," he said.

"The rock must have shifted over the years," Magadon observed. "This tunnel must once have been at ground level."

Cale nodded and said, "Or it could be just as likely that this corridor was once attached to the upper levels of a soaring tower."

Roads spanning the sky had not been uncommon in that city. Cale could sense it. The magical skill evidenced by the spire suggested to him that the ruined metropolis, that even Skullport, had once been places of grandeur. He wondered at the true origin of the Skulls.

Putting the awe out of his mind, he eyed the ruins below, searching for any sign of the slaadi. He did not see them.

"We need to get to that spire," he said. "The slaadi must be heading there. That spire is the origin of the lattice, and that's where Azriim will use the Weave Tap."

As though affirming his words, the shadows leaking from Weaveshear floated into the air and across the cavern toward the spire. The height at which the companions stood was about two-thirds of the way up the tower.

"Teleport us there, Cale," Riven said.

Cale shook his head and replied, "I can call upon the shadows only infrequently. I can shadowstep often, but teleport only rarely. The slaadi, on the other hand have no such limitation with their teleportation rods. Likely, they're already inside the cupola. We need another way."

Cale ignored the look of satisfaction in Riven's eye, and realized then that the assassin cared more about being Mask's second than he did about stopping the slaadi. He didn't have time to give it further thought.

"Look!" Jak said, pointing at the tower.

The slaadi emerged from around the back of the tower, loping up the crystalline staircase for the cupola. The largest of the three hobbled along with a limp.

"Why didn't they teleport into the cupola?" Magadon asked of no one in particular.

"The magic of the tower must interfere with transport magic of that kind," Cale said. "They probably teleported to near the tower's base. We weren't that far behind them and yet they're already halfway up the tower."

"I can get us there," Magadon said. "Without magic."

Cale turned to face the guide and asked, "What can you do?"

Magadon, already drawn and haggard from all of the psionic energy he had expended in recent hours, said,

"Attune our bodies to the air. We'll be able to run above the city to the tower."

"Dark," Jak whispered.

"What will you have left?" Cale asked him.

Magadon shook his head and replied, "I'll drop the mindlink. But still, not much."

Cale took only a moment to decide.

"Do it."

Magadon nodded and held his left hand to his temple. A dim white light originated at the crown of his head and spread downward until it sheathed his entire boy. There was a sound like the *whoosh* of a wind. Magadon touched each of Cale, Riven, and Jak in turn, causing a similar light to limn their bodies, eliciting a similar sound.

"Now," Magadon said, and the light flared.

A tremor ran the length of Cale's body. He felt lighter, as ephemeral as a spirit. The white light rapidly diminished to nothingness, but the feeling of insubstantiality remained.

"Walk on the air as though it's solid earth," Magadon said. "Vertical movement is controlled by your mind. Imagine stairs or a ramp as you run, and you'll move up or down."

Without another word, the guide stepped off the corridor's edge and into the open air. Jak audibly gasped, but instead of plummeting to his death, the guide stood suspended on nothing.

Cale took a deep breath and followed suit. The air felt spongy under his feet, but solid enough. He could see the ruins of the city far below and had to fight down a wave of dizziness.

He said to Riven and Jak, "Come on."

They did, and when all four had tested the air, they turned and ran across the sky for the tower. Magadon and Cale led. Jak and Riven followed hard after.

With nothing but air and orange light around him, Cale felt exposed, visible. He yearned for the comfort of shadow. He toyed with the idea of making himself invisible but saw no point. He could do nothing to hide his comrades, so he would stand with them.

When they had made it halfway across the city, the biggest of the three slaadi—Dolgan—saw them. The fat slaad, wobbling on his wounded leg, made an obscene gesture in their direction and shouted to his fellows.

The creatures were almost to the cupola. One more twist around the tower and they would be at the top.

Cale could see Azriim's fanged grin, even from that distance. An itch manifested deep in the base of Cale's brain, an itch that became a whisper, then a voice.

It is my pleasure to see you again, Azriim said into Cale's mind. Unlike the feeling elicited by Magadon's mindlink, the slaad's psionic touch felt greasy, hostile. *You are a persistent creature.*

I'm going to kill you, Cale projected back.

Hardly a novel plan for you, priest, Azriim replied with a mental sneer.

The slaad broke the contact and spoke to his fellows. As one, the three slaadi pointed in the direction of Cale and his companions, each mouthed an arcane word, and fired three pea-sized orange balls from their outstretched palms.

"Cover!" Cale shouted, and immediately realized how foolish the exclamation sounded.

They were running across the open air. There was nowhere to hide.

He turned, grabbed Jak, and threw himself face down over the halfling as orange fire exploded in their midst. He prayed that Magadon would survive the blast, knowing that if the guide was killed, their ability to walk on air would cease.

One ball of flame exploded, then another, and another. The blistering air rushed past and over Cale. Jak hissed against the pain. The heat and flames enshrouded them. Cale grimaced against the expected agony but the pain did not come. His shadowstuff-suffused body resisted the spells of the slaadi and sheltered Jak from the worst of the blast. Cale waited for the fall to come, his heart in his throat.

The air remained as solid as earth under his boots.

He climbed to his feet, pulling Jak up by the cloak. The halfling already had his holy symbol in hand and he began to chant.

To Cale's right, Magadon and Riven clambered to their feet, skin raw, clothes smoking. Riven pulled shadows from the orange-tinted air, twirled them around his fingers, and touched them to his flesh. His wounds disappeared. Magadon swayed but seemed all right.

In the meantime, the halfling completed his prayer. White fire flew from Jak's outstretched hands and broke on the slaadi like water on rocks, seemingly to no effect.

Recovered, Magadon unshouldered his bow, knocked an arrow, and let fly. The arrow took Dolgan in the shoulder. The impact drove the fat slaad against the tower and he howled, stumbling on his wounded foot.

"Move!" Cale said. "We have to keep them from reaching the tower!"

Together, they pelted for the spire, Cale and Magadon in the lead. They had a full bowshot of open air to cover before they reached the tower.

Seeing them charge, Azriim barked something to his fellow slaadi, turned, and raced up the crystal stairs, taking them two at a time. He spiraled around the tower and went out of sight. Meanwhile, Dolgan jerked the arrow from his flesh, threw it over the side of the staircase, and pulled a thin iron rod from a leather tube on his thigh. His fellow did the same, except that his wand appeared to be made of wood.

"Wands!" Magadon warned as they ran.

"Spread out!" Cale shouted, and began to incant his own spell.

The comrades opened some distance between them as they charged, to make targeting them with the wands more difficult. Cale finished incanting his spell, a dweomer that cancelled other magic. He targeted it on the gray-eyed slaad's wand hoping to disable it. His spell took effect, met the magic of the wand, and failed. In that failure Cale caught a sense of the power of the mage who had crafted the wand: the Sojourner.

"Dark and empty," he whispered.

Dolgan's fanged mouth formed an arcane word and the tip of his wand flared. A mass of churning green gas formed in the air near Jak and Riven, a noxious, sick-looking little cloud. The halfling tumbled aside, but Riven ran right into it. The vapors swallowed him. The gas was so thick Cale couldn't see within.

"Riven!" Magadon said.

Unwilling to leave Riven behind, Cale and Magadon aborted their charge and turned back.

Quickly, Jak sheathed his blade, pocketed his holy symbol, and said, "I'll get him."

The halfling took a great gulp of air, held it, and rushed into the cloud. He emerged a moment later pulling Riven by his cloak. The assassin was bent double, coughing and vomiting. He pushed Fleet away and gestured toward the tower.

"Go," the assassin spat at them. "I'll follow."

He retched again, raining the contents of his stomach on the ruins far below. The cloud of gas, evidently heavier than air, began to slowly sink toward the ruins below.

Cale turned just in time to see the gray-eyed slaad fire a thin green beam from the tip of his wand. Magadon saw it too, and danced aside as the beam streaked past his hip.

Azriim came into view again around the near side of the tower, still loping hard up the spiral stairway. He was nearly to the archway that opened onto the cupola. Cale knew then that they would not be able to stop him. His heart sank.

Orange light streamed out of the archway in a cascade of beams. And in that light, Cale suddenly saw a way to stop the slaad.

To Magadon and Jak he said, "You two take the slaadi on the stairs. I've got Azriim. Go!"

"Do not delay, Erevis," Magadon said, and Cale could see the fatigue in the guide's eyes.

He would not be able to keep them attuned with the air for much longer.

Cale nodded and said again, "Go."

The guide and the halfling charged forward together. Cale stayed back, drawing his own shadow close around him, eyeing Azriim, waiting. He spared a look back at Riven, who appeared to have gathered himself.

"Meet me in the cupola," Cale said to the assassin.

Riven wiped the vomit from his mouth, eyed him, and nodded.

❂ ❂ ❂ ❂ ❂

Jak knew he had to do something about the wands. He and Magadon were thirty paces from the slaadi. The creatures would get another shot at them before they could close.

"Cover me, Mags," Jak said.

The halfling pulled his holy symbol and began to incant a prayer as he ran.

The guide did not ask questions, instead he unshouldered his bow and began to fire. The guide fired rapidly, if inaccurately, even while running. His archery was astounding. The slaadi dodged the streaking missiles, though the effort nearly caused the fat one to fall from the tower.

Jak finished his spell and targeted the mind of Dolgan, overwhelming the slaad's brain with conflicting, confusing ideas and images. He knew it had worked when the huge creature gripped his head between his clawed hands and began to mutter. The slaad set down his wand and looked from Jak to his fellow slaad, then to the top of the tower and to the ruins below.

"Well done!" Magadon said.

The guide reshouldered his bow and drew his sword. Jak unsheathed his own blade, reserving his other hand for his holy symbol.

"He's only confused," the halfling explained. "He's still potentially dangerous, but for now, focus on the other."

Magadon nodded and they raced across the solid air at the slaadi.

The slaad unaffected by Jak's spell fired his wand again. Jak dodged, but the beam struck him in the side. His body went soft, amorphous. He felt his form begin to shift, felt the components of his body begin to metamorphose. . . .

"No," he said between gritted his teeth.

Still running, even as his legs began to shrink and thin, he willed himself to stay whole, to resist whatever transformation the wand sought to force.

The effect ceased. He'd done it. Jak came back to himself, grinning fiercely.

The gray-eyed slaad, seemingly untroubled, replaced his wand in his thigh sheath and pulled a huge falchion from a scabbard over his back.

Magadon and Jak spaced themselves as they ran to come at the slaad from different angles.

But before they could close, the slaad confused by Jak's spell growled something unintelligible, turned to his fellow slaad, and lashed out with a claw. Red tracks opened in the skin of the gray-eyed slaad's chest. He bounded backward and down a few stairs, shouting urgently in a tongue Jak didn't recognize. The wounds on the slaad's chest began to close, while the larger one advanced on him in a fighting crouch.

Jak's spell was working better than he could have hoped. Tymora and the Trickster always smiled on the brave.

Still, it sometimes paid to be cautious. He slowed his charge long enough to allow him to utter the words to another spell. When he finished, his hands and feet grew sticky. He knew they would adhere to walls and ceilings, helping prevent a fall from the tower.

Meanwhile, Magadon took advantage of the confused slaad's attack on his brother. Shouting, the guide charged the gray-eyed slaad, blade bare. He closed in a final lunge and sent a cross cut at the slaad's head. The creature parried the blow, ducking and answering with a quick thrust that Magadon avoided only by bounding backward onto the air. The larger slaad attacked his brother again, but the gray-eyed creature twisted out of the way and opened a slash on his fellow's arm.

Jak realized that the guide's skill at archery exceeded his bladework. Only Riven or Cale could match the speed of the small, gray-eyed slaad.

Dolgan raised a claw to strike at his brother again but stopped in mid swing, a dumbfounded look on his broad, flat face. As suddenly as it had started, the confused slaad left off the attack on his brother, sat with a sigh on the stairway, and looked at his bloody claws as though they belonged to someone else. He began to dig his talons into his own arms, moaning in either pain or ecstasy—Jak couldn't tell which—at the sensation.

The smaller slaad grinned, feinted at Magadon to draw his blade out of position, and stabbed the guide through the shoulder. Magadon groaned, waved his blade defensively, and staggered backward down three steps. The slaad took them all in a single bound and pressed the attack. Magadon backstepped, using his blade as best he could to ward off the slaad's lightning-fast attack. Wound after wound opened on the guide. He was weakening.

Jak decided to gamble. He whispered the words to another spell and when he was done, he ran forward to the stairs, putting himself between the slaadi, right at the edge of the staircase. The confused slaad paid him no heed.

"Try me, you son of a diseased toad," Jak called.

He knew the insult was silly but that didn't matter. The magic of his spell lent the words power and significance. If the casting worked, the slaad would not be able to resist attacking him.

The slaad opened a gash in Magadon's stomach and whirled around to face Jak, hissing in rage. From the look of hate in the slaad's gray eyes, Jak knew that his spell had worked.

He added further insult by waving his short sword and saying, "I'm going to cut out your maggot-infested tongue and stick it so far up your polluted arse that you'll be able to lick your eyes."

He could not help but grin at that one.

The slaad dropped his sword, apparently intent on using his claws to rip out Jak's throat, and bounded up the stairs with terrifying rapidity.

Jak feigned fear, raised his blade awkwardly, and fumbled backward. The slaad rushed him. His claws closed on the halfling's chest and face. Pain blossomed.

Jak fell backward over the side of the staircase. The momentum from the enraged slaad's charge carried the creature right after.

Jak slipped from the slaad's grip, flipped in midair, and slammed his hands against the side of the tower. It occurred to him too late that the stone might hold an enchantment that would defeat his spell. His heart found his throat.

But his grip held.

Jak enjoyed a moment's satisfaction as the slaad fell, the beginnings of a scream erupting from the creature's throat.

His satisfaction vanished as clawed hands closed on Jak's ankles in a grip stronger than a vice. The weight of the falling slaad nearly dislodged the halfling, but his spell held them both hanging from the side of the tower at a height of four bowshots above the ruins. Jak kicked his feet, trying to shake the slaad loose. No use.

Jak tried to step onto the air and found that he could no longer walk on it. Magadon's psionic effect had ended. Was the guide dead? What had happened to Cale and Riven? He had no time to pay the questions further heed.

"You will pay for this, little creature," growled the slaad below him.

The creature's claws sank deeply into Jak's calves. The pain was excruciating and Jak could not contain a scream. The slaad began to scale him as he might a rope.

One claw released his calf only to sink into his thigh. Jak was dizzy with agony. Warm blood coursed down his leg.

"Magadon!" Jak screamed, praying that the guide was still alive. "Magadon!"

From above, all he could hear were the dumb moans of the enspelled slaad.

"Pain. . . ." the slaad hanging from his legs said.

The creature sank a clawed hand into Jak's shoulder and began to pull himself up. Jak cried out in agony. He couldn't hold on much longer. He could imagine the creature's huge, fanged mouth just behind his head.

"I'll drop us both, you stinking frog!" Jak threatened, and he meant it.

The slaad tensed at that. Jak prepared to let go of the wall, praying to the Trickster that the impact of the fall would kill him quickly.

Magadon's face appeared over the ledge, and the glowing tip of a knocked, psionically-enhanced arrow followed.

As absurd as it was, Jak could not contain a smile.

"Mags!" he said.

He felt the slaad on his back tense, and could imagine the look of shock on his froglike face.

"Take your fill of this," Magadon said, and fired.

The impact blew the slaad from the halfling's back. Jak heard an aborted scream of pain and looked down between his feet to see the creature plummeting toward the ruins.

"Jak!" Magadon said. "Here."

Jak looked up to see Magadon's extended hand. Jak took it in his own sticky grasp, and the guide lifted him up to the stairway. Magadon was covered in wounds, some of them deep.

Near them, the confused slaad continued to sit on the stairs, wounding himself and muttering.

Jak ignored the creature, touched his friend, and spoke the words to healing prayers. Most of Magadon's wounds closed, and color returned to his face.

Afterward, still eyeing the confused slaad warily, Jak used more healing prayers to close the gouges in his own legs and shoulder.

They looked up toward the top of the tower, and Jak prayed to the Trickster and Tymora that Cale had made it to the top before Magadon's psionic effect had ended.

They looked at the enspelled slaad, then looked at each other.

"We'll go past him if possible," Jak said. "Through him if need be."

"Through him," Magadon said grimly.

As he advanced up the stairs toward Dolgan, the non-plussed slaad looked a question at him.

Magadon slashed open the slaad's throat with a hard cross slash. Dolgan fell backward on the stairs, surprise in his eyes, gurgling and spasming.

Magadon walked over him and up.

"Don't slip on the blood," the guide said to Jak.

Jak nodded and followed.

         ◉ ◉ ◉ ◉ ◉

Cale waited until Azriim stepped into the glowing archway. When he did, the slaad's body blotted out the orange light and cast a long shadow behind him. Cale sensed the semi-comprehensible space-between-space that connected the shadows he'd gathered around him and the shadow that Azriim cast. As always, it was not but a step in a direction that could not be represented on a map, that most beings could not see or sense. He readied his blade, prayed that the tower did not interfere with his ability, and took the step.

A moment of motion and he found himself standing behind Azriim. The slaad must have sensed him for he started to turn, but too late. With gritted teeth, Cale drove Weaveshear into Azriim's back, through his spine, and out his green-skinned chest. Azriim screamed in pain, bared his fangs in agony, and started to fall. Some small thing the slaad had held in his hands went skittering across the floor of the chamber beyond the archway. Warm, black blood cascaded down Weaveshear's hilt and over Cale's hands. He twisted the blade as Azriim collapsed, eliciting another hiss. He put his foot into the semi-prone slaad's back and kicked him off the blade and through the archway.

The chamber under the cupola was nothing more than an open space covered with a metal roof. Arcane symbols were engraved into the metal. Cale had no idea what the cupola's purpose might once have been.

In the center of the chamber, erupting from the stone of the tower like the edge of a giant knife, was a faceted wedge of crystal taller than Cale. It pulsed with power and sent its orange beam of arcane might sizzling through the hole in the cupola and toward the top of the cavern.

"I said I would kill you," Cale said, and was surprised to hear in his words the same emotionless tone he sometimes heard in Riven's voice—the tone of an assassin doing his work.

The slaad apparently could not move his legs. On all fours, he dragged them behind him like dead things as he tried to move away from Cale.

So you did, Azriim replied, and even his mental voice seemed strained with pain.

With surprising suddenness, the slaad whirled around, pointed a palm at Cale, and uttered an arcane word. A fan of clashing colors flew from his hand and exploded around Cale—

—and drained harmlessly into Weaveshear. Cale felt the blade pulsing with the absorbed power, vibrating from its proximity to the magical beam.

Azriim's mismatched eyes went wide. He turned and dragged himself after the item he had dropped. Cale saw it lying on the floor not far from them: a silver nut latticed with black veins, about the size of Jak's closed fist. A seed.

Cale jumped forward and put his boot into Azriim's back. The slaad hissed in pain and collapsed onto his belly.

You would not kill me in these clothes, would you? Azriim asked, and Cale almost laughed at the absurdity of the question.

Cale saw the wounds he had inflicted with Weaveshear beginning to close. The slaad's leathery skin was sealing itself. Soon, Azriim would have the use of his legs again. The creatures regenerated quickly, perhaps more quickly than Cale himself. He knew then that he would have to finish Azriim with brutal, overwhelming, final violence.

Cale hesitated for a moment, wondering if he should spare Azriim, force him to tell all he knew of the Sojourner.

No, Cale decided. He would learn what he needed to know some other way. Azriim had to die. At that moment, *chororin* required it.

He raised Weaveshear high for a decapitating strike.

"This is over," he said, and was pleased to hear that his voice was his own and not Riven's.

Azriim turned to face him, turned to face death. His mismatched eyes did not show fear, but they did go wide.

By the time Cale realized that Azriim's eyes were wide from surprise, not fear, it was too late.

Agonizing pain exploded in Cale's back. Magical steel pierced his flesh, his kidneys, and scraped against his ribs and spine. He looked down to see the tips of two blades making little tents of his cloak before poking through. Two saber tips.

Riven's sabers.

Warm blood poured down Cale's back, and trickled down his front. Sparks exploded in his brain. His vision went blurry, but somehow he managed to keep his feet. Riven pulled both blades free. Cale hissed at the shot of agony that ran through his frame as the blades withdrew. He tried to turn around but his body would not respond. It was all he could do to stay upright. He clutched Weaveshear hard in his fist but felt it slipping from his grasp.

"It's over, Cale," Riven said, his voice as frigid as a winter gale. "It's over."

A saber stab again impaled Cale's organs. Another. He could not even groan. The strength went out of his legs. He collapsed to the floor, and the fall seemed to take forever. His hearing went dull. Sounds seemed to stretch impossibly long, into a scale he'd never before noticed. Only the rasping of his breath and the irregular hammering of his heart sounded clearly and normally in his ears.

Cale lay on his side, his eyes open, his breathing labored. He felt his shade flesh struggling to regenerate, but feared it would fail. Riven had done a lot of damage. Like Cale, the one-eyed assassin knew how to kill. And the assassin knew how to betray.

In some distant part of his brain, Cale wondered when Riven had made the decision to turn on them, wondered whether the assassin had planned it all along. For a reason he could not explain, Cale thought of the Plane of Shadow. He cursed himself for a fool, a trusting fool. In his mind, he could hear Azriim laughing.

Riven walked past him, past the prone slaad, and retrieved the silver seed. Sabers still bare and bloody, he walked back to stand over the slaad. Two saber tips pointed at Azriim's heart.

"My mind is open," Riven said to the slaad. "Read it."

Azriim's mismatched eyes narrowed and Cale sensed the flow of mental energy. A fanged grin spread across the slaad's face.

"I come with you, and participate in what's to come," Riven simultaneously asked and ordered.

Azriim nodded. Riven sheathed a saber and extended a hand to help the slaad up. Azriim took it and climbed slowly to his feet. His regeneration had returned the use of his legs.

"Give me the seed," Azriim said.

Riven ignored him, and Cale could imagine but not see the assassin's sneer.

Still holding the seed, Riven turned to Cale. He knelt down on his haunches so that he and Cale could see into each other's faces. Riven's eye was cold, the hole in his other socket black and deep. Cale thought back to an alley in Selgaunt, when Riven had been helpless before him. He should have killed him then.

"I side with the winner, Cale," Riven said. "You don't see it, you never saw it, but you've already lost." He stood, spat a glob of saliva onto Cale's cheek, and added, "And I've been Second long enough."

Cale tried to grab his boot, failed, coughed up blood, but managed to groan, "You'll always . . . be Second . . . to me, Zhent."

Riven stood still for a moment, and Cale waited for the finishing saber cut. It did not come, and when the assassin spoke, Cale could hear the sneer in his voice.

"It doesn't appear so now."

Together, Riven and Azriim walked to the huge crystal in the center of the room. They stood for a moment before the crystal and looked at the orange beam, the beam that powered the Skulls, that kept Skullport from collapsing.

Without ceremony, Riven handed the seed to Azriim. The slaad appeared startled by the gesture, but took the seed.

Azriim looked at Cale and said to Riven, "If he lives, he'll come looking for you."

Riven eyed Cale coldly and replied, "I hope he does."

"We need to get you some new clothes," Azriim said with a smile, then he slipped the seed into the beam.

The moment the silver seed touched the orange light, it disintegrated into a million glowing particles, all of them streaking upward like a swarm of fireflies, spreading along the net of power. The orange glow darkened, turned crimson. The air changed. Cale's ears popped. A low, vibratory hum sounded, growing louder and louder. The entirety of the chamber bucked, shook. The tower rattled. The huge crystal cracked and a million fine lines manifested along its facets.

Cale turned his head and saw that outside the cupola, stalactites detached from the ceiling, fell gracefully through the air, and crashed thunderously amongst the ruins. Clouds of dust went up from the point of impact. It was raining stone.

It was at that moment that Cale realized that the bleeding in his back had stopped. His flesh closed the wound. Though still weak, he reached into his cloak pocket and found his holy symbol. The feel of its soft velvet in his hand comforted him.

I'm the First, he thought. I'm the First.

He searched his mind for a spell, something to stop Riven and Azriim. He found one, tried to utter the words, but was unable to maintain his concentration. He could only watch them, could only bear witness to his failure.

Azriim, grinning like a lunatic, took out his teleportation rod. Riven grabbed the slaad by the arm.

"I'm coming with you," he said.

Still wearing that stupid grin, Azriim nodded and said, "I wouldn't have it any other way."

The slaad began to manipulate the rod.

From behind him, Cale heard a voice—Jak's voice—exclaim, "Riven! I knew it, you black-hearted whoreson!"

Azriim and Riven looked up in surprise.

Cale turned his head to see Jak and Magadon standing in the cupola's archway. Both looked to Cale. He tried to indicate to them that he was all right, that he would live, but managed only to blink at them.

Jak's mouth went hard.

"Bastard," he said to Riven.

As fast as a lightning strike, the halfling pulled two throwing daggers from his chest bandolier and whipped them across the chamber.

Cale heard one sink into flesh. Riven grunted, and Cale turned to see one of the blades buried to the hilt in the assassin's shoulder.

"I'd kill you for that, *little man*," Riven said, grimacing as he pulled the dagger free. "Except that you're already dead. And I'm leaving."

The assassin had something in his hand. He hurled it back at Jak. The halfling couldn't dodge it, and the small wooden object thumped into Jak's chest, doing no damage, and fell to the floor.

Jak's pipe.

"Be thankful it's not steel, Fleet," Riven growled.

"You've wanted this," Jak said, and started to advance across the chamber. "Now you've got it. Come on, Zhent!"

Magadon walked beside him, blade bare.

"You won't get away, Riven," the guide said.

"I already have, tiefling," Riven replied with a sneer.

Azriim continued to twist the teleportation rod. Cale tried to shout at Magadon to connect psionically to Riven, but he could not say the words.

Riven looked past Jak and Magadon and toward the cupola's archway.

"They don't look happy," the assassin said, and he and Azriim winked out.

"Coward!" Jak shouted at the empty air.

Cale followed the assassin's gaze and saw six of the Skulls streaming into the cavern. Though they were still far away, Cale could see that their mouths were open, and he heard the howls of rage and dismay that went before them. Lines of energy crackled around the guardians like lightning.

The chamber continued to shake. Stalactites fell in increasing numbers. The net of power formerly visible along the ceiling crackled and sparked, its power failing. It felt to Cale as though the entire chamber was in danger of imminent collapse.

Jak and Magadon rushed to his side and sat him up. Cale hissed with pain as he rose slowly to his feet.

Jak said, "Cale, are you—Trickster's toes! You're soaked in blood."

Leaning on his friends, Cale said, "I'll be all right."

His shadow-infused flesh continued to work its miracle.

A lightning bolt exploded through one of the cupola's archways and blew them across the floor. They all fell face down on the stone. The hairs on Cale's arms stood straight up.

The Skulls are coming, he thought. And they're angry.

"Come on," Cale said, slowly clambering to his feet.

Jak and Magadon at his side, he limped across the chamber to the opposite archway. They stood there on the edge of the tower, looking down on the ruins far below. Soon the lost city would be covered in rock, the chamber forever lost to history.

Above them, the ceiling of the cavern was aglow in intermittent flashes of crimson lightning and showers of sparks. Cale saw some of the Skulls wheeling frenetically around the cavern, preventing what destruction they could, and patching the net of power where possible.

But two others were coming for the tower. Keening, aglow with power, rage, and despair, they blazed toward the comrades.

The tower shook under Cale's feet, nearly knocking him off the side. The world shook above them.

Still bleary-eyed from his wounds, Cale said, "Hold on to me and get ready to jump."

Magadon and Jak went wide eyed.

"What?" Jak asked.

Cale gathered what darkness he could around him. He needed more. It was too bright at the top of the tower.

"Jump, little man," he said. "Together."

Still they hesitated.

Two Skulls streaked into the cupola.

"Your transgression shall result in your slow flaying and prolonged torture, you—"

"Now, godsdamnit," Cale ordered.

Beams of energy fired from the Skulls' eyes.

Jak and Magadon, clutching Cale between them, jumped.

CHAPTER 20

REAPING THE HARVEST

Levitating in midair in the nursery, Vhostym pressed his ear to the trunk of the Weave Tap and blinked against the increasingly bright pulses of power that ran the length of the artifact. Most creatures wouldn't have been able to see much beyond their own hands in the light of those pulses, but even that dim luminescence stung Vhostym's eyes.

From the burgeoning upper limbs and thick, twisted roots of the Weave Tap hung the desiccated, blackened corpses of the captive devas and demons whose life-force had fed the Tap's early growth. Their mouths were thrown open with the pain of their slow, agonizing deaths. The impaled corpses looked like some macabre fruit, as wrinkled, dry and twisted as prunes. Had he touched one of the corpses, it probably would have crumbled to dust.

Vhostym looked upon the dead celestials and

fiends without emotion. The weak, he knew, must always suffer the will of the strong. And Vhostym was strong. The creatures died to serve Vhostym's purpose, speeding the growth of the Weave Tap's first seed.

His slaadi had planted that seed at the provenience of Skullport's mantle. Already the seed's tendrils had spread throughout the city, harvesting its power, pooling it. On the other side of Faerûn, a wave of arcane energy was gathering and would soon course along the Weave from the blossoming seed back to the Tap, where it would be stored. Vhostym could feel the power rising through the fabric of magic like a gathering tide, could feel it preparing to race toward him like a gale-driven storm.

Vhostym's heart beat faster than it had in centuries. He braced himself for the rush and attuned his vision to see magical power.

The sentience in the Weave Tap also seemed to feel the pooling power. Its roots began to squirm, its limbs to writhe. The movement was so slow as to be almost imperceptible, except that the dried corpses of the demons and devils broke apart in that movement, crumbling into a million black snowflakes.

The silver beat of the Weave Tap's pulse accelerated, faster and faster, gaining intensity. The slight increase in light caused daggers of pain to stab behind Vhostym's eyes, but he endured. He would witness the success of the first step in his plan.

The power was coming . . .

And there it was.

Without a sound, the spirals of diamond embedded in the circular cyst of the nursery began to glow with magical luminescence. The light—not real light, but a perception funneled through the lens of his magic-detecting vision— caused Vhostym no harm. The diamonds flared with the brilliance of a sun as more and more magical energy flooded them. The entire nursery began to thrum with power. The flakes of the demons and devas swirled around the nursery like dust devils. The limbs of the Weave Tap stretched slowly for the diamonds. Its roots squirmed toward the floor, as though attempting to brace itself more fully in the Shadow Weave, against the expected influx of magic from the Weave.

Vhostym waited, savoring the moment. His eyes boiled from the silver pulse of the Weave Tap, and his soul burned with the knowledge that he had succeeded.

With a suddenness that took even Vhostym aback, three thousand nine hundred and fifty-nine diamonds emitted finger-thick rays of magical energy into the Weave Tap. The living artifact was suspended in a grid of arcane power as fine as a fisherman's net. The tree throbbed with power, faster and faster. It's limbs squirmed as though in ecstasy, until its formerly bare stalks exploded amber leaves, each of them throbbing along their black veins with the arcane power contained within.

Abruptly, the connection between seed and mother tree ended. The nursery went quiet. The seed had exhausted itself, had been born, thrived, and died all within a span of heartbeats. In its death throes it had sent the energy from its "soil" exploding along the lines of the Weave, all to be harvested by the Weave Tap, used to grow more seeds, and stored.

Vhostym looked upon the Weave Tap and thought that even partially-powered it was among the most beautiful things he had ever seen. Within the glowing, amber leaves lay encapsulated the power of an archmage—several archmages—and Vhostym could draw upon that stored power at any time.

But he would not yet do so. He had two more steps to complete before he could complete his plan, and for those steps, his own power would have to serve.

His thoughts turned to his children, his beloved slaadi. They had served him well. He would reward them with transformation to gray, but he would not yet give them their freedom, for he still would need their assistance.

He thought of Skullport, and wondered in passing what destruction had resulted from the Weave Tap's draining of the mantle. Perhaps the Skulls had been able to save the city; perhaps not. Vhostym didn't care. He would do what he willed.

He sent his consciousness searching for his sons. He quickly located Azriim and Dolgan. The largest of his sons was alive but sorely wounded. Serrin he could not locate. He wondered without sentiment if his third son had died.

Azriim and Dolgan were on Faerûn's surface, no doubt having used their teleportation rods to escape the destruction of Skullport.

Well done, my sons, he projected, and caressed the pleasure receptors of each of his brood. *Well done, indeed.*

To Azriim alone, he projected, *Where is Serrin? And the priest and his comrades? Did you kill him, as you had so hoped?*

He sensed hesitation.

Serrin is dead. And I did not kill the priest, Azriim returned, with some disappointment. *But we believe he is dead, he and two of his comrades. The other . . .*

The other? Vhostym pressed.

Azriim's confusion carried through the connection.

The other saved me and offers alliance. We're bringing him to you. He wishes to join the brood.

Vhostym frowned, unsure of Azriim's meaning. No matter. He would deal with the priest's ally when he arrived back on the pocket plane.

Bring him, he projected to his slaadi. *I would reward you both.*

He sensed the excitement of his sons through the mental connection. Azriim and Dolgan were imagining their transformation into gray slaadi.

Azriim's mental voice answered, *We are coming now.*

An Excerpt

R.A. Salvatore's War of the Spider Queen
Book V

Annihilation

Philip Athans

Valas could tell that Danifae didn't know the drake was behind her until the second his arrow sliced through the fine membrane of its wing, surprising it. It made a noise deep in its throat, the arrow made a wet ripping sound as it entered, and the drake's smooth motion ended in a jerk. All that was enough for anyone to sense some disturbance behind her and turn—and it was that simple reflex that saved Danifae's life.

Though the drake forgot its intended target, it landed hard in a skidding roll and would have bowled her over if she hadn't jumped clear—and she barely managed that.

The portal drake whirled in the direction from which Valas's arrow had come. Saliva dripped from its open mouth, curling around jagged teeth and collecting on the cave floor in steaming pools. Valas saw the intelligence in the thing's eyes, the great age—centuries spent stalking the alluring magical portals of the Underdark—and the cold, hard anger.

The drake searched the darkness for him, but Valas knew it wouldn't see him. Valas didn't want to be seen, it was that simple.

Behind the creature, Danifae scrambled to her feet, drawing her morningstar at the same time. Valas already had another arrow in his hand, and as he slipped sideways along the edge of a deep shadow he set it to his bow and drew back the string. The drake mirrored that expansive movement by drawing air into its lungs. It couldn't see Valas, but it had apparently come to the conclusion that all it had to do was get close. And that was a conclusion Valas was unable to find fault with.

After taking a heartbeat to aim, Valas let the arrow fly. The drake exhaled, releasing a billowing cloud of greasy green vapor into the air. It rolled and expanded as it left the dragon's mouth. The drake began to strain to get it all out.

Danifae struck with her morningstar from behind it—a weapon enchanted with the power of lightning—and the portal drake jerked forward. Valas's arrow bit deeply into its chest, finding the half an inch it needed between two hard scales. The thing's armored skin quivered, and muscles rippled and jerked. The breath caught in its throat and its cloud was cut short. Still, the gas rolled in Valas's direction.

The scout could see it coming, and it was aimed toward, rather than at him, so he flipped backward away from it. He had no way to protect himself from poison gas. It was a weakness in that situation that Valas found frustrating. All he could do was avoid the gas, but avoidance, at least, was something the scout was well versed at.

"Hide in the dark there if you wish, drow," the portal drake hissed in Undercommon. It's voice was cold and sharp, almost mechanical, and it echoed in the high-ceilinged chamber with a sound like glass breaking. "I can't see you."

The creature turned to face Danifae, who was whirling her morningstar, looking it in the eye, and backing up.

"But I can see her," the drake said.

Danifae smiled, and the expression sent a chill down Valas's spine. He stopped, noting the sensation but utterly confused by it.

When the battle-captive lashed out with the enchanted morningstar again, the drake dodged it easily.

"What are you expecting, lizard?" Danifae, nonplussed by her failed attack, asked the drake. "Do you think he'll reveal himself to save me? Have you never met a dark elf before?"

Valas, about to draw another arrow, let it drop silently back into his quiver. He slipped the bow over his shoulder and made his way around the back of the drake, skirting the edge of the cavern wall toward the giant face. He quickly estimated the number of steps, the number of seconds, and gauged the background noise for sound cover.

"Dark elves?" the drake said. "I've eaten one or two in my years."

Danifae tried to hit it again, and the drake tried to bite her. They dodged at the same time, which ruined both their attacks.

"Let us pass," Danifae said, and her voice had an air of command to it that got Valas's attention as well as the drake's.

"No," the creature answered, and Danifae stepped in faster than Valas would have thought her capable of.

The morningstar came down on the portal drake's left side and Valas blinked at the painfully bright flash of blue-white light. The burning illumination traced patterns in the air like glowing spiderwebs. The creature flinched and growled again, its anger and pain showing in the way its lips pulled back from its teeth.

Danifae stepped back, setting her morningstar spinning again. The drake crouched and Valas stopped, stiffened. It didn't lunge at her—it burst into the air with the deafening beat of wings. In less than a second it was high enough to disappear into the gloom up in the cathedral-like space.

Valas stepped forward and let his toes scrape loose gravel on the floor. Danifae looked up at him.

Run back to the tunnel, Valas traced in sign language. *Go!*

Danifae saw him, didn't bother to nod, and turned to run. Valas slipped back into the darkness, drew his *piwafwi* up over his head, and rolled on the floor until he knew he was back in a place where no one would be able to see him.

Valas watched the battle-captive run, knowing she wouldn't be able to see the portal drake. He drew another arrow slowly so that it wouldn't make a sound as it came free of the quiver. He turned and twisted a fraction of an inch here, a hair's breadth there, so the steel tip would reflect no light. Breathing slowly through his mouth, the Bregan D'aerthe scout waited—but didn't have to wait for long.

The sound of the portal drake's wings echoed from above, then doubled, then doubled again, and more—not just echoes.

Five, Valas counted.

Still cloaked in auras of invisibility and the gloom of the long-abandoned cavern, Valas started forward.

The five portal drakes swooped out of the shadows in formation, then the two at the far ends swept inward, and two others shifted out. They changed positions as they flew, but their target was the same.

Danifae hesitated. Valas could see it in her step. She heard them, and knew they could fly faster—many times faster—than she'd ever be able to run. To her credit, though, she didn't look back.

The five portal drakes were identical in every detail, and no one who had traveled as extensively as Valas had could have been fooled for long. Only three wing-beats into it, Valas knew what they were.

Not all of the trinkets the scout wore were enchanted, but the little brass ovoid was, and Valas touched it as he ran. The warmth of his fingers brought the magic to life, and but a thought was needed to wake it fully. It happened without a sound, and Valas never missed a beat, or revealed himself at all.

Danifae stopped running anyway, leaving Valas to wonder why.

Similarly confused, the portal drakes drew up short, all five of them fluttering to a halt, crossing each others' paths, and coming within fractions of an inch from collision.

Danifae smiled at the dragons—all five of them rearing up to shred her with claws like filet knives—and she said, "Careful now. Look behind you."

The toothy sneer that was the drake's reply played out simultaneously on all five sets of jaws.

Valas let his arrow fly, and all four of his own conjured images did the same. The little brass ovoid—a container for a spell that had been very specially crafted by an ancient mage whose secrets had long ago been lost—had done its work, and for each of the five portal drakes, there was a Valas.

For each of the five portal drakes there was an arrow.

The dragon might have heard them, or sensed them in some other way, or maybe its curiosity had gotten the better of it. The creature whirled around and met the arrows with its right eye. Four of the arrows blinked out of existence the instant they met with the false drakes, and those illusionary dragons disappeared as well. The barrage left only one real arrow, one real portal drake, and one real eye.

The force of the impact made he beast twitch, then stagger back a step.

Valas could tell that the dragon could see him—all five of him—with its one good eye.

"I'll eat you alive . . ." the portal drake rasped, "for that."

Valas drew his kukris and his images did the same. The dragon, blood pouring from its ruined eye, didn't bother to pull out the arrow that still protruded from its socket. Instead it charged, wings up, claws out, and jaws open.

Valas stepped to the side, into its blind spot. The drake had obviously never fought with only one eye before and the creature fell for the feint. Valas got two quick cuts in—cuts each answered with a deep, rumbling growl from the portal drake.

It lashed out and Valas stepped in and to the side, letting one of his images cross in front of the attack. The portal drake's claw touched the image's shoulder, and by the time the talon passed through the false scout's abdomen the illusion was gone.

The drake grumbled its frustration and Valas attacked again. The creature twisted out of reach and snapped its jaws at Valas—coming dangerously close to the real dark elf. When the dragon's single eye narrowed and smoldered, the scout knew the dragon had pegged him.

Valas danced back into the drake's blind spot, stepping backward and spinning to keep it off balance and to keep his mirror images moving frenetically around him. The drake clawed another one into thin air, then bit the third out of existence.

Valas watched the image disappear, and followed the portal drake's neck with his eyes as it passed half an arm's length in front of him. He looked for cracks, creases, any sign of weakness in the monster's thick, scaly hide.

He found one, and sunk a kukri between scales, through skin, into flesh and artery and bone beneath it. Blood was everywhere, pumping out of the creature in torrents. The dragon flailed at Valas, though it couldn't quite see him. As it died it managed to brush a claw against the last false drow. The drake started to fall, and Valas skipped out of the way. Its head whipped around on its long, supple neck, and the jaws came down on Valas's shoulder, crinkling his armor and bruising the black skin underneath.

The scout pulled away, rolled, and came to his feet with his kukris out in front of him.

No new attack came. The portal drake splayed across the floor of the cavern. Blood came less frequently, and with less urgency, with every fading heartbeat.

"Always knew . . ." the dying dragon sighed, "it would be . . . a drow."

It died with that word on its tongue, and Valas lifted an eyebrow at the thought.

He stepped away from the poisonous corpse and sheathed his kukris. There was no sign of Danifae. Valas didn't know if she'd kept running back the way they'd come, or if she was hiding somewhere in the shadows.

With a shrug, and a last glance at the portal drake, Valas turned and went to the abandoned monastery. Assuming that the Melarn battle-captive would eventually return to the cavern, and the portal that was their goal there, Valas climbed into the great down-turned mouth.

Inside the semicircular structure were two tall, free-standing pillars. Between them was nothing but dead air and the side of the cavern wall. The interior was shrouded in darkness, and there was the sharp smell of the portal drake's filth.

Danifae stood between the pillars, her weight on one foot, her hand on her hip.

"Is it dead?" she asked.

Valas stopped several strides from her and nodded.

The battle-captive looked up and around at the dead stone pillars and the featureless interior of the huge face.

"Good," Danifae said. "Is this the portal?"

When she looked back at Valas, he nodded again.

"You know how to open it," she said, with no hint that it might be a question.

Valas nodded a third time and Danifae smiled.

"Before we go," she said as she pulled a dagger from her shapely hip, "I want to harvest some poison."

Valas blinked and said, "From the portal drake?"

Danifae walked past him, smiling, spinning her dagger between her fingers.

"I'll wait here," he told her.

She kept going without bothering to answer.

If she survives that, Valas thought, she might just be worth traveling with.

**Available in Hardcover
From Wizards of the Coast
July 2004**

FORGOTTEN REALMS®

NEW YORK TIMES BESTSELLING SERIES

R.A. SALVATORE'S
WAR OF THE SPIDER QUEEN

The epic saga of the dark elves concludes!

EXTINCTION
Book IV

LISA SMEDMAN

For even a small group of drow, trust is the rarest commodity of all.
When the expedition prepares for a return to the Abyss, what little
trust there is crumbles under a rival goddess's hand.

ANNIHILATION
Book V

PHILIP ATHANS

Old alliances have been broken, and new bonds have been formed.
While some finally embark for the Abyss itself, other stay behind to
serve a new mistress—a goddess with plans of her own.

RESURRECTION
Book VI

PAUL S. KEMP

The Spider Queen has been asleep for a long time, leaving the
Underdark to suffer war and ruin. But if she finally returns, will
things get better...or worse?

www.wizards.com

THE TWILIGHT GIANTS TRILOGY
Written by *New York Times*
bestselling author
TROY DENNING

THE OGRE'S PACT
Book I

This attractive new re-release by multiple *New York Times* best-selling author Troy Denning, features all new cover art that will re-introduce Forgotten Realms fans to this excellent series. A thousand years of peace between giants and men is shattered when a human princess is stolen by ogres, and the only man brave enough to go after her is a firbolg, who must first discover the human king's greatest secret.

THE GIANT AMONG US
Book II

A scout's attempts to unmask a spy in his beloved queen's inner circle is her only hope against the forces of evil that rise against her from without and from within.

THE TITAN OF TWILIGHT
Book III

The queen's consort is torn between love for his son and the dark prophesy that predicts his child will unleash a cataclysmic war. But before he can take action, a dark thief steals both the boy and the choice away from him.